ABANDONED
In Exile

A.L. McDonnell

Published in Australia by Thestel Books Pty Ltd.
Email: author@almcdonnell.com

First published in Australia 2021
This edition published 2021
Copyright © A.L. McDonnell 2021
Cover design, typesetting: WorkingType (www.workingtype.com.au)

McDonnell, A.L.
Abandoned: In Exile
ISBN: 978-0-6450821-0-4
pp436

ABOUT THE AUTHOR

A.L. McDonnell is a medical practitioner and psychologist who lives in Queensland's Lockyer Valley. She has written many scientific pieces and articles for lifestyle magazines and, as a medical practitioner, has worked extensively throughout the outback which is home to some of life's most colourful characters. Odd experiences are often the norm in the remote far west, and she was fascinated by the way individuals could spin their yarns, in pubs or around the campfire, turning ordinary events into something beyond this world and, even more, the many methods they claimed to have used to confront their bizarre encounters. *Abandoned* grew from such a tale when she was asked what she would do if a spaceship landed in one of her own paddocks …

For more **http://almcdonnell.com**

To Mauryeen –
You left us far too soon.

ACKNOWLEDGMENTS

Without Barry, this novel would still be gathering dust in the bottom draw of my desk.

My thanks to my lovely writer's group for all their help and encouragement — Jill, Kate, Jan, Danae, Bryce, Ruth and Barbara — and all the editors and instructors who helped with early drafts.

Thanks to Mark Griffiths for his military knowledge, and my apologies to Mark for the number of times I ignored his sound advice for the sake of a good story.

CHAPTER 1

Springbrook Mountain,
Gold Coast Hinterland, Australia

Thursday, 20th February 2020

After three fruitless hours of research, hunched over the viewing equipment in her hide, Jemma had been about to give up when an intense blue light exploded through the rainforest. Reeling back, she knocked her head on the low roof of the hide. Cursing the cramped space, she dropped back over the screen for a better look. Bizarre though the light was, the man that she'd seen at the edge of her viewing zone had her more worried. He'd been standing as still as the gums and melaleucas that surrounded him, but he was gone. Sure she hadn't imagined him, she adjusted the screen and re-angled the lens, but no amount of fiddling brought him back in to view. In all the years since she'd first begun to work in this restricted section of the rainforest, she'd not seen another person here at night. She doubted this man had any right to be here now.

Scrambling out through the small flap, she gripped the

canvas and pulled herself up to peer through the shadows that danced in the eerie luminescence still flooding the bush. She searched for any sign of movement, but all was still. The light cast a vivid palette of blue around the branches and the dense undergrowth of ferns and bracken that blurred the gaps between the massive, ancient trees.

Something crunched on the dry forest litter behind. She swung around. The man was less than fifty metres away and walking swiftly in her direction. A heavy jacket, with a hood pulled forward, covered his head and a balaclava obscured his face. Her breath caught as she scanned the bush for an escape route.

'Wait,' he called, when she began to turn. 'We need to talk.'

'No chance,' she muttered, and charged onto a narrow path into the rainforest. There was no way of predicting how far the track would go, but it was her only option. The light helped her weave her way across the tangled web of strangler fig roots that criss-crossed the ground although she stumbled several times in the washouts and flowing streams. Tripping on fallen logs and scattered rocks, branches clawed at her skin, flicking dew from the leaves into her eyes but, through it all, she managed to stay upright. Suddenly, as if someone had flicked a switch, the light receded to a thin, intense strip of blue that shot up into the night sky like a high-powered spotlight. Her eyes couldn't adapt to the cloying darkness that now shrouded the forest. Unable to stop, she caught her foot on the edge of one of the gnarled roots. Hurled face-first onto the rotting leaves of the forest floor, her forehead slammed onto a half-buried rock and everything went black.

When her mind started to clear she heard a groan, but it wasn't until she felt the vibration in her throat that she realised she'd made the sound herself. As she tried to sit up, she had no idea how long she'd been lying there, or what had happened. Something wet streamed down her cheeks. It made her eyes sting, tasted metallic, salty. She reached up to press her hand against her throbbing head and her fingers dipped into a large gash on the right side of her forehead. She couldn't focus her thoughts, nor could she remember why she'd left her hide until the vision of a man flickered through her foggy brain. Then it all flooded back, running from the man, the light going out, tripping and falling. She had no idea if he'd followed her and, surrounded by some of the thickest forest on the mountain, she had to find a way out. It would be hours before anyone would come looking.

Pressing one hand against the wound, she gripped the trunk of a small tree with the other and forced herself into enough of a sitting position to look around. The strip of light, flickering through the trees, couldn't be more than a hundred metres away, but she couldn't make out what was producing it. Something between the source and where she sat obscured its base. Exhausted and hurting, she rested back against a tree to decide what to do, listening hard for any sound, any hint the man might have followed, but all was quiet. She knew she should find somewhere with a mobile phone signal and call for help, but she wasn't about to walk away from something as bizarre as this light without identifying its source.

Pushing up onto her knees, she tried to stand, but her muscles were like jelly and she collapsed back down. Determined to find out what was there, she rolled onto her stomach and gripped clumps of grass and small saplings. On her hands and knees, she clawed her way up the mound, grabbing whatever she could find to pull herself forward until she was able to peer over the top. She couldn't believe what she saw. A clearing; bigger than a football field. She blinked hard, convinced she had to be hallucinating. But, when she looked again, it was still there. The forest had been part of her life for the past fifteen years. It was like a second home and had become her refuge after her parents died. A place where she could be herself and not have to deal with the demands of other people. She knew every square inch of it, and she couldn't understand how she could have missed something like this.

It wasn't just the clearing. Dozens of men and women dressed in white flowing robes were gathered in it. They chatted and stretched, like people in an airport lounge after a long-haul flight. Around the perimeter others, dressed in maroon jump suits, their faces masked by a thick fabric, had high-powered rifles slung over their shoulders. Their gait was awkward, and they moved slowly. Some of them watched the people in white. Others stared into the forest as though they were searching for something.

The light now extended well up into the night sky. Its base was on the far side of the field although she couldn't make out what was producing it through the blinding glare. Three more people in white emerged through the glare and walked out to join the others. She edged closer but didn't notice a small patch of dry leaves until they crackled under her weight. Dropping down, she flattened herself against the grass, and hoped they hadn't heard, but one of the armed men swung around and pointed his weapon in her direction. She winced when she saw him raise his free arm to alert the others. She had no hope of getting away, she could barely move. Half of the men formed a tight cordon around the people in white. The rest edged toward the small hill where Jemma lay, frozen.

Pins and needles tracked through her arms and legs and her chest burned as she desperately tried to push herself up. Pain seared through her body each time she moved, making her head spin. There was no way out. She flattened herself down on the grass and prayed they wouldn't find her but suddenly a hand clamped her mouth, and a powerful arm grabbed her around the shoulders.

'They heard you,' a man's voice growled. His hand gripped her mouth so hard she couldn't scream, but there was no way she'd give in without putting up a bloody good fight. She bucked, fisted her hands, and swung at him, but didn't have the strength to break away.

When she bit down on one of his fingers, his hand loosened. 'Let me go,' she spat.

He firmed his clasp and growled, 'Shut up. With me, before you get us both killed.' His right arm held her against him, and his left hand remained across her mouth as he reefed her to her feet, but her legs gave way when he turned her to run. He hesitated just long enough to look at her, but she wasn't having any of it. She mustered all the strength she had left to swing around and punch at him.

He picked her up and tossed her over his shoulder. 'You make one more sound, I'll drop you. They can have you. Work it out for yourself.'

His words stopped her from fighting long enough for him to take off, but she knew the forest better than anyone. If she could just get away from him, she'd be able to hide until her head cleared, and then make her escape. She punched at his back and rammed her knee into his stomach but no matter what she did, she couldn't loosen his grip. Her head still spinning, she had to give up. She reached down, grabbed his belt and hung on as he ran behind trees, doing her best to protect herself against the prickly bushes and overhanging branches. He pushed through a thicket until he reached a small cave wedged between overhanging rocks.

'In here.' He set her down in a narrow, musty passage and turned on a small but powerful torch, then reached out his arm to support her. 'Can you walk?'

She swayed when he let go, although she managed to stay on her feet and started to edge away, but he was too quick. Pressing his hand firmly against the centre of her back, he pushed her through the narrow cave and around a sharp corner until they were out of sight of the entrance. Then he swung her around to face him.

'What the hell were you doing there, in the middle of the night?'

'My job.' She slapped his arms away and glared back at him. 'I'm a scientist. I'm investigating a virus that's killed dozens of animals in the last couple of months, a lot of them endangered like the spotted-tail quoll, my research target. More to the point, why are you here in the middle of the night? Who the hell are you? And why were you watching my hide?'

'What hide? I saw you gawking at their compound.'

She stepped back and arched her head upwards to meet his eyes. The man she had run from was her height, nothing like this fellow. But how could she know they weren't together, or that he wasn't something to do with all those people around that blue light. 'Who was the man who approached my hide then?'

'How would I know? When was this?'

'Just after the light appeared. Is there someone here with you?'

'No, I work alone. What did this man look like?'

Raising her hand, she rubbed her forehead, which now throbbed. She had no idea if she could trust her captor, but trapped here with him, there didn't really seem to be any reason not to tell him what had happened. 'I couldn't see him very well. He had a hood, and something covered his face.' Struggling to remain upright, as the pain continued to pulse through her head, she found a small ledge and eased herself onto it.

'It wasn't me, and I didn't see anyone else.' He squatted in front of her, assuring her they'd be safe in the cave, but his jacket fell open exposing a pistol in a shoulder holster and she could see something poking out of his boot; it looked like the handle of a knife. She shrank away even as he adjusted his shirt to cover the gun.

'Sorry,' he muttered, holding out his hand. 'Sean. I'm part of a joint task force with ASIO, CIA and MI5. My people have seen these lights before in other countries. People disappear around them.'

Afraid to take her eyes off him, she rubbed her forehead again, wincing when her fingers dipped into the wound.

'Here, let me look. That's one hell of a cut.' He reached out his arm to steady her.

She pulled back, 'I'm fine.'

'Ma'am, I understand you have no reason to trust me, but I'm the best hope you have to get away from here safely.' He took hold of the top of her head and eased her chin upwards to get a better look at the wound on her forehead. 'Nasty.'

She stared at him. He expected trust. That wasn't something she could do easily at the best of times, but he had a gun ... and he'd forced her to come with him. But realistically, if he'd wanted to do her some harm, he could have easily hurt her multiple times.

He sighed when she said nothing. 'At least let me dress that wound.'

She sat upright on the ledge, still looking around for any possible way to escape as he moved closer to inspect her wound. For such a strong man his touch was surprisingly gentle as he brushed away her blood-soaked hair and somehow, she realised, she'd started to feel safe in his presence. She dropped her hands and let him examine the wound, but she wasn't about to drop her guard trapped in a cave in the middle of the night with a total stranger. She had no idea who he was or why he was here. Talk of a task force was fine, but she had no proof that that was the truth.

He didn't take his eyes off her as he extracted a small package from the pocket of his cargo pants. 'Snake kit,' he said. 'Not ideal, but it'll have to do.' Using one of two bandages in the kit and a bottle of water from his belt, he cleaned her forehead then tore open another pack. He covered the wound with a cotton pad, deftly wrapped the second bandage around her forehead, then picked up all the wrappings and shoved them back in his pocket. Finally, he helped her sit further back onto the ledge.

Surprised that the cool, damp granite rock soothed the pain, she felt her eyes starting to droop, but she didn't dare allow them to close. She sat up, forcing herself to be more alert and, using the glow of the torchlight, took a good look at Sean. He stood straight despite his height. He had to be well over six foot and was fit and muscled. He probably was military. His iridescent green eyes seemed to penetrate right through her. Like it or not, she was going to have to rely on his help, at least until she recovered a bit more from the bang on her head. She extended her hand. It couldn't hurt to be polite. 'Jemma Anderson. What do we do now?'

'Hello, Jemma Anderson. We sit tight. Let them make the first move.'

'Who are they? The people in white weren't worried. Who were the men with the weapons? They looked … odd. And what was that blue light?'

'Don't have answers,' he replied. 'A laser maybe?'

'No, it shot up too high for a laser and it started as a floodlight like it had to gear up before it could produce the narrow beam. Lasers don't do that.'

'Okay,' he replied. 'People in white, no idea. Religious zealots maybe. Not security. Most of them had grey hair, some were on walking sticks.'

'Religious communes don't have people walking round them with rifles.'

He shrugged. 'No, probably not. I'm not familiar with those weapons. The ones in the maroon uniforms had to be primary alert, not fast enough for anything else. They looked disabled. Doesn't make sense for them to be in a front-line security role.'

'But they chased us,' said Jemma.

'No, I don't think so. There was a changeover, although I'm not sure when that happened. The ones who chased us were military. Army cams, army issue rifles and they were fast.' He grinned at her. 'Luckily, I'm faster.'

'None of this makes sense,' said Jemma, although she couldn't help a smile.

'That's better,' he said. 'Just try to relax a bit. You're concussed.'

She leaned back on the ledge and this time her eyes did fall shut, but she jerked forward when she heard a noise outside. It sounded like someone had stood on a twig and snapped it. She worked to control her breathing and felt like she might throw up.

Sean rested one hand on his gun, the other on her shoulder. He flicked off his torch and whispered, 'Quiet.'

The sound of boots rang out at the cave entry, and lights shone down the tunnel. She wondered if she should call out. If Sean was right, and they were military, then surely they'd help, but all she had was Sean's impression. They might be one of those quasi-military mercenary type groups. She sat still and, as her eyes began to adjust to the dark, was able to make out Sean's outline. He was crouched and ready to spring. It could have been a charade, but she couldn't see why he'd do that. Gripping the rock on which she sat, she waited for the lights and the noise to fade, jumping when Sean touched her shoulder.

'Okay?'

'No, not really, but I'll deal with it.'

He stood but didn't turn the torch back on. 'Jemma, I need to look for another way out of here. Will you be okay if I go and explore the back of this cave?'

'I'm fine. Don't worry about me.' She sat straighter and made herself smile until he backed further into the cave. A faint flicker of light appeared from the direction in which he'd gone. He must have turned the torch back on. She leaned against the hard rock wall, her mind whirling. Perhaps this was her chance to escape, maybe she could find out if the people who'd chased them were military, but she doubted she could walk as far as the end of the cave yet. She tried to relax, but around an hour later, when he hadn't returned, she eased herself down and, although wobbly, managed to stand. Her head still hurt but it no longer pounded if she moved slowly. Steadying herself against the sides of the cave, she edged back to the entrance. It couldn't hurt just to look. She'd be careful, and retreat if she didn't like what she saw. Besides, Sean had been gone so long, he might have found another way out and left her to fend for herself. She took care to remain in the shadows cast by the moon light, but she couldn't see anyone, or anything, out of place, just the pristine rainforest.

'Jemma,' Sean whispered behind her. 'Back this way. You don't want to be seen.'

She jumped at the sound of his voice, 'The guards are gone.'

'No, they're there. If they see you, they'll pounce.'

'I don't think so. It looks clear.'

'I know what I'd do.' He extended his hand, clearly expecting her to follow.

She frowned and stepped back. She didn't enjoy being told what to do, but she couldn't come up with any other option. When she took his hand, an amused look crossed his face. She swore and retracted her hand but continued to walk with him until they were out of the line of sight from the entrance.

When he stopped, his look was much more serious. 'You didn't see any aircraft out there, did you?'

'No. Do you think someone might be searching for us?'

'I doubt it. Too early. I thought I saw something just above the trees before I moved you last night. It was big, and round, maybe twenty metres across. It just hung there. Don't know what it was, but it made me uneasy. It felt like someone was looking my way.'

'Sorry, I didn't see anything.'

'Alright. Forget it. I've found a break in the cave roof. Stick with me a bit longer, I'll get you home. Okay?' He led her back towards a streak of light. 'Bit of a climb. Are you up to it?'

'Of course. I don't just curl up in my hide. I've climbed most of the rock-faces on this mountain.'

'Good.' He grinned as he scooped his arm behind her back and assisted her up. 'Let me check outside first.'

She realised as she looked back at him that she had started to trust him, but when his powerful arm came around her, drawing her in so he could help her up, something that she could only describe as an electric shock charged through her body. She shrank back, and Sean jumped which made her think he'd felt the same thing.

'Static electricity,' he said, staring at her. 'Come on. Let's go.'

'Yeah, okay.' She grabbed a handhold in the rock, trying to control the tornado of thoughts that whirled through her still foggy brain. Static electricity didn't make sense. This place was entirely rock, no metal, no electric currents, nothing to produce that sensation, yet her hands were still stinging.

'Damn it,' Sean muttered, when he lifted his head through the opening. 'They're everywhere. The bastards know we're here. They're waiting. There's a track. Over to the west. Can't see any guards there. It might be a way out. We'll have to stay down so they don't see us, then there'll be a climb. This isn't easy, Jemma. I can find you somewhere to hide while I go for help, if you like.'

'Not on your life. Just tell me what to do.' Despite his strength and power, she doubted he could take on all those guards alone.

An electronically enhanced voice suddenly broke the silence. 'We know you are here, Colonel Bellamy. Please show yourself. We will not harm you or the woman.'

'Yeah, right,' growled Sean.

Jemma pulled away from him. 'Colonel Bellamy? That's you? For God's sake, who are you? Really?'

'Shit.' He sighed. 'Like the man said. Lieutenant-Colonel Sean Bellamy. We don't have time for this. Let's go.'

She hesitated. 'Are you one of them?'

'No, I'm not. But I know a bit about them, and I don't trust them, okay?' He pulled himself through the opening and cupping his arm under hers, eased her closer to him. 'Ready?'

She nodded, just happy there wasn't another shock as she started to pull herself up.

The voice began again. 'We will commence smoking the caves if you do not show yourselves. You have five minutes.'

'They obviously don't know exactly where we are,' said Sean, reaching back to assist her further. 'They're trying to bluff us.'

She hesitated as she looked out. He could be leading her into a trap. But he hadn't harmed her so far, why would he start now? With a sigh she took hold of his arm and did her best to climb up although he mostly pulled her out. She shivered when he checked the gun in its holster before steering her towards a track twenty metres away and up an incline. Well into the cover of bushes he stopped, helped her to stand and pointed towards the road.

'You're much better than you were. Do you feel strong enough to drive? I can call an ambulance if you're not.'

'My head hurts, but I'm fine,' she replied, determined not to let him see how weak she really felt.

'Alright, go quickly. Don't stop until you reach your car. Go straight to a hospital. I saw bone when I dressed that wound on your head. It needs attention.'

'I need to check on my hide.'

'Not now. I'll pack it up later. Go.'

She started to move, then turned back to thank him, but he was gone. What a strange man. Then again, what a strange night, and standing here trying to puzzle it out wasn't going to get her the help she needed. With a shrug she kept going along the narrow track, using branches on either side for support, and made her way to the carpark. No idea if she'd ever see him again, she looked back as she unlocked her car door.

'Thank you, Sean Bellamy,' she called. *Or whoever you are.*

Although she hadn't been prepared to admit it to Sean, she was still dizzy if she moved quickly. Not knowing if any of those armed guards had followed her, she got in her car and locked herself in. She was too frightened to call an ambulance herself. That would mean waiting alone in the deserted carpark until they arrived. And she knew this road well, she should be okay. Concentrating hard, she made it down to the bottom of the mountain and had almost regained her confidence until she tried to merge with the highway. She had to swerve as another car blasted her with its horn. Shaken, she pulled over at the next servo to grab a bottle of water. After sitting for a few minutes, sipping on the water, she started to wonder if she might have hallucinated the events of the night. She had, after all, taken a heavy knock to her head.

Once she'd begun to relax, she restarted her car and headed the rest of the way to the hospital, unaware of the car that followed behind. Relieved to finally reach the hospital carpark, she found the closest spot to the entrance, but she still had to get to the emergency department. Feeling much worse now than when she'd left Sean, she regretted refusing his offer of an ambulance. The emergency department was only a few metres away, but the way she felt right now it might as well have been on the other side of the country. She took a deep breath and started to walk but had to stop every couple of metres to rest. Covered in sweat, and within metres of the entrance, she gripped the nudge bar of the neared vehicle and leant over the bonnet.

'Are you alright miss?' A woman in nurse's uniform ran towards her. 'Your head's bleeding.'

Jemma reached up to feel her forehead. Her mouth was again parched, and she had to wet her lips before she could answer. 'No, I'm …' She felt the woman's arm around her waist.

'Okay dear. Come on now, let's sit you on the ground. What's your name?'

'Jemma,' she replied as she let the woman help her sit.

'Alright Jemma. You're safe here.' The nurse called to someone to get a wheelchair.

Everything seemed to slow down. People fussed and said things she couldn't comprehend. A couple of men bundled her into a wheelchair. Someone said to hang onto him, but she couldn't co-ordinate her hands, and her arms fell heavily to her sides. Next thing she knew, she was on a bed and several people stood at the foot of it.

A man with a stethoscope around his neck moved forward and touched her arm. 'You've got quite a nasty head injury. Can you tell us what happened? Did someone hurt you?'

His voice was fuzzy, although she understood what he said. She rubbed her ears. 'No, I got a fright. I tripped on a tree root and fell.'

He frowned, 'If you're afraid of someone, please tell me. I can get help for you.'

'I'm not afraid of anyone,' she replied. Not quite true, but she wasn't going to tell him about what had happened overnight.

He turned to the nurse. 'Get her to CT. That wound's deep. Need to check for a skull fracture. I'll organise a surgical review.' He shook his head as he turned to walk away. 'Might pay to get the social worker down here too. And call the police.'

Jemma looked down at her arms. There were needles

in both, and blood on the sheet. A bag of clear liquid was attached to a stand beside her bed.

'It's just fluid,' said the nurse, following her gaze. 'You were dehydrated when you arrived. I've no idea how you drove yourself here. You must have been running on adrenaline. Let's get some details from you now, then I'll get you round to radiology. So, who's your next of kin?'

'Professor Chang.'

'And Professor Chang's first name?'

'Eric or Mary, either one.'

The nurse raised her eyebrows. 'Would you like me to call them?'

'Yes please.' Eric, the dean of her faculty, and his wife Mary, a professor of engineering, had stepped in to help her after her parents died. She had no idea how she'd have managed without them. The nurse pulled a blanket over her and dimmed the lights before leaving to make the call. Jemma allowed herself to doze until she heard a concerned, but familiar voice outside the curtain talking to the doctor who'd been so convinced that she'd been hurt by someone.

When he poked his head into her cubicle, she broke down. 'I'm sorry,' she said, between sobs. 'I'm so glad to see you.'

He reached down and, sitting on the edge of the bed, gathered her into his arms and murmured soothing noises.

As the tears subsided, she realised he had someone with him, and she forced herself to sit up. 'I'm sorry,' she said again.

The man stepped forward. 'No, no. I'm Dr McGregor. Plastic surgeon. Let me have a look at that laceration.'

'Friend of a friend,' said Eric.

That made Jemma smile. Eric always had a friend, someone who'd have the skills to organise whatever he needed. She gripped his hand and, even though she knew it was irrational, she felt afraid that if she let go, he might disappear, and she'd be back in the forest.

'I've had a look at the CT,' said Dr McGregor. 'No fracture, but the wound's been open, and the bone's been exposed, far too long. It needs a surgical washout.'

Eric stayed with her until she was wheeled into the theatre. Then everything became even more surreal. The smell of antiseptic, the hushed voices and the bright lights. She jumped when another doctor took her hand and introduced himself as the anaesthetist. A few minutes later everything was again black. Her first word when she woke from the anaesthetic was, 'Eric.'

'I'm here, sweetheart,' he replied, stroking her hair.

She tried to speak but couldn't stop herself from drifting back to sleep until she felt a nurse rubbing her hand and calling her name. Eric, who didn't look like he'd moved, introduced her to a police officer who sat beside him, Sergeant Parker.

'Hello Jemma,' said Parker.

'Hello.' Her mouth was so dry, she gratefully accepted a glass of water from Eric.

'Do you feel up to telling me what happened.' Parker's voice was gentle, encouraging.

'Sure.' She recounted her story as much as she could remember.

The police officer took copious notes and didn't interrupt until she'd finished. 'Could you answer a few questions?'

'Okay,' she said, although she'd rather have gone back to sleep.

'Any idea who the hooded man might have been? Can you describe him? Could he have been another scientist?'

'No idea. He was my height, average weight. I couldn't see his face.'

'Hair colour?'

'His head was covered too.' She rested back on the pillow. 'I really don't know anything more.'

'Just one more thing,' said Parker. 'The other man, Sean. Did he say why he was there?'

'Some sort of task force. CIA, ASIO and someone else.' She slapped her hand on her thigh. 'Oh, I know, MI5. Said he was investigating the blue light.'

'Right. The blue light. We've had a few reports of it, too. Did he say what it was or why he was investigating it?'

'No, only that people had gone missing near those lights in other countries.'

'Okay, I'll need to talk to you again, but rest for now.'

Eric lightly kissed the bandage on her forehead, then stood and walked with Parker to the door. She couldn't hear the discussion but suspected they were planning something. He was smiling when he returned. 'I'll stay with you,' he said, pulling a recliner chair close to her bed.

*   *   *

That afternoon, when Sean arrived at work, all eyes were on his boss's office. It occupied one corner of a large room. His own office was in the opposite corner and he considered sneaking around the two-metre-high screens that separated the ordered rows of back-to-back desks, to get to it. Dan O'Leary, his partner, tried to push him back out the door but he faltered and when his boss, General Alexander Hunt, yelled into the phone at someone, he missed his opportunity to slip away. Hunt slammed the phone down and glanced up. He locked eyes with Sean, before bellowing at him to enter.

'Are you out of your fucking mind?' Hunt hurled a document onto the desk. 'ASIO, MI5, CIA? Are you sure you didn't forget someone? What about the KGB or oh, I don't know, Mossad?'

'What's the problem?' Sean swore under his breath.

'You let the girl go to a hospital. They called the police.'

'Of course, she had to go to a hospital. She had a head wound.' Sean paused. 'She didn't say I hurt her, did she?'

'No. She told them you rescued her when she was chased by some man.' Hunt slammed his chair against the desk and strode around it to stand in front of Sean. 'What the hell did you think you were doing?'

'What was I supposed to say? Oops, you'd better move away, there's top secret government business here.' Sean drew himself up to his full height, grabbed the report and waved it back at Hunt. 'It's easy for these bastards to criticise when they weren't there. It wasn't just that blue light; there were people, lots of them, and guards with bloody big weapons.

Then there was a trapped civilian, terrified out of her wits.'
And no way was I going to leave her there to fend for herself
against those weapons.

'Your job was to ensure the security of that facility, and
everything that goes with it, not play superman.'

'Then maybe they should have told us about the *everything*
that goes with it.'

'You don't get it, do you, Bellamy? You used your own
name. For Christ's sake. I've had the Australian Prime Minister on the phone abusing me. He's had the British Prime
Minister screaming at him.'

'No, I didn't use my name. The bastards who chased us
broadcast my name over a loudspeaker. They must have seen
me near their site, although I don't know how. Jemma obviously picked it up, but I didn't expect her to go to the police.'

'Jesus, now it's *Jemma*. You were besotted by a good-
looking girl. You've managed to get us slammed across the
international police networks. All their radars are gunning
for us.'

'I had to come up with something fast to get her out of the
way. Are you saying I should have let them grab her, and do
God knows what?'

'Yes.' Hunt paused before he spoke again, his voice now
quieter. 'They wouldn't have harmed her, and it might still be
the best place for her.'

'You can't be serious. How the hell do you know they
wouldn't harm her? You don't even know who they are. Or is
there something you're not telling me?' He tossed the report

back on the desk and stood, his arms folded across his chest, and glared back at Hunt.

An odd look crossed Hunt's face, not a frown, more like irritation. Sean knew that his orders had come directly from the Chief of the Defence Force. He'd been directed to look for an intruder around the source of that blue light. The chief had called it the Springbrook Communication and Research Facility. In quieter moments, he'd called it SCARF. They'd met with SCARF's executive commander, Brigadier Charles Everson, but neither he nor the chief would explain the facility's purpose or what an intruder might be after. They said it was a simple research facility. Sean knew Hunt would have tried to get more information but, from his look, he'd failed. He was out of the loop and didn't like it. Now he looked everywhere except at Sean.

'They're military, and that's enough,' Hunt snarled. 'I've had orders to pick her up and hand her over to Brigadier Everson.'

'For Christ's sake, she's in hospital. I can't just head in there and grab her. And who the hell is Everson? We don't know anything about him or what he does up there. I did some searches after I left the mountain this morning. I couldn't find any mention of him or SCARF on any website, not even the encrypted ones. If it's a research facility like they claim, why don't they have a building. It was just a grassed-over clearing with a beam of light in the middle. All we know for sure is that he's got the chief jumping to his bidding.'

Hunt sighed and sat back down behind his desk. 'I've

told you all I know. Get surveillance on the woman. We'll decide on further action later. In the meantime, make sure she doesn't become a problem.'

'How do you propose I do that?'

'I don't bloody care. Just do it.'

'I might stand a chance if I knew what it is that I'm supposed to be investigating.'

'You know all you need to know.' Hunt glared, then hurled the report back at Sean. 'Now get the hell out of here and fix your mess. And next time, give me the ammunition to return fire before I get a rocket from the chief.'

Sean slammed the door as he left. 'Dan, my office,' he snarled. Hunt was right, he should have been informed, but that was no excuse to shout at him, especially in front of his staff.

Dan grimaced. 'That kind of day.'

'I suppose you heard.'

'Most of it.'

'My butt's on the line.' He tossed the report across the desk. 'Everything went wrong overnight. The woman's name is Jemma Anderson. She's a university lecturer. I need to know which university and where she lives. I'm going back up there to pack up her gear.'

'Will I take her into custody when I find her?'

'No. Call me.' Sean stopped. 'And get on to the Air Force. Ask them about experimental aircraft in that area. I glimpsed something before I grabbed her. When I looked back, it wasn't there. Could have been a blimp, the type tyre companies use for advertising. It was stationary, and much bigger, about the size of a Dash 8, but no wings. Spherical. I know it's ridiculous, but I had the feeling it was watching me.'

'Watching you? Right. Could you hear any engine noise? Or rotors?'

'Nothing, it just hung there. I didn't get a good enough look.'

Dan sighed. 'Okay, find the woman. Then identify an aircraft that was watching you but vanished before you could see it. Goodo.'

'You've got it. On your way.'

Sean flopped into his chair and stared back at Hunt's office. He'd have to work out for himself what Everson was up to, why that man had chased Jemma, and what it had to do with the blue light. Despite Hunt's rant, he wouldn't allow himself to get too close to a subject no matter how much he was attracted to her although following up on Jemma would be a pleasure. She was tall and lean, with the face of an angel, but it was the strength of character shining through those intense hazel eyes that had him fascinated. When he'd growled at her, she'd snapped back and despite her injuries, she'd stood up to him, more than most would. She reminded him of his twin sister Cheryl, not in looks but the same determined attitude.

When they were just ten years old their father had died, and their mother abandoned them. Cheryl had become fiercely independent, determined to accomplish everything herself, refusing help from anyone, including Sean at times. Jemma had fought against him in much the same way, and he presumed she'd reject his ongoing efforts. He could set up covert surveillance. She didn't have to know it was there. Besides, she didn't know anything that could compromise SCARF. Hell, he didn't know anything himself and, despite the chief's assurances that Everson was legitimate, Sean wasn't satisfied that Everson wouldn't go after her.

CHAPTER 2

Jemma did her best to stay awake so she could chat to Eric after Sergeant Parker left but she couldn't stop herself from drifting off. For the rest of the afternoon, and right through the night, whenever she moved, he'd jump up and check on her, offering water, pillows, extra blankets. It was a relief when, early the next morning, the surgeon cleared her to go. Eric insisted she come home with him, so he and Mary could look after her. She smiled as he helped her to sit up. If anyone else had smothered her this way, even in her current state, she'd have argued.

She baulked when he demanded she get into a wheelchair to leave the hospital, but he stood in front of her, arms crossed, until she gave in. She threw herself into the chair, but when he went to put a blanket over her legs in the car, that was too much.

'Jesus, Eric. It was just a cut. You're treating me like I'm an invalid.'

'You were seriously injured on that mountain and chased by multiple unknown males. I don't plan to allow anything else to happen to you.' A tear rolled down his cheek and he drew her into a hug. 'We're not going to lose you.'

Shocked by the strain in his eyes, she swallowed her retort and returned his hug. 'I'm not going anywhere.'

He squeezed her hand before shutting the door and, after thanking the nurse, walked round to the driver's side, got in and started the car. He drove slowly out of the carpark as though he was afraid that she might break.

'Eric, I'm fine,' she said, with a sigh.

He looked at her as he waited for a gap in the traffic to turn out onto the main road. 'I know, sweetheart, but you'll have to forgive me for worrying. When that emergency nurse rang to inform me that you'd been injured, and I had no idea what had happened, my brain went into overdrive. When I told Mary, I thought she was going to have a heart attack.'

'I'm so sorry.'

'No, don't be sorry. None of this was your fault and that's part of my problem. I don't know who did this to you, or why, so we don't know who to watch out for.'

'Nobody did anything to me. I fell.'

'Yes, but you wouldn't have fallen if someone hadn't chased you. Then this Sean fellow forced you to go with him. I accept that, in the end, he helped. But still …'

'I know. It's all really weird but it's over now, and I have to get past it and go back to being normal.'

'Yes, I understand,' he replied. 'But not yet. Humour us and let us look after you for a while.'

They drove in silence up the coast road, past the sparkling blue of the Broadwater and, as they skirted the esplanade, most of the tension seemed to drain from her body, and she allowed her eyes to fall shut. She jumped when she felt Eric stroke her face to let her know they were home. He draped his arm around her as they walked up the stairs, but she was surprised to see the police officer from the night before in the lounge room, chatting to Mary.

'Do you need anything,' Sergeant Parker said to Eric. 'I'm ready to go as soon as you are.'

'Go where?' said Jemma.

'We're going up the mountain to find your hide, sweetheart,' said Eric.

'I'm going with you,' she said, staring at him. It didn't take a genius to work out that's what they'd been cooking up when she'd seen them whispering in her hospital room.

'No, we've got this,' replied Eric, returning her stare.

'Mate, we don't know what we'll find there,' Parker added. 'It's better if you stay here.'

'I know where my hide is. I can take you straight to it.'

'I helped you set it up,' said Eric. 'I know where it is too.'

'Stop treating me like a child.'

'Stop acting like one.' Eric stood in the doorway, smiling. 'We can handle this, and you can rest.'

'Come on, dear,' said Mary, dragging Jemma from the door. 'We'll have a cuppa while we wait for them.'

Too tired to resist, she followed Mary to the kitchen, slapping the palm of her hand on the bench when Mary crossed to the tap to fill the kettle.

'Enough,' said Mary. 'Let the police do their job. I'm much happier to have you safe here with me than trekking around that mountain with them.' She stood, hands on hips, and glared.

Jemma opened her mouth ready for a fight but the look on Mary's face made her laugh. 'God, I love you, Aunty Mary.'

Mary flicked her with a tea towel, then pulled her in close which took Jemma back to the early days. Just eighteen when her parents were swept off the bridge in the 2011 floods, she'd spent much of the following weeks consoled in Mary's embrace.

It was several hours before Eric returned with Sergeant Parker.

'Am I pleased to see you,' said Mary, as he walked through the door. 'Almost had to tie her down to have a sleep. She's been pacing for the last hour.'

'About to get worse,' he replied, hugging her.

Jemma slipped past them down the stairs to the police Land Cruiser. She ran around the car, then back to Sergeant Parker and grabbed his arm. 'Where is it?'

'No luck,' he replied.

'I told you Sean said he'd pack it up.'

'Yes, and it looks like he has, but we had to check,' said Eric, steering her back towards the house. 'Now settle down and we'll go inside and decide what to do next.'

She couldn't see how more talking would help, but she didn't have a better plan, so she followed him up the stairs and sat with them at the table. They talked for more than an hour until finally Parker assured Jemma that the police were doing all they could, which she took to mean that they had no idea what was going on.

Sergeant Parker spoke to her almost every day after that, usually with more questions, concerned that he'd found no trace of the man who'd made her run in the first place. He also took a dim view of Sean's actions, referring to it as 'deprivation of liberty,' even though she repeatedly told him Sean had rescued her. She wished she'd never mentioned Sean, although she'd had to explain how she got away. But it was the look on Mary's face each time he said he had nothing new to report that stopped her from expressing her wish to go home. She understood Eric and Mary's fears for her safety. Their only son, Anthony, had disappeared five years earlier after he was transferred by his organisation to New York for a major promotion. Police had suspected foul play. She knew that Eric and Mary saw her as their adopted daughter and were terrified of losing her too, but even so, when two weeks later the police hadn't located Sean, or the man who had made her run from her hide, she insisted on going back to her apartment.

Early the next morning she packed, put her bags in the car and returned to say goodbye. She declined Mary's offer of breakfast, scooted down the stairs, jumped in her car, and started the engine before she could change her mind. She looked back and waved, just in time to see Mary wipe a tear from her eye. With a sigh, she firmed the pressure on the accelerator and reversed out, braking to allow a medium sized, grey SUV which had pulled out from across the street to pass. She waited at the edge of the driveway, but it was taking so long, she turned around to look. Its windows were heavily tinted, and she couldn't see the occupants, although she thought there were two, but she had the impression they were looking her way. Once they'd passed, she backed the rest of the way out of the driveway, flattened her accelerator and turned left into a cross-street. For the next three blocks she repeatedly checked in the rear-view mirror but didn't see the SUV again.

'For crying out loud,' she growled at herself. 'You're being paranoid.' She kept talking to herself as much to distract as to re-assure until she turned into the carpark of her apartment block. A similar grey SUV drove past behind her. Eric had spent so much time, not just now, but for years, drumming into her to keep her eyes open, use her peripheral vision, be aware of her surroundings and to act if anything didn't seem right. She zipped into her allotted parking bay, stepped out, grabbed her suitcase from the boot, locked her car and turned towards the lift only to see the grey SUV drive slowly behind her. It rounded a corner and headed deeper into the multi-level carpark. It could be a coincidence but, mindful of Eric's training, she picked up her pace and ran towards the lift. The vehicle must have turned around as it suddenly swerved in front of her, trapping her against a pillar. The car's doors flew open and out jumped Sean.

She dropped her bags on the ground and shouted at him, 'How dare you? You just scared the living daylights out of me.'

'Sorry, but I need to talk to you,' he said, pointing to another man who'd also been in the car. 'This is Dan. My partner.'

She nodded to Dan but didn't take her eyes off Sean. 'Answer me. What the hell did you think you were doing?'

'Protecting you. I followed you down the mountain that night and I've had you under surveillance since you left the hospital.'

'You don't think you could have found a way to approach me without giving me a heart attack? And why on Earth would you have me under surveillance for God's sake?'

'First chance I've had to *approach* you that you weren't surrounded by other people. That uncle and aunt of yours know how to set up a tight security net. Surveillance is standard procedure, and that's the reason I'm here. We've observed someone who we believe is watching your apartment, probably waiting for you to return. We have surveillance cameras around the outside of your building and in the carpark and we've used face-recognition software to come up with one stand-out image. A man, Caucasian, about 175 centimetres, 75-80 kilograms, early fifties, brown hair. I'd like you to look at some photos, see if you recognise him. If we've got the right person, we should be able to ID him.'

'Have you told the police?'

'Not yet, but we will once we know who he is.' He picked up her bags and steered her towards the lift. 'Mind if we come up with you, check your apartment?'

'Yes, I mind, but since that night on the mountain nobody seems to take any notice of what I think.'

He laughed as he pressed the button for the lift. 'I am interested in your thoughts, but I'm more concerned about your safety.' He walked into the lift with her bags and, still smiling, held the door open waiting for her to join him. Dan, following behind, glanced at Sean, then turned back to face the door, his hand on his weapon.

Jemma pointed at Dan's hand. 'You've got to be joking.'

'Understood,' replied Sean, but when the doors opened on her floor, he held her in the lift until Dan had checked the corridor and the stairwell.

'I don't believe this,' she muttered when he released her. She walked ahead of them towards the penthouse apartment that she'd bought from her parents' estate. The only one on the top floor, it had views that stretched out over the ocean to the horizon and a balcony bigger than the average urban backyard.

She resisted Sean as he wrested the keys from her hand, but his strength won. Why was it that no one seemed to think she was capable of doing anything for herself since that night?

'Did you secure the deadlock before you left?'

'I did.' She moved closer to the lock. 'Eric came in to clean out the fridge and pantry, but he's really conscientious about locking up, so he'd have fixed it even if I did leave it open.'

'It's unlocked now. Wait here,' he commanded. The men stood on either side of the door, nodded to each other, then Sean pushed the door open.

Bristling at his expectation she'd obey his order, Jemma nevertheless stood back and waited, peering inside each time she heard them open or shut a door or fiddle with locks. Finally, Sean beckoned her in. She picked up her bags and brushed past him without speaking but, in the doorway to her bedroom, she froze. She'd left the bedspread down because she'd planned to change the sheets the next morning. It was now arranged neatly over the bed. Eric wouldn't have done that. He saw making beds as a woman's work which annoyed Mary no end. There was no way he'd have made her bed. Her skin crawling, she dropped her bags and walked through the lounge, into the kitchen, where she saw two plates that she knew she'd left in the sink to soak, stacked neatly on the drainer. Eric was a creature of habit. If he'd done that, he'd have dried them and put them away.

'Someone's been here,' said Jemma.

'My impression too.' Sean gently lifted her face until her eyes met his. 'Your balcony door was open. I've locked it now. Does anyone else have a key?'

'Only Eric. God Sean, who's doing this? What do they want?'

'I don't know, but I'll figure it out.'

'Yeah, right. You sound just like the police.' She dropped her voice low. '*Let me assure you we're doing everything we can.* Meaning they haven't got anything.'

'Come on.' Laughing, he steered her towards the sofa and told her to sit, then flopped down beside her. Dan sat opposite and while Sean focused his attention on her, Dan's eyes kept moving, following sounds and movements and continually checking doors and windows.

Sean pulled something from his pocket. 'Jemma, would you look at this please? This is the man we've noticed. Have you ever seen him?'

She grabbed the photo. 'Oh my God. Yes, I have. A couple of weeks ago. He came to my office.'

'What did he want?'

'Told me I should stay away from the rainforest. That is was dangerous.'

'Did he explain what was dangerous?'

'No. Told me to trust him. But why would I? I didn't know him. Besides, he was just too friendly. Looked the same as he does in the photo. That hat with the narrow brim and the pleat in the crown. And the same dark-coloured sunglasses so I couldn't see his eyes. He gave me the creeps.'

'Did you get a name?'

She shuddered as she shook her head. 'Do you know who he is?'

'Not yet, but I've sent it out. We usually get a quick response. Would you consider coming with us? We can organise a safe house until we know what's going on,' said Sean.

'I need answers Sean, not protection.'

'I don't have them. Once we find out who he is, I might be able to give you more. In the meantime, I think you do need protection, either with us or go back to your aunt and uncle for a while.'

Before today, she'd always felt safe in her apartment and in her normal, organised world. She taught at the university during the day and conducted her research in the mountain rainforest at night, her biggest highlights international conferences. Her worst stress was coping with the volume of students in the first-year class she taught one semester of each year. 'I don't want to go anywhere else,' she said quietly. 'I'll be careful, keep everything locked tight.'

'Alright, I can't force you to come with us. I can keep surveillance on you.' He handed her a card. 'Call me, anytime. My people will be close by, and I'm not far away.'

'That's what the police said.'

'I'd rather you called me. We're better at extracting people if things turn nasty.'

'How much nastier can it get?'

'It won't if you'll trust me and let me help.' When she didn't answer, he stood and walked to the door, but stopped to look back before opening it. He held his hand to his ear mimicking a phone: 'Call me.'

After he left, she locked the door, then threw herself back on the sofa and hugged a cushion. His scent and body warmth lingered where he'd been, and an image flitted through her mind of Sean still there, his arm around her, comforting her. With a sigh, she buried her head in the cushion, but the image wouldn't go away, so she got up and walked out through the balcony door, hoping to distract herself by watching a group of people on the foreshore feeding seagulls. One of the greedy birds swooped close to a small child, making her cry. Jemma smiled as older children chased the birds, yelling at them to go away. The birds flew up and around a large pine tree, then swooped back to the table, drawing her eyes to a man who stood behind the youngest child. She gripped the balcony rail. It was the same narrow-brimmed hat, the same sunglasses. And he stared up at her.

She fled inside and secured the door. Sergeant Parker had keyed his number into her phone, so she hit it first, pacing between the kitchen and the balcony door until he answered. He instructed her to check all locks and not to open the door to anyone until she heard his voice. As if she would. Then, despite her earlier annoyance with Sean, she reached for his card but stopped, her arm still outstretched when a bright blue light crept around the front door lock. The door handle turned, and the door that she knew she'd locked after Sean left, creaked open. She grabbed a large saucepan, the only thing within reach heavy enough to use as a weapon. It slipped through her clammy hands. The man stood in the doorway, still wearing his narrow-brimmed hat, still smiling. She tried to run for her bathroom, the only room she could lock herself in, but he caught her arm and pushed her further back into the apartment, pinning her against a wall, his grip too strong for her to break.

'Hello, Jemma,' he said. 'Good to see you again. Now, I'm not going to hurt you, but we do need to chat.'

'How did you get in? Who the hell are you? … And what do you want?'

'You know who I am, we've met before. I've been watching you for months, long before that night you ran away from me on the mountain.'

'It was you stalking my hide?'

'Of course.' He sighed. 'I wasn't stalking, I'm trying to protect you. I told you not to go there, but you wouldn't listen.'

'Why would I listen to you?' She kicked at his knee but, too fast, he grabbed both her hands, jamming her against the wall with his body.

'Because I'm trying to help you. The virus you discovered on the mountain. I've seen it elsewhere. It can infect people as much as animals. My staff are working hard to find a vaccine and a cure. I'm told you're close to a vaccine.'

'Not really, but if your people contact me, I'll give them everything I've got. Besides if I do develop a vaccine, I'll publish my findings.'

'No, no,' he said, firming his grip. 'I can develop it commercially. Make you wealthy beyond your wildest dreams.'

She shook her head. 'There's no money to be made. It's an isolated virus.'

'We can fix that,' he replied.

'What?' She gaped at him. Surely, he wasn't suggesting he'd deliberately spread a virus to do harm. 'You can't be serious.'

'How do you think it got to the mountain?'

'You released it there?' She shrank back as far as she could, given he still had hold of her, very aware that if he was prepared to kill so many animals, he'd have no qualms harming people. 'How could you do that?'

'Are you really that innocent?' He smiled, a quizzical look on his face as he stared back at her. 'You're so like your mother. She fought to the end. Pack some things. I'll take you somewhere safe.'

Jemma remained rigid against the wall, even as he relaxed his grip. His strength and the cold, hard look in his eyes left her in no doubt he'd hurt her if she didn't go along with him, but his words had more impact than anything he could do physically. Not just his suggestion that he'd spread the virus, but he knew her mother. Eight years had passed since her parents died, yet she still grieved for them every day. Multiple scenarios regularly flitted through her mind, all of which involved convincing her parents to stay off the bridge where the wall of water had raced down Murphy's Creek washing their car off the bridge and smashing it into a tree. The car flipped, and her parents had both drowned. Yet bizarre though the event had been, it had never occurred to her until this minute that their accident might not, in fact, have been an accident.

'What do you mean, *fought to the end?*' Her voice sounded weak, even to her, and a long way away.

He looked quite surprised. 'I was sent to stop her from claiming her title. She wouldn't listen.'

'What title?'

'Give me strength,' he muttered. 'Do you not know where you come from?'

'I was born in Brisbane.'

'No.' His stare penetrated through her as though he was trying to determine whether she really didn't know. 'Did she tell you where she came from?'

'Northern Ireland.'

He stepped back and stared at her.

Her eyes flitted around for an escape route, but she didn't move. Whatever he knew about her mother, she had to hear. 'How well did you know my mother?'

'Very well, and I respected her. It was a pity we were on different sides. It didn't have to be that way. And you're her heir.'

'Her heir?' Afraid now to even look at him, she whispered, 'Did you kill my parents?'

'Not me, no. But she should have listened.'

She could barely hear her own voice. 'But someone did?'

For a few seconds, he glared back. Then his eyes relaxed and he softened his voice. 'Come on now, pack a bag and I'll get you back to your family.'

'My family perished in the floods.'

'Not everyone.'

She shrank away. Her younger sister had been in America when the floods hit. Her supervising family had stopped her from returning initially, but she'd disappeared shortly after, and all Jemma's attempts to find her had failed, but she couldn't believe her sister would have anything to do with this man. No idea what his intentions were, she followed him to the bedroom, all the while looking for anything she might use, to overpower him. She picked up a suitcase from the walk-in-robe, put it on her bed, then turned to go back for her clothes. In that instant, she noticed him look away. She dashed to the ensuite. It had an unusually solid lock, although her shaking hands made securing it difficult. Once she had, she flicked the toilet seat down and sat on the closed lid. She didn't have Sean's number in her phone, so she redialled Sergeant Parker, and had just finished telling him what had happened when a beam of blue light streaked through and around the lock. The door sprang open.

The man charged in, waving his weapon at her. 'Do you want me to use this on you?'

She backed into a corner and shook her head, too frightened to speak.

'Forget the clothes, we're going.' He dragged her into the lounge, but a knock stopped them a metre inside the front door.

'Police. Open up.'

The man aimed his weapon towards the door. 'Answer it, but don't let them in. I won't hesitate to use this. Do you understand?'

'Clearly,' replied Jemma, her eyes fixed on the strange weapon. A small screen glowed at the top, but there was no trigger, or hammer, or anything else to fire the thing. She'd learned from a young age to use rifles, shotguns and even pistols on the farm. It had always been presented as self-protection against wild dogs, feral pigs and venomous snakes but with this man's talk of a title, was it possible that her parents had been training her for some other kind of threat?

The man backed towards the balcony door. She grabbed his arm. 'What's your name?' He hadn't answered when another sharp knock interrupted them.

'Police. Open the door. Now.'

He shrugged and ran to the balcony.

She had no idea if he'd fire his weapon and was horrified by the thought that any police officer could be shot protecting her so, irrespective of Parker's commanding tone, she took her time to open the door.

Parker pulled her outside, then ran with two other officers into the apartment. She squatted in the hallway, clamping her hands over her ears to drown out the repeated calls of 'clear.'

'I didn't expect to find him,' said Parker as he helped her up. 'But the balcony door's open.'

'That's where he went.'

'Okay, we'll take you to a safe house, until we work out what he wants.'

'He's after me,' she replied, without moving. 'He's only after me.'

'Do you know why?'

She shook her head but didn't resist Parker as he gently pushed her towards her bedroom and told her to pack. He waited outside while she threw some clothes in the suitcase that was already on the bed. She grabbed her computer then followed him into the lift that would take them down to the carpark. When the lift doors opened in the basement, he slipped his hand through her arm and held her back from the door, just like Sean had. The other officers stepped out, both with their hands resting on weapons. An unmarked car pulled in and Parker pushed her into the back seat before jumping in beside her. He ordered the driver to take off and the other officers ran to a police car parked on the other side of the lift. The driver of Jemma's car carefully surveyed the street then zipped into the heavy traffic before turning south onto the Pacific Highway. When he took the Mudgeeraba off-ramp, she glared at Parker. This was the road that led to Springbrook and that blue light. She started to question where they were going when the driver veered off onto a concealed driveway.

'It's alright Jemma, I've requested higher level protection,' said Parker as they neared a two-metre-tall chain mesh fence with razor wire along the top.

'This is a nightmare,' said Jemma, staring up at him.

'I know.'

The driver parked near the front door of a house. Parker grabbed her suitcase and helped her from the car, then introduced her to two men, one from the CIB, one from ASIO.

She couldn't believe her ears. CIB okay. That she understood. But ASIO? What on Earth had she got herself into?

'I don't understand why I need looking after.'

Parker shrugged. 'Neither do we but until we do, we have to see that man as a serious threat.'

*   *   *

Hunt exploded when Sean called to say he'd lost Jemma. 'How the hell did this fellow get past both you and the police?'

'He's slippery,' replied Sean. 'I only saw him when he ran out of her balcony door and climbed onto the roof. There was low cloud cover and I lost him after that, but I've got two of our people searching. I didn't see him go in. Two police cars arrived, and they rushed her away before I could intervene. She should be safe with the police, but I need to be sure she stays that way.'

'Damn it,' Hunt snarled. 'It's a fucking debacle. The chief told me this morning that there's something important about

Jemma's past, but he won't elaborate. We're to protect her, and if we can't achieve that, hand her over to General Everson.'

'Jesus. If there's something special about her, I'm sure she doesn't know what it is. Why does he keep wanting to involve Everson? We've got more capacity to protect her than any ordinary unit.'

'Yes, I agree, although I don't think SCARF is an ordinary military unit. I don't know what it is. But we need to get hold of her now, ask questions later. If I go through official channels to override the police, it'll take days. I've texted you the co-ordinates for the location of the police car. Get up there and remove her before that other arsehole interferes. What do you need?'

'Chopper on standby.'

'Right. Send O'Leary to the airfield. Do you want another team to join you?'

'No, I'm best alone. Keep them available in case I need backup.'

'Done.'

'Check your inbox,' said Sean. 'We got a photo this morning of the fellow who's been following her,' said Sean.

'Already onto it. His name is Fredrick Pritchard. Owns a pharmaceutical company. Headquarters in New York. No police record that I can find, there or here.'

'What the hell does he want?'

'Don't know. I've put another team onto finding him.'

'Can you speak to Everson, see if he recognises him, or if he knows anything about Jemma's past.'

'Already tried. He won't give me anything. I'll keep trying,' sighed Hunt.

'Sir, that's crap. He's supposed to be working with us. What the hell's going on?'

'Wish I knew. Whatever it is he and the chief are hiding, they're as keen as we are to get hold of Pritchard and find out what he's up to, but that's as far as I can get.'

Hunt remained seated at his desk after the call. It'd probably be easier to knock down a brick wall with his bare hands than get the information Sean wanted. Trying to protect Jemma, when everybody from the chief of the defence force down had refused to reveal everything they knew, was next to impossible.

It was the chief himself who'd insisted on Sean taking command of this project, over-ruling Hunt's intention to allocate a junior officer to what he thought was a simple surveillance job. That'd been his first hint of something astray. But his mind kept returning to the chief's instruction earlier that morning, to *allocate surveillance for Jemma's guardians.* That just didn't make sense. Jemma had legally been an adult when her parents died, and despite her close relationship with the people who'd helped her, they weren't *guardians.* Friends, helpers, even stand-in parents, not *guardians,* but that word took him back to an event he'd witnessed twenty years earlier.

Hunt's first commanding officer had been General Eamon Bellamy, Sean's father, although Sean didn't know that. He didn't think Sean even knew his father had a military background, let alone such a high rank. Hunt, along with the rest of his unit, had driven off the insurgents who'd ambushed General Bellamy, but he'd already sustained critical injuries. He was evacuated to a major Brisbane hospital, and Hunt clearly remembered his one and only visit to the hospital. The children, Sean and Cheryl, stood clinging to each other, crying, with no adult in the room to help them.

Outside, General Bellamy's wife argued with an army officer, not someone Hunt knew, but he remembered her words as if they'd been uttered just minutes ago.

'You bastards forced me into that marriage against my will. You stole my last baby. Now you can have the bloody lot of them.'

The officer frowned, and Hunt had readied himself to intervene as the fellow moved closer to her. 'Now is not the time or place,' said the officer. 'You must discuss this with the guardians.'

'To hell with the guardians,' she shouted. 'Tell them to take over. I'll have no further part in this.' She swung around and raced towards Hunt, almost knocking him down in her haste.

He reached out to balance her, 'Who are the guardians?'

'As if you didn't know,' she snorted, trying to break away from him.

'No, honestly, I don't know.'

She glared at him for a minute, then snapped, 'Ask your father, he organises them.' This time she broke his hold and ran from the hospital, ignoring both her husband and her children.

Hunt could only stare after her. How would she know anything about him, or his father? When he'd asked later, his father professed ignorance, but Hunt had seen something cross his father's eyes before he'd smiled and changed the subject. In that instant, Hunt knew he had to keep an eye on Sean and Cheryl. The neighbours stepped in as surrogate parents for the twins, which made him suspect they were the guardians. Shortly after, he discovered that the principal of the twin's boarding school was ex-military and he made himself known to her. He couldn't remember what excuse he'd used, but she'd accepted it and expressed her own concerns about the twin's welfare. Cheryl's independence shone through quickly but Sean, although also independent, exhibited a vulnerability which had opened him up to bullying. Hunt suggested to the principal that she send Sean to a karate school where he instructed. Later he'd suggested to Sean to try out for the school's army cadet corps. After that, it was a simple task to guide him into a military career and, once he'd graduated from Duntroon, Hunt had taken him over.

Proud of the man that Sean had become, Hunt regretted having never revealed to Sean his father's military history, or even that they'd worked together. The current chief had ordered him to keep his mouth shut, but perhaps he should have used his own judgement. He sighed. Today, Jemma's safety. It seemed far-fetched that these guardians could represent a link between Sean and Jemma, and possibly himself, but that investigation would have to wait.

CHAPTER 3

Jemma had never felt so helpless as she followed the detective through the house. He stopped in a large room with a traditional fireplace which was unusual in a Queensland home. On the opposite side of the room was a modern sofa, but it was otherwise bereft of furniture. The detective placed a wooden kitchen chair directly in front of her so as he sat, he looked down on her.

Parker sat beside her on the sofa and glared at the detective. 'She's been through enough.'

The detective's forehead wrinkled, and he returned Parker's glare, but said nothing as he turned his attention to Jemma. 'I need you to go through everything. This man who chased you, the blue light, the military person,' he glanced at his notes, 'Bellamy. And everything that happened this morning.'

Jemma bristled but managed to hide her annoyance. He clearly hadn't reviewed the case given he couldn't remember Sean's name. She took a deep breath and focussed on her feet before recounting the events. She'd told her story so many times now, that it felt like a rehearsed speech, but she did her best to include every detail. The detective continually interrupted, mostly demanding details she'd already given. When he finished the ASIO man stepped forward. He introduced himself as Luke which was better than the other fellow whose name she still didn't know.

Perhaps it was Luke's slow southern US drawl, but his voice sounded kinder than the detective, sympathetic. 'This title. Did the fellow give you any idea which country?'

She shook her head.

'Okay, what about the weapon? It gave off a blue light, you said. Did he attempt to fire it at all?'

She shook her head again.

'So, you don't know for sure it was a weapon?'

'No. Could have been a prop. He might just be a crazy person, but he scared me too much to argue, and he did somehow open those locks without a key.'

'Thank you,' he replied. 'That gives me something to start on. You need a break now, but I'd like to talk to you again later.' He smiled and extended his hand to help her stand. Sergeant Parker then led her to her temporary room, but before they got there, she heard the detective's raised voice.

'Just ignore him,' said Parker. 'He was trying to impress the ASIO man.'

'I don't think it worked,' she replied.

'Neither do I. Now, you're free to come and go as you please. Your bag's already in there. Freshen up, then come back out when you're ready.'

She made herself smile as she thanked him, but once he'd shut the door, she leaned back against it, and sank to the floor. Her parents had been academics, both successful and both well-liked. Why would anyone want to kill them? And why didn't she know her mother had a title? That had seemed to strike a chord with Luke although he didn't say why. She closed her eyes. Alternating images of her parents and the man with the strange hat and sunglasses, consumed her thoughts. She slammed her fist on the floor. 'Why?'

'Why what?' Sean jumped down from the manhole in the ceiling.

She jumped up, but he was too quick. He rammed himself against the door, barricading her only exit.

'Get out,' she hissed. 'What the hell are you doing here?'

'You could have said hello, or nice to see you Sean. And who's a bastard?'

'Answer my question. Why are you here?'

'To formulate a plan for your escape, and ongoing survival.'

'Why would I need to escape from the police? Talk to them. You could sort this out.'

He groaned. 'Out of the mouths of babes. My only interest is your protection.'

'I'm not a babe. I'm an intelligent woman caught up in something I don't understand. Give me an intelligent answer.'

Her voice grew louder, and someone knocked on the door. 'Everything okay in there?'

'Yes thanks,' she replied, pushing Sean away. 'I fell asleep. Bad dream.'

'Okay, call if you need anything.'

Sean led her away from the door. 'Good, I take it you'll listen to me.'

'You've got five minutes. You'd better be pretty damned convincing.'

'You drive a hard bargain, but I'll do my best.' He grinned with the same mischievous twinkle that'd won her over that night in the cave.

'Four-and-a-half minutes,' she snapped, flopping onto the bed, surprised to see him take a deep breath as though he was carefully choosing his words.

'Jemma, I walked across an open yard, no alarms, no one patrolling, no dogs. I climbed a tree, removed tiles from the roof, and crawled through the roof-space to get here. Someone should have stopped me. Do you understand what I'm saying?'

'Their security isn't very good?'

'Worse than that. It's non-existent. The fellow who called to you just now. He should have come in and checked properly, simple police procedure.'

'Are you saying he wasn't police?'

'I don't know who's out there but you're right, I don't think they're police.'

'Let's just go out and have a look then,' said Jemma, throwing her hands in the air, but before she could stand, his hand pressed firmly on her shoulder and pushed her back down.

'No. We don't know who they are, how many are out there or what weapons they have.'

She stared back at him without moving. 'You think it's that man again?'

'He's my first thought. We have his name now, Fredrick Pritchard. Does that ring any bells?'

She shook her head.

'Alright. Jemma, I don't know if it's him, and we won't find out standing here talking about it.'

'He says my parents were murdered.' She inhaled sharply. 'Said someone else did it, but he was involved.'

'Jesus.' Sean gently eased her up. 'Mate, I have no idea if that's the truth, but I do know you have to get out of here now.'

'How do you propose I do that? There's bars on the windows and, if you're right, I can't just walk out the door.'

'Oh, I don't know. Would you like me to help you?'

'Depends on how high a price I have to pay for your help.'

'No price. All part of the service, ma'am.' His face became serious. 'I didn't anticipate a problem after that night. Obviously, I was wrong and should have organised better protection for you at the time. Fair enough?'

'Maybe.'

'Right, if we're going, we'd better start. I need to get you into the roof-space which means climbing onto my shoulders, so I can push you up there. Are you up to it?'

'I can only try.'

'Okay, on the bed.'

'Really? I don't think that's part of the deal.'

'Bloody hell. I suppose I deserved that. Would you please stand on the bed? From there I will squat down, and you will climb on my shoulders. I will then boost you up into the ceiling. Was that phrased appropriately enough?'

'Hurry up then.' She clambered onto his shoulders when he squatted down but didn't have the strength, even with his help, to lever herself through the manhole. He took a deep breath then reached down to her lower legs and heaved her into the ceiling space. She watched as he pulled the bed under the opening and lifted himself through the manhole, his muscles rippling with the pressure.

'Let's go. I want to be out of the compound before they decide to check on you.'

She followed him through the narrow ceiling and onto the roof tiles, then watched him slide down the tree, and made sure she was beside him before he turned back to assist her. The fine sliver of a moon made it hard to see very far, but the yard looked clear and she stepped out from behind the tree.

'Wait,' Sean said, pulling her back. 'Run to the southern fence line. It's the shortest path, less chance of being seen.'

Still wondering if his concern was really warranted, she shrugged. 'Alright, lead the way.'

'Let's go.'

Half-way across the yard she tripped on something. It felt like a log, although it moved as she touched it. She turned as she picked herself up, and gasped. A man lay on the ground, not moving, a sizeable hole in his forehead.

'Quiet,' snapped Sean, crouching beside the man. 'Still warm, but there's no pulse, not breathing.' Sean gently closed the man's eyes, searched the pockets for an ID, then stood and look around. He grabbed Jemma's arm. 'Let's go. We've got to get out of here.'

'I couldn't see him properly. Did you recognise him?'

'No.'

She had no choice but to go with Sean as he pulled her along the fence panels until they reached a cut section, presumably the way he'd come in. He skidded to a stop as he neared a parked car, pointing to pieces of plastic-coated wire strewn under the front.

'Arseholes,' he muttered, whipping out his mobile phone. 'Vehicle's compromised. We need urgent extraction.'

'Tell me what's happening, or I go nowhere,' said Jemma. She tried to sound firm, but her voice trembled.

'Christ Jemma, I'm trying to save your life. Mine as well now. Stay here if you like, but you won't live through the night. I'm getting out. Are you coming or not? He won't wait for us.'

A noise behind made her swing around. A flashlight shone through the yard they'd just left. Sean grabbed her around her shoulders and propelled her forward.

Twang. Something hit a tree near them. *Twang* again.

'What was that?'

'Shots. Keep moving, it's our best chance.'

A helicopter soared past overhead. 'Hurry,' he yelled, but in the swirling wind from the rotors it was difficult to run. He firmed his grip on her shoulders and half carried her the last few metres, then pushed her through the open door and into the cabin. Someone inside helped her up and Sean hauled himself in, then dragged the door shut, and yelled, 'Go. Go. Go.' Another *twang* and the thud of metal on metal. 'Move. We're under fire. Get out of here,' he shouted to the pilot.

The helicopter rose vertically, before banking sharply east. She started to slip but Sean leaned across and fastened her seatbelt. 'Should be out of firing range now.'

Once she'd righted herself in her seat, she turned to face him. 'Okay, time to tell me what's going on.'

'Yeah, big guy. Tell us,' said Dan, who sat opposite.

Sean leaned back and sighed. 'The police should have been on patrol. I suspected they'd been removed when I went to Jemma's room and they didn't check on her. I'd say the intruders weren't quite organised which was lucky for us, allowed us to get away. I grabbed a wallet from that body. Hopefully, it'll give us something.'

'Dear God, this is a nightmare,' she whispered.

Dan took the wallet. 'Go ahead, I'll look through this. Why didn't you take the car and get out?'

Sean shuddered. 'Wire underneath the front. Didn't have time to check for a bomb or defuse it. Then the flashlight, and the shots.'

Dan held the wallet up. 'It's probably fake, but the passport's American. I'll run the name through our databases. Doubt I'll get anything.'

'One of the guys in the suits had an American accent, but he introduced himself as ASIO,' said Jemma. 'He wasn't wearing a suit when we found him though. Can I have a look at the passport?'

'Sure.' Dan held it up.

'Oh, my God. That's Luke. He was from ASIO.'

Sean sat back in his seat and rubbed his eyes until the pilot interrupted. 'Sir, I've been ordered to head to your property at Kilcot.'

'Good,' replied Sean. 'Is anyone meeting us there?'

'One team is on the ground now. There's another on the way from the northern office. Should be there before we arrive.'

'Shit, what the hell's that?' Dan moved as close to the window as he physically could and pointed to a large spherical object, around a hundred metres away, that flew parallel to the helicopter.

'Got it,' said the pilot. 'I'll check with air traffic control.'

Sean leaned across Jemma to follow Dan's line of vision. 'That's the thing I saw that night on the mountain. Strange it's here too.'

'Yeah,' said Dan. 'Very strange.'

'Air traffic control can't see it on their radar,' said the pilot. 'It's gone now anyway. Maybe it was an optical illusion.'

'Don't be ridiculous,' Sean snapped. 'Four of us saw it. Unless you're piping something funny through the air-conditioning, it was real.'

It was only minutes until Jemma felt Sean move and the landing rails touch down. He pulled her with him as he jumped out into a small clearing. Tiny solar garden lights illuminated a path up to the house, creating shadows that seemed to move around her as the trees shifted in the wind.

'It's okay,' said Sean. 'This is my place. We set it up a few years ago so I could use it as an emergency safe house. There's a team waiting inside for us.' Motion sensors set off a string of floodlights near the house and five metres from the back veranda, intense spotlights flashed on, bathing them in daylight. Sean pointed to a tiny camera above the door and explained his team had them under surveillance.

'But it's your house, and they know it's you. Why would they have you under surveillance?'

'They'll want to be absolutely sure it's me, and that I'm not under duress.'

A red light next to the camera blinked when he touched the door handle and he rushed to disable an alarm.

She took his arm when he held it out for her and walked with him through the front door. An enormous German Shepherd bounded across the yard and headed straight for her.

'Meet Max,' said Sean.

She laughed as she bent down. 'Hello gorgeous.' Once Max had joyously licked her face, he rolled on his back, thumping his tail on the floor. 'He's just a great big teddy bear,' she exclaimed.

Sean chuckled. 'Let me demonstrate. Max, here.' Max ran to him and sat neatly by his side. 'Max, guard. Now just move a step or two towards me.'

Jemma shrugged, and took a step, but stopped when Max lifted his lip and growled. 'Alright, I get it. He's well trained. Can I have the teddy bear back now please?'

'Max, leave.' He walked, with the dog, back to her. 'She's okay, mate.'

Max bounded over again and rolled for his tummy rub. She laughed. 'He might be good, but he's still gorgeous.'

'Do you feel a bit safer now?' He grinned at her. 'Max'd eat me alive if he thought I was hurting you.'

'Go Max.' She returned his grin. 'So long as I don't have to clean up the blood.'

'Come on, you need to freshen up and get some rest.' He showed her to his sister's room and told her to use any clothes in the wardrobe. Then he pointed to the bathroom and left her alone.

After her shower, Jemma sat on the edge of the bed, Max's chin on her knee, and listened to Sean humming. He'd shown up to help each time she'd been in trouble. He made her feel safe, she wasn't even sure how, but he couldn't be there every minute of every day.

'I know you're worried,' said Sean, leaning against the door. 'Try not to think about it. Focus on what we do now.'

He looked so relaxed. Yet to her it was a nightmare, and she wanted to wake up. 'I don't like to be this far out of control. I have no idea what to do next.'

'Understood. One foot after the other. Don't think too far ahead. Come downstairs. You'll feel better after dinner.'

Dan was already seated at the table. He stood as she entered the kitchen and pointed to a chair beside him. The smell of the food made her realise she was hungry, and it didn't take long to devour a bowl of thick vegetable soup, or the beef stew that followed.

'I cheated,' said Sean, with a wink. 'I often cook up a pot then divide it up and freeze it. The microwave's my best friend.'

'I'm impressed. This is really good,' she said, surprised by how comfortable she felt at the table having dinner with him. He was full of self-confidence and an entertaining companion.

But he took control away from her and demanded she follow his orders, something she'd never allowed anyone to do.

'Jemma,' he said, leaning across the table, 'I'll be gone early in the morning. There'll be a team outside, and I've got a mobile phone for you. If you feel at all unsafe, I want you to call me. I've keyed in my number. I should answer straight away. If I don't, I've also stored Dan's, and two others.'

'Where are you going? Why can't I come with you?'

'You're best here with Max and I'll have guards stationed outside. We'll be back as soon as we can but just in case, there's something else I want to show you.'

As she rose to join him, he turned to Dan. 'Go and check on the team outside. I won't be long here.'

After Dan left, she stared at Sean, 'Don't you trust him?'

'Not many I'd trust more, but he doesn't need to know about this.'

'And what is this?'

He smiled. 'An escape route. Let me show you.' Taking her hand, he walked her through the house, to a small study at the back with one door and no window. She looked at him, puzzled, and he nudged her towards a painting behind the desk.

As she reached up to touch it, he leaned in behind her, pushed the painting to the side, and pointed to a green button on the wall.

'Press the button,' said Sean.

The very thought that she might need an escape route made her shake and she gripped the painting's frame with one hand to steady herself, so she could reach up with the other hand and press the button.

He moved closer and gently put his hand on her shoulder. 'Okay?'

'Yeah. I just don't know how to handle this.'

'Okay, but I want to see you press the button to know that you can in an emergency. Jemma, keep in mind that this is a precaution, I don't expect you to need it.'

She reached up and hit the button, which moved quite easily. The wall slid in the direction of the painting, revealing a cavity, and lights flickered on. Feeling the warmth of Sean's body close behind, she jumped forward, and stared back at him.

He looked into her eyes. 'Jemma it's okay, you've trusted me this far. I'll work out how to get you through this, I promise.'

'I know you'll do your best, but we don't know what *this* is. It's got to be Pritchard, but why? There has to be some reason, something to do with my mother, but I have no idea what it is.'

'I know. One day at a time.'

'That's what she would have said.'

'Then she was a wise woman.' He smiled. 'There's another green button on this side. It closes the wall and returns the painting to the right place. Once you've secured it, run down the tunnel. Every twenty metres, you'll see another button. Press that and a door will drop down behind you and lock into place, isolating each section. Understand?'

Breathing too hard to speak, she nodded and stared down the long, dark tunnel.

'Text me if you have to use it. And take Max with you.'

CHAPTER 4

When the dawn light seeped through the bedroom window, Sean stretched, dressed and looked in on Jemma. She looked so peaceful now, her hair mussed across the pillow, all the strain melted from her face. He desperately wanted to make sure she stayed that way. Ordering Max to guard her, he crept down the stairs and spoke to his people, then left through the back door. He checked every shadow and hiding place, pausing only to watch a startled pretty-faced wallaby hop protectively towards her joey. His favourite time of day, dew on the grass, soft mist over the dam, butcher birds singing up the sun, nothing to interrupt the peace and quiet of the bush. His memories of standing in this spot with his father and watching the animals had dimmed over the years, but it remained a special place. Sometimes even now he'd walk down here, talking to his father as though he were still beside him. He'd never admit even to his sister how much he missed his father, but there was a void that at times still threatened to overwhelm him. He sensed that, despite Eric and Mary's support, Jemma had a similar void.

When his phone rang, shattering the early morning

silence, he jumped, and it slipped from his hand. He missed the caller ID as he scooped it up to answer, 'Dan?'

'No, it's me,' replied Hunt. 'Just listen, Bellamy. Is the girl safe?'

'Yes, sir, she is.'

'Are you sure?'

'As sure as I can be,' replied Sean. 'Are you sure that SCARF bunch are legitimate military?'

'Like you, as sure as I can be. I've spoken to the chief. He insists they are. We have to accept that.'

'Then there has to be someone else,' said Sean. 'We tripped over a body last night.'

'Christ almighty. You've got to think Pritchard. I'll raise the priority, get more teams onto it.'

'He's clever' said Sean. 'Warn them he'll come out fighting.'

'Right. Everson wants to meet. Secure the house and come straight in.'

'It's secure. Why does he want a meeting?' Sean instinctively scanned the house yard again.

'He said to clear the air and plan future security.'

'Obviously, you think otherwise. So, who the hell are they?'

'I don't have anything further, but he sounded genuinely surprised when I asked about the police safe house. I'm satisfied he wasn't involved.'

'Then what the hell does he want?' Even though the chief had vouched for Everson, it didn't explain the blue light, or Pritchard, and if Pritchard was also SCARF's intruder, finding him had to be top priority.

'Don't know what Everson wants, but it's our best chance to get some information out of him. I'll stall until you get here.'

Sean tapped the phone against his chin after Hunt ended the call, then hit Dan's number. 'Come on, get up.'

'I'm right behind you.'

'Good. Let's get going.'

He donned a Kevlar vest, and threw another one on the passenger seat just as Dan opened the door, then he checked his holster, and the knife in his boot. Dan picked up the vest and threw himself into the front seat.

'Are you fully armed?'

'Yep, and good morning to you too,' muttered Dan.

Sean relayed his conversation with Hunt. 'Nothing gels. Stay on your toes.'

He cursed the peak hour traffic as he drove up the hill towards the rear entrance of his inner-city office building, Not interested in another ambush, he checked up and down the street before proceeding into the carpark. There were a few people around cars or walking towards the lifts. All looked benign, so he turned around on the bottom level and headed back up.

'Hang on. Check that,' said Dan, partway through the next level.

A man leaned against a car. He looked innocent enough until Dan pointed to the butt of a pistol poking out of his jacket.

'Get the number plate and run it,' said Sean.

Dan tapped into the small computer under the dash and,

seconds later, threw back his head and laughed. 'Military. Belongs to a unit based in Springbrook, called SCARF. Funny that.'

'Hilarious. Probably Everson's driver, but keep your eyes peeled.' Outside the carpark, Sean drove to the front of the building and squeezed into a vacant spot. He slipped an *official military business* sign on the dash, then secured the car and took a last look around before heading inside their building. The ten-storey, architecturally bereft, cement block structure wedged between other similar government office blocks, was designed to blend in, given the nature of their business. It housed various military units, all involved with advanced security of one kind or another.

'You take the lift to the top,' said Sean. 'Come down the stairwell to the meeting room. I'll take the stairs up from here.' He pulled a small bug-detector from his pocket and set it to a ten-metre radius then strolled through the large, glassed-in foyer, taking in everything and everyone in his surrounds. Three people to his right, each of whom checked their watches. Waiting for something, or someone. Two individuals to his left sat with briefcases beside them. Both looked nervous. Job seekers. All the men were dressed in suits, the women in fashionable but understated outfits, the colours all neutral. He grimaced. His old jeans, torn at the knees and his sloppy green jumper under the tatty old leather jacket stood out against the suits and the government issue grey all around him. Even the security contingent's suits were grey, although they too were military. Nothing to alert the casual observer to the kind of business encased within these walls. He'd noticed one of the guards scrutinise him as he entered and paused to chat to the fellow until he'd relaxed, then moved on to the stairwell door and casually opened it. Dan should have reached the top floor by now and be heading back down. Once the door had shut, he charged up the stairs and checked out the first floor, repeating the process on each floor until he reached the fifth level where he waited for Dan. Outside the meeting room they paused to listen. A heated conversation, mainly about what he had done with Jemma, halted as they entered and all heads turned towards them. Five people sat around the conference table, Hunt, Everson and three others, one female and two males. Hunt, normally the consummate bureaucrat, sat at the head of the table toying with a microphone jack and looked annoyed which made Sean ease his hand to the shoulder holster hidden inside his jacket. Equally unobtrusively, the people on the other side of the table did the same.

Hunt rose, 'May I present Lieutenant-Colonel Bellamy and Major O'Leary?'

Surprised by the formal introductions, Sean found a chair close to the exit. Dan sat beside him, and both men turned their chairs slightly towards the door. Sean leaned forward and shook hands with each person on the other side of the table. None of these people, apart from Everson, had been at the first meeting. He sat back, expecting Hunt to break the awkward silence, but Hunt also leaned back, his arms folded.

Everson rose and walked to the window that overlooked the main street where Sean had parked his car. 'We had a situation, a couple of weeks ago,' said Everson. 'You were to keep people away from our site, but you allowed a woman access, then hid her from us.'

'No, I found the woman staring at your site, and removed her. Is there a problem with that?'

'Not at all,' continued Everson. 'But it has created a problem that must be corrected. She's already told the police too much. If you would deliver her to us, we have safe places for people like her.'

'What does that mean?' Sean stared at Everson. *People like her?*

Everson leaned forward, resting clenched fists on the table. 'People who've seen things they shouldn't.'

'What is it that she's seen, the things that she *shouldn't?*'

'You know exactly what I mean.' Everson pushed himself off the table and, hands still fisted, glared at Hunt.

'No, I don't,' said Sean. 'But it's a moot point. I can't deliver someone I don't have.' Everson had a weapon tucked inside the front of his jacket, larger than the side-arm most agents carried, not a weapon Sean knew, which was unusual given his expertise in small arms. Jemma had described something similar on the man who'd invaded her apartment and that had to be more than coincidence.

'We found some of her blood near our site, Mr Bellamy,' said Everson. 'Was she wounded?'

'She was.'

'We analysed that blood. It was odd. Tell me, did you find any of her behaviour strange?'

'In what way?'

'Oh, I don't know. Did she mention where she comes from?'

'No, not that I can recall.'

Hunt sat straighter in his chair. 'Your point, Mr Everson?'

Everson clasped his hands in front of his chest and bowed his head. 'No point just interested. We know you have her, Mr Bellamy. Let's be gentlemen about it. One way or another, we will get her.'

'More to the point,' said Sean, 'you asked us to check for intruders to your facility. She was chased by a man who we now know is Fredrick Pritchard. That was why she was near your facility. Is he also your intruder?'

'My people agree he is the same man, although he is not usually alone.'

'So, who is he? What does your facility have that he'd want?'

'I cannot say who he is or what he would want, but the purpose of our facility is on a need to know basis, and way above your clearance level,' replied Everson.

'Crap,' replied Sean. 'We all have the highest-level clearances, and you can read us in on any *need to know*.'

'We need you to set up surveillance, nothing more. But right now, we need you to return Dr Anderson and I believe you've received an order from the chief to that effect.'

Hunt jumped in. 'Not quite. The chief's ordered us to protect her, or to hand her over if we can't, and I'm sure that won't be necessary. Did he tell you why he considers her important?'

'No, I'm not privy to that information. But from my perspective, I need to prevent her from talking about our facility. We are designated above top secret for very good reason,' said Everson. 'The chief knows I can protect her from whatever it is that concerns him. So, if you place her in my custody, I can cover both bases.'

Sean shrugged, there was no point arguing, although he was surprised that Hunt hadn't pushed a bit harder. Despite the chief's assurances, Sean wasn't comfortable with Everson and there was no way he'd give Jemma up.

* * *

Jemma roused herself a couple of hours after Sean left. Dressed in jeans and a t-shirt that belonged to his sister and with Max by her side, she walked down the stairs. Although she presumed the guards were still outside, she couldn't see them, so she walked around checking the locks on every window and door then sat on the sofa. Max snuggled into her as though he truly did understand her pain.

'Just us, mate. Suspect they're out checking the grounds. They'll be back soon. I can smell coffee. Shall we see what we can find?'

The dog wagged his tail and followed her to the kitchen. Sean had set the coffee pot to come back on at 8am. Coffee and toast, just what she needed. Max trotted around beside her, probably after some of her toast rather than keeping her company, but his presence helped her relax.

The pleasant country kitchen looked like it could do with a good scrub and, desperate to distract herself, she cleaned out the fridge and scrubbed it from top to bottom. She stood back to admire her handiwork until, out of the corner of her eye, she sensed something move outside the kitchen window. Probably one of the guards. Leaning across the sink for a better look, she automatically extended her arm around Max as he jumped up beside her, resting his paws on the edge of the bench. The top of his head was almost level with hers.

'We're being paranoid, Max,' she said, turning away from the window. 'The guards must've turned the motion sensors off. I'm sure they'll walk back in any minute. All that talk from your dad about escape routes last night. It's got us on edge.' From then on, Max hugged her side. She wiped her hands on a tea-towel and stroked his head. 'Come on, let's get on with it. He'll be back before we know it.'

After sweeping and mopping the kitchen and downstairs bathroom, she looked around for a vacuum cleaner. 'Alright Max, where is it?' There had to be one somewhere, perhaps upstairs.

Max growled. It was barely audible, but his ears were back, and the whites of his eyes flashed. He took a couple of steps towards the front door as a shadow crossed the frosted glass insert. Jemma froze, still with one foot on the bottom step. With a deep breath, she gripped the stair rail to steady herself, then crept across the room to look through the peephole.

Max growled again, this time louder, his lips curled

upwards. One foot was raised, and his body leaned forward, ready to lunge.

Where the hell were the guards? 'Okay mate, we'll press that button. I'll text your dad once we're locked in.'

She crept towards the study. 'C'mon Max.' He half turned to follow but kept his eyes trained on the front door, knocking over furniture as he edged towards her. A loud bang from the living room, followed by the unmistakeable clink of glass shattering on the hard-wood floor, made her pick up her pace. She ran, Max by her side, to Sean's green button and punched it. The wall panel slid aside, and she shot through, hitting the button on the other side to close it as soon as Max's tail was clear, then locked it from the inside as Sean had instructed. Max continued his soft growl and she had to call him through each time she locked another section. After the third section, she pulled the phone out of her pocket. The possibility she might not get a signal in the tunnel hadn't crossed her mind, but no matter which way she held the phone, it didn't. She just hoped there'd be a signal at the other end of the tunnel, although she had no idea where that might be. She called Max and ran as hard as she could until they reached a metal structure that looked like an old garage. It didn't appear particularly secure but heavy locks adorned each door and metal bars secured the blackened windows. Now she had a signal, so she sent the text. 'Pressed the button.'

*   *   *

Sean felt Hunt's eyes bore through him when his phone pinged, and everyone else in the meeting stared at him. He checked the message, then glared at Everson. 'Do you have someone at my property?'

'No.' Everson stepped back, looking surprised. 'Check with Colonel Williamson,' he said to one of his people. 'It's highly unlikely he'd proceed to your house without my knowledge, but we'll verify. My people can help you.'

'Thanks, but it's covered,' replied Sean. 'That was my northern office. They'll be there within ten minutes, quicker than we can get there. If we're finished, I'll head out too.'

'We're not finished, we still need to resolve the issue of Dr Anderson,' snapped Everson. 'Presuming she's at your property, your protection is clearly inadequate.'

Sean winced. He could hardly disagree. His phone pinged again with the text from Jemma. He muttered an apology, beckoned Dan, and backed out of the meeting room.

'Damn it,' snarled Sean. 'Jemma's in trouble. We need to get to her fast.' He ran towards the stairwell.

'Not that way, mate,' Dan called, steering him to an external staircase that led to the roof. 'I've got a chopper waiting. Had a hunch there might be a problem. Pilot's a mate. He's safe.'

'We can't be sure of anyone at this point. I've just had word that my motion sensors and all the cameras, except one we hid in a tree a few months ago, were taken out. And they can't raise the guards on their phones. Jesus how do these bastards keep doing this?'

'They're tracking her somehow,' replied Dan. 'What's that about a button?'

'Escape route. I showed it to her last night. Let's go.' The pilot had started to gear up when Sean jumped in.

Dan levered himself in behind, pulled the door shut and yelled to the pilot to lift off. They lost height as the chopper fought against a strong westerly wind, and Sean's stomach dived with it. Flying was never his preferred option and he gripped the seat as the craft slowly rose and headed north.

'Hang in there, fellas,' yelled the pilot. 'You've still gotta tell me where we're goin'.'

After handing across the co-ordinates, Sean peered below for anything that might have followed. It'd be easy enough to track them by radar, but so long as he could get to Jemma before anyone worked out her escape route, he'd still have the advantage. Watching out the window, he spotted the outskirts of Kilcoy and, as the chopper headed down towards the tree line, he saw Dan start to remove his harness, so he did the same. As soon as the landing rails of the chopper hit dirt, they leapt out and ran through thick scrub towards a dilapidated metal shed, its walls covered in vines, and barely visible in the encroaching bush.

A few metres from the shed, Dan stopped dead and shot out his arm, knocking the wind from Sean's chest. 'That bloody metal sphere again. It's following us.'

Sean followed his gaze above the trees. The damned thing just seemed to be hanging there. No noise, no wind, no movement. 'I suspect you're right. Remember I said the first time I saw it that I felt it was watching me, but no one's been able to identify it as yet. Air traffic control still can't get it on radar. Concentrate on getting to Jemma now. Anything else can wait.' Sean grabbed a rock, smashed an old lock and opened the door. He tapped in some numbers and it swung back to reveal a small space and another door opposite with a small box to one side. He leant down so his eye was level with a retinal scanner at the base of the box which then lit up with the message, *speaker active*. 'Jemma, it's me. Key in the combination.'

Holding his breath, he waited but there was no response, so he tried again. '9537. Key the numbers in.'

CHAPTER 5

Max ran towards a recessed panel beside the exit from the tunnel and wagged his tail. Jemma ran her hand over it. No handle or catch. 'Can't be anything there, Max. Look,' she said, thumping the panel. 'See?'

Max's tail wagged harder, so she pushed the panel again. It slid back revealing a door with a keypad. Now she could hear Sean's voice telling her to key in the number he'd given her the night before. She stared at it; her mind blank. Even when he repeated the numbers, she had to concentrate to lift her hand and tap them in. She didn't wait for the panel to fully open, she pushed through, sobbing as she sank into Sean's arms.

'Charming,' muttered Dan. 'I'll pat the dog while you two sort yourselves out.'

Sean eased her back, without removing his arm. 'Okay?' he said, ignoring Dan.

'Yeah, I'm fine. I just didn't know what to do. Max told me someone was there, then I heard an almighty bang. So, I ran.'

Dan spoke louder. 'If it's not too much trouble, we need to think about getting back to the chopper. Whoever broke in could still be around somewhere.'

'Back off,' growled Sean. 'You did the right thing, Jemma.

My team's in the house now. Hopefully, they'll get some clues to identify the intruder, but we'd better move before Dan has a seizure. Just have to call the boss first.' He moved away and spoke into the phone.

'Right sir. We'll do that.'

'Do what?' said Jemma.

'We're not going in the chopper. He's sending a decoy team to the chopper and we're to get out of here by road.'

She turned to look around the garage. 'There's no car.'

'Follow me.' A large tarpaulin covered something stacked at the other end. He pulled it back to reveal three older-style Yamaha 750cc motorbikes.

'These are amazing,' she exclaimed, 'and their condition's superb. Do they work?'

'My hobby,' replied Sean. 'I try to take each of them out at least once a month, so yes, they work well.'

She ran her hands over the closest one. 'You must spend a lot of time on them.'

'I do, but we can admire them later. The boss wants to see if the sphere follows the chopper or us. We need to get on our bikes and get out of here.'

Jemma didn't move. 'But what if it doesn't work and the sphere follows us?'

'We'll deal with that if it happens. Dan, you take one of the bikes, and Jemma can ride behind me. Do you think you'll be alright doing that, Jemma?'

'On the other hand, how about I take one and you ride behind me, that's if you feel you can hang on.' She laughed at

Sean's expression. 'I've been riding bikes since I was ten years old. Best way to muster cattle in the outback.' The memory of her uncle and his farm in far western Queensland made her smile. He'd been such a stickler for safety, and she'd learned well from him. Vast distances, many miles from the farm, no satellite phones back then, and UHF radios that only worked near a receiver meant accidents often ended in tragedy. She'd just started learning to fly the ultra-light helicopter when the floods consumed her family. Her smile faded. Her uncle had disappeared from the farm during the flood that took her parents, and it only now occurred to her that he might also have been murdered. She looked up to see Sean staring at her.

'Okay?'

'Yes … yes, I am.' She shook herself down and reached for a leather jacket and a helmet on the back of one of the bikes. Dredging up memories of the past could wait. She smiled as sweetly as she could manage. 'Are the gears up or down?'

'Alright, smart-arse. One down, three up. We'll go through a bit of bush but it's flat, so these bikes should handle it fine. I know an abandoned property with some old workers cottages that we can use for shelter. Even if someone comes looking, we shouldn't be seen.'

'Sounds good,' said Jemma. 'I don't want to be followed.'

'Okay. We'll keep a close eye and take some detours. Should be able to shake them. Before we go, does anyone have anything electronic that could be used to track us?'

Jemma checked her pockets. 'I've a small iPad, but it's turned off.'

'Doesn't matter, it'll have a GPS, and if they know what they're doing, they can turn it back on. Put it under the tarp,' said Sean. 'We can come back and get it once we're safe.'

He had a habit of standing with his hands behind his back staring at her, as he waited for her to comply with his orders, which irritated her so much more than his words. In the end, she sighed and placed it under the tarp, then mounted her bike. 'Right, let's go.'

Sean pushed his bike to the front. 'Stay together. I'll lead the way because I know this country well. Now, I know you're a far better rider than myself, Jemma, but please don't try to prove it. Humour me, and keep in a strict convoy until we get to where we're going, okay?'

'Certainly, I'll slow to your pace.' She rode the bike outside and, while she waited for Dan to close the doors, took in the breathtaking vista that stretched out in every direction. Rich green pasture and rolling hills were punctuated by glistening blue dams and dotted with black and white dairy cows. She touched Sean's arm. 'Who looks after Max?'

He reached down to pat the dog. 'Next door mate. Go.' Max obediently ran towards the next farm. 'After my father died and my mother took off, our neighbours became our guardians. We stayed with them every school holiday and they treated us like their own kids. Max lives with them, but he's my dog and always comes to me when I'm home.'

'At least I was eighteen when my parents died,' said Jemma. 'It must have been incredibly hard for you at such a young age.'

'True, but my guardians stepped in quickly, and heaps of

people helped us. You just learn you've got to get on with it. No point wallowing. And that includes now. Let's go.'

They rode a couple of kilometres down a well-worn path, around a sharp turn towards an old gate, then waited while Sean jumped off his bike, opened the gate, and waved them through. Jemma stopped beside Dan then together they followed Sean onto the highway. They passed through Harlin then beside the township of Toogoolawah, turning just before Esk onto an overgrown block. As they neared the homestead, she stood upright on her bike hoping to see the workers' cottages Sean had described, but he waved her down. In her mind she swore at him, but she did as he demanded, slowing so that she was again between the two men. Sean scrutinised every pathway between the trees and in the rear-view mirror, she saw Dan doing the same. She didn't enjoy being a passive observer but given the events of the last few weeks she had to accept they were in charge. When Sean pulled in to the rear of one of the old cottages, she pulled up beside him waiting until he indicated it was safe to park, then stayed with the bikes while the men finished checking the house.

She pulled off her helmet and shook out her hair. Something stung her face and she yelped as she swatted it away.

'Better go inside,' said Sean, walking back towards her. 'The mozzies are everywhere after the rain, and they're the type that carry Ross River virus.'

She ran for the house, wiping away cobwebs as she stepped inside. A layer of dust covered the small amount of furniture that remained, a few chairs, a table, and a couple of old beds. She wiped the dust from the kitchen bench and the outside of an old stove-top kettle. A cupboard above the sink had some old, although clean and usable, mugs but there was no water or power. She sat on one of the chairs and leaned across the table just as Sean opened the door.

He pulled a chair close to her and rested his hand on her shoulder. 'Jemma, it's temporary. If we work together, it'll be over soon.'

'God, I hope you're right.'

'The good news is that we haven't seen any further sign of that metal sphere. I'm going back into town to get some food. Dan will stay with you. Anything you'd like me to get you?'

She shook her head. She'd have preferred to join him, but knew he'd decline. After he left, she busied herself looking for plates and cutlery and chatted to Dan. An hour later, Sean returned with a couple of shopping bags, bottled water, a portable butane gas burner, and a Thai takeaway. He seemed to be doing his best to join in on the conversation, but she could tell he was distracted. She wanted to ask him what was wrong but the look on his face told her to leave it be.

When they'd finished, he ordered Dan to head outside and patrol the house and grounds.

Dan groaned, 'Alright, boss.'

Jemma raised her eyebrows. 'Boss?'

'Army rank. I'm one higher,' muttered Sean as he followed Dan to the door. He said something Jemma couldn't hear before returning to sit beside her. Resting his hand on her arm, he started to speak. Then he stopped, sighed and started again. 'Jemma, there's no easy way to say this.'

'What's wrong? Has something happened to Eric? Or Mary?' She pulled her knees up to her chest, hugging her legs and rocking as she stared at him.

'What? No, they're fine.' He stared at the table, and appeared to be struggling for words. 'The policeman who took you to the safe house … Mate, I'm sorry to have to tell you he was killed. Three others, including the ASIO man, were also killed. Murdered. There's a major police investigation under way.'

'Oh God.' She dropped her head into her hands. 'Oh God. He was only there to help me. He's got children. A wife. And the others. They're all dead because of me.' She looked back at him and tears streamed down her face.

'No,' he replied, as he gently wiped the tears from her eyes. 'He's dead because of the bastard who's pursuing you.'

'Did they kill the guards at your house too?'

'No, thankfully. They were knocked out and locked in the garage.'

'Can I use your phone to call Eric and Mary? They'll be out of their mind with worry.'

'No, I'll have someone visit them and let them know you're safe.'

'I need to talk to them.'

'I know, but right now it's not safe for them or you.'

'Oh my God. Are you saying they're at risk?'

'I don't know but we've got surveillance on them, and I've asked for that to be increased. Jemma, I have to ask you something. I told you we'd identified that man, Fredrick Pritchard. He runs a Pharmaceutical Company. Have you ever heard of Pritchard Pharmaceuticals?'

'I don't think so, although it does sound familiar.' She rubbed her forehead. The wound she'd sustained running from Pritchard still hurt when she was tense. 'Oh heavens, I know. Eric and Mary's son, Anthony. He worked for Pritchard Pharmaceuticals. They transferred him to New York. He was only there a few weeks and he disappeared. That was five years ago.'

'Do you have any idea why Pritchard would be following you?'

'No. It was Anthony's job. Nothing to do with me. What's going on, Sean?'

He shook his head. 'I don't know, but my people are working on it.'

She stood, walked to a window and stared out to the back of the property which sloped gently down to the upper reaches of the Brisbane river. 'I used to sit at the back of my uncle's house on the farm, and dream of living there all the time.' She smiled. 'I could happily live in a place like this, with a couple of hundred head of cattle, grow my own veggies, and leave the rat-race behind.'

'I thought you loved your research.'

'Yeah, I guess. Truth is, I'm not quite twenty-seven and I've pretty much achieved everything I planned. I've got my PhD, I'm a lecturer at a good university, and I've had a lot of recognition. I can't see that there's anywhere left for me to go, and I hate the bureaucracy so getting promoted up the ladder doesn't do much for me. You're right, I do love my research, but I don't love everything that goes with it.'

'You'd be surprised how much of that I understand,' said Sean. 'I'm four years older than you and I've been promoted well before I'd expected. I think that's happened because I've always gone headlong into whatever I do, and I wouldn't change any of it, but when Dad was alive, we had our own cattle, and I learned to ride a horse the same way you learned to ride a bike, mustering cattle. Sometimes I still dream of setting up a property with my own cattle.'

'Sheep too,' murmured Jemma. 'I could have my own loom, start a business with my knitted products. And I prefer lamb to beef anyway.'

'Well, I could make leather goods. You know, belts, whips.'

'Or handbags and leather skirts.' Jemma laughed, but tears ran down her face.

'Oh hell, mate, I'm sorry,' said Sean, wrapping her in his arms. 'I was trying to distract you.'

'Don't be sorry. I appreciate it. I just don't know what to think, or how to feel. I can't believe this is happening.'

'I know.'

She pulled back enough to look him in the eyes. 'Do you think we'll ever work it out?'

'Of course, we will but, in the meantime, we have to ensure your safety.'

*   *   *

Happy to give Sean and Jemma some space so he could untangle his own mind, Dan walked swiftly down the hill, increasing his speed with every step. Not only were the police deaths senseless but his team was no closer to nailing the perpetrators, and that just wasn't good enough. They'd have to work out what they'd missed, there had to be something. There could be little doubt that Pritchard was behind it all, but they didn't have any substantial evidence to link him to anything apart from breaking into Jemma's unit. And even then, it was his word against hers.

By the time Dan reached the entry gate, he'd worked up to a full run. Lathered in sweat, he leaned against the fence post for a couple of minutes to catch his breath. He kicked the old gate when the rusted latch refused to give way, and almost fell through when it swung open. Swearing, he made his way across to the next paddock and the old homestead. The sprawling building, although shabby, appeared structurally sound and, inside, the rooms all looked to be in good repair with their high, pressed metal ceilings and ornate archways. He couldn't help but wonder why a family would just walk away from all this, but there was no sign of anyone anywhere, so he shut the front door and stepped back onto the wide front veranda. As he turned to leave, his thoughts were halted by a shadow that moved slowly across the veranda and blocked the sun from the whole front yard.

Not sure what he might see, he slowly turned his head and looked up. A metal sphere, like the one they'd seen from the helicopter, hovered around ten metres above the house. It was at least twenty metres in diameter, and he could see clear and evenly spaced markings on its underside, possibly landing gear. Jesus, when he'd seen it before he'd thought that it could be a weather balloon, or something under remote control, but this was some kind of craft and he sure as hell wasn't going to hang around to find out. He unlocked the door, charged back inside, and crouched beneath a sash window. With no clue what to do next, he waited. The thing made a soft, whirring noise.

Ten minutes later, the noise began to fade, then stopped completely. He raised himself up, so his eyes were level with the bottom of the window and peered out. As with every other sighting, the sphere had disappeared. He cracked open the door and eased out onto the veranda. All remained clear, so he ran across the yard and up the long driveway towards the cottage. Knowing it was a good two kilometres away, he ran hard, ignoring the muscle cramps and his need to suck in air. If Sean and Jemma hadn't finished their discussion, too bad, he wasn't dealing with this alone. Fifty metres from the cottage, and with almost nothing left in the tank, he started to slow down, when he heard the noise again and sensed the shadow. The craft hovered above him. Without warning, a two-metre circle of light snapped on at its base. He ducked behind a thick clump of bushes as a shaft of bright blue light shot down towards him. The light moved forwards and backwards and appeared to be searching. He waited for it to move behind him then, not knowing if it would follow, he charged through the back door of the house and slammed it shut. Leaning against the door, he bent forward and heaved in some air.

'Dan,' cried Jemma. 'Dan, what's wrong?'

He tried to speak but couldn't.

'Take a breath, mate.' Sean pushed him into a chair and grabbed another to sit opposite him. 'Ignore everything else. Focus on me.'

He nodded and, gripping the chair, looked directly at Sean. 'Bloody metal ball again… like the one at your place … hovering … made a noise, kind of whirring … wouldn't have been more than ten metres above me … tried to get a good look. The bloody thing was bigger than this house.'

'It's alright mate, keep going,' said Sean.

'The whirring stopped. A patch of light appeared at the base. I ducked for cover, but a dirty great light shot down. Seemed to be looking for me. Didn't know what the hell it was. I took off.'

'Are you hurt?'

'No. I'm okay, but we've got to work out what that thing is. It bloody well fired at me. Sean, it's following us. It might still be there.'

'Agreed. We can't do much tonight. I'll take the first watch. You settle down for a bit. I'll go out and check.'

*   *   *

Jemma watched Sean walk outside, shuddering when he drew his pistol. There wasn't much she could do to help him, so she turned her attention to Dan. 'Come on, I'll get you a cuppa.'

After settling Dan, she waited at the door to tackle Sean.

As soon as she heard his footsteps, she slipped outside and barred his entry. 'Dan's not in a fit state to take a watch. I'll take his turn.'

'No. You need to rest. We don't know what tomorrow's going to bring.'

'I'm a grown-up Sean. I can deal with the unknown as well as you can.'

'I know you can, but my job is to protect you and that means you stay inside, and Dan and I do the watches. I'll call for back-up if I have to. It's not up for discussion.'

She turned on her heel and walked into one of the bedrooms, checked the old mattress for bed bugs and other creepy-crawlies, and threw herself onto the bed. She tossed and turned most of the night, giving up as the first rays of light crept through the window. Knowing the men had been up all night, she headed to the kitchen and busied herself putting breakfast together. Relieved the little burner still had some gas she boiled the kettle, set them each up with a cup, then found the coffee and the bacon and eggs that Sean had bought the day before.

She heard footsteps behind, and said, 'Good morning,' without turning to look.

'Good morning,' replied Sean. 'Smells good. I'm going back up to the SCARF site. See if I can lure Pritchard out, maybe find out more about Everson.'

'Good,' she replied. 'I'll join you.'

'No, mate, there's a chopper coming for you. I do this one alone.'

'Damn it, Sean. You need to include me.' She turned back to the little gas stove.

CHAPTER 6

Given Sean had no idea how much risk the metal sphere posed, he had to be as certain as he could that it was gone before he left. He cringed at the sound of dishes clattering in the sink as he walked outside to check around the house. Satisfied all was quiet, he went a short distance down the road. A few birds flitted through trees, and a couple of kangaroos grazed on the flats, but nothing seemed out of place, so he headed back to the house where he heard the breakfast cutlery and plates still being slammed around. He understood her frustration but wasn't prepared to risk putting her in any more danger. Snatching his leather jacket from the hook just inside the door, he put it on, picked up his helmet and retreated to his bike.

'She's cranky,' muttered Dan, following him out.

'Can't say I blame her,' replied Sean. 'But it's our job to keep her safe, and if that pisses her off, so be it. I'm not handing her over to Everson, whatever the chief says. He's an arrogant arsehole and I'm damned sure he knows more about Pritchard than he's saying.'

'Does General Hunt know where you're going?'

'No.' Sean slapped him on the back. 'If I don't return, you'd better tell him.'

'Jesus, Sean, I wouldn't like to be in your shoes when he finds out. If I don't hear from you every hour, I'm going to notify him. You might enjoy a good lashing, but I don't.'

'You'd better toughen up then if you're going to be my stand-in,' replied Sean, laughing. 'Request a chopper. Head to the Nerang warehouse and we'll call the boss from there.' He grinned. 'That is, if I survive the mountain.'

'You'd better. I don't want to become his next punching bag.' Dan looked down at his feet. 'And if you're considering not coming back…'

'Come on. Whatever it is, spit it out,' said Sean.

'Is there something going on between you and Jemma?'

'Don't be ridiculous.' Sean pulled on his leather jacket. 'I'm responsible for her safety. She needs our help.'

'Okay. Then you don't mind if I try to get to know her better?'

'You keep your hands off her.' He glared at Dan. 'I mean… the last thing she needs now is you chatting her up. Just concentrate on doing your job.'

Dan had a wide grin on his face. 'Sure. Got the message.'

Swearing, Sean jumped on his bike and roared away. He'd long ago recognised his lifestyle didn't allow for relationships. They never lasted anyway. His sister had clung to him when his father died, the same way Jemma did last night, but when Cheryl turned seventeen, she'd taken off to America supposedly to study, then she met a man and married before she was twenty. His mother had never been there for him, although he'd developed a sort of relationship with her as an adult. He had the sense that something terrible had happened to her but, whenever he raised it, the pain in her eyes sent a knife through his heart.

He was an hour late to call Dan, when he finally pulled off the highway and found a spot beside a river to secure his bike. Sitting at a table, close to the water, he drank in the sound of laughter from children paddling in the shallows. Their parents stood arm in arm, watching. They looked so happy. That's how he remembered his own parents when he was a small child.

Dan wouldn't dob him in, they'd been covering for each other for years. He pulled out his phone and made the call, amused when Dan demanded another call within the hour, or he'd report to the boss. He'd make the same threat if their roles were reversed. After a last look around he got back on his bike and headed for the highway. Not far along, he turned off onto the Mudgeeraba exit and then the Springbrook Mountain Road. Almost immediately, the road changed from a well-designed city carriageway to a narrow, twisting mountain road with sharp drop-offs that led down into steep ravines filled with thick, impenetrable scrub.

He stopped at a rest area two hundred metres from the carpark used by the SCARF team and parked his bike. As he jogged the rest of the way up, he passed an odd mix of touristy lookouts, houses, stretches of native scrub and the occasional shop before turning onto a two-kilometre track cut out by wildlife. It was the only access from the carpark to the SCARF site and several times he heard movement nearby, mostly small animals scurrying out of his way. But sometimes he saw nothing, and that left him with an uneasy sense that he was being followed.

Not far from the mound where he'd found Jemma that night, he took cover behind a massive gum tree. All seemed quiet, so he crawled to the top of the mound, and crouched just below the top. The night he'd rescued Jemma, intense glare had obscured everything other than the light itself. Daylight painted an entirely different scene. A large granite boulder on the far side of the clearing, sat up high on its base. Most boulders were buried deep into the ground. The diameter of this one was at least ten metres and it was the height of a single-story house. The massive rock had to weigh hundreds of tonnes. A platoon of soldiers wouldn't shift it manually, and it would take a highly sophisticated artificial platform to hold that kind of weight. Yet, the light had come through it, as had the people in white. He walked cautiously into the clearing and ran his hand across the granite. A damned good façade, or a hidden entrance, but he couldn't identify either.

Without warning, the boulder and the ground around it began to shake. He tore back to the mound, hurled himself up and over, then crouched on the other side until the tremor stopped. Edging up, he used a small bush for cover, until he could just see over the top of the mound. The boulder had moved back three metres and Charles Everson stood at the entrance, flanked by three armed men in Australian Army uniforms. He touched a small object on his shirt, about the size of a credit card, and his voice boomed across the clearing.

'Mr Bellamy, I know you are here. Please show yourself, we need to talk.'

'Not on your life,' muttered Sean, cursing that he'd failed to trust his own instincts. The bastards *had* followed him through the bush. No way would he show himself to Everson here, without back-up. He wriggled down to the base of the mound, and drew his weapon, a simple Glock, but it was all he had. He didn't know how much use it'd be against the weapons these men held, possibly high-powered rifles, but not like any he knew.

Again, the voice rang out. 'Mr Bellamy, we must talk. If you return Dr Anderson to us, our original arrangement can remain in place. Show yourself so we can speak, one gentleman to another. I don't wish to send my people out to find you.'

Everson still stood with his hands clasped in front of his chest but, after a couple of minutes, he nodded to the soldiers. Sean didn't wait to see what they'd do, he took off back down the track, desperately casting around for a hiding place. His best hope looked to be a heavily treed copse on the far side of the car park. He tore through the trees and only just stopped in time to avoid going over the edge of the plateau. Staring down, he spotted a ledge, ten metres below that was shielded by a rocky overhang. Getting to it without falling would be a trick, and the odds of surviving a fall, miserable, but it was the only option and, if the alternative was to be taken by Everson's people, he had to give it a try.

As he eased himself over the top, his foot dislodged some small rocks. They clattered down, eventually splashing into water. It had to be hundreds of metres below. With no time to look for other options, he felt around for a foothold. Gripping exposed tree roots, he levered himself down as far as he could. Three metres above the ledge which jutted out from the volcanic rhyolite cliff gouged out by centuries of moisture and erosion, he ran out of footholds. Nothing else for it, he took a deep breath and jumped. The ledge crumbled under his weight. Flailing around for anything he could grab, he swore and clawed at the rock, until he hooked his right hand under an old fig root.

Clinging to the root with his right arm, he swung his body up towards the ledge until his left leg hooked over the more solid inner ledge, anchoring behind an exposed rock. Grabbing another tree root with his left hand, he used both arms to pull himself up, then heaved his right leg up until he'd steadied his body on the more solid inner surface, then rolled across to sprawl beneath the overhang, gasping for air.

Once his breathing steadied, he peered round for an escape route. On his right was a sheer granite rock face, covered by a thin spray from a waterfall. No way he'd be able to climb a slippery surface like that. Multiple areas of washouts and erosions, much like the spot he now occupied, were on his left. Dicey, but there might be enough handholds to go up. He pushed himself to the outermost aspect of the ledge, checking it wouldn't crumble with each move forward, and peered over the edge. The same sort of terrain stretched down as far as he could see, washouts, fig roots, small trees and crumbling rock. He could probably climb down using roots and rocky outcrops but at the bottom was some of the thickest rainforest he'd ever seen bordering a fast-flowing stream. His best chance would be up, although he'd have to wait for nightfall and then footholds and snags might be hard to see in the dark, but he didn't have much choice. Without a phone signal he'd have to sit tight which would leave Dan with a dilemma. By rights Dan should call Hunt, but Sean knew Dan wouldn't want to dob him in.

He laid back and stared at the sky but, before he could feel too sorry for himself, footsteps sounded above and he scrambled back beneath the ledge.

'Sean, is that you?' It was a male voice, familiar but he couldn't put a name to it, and he didn't dare look up. Too late, he realised his foot was exposed beyond the overhang.

The same male voice again. 'Answer me, damn it. The others aren't far behind. It's Tom Lambert.'

It couldn't be. The last time he saw Tom, he was in rehab and couldn't walk without crutches. Sean eased out, grabbed a tree root, and steadied himself before looking up. He wasn't sure whether to laugh or snarl when he recognised Tom. 'Bit of help'd be much appreciated, mate.'

'Grab the rope. I've hooked the other end around a tree. Do it fast.' Before Sean had pulled himself up and over the edge, Tom, although still talking, had started to walk away. 'There's a warrant out for your arrest. Reckon you murdered four police officers. Come on. In the car. Move.'

Sean stood stock-still and stared. They were trying to pin the murders on him! Once he'd caught his breath, he had to run through the trees and up to the road to catch up with Tom. 'Are you serious?' he said, as he opened the passenger door.

Before the car doors had shut, Tom hit the accelerator. 'Yes, I'm serious. Where's your vehicle?'

'Couple of hundred metres down the road,' replied Sean, gaping at Tom.

'Okay, I'll drop you there,' said Tom, sneaking a look at Sean which made him take a corner too fast. Both men swore as the front wheel slewed into the softer verge and they stared into a void down the side of the mountain. Tom managed to reef the steering wheel around and swerve back onto the road.

'Jesus, mate,' muttered Sean. 'I'd like to live through this day.'

Tom jammed on the brakes when he reached Sean's bike, stopping within centimetres. 'I'll meet you at the café in the shopping centre at the bottom.'

'That's if you get there in one piece.'

'Just get on your bike and move,' snarled Tom, looking behind them. With a grin, he turned back to Sean, and added, 'Sir.'

'Yeah right.' Sean jumped out and swung the car door shut. It hadn't fully closed, before Tom took off. Donning his helmet, he mounted his bike and followed Tom's lead, taking off at speed.

When he reached the shopping centre, Sean had recovered enough to demand more. 'What do you mean I'm wanted for murder.'

'Just that. I've seen the warrant. Two officers shot, two

with their throats slit. They claim you were there, and abducted a scientist, Jemma Anderson. She's still missing.'

'Jesus Christ. Throats slit?'

'Correct. Throats slit.'

'Jemma's in our protection,' said Sean. 'I assumed it was your people. Are you part of this SCARF project?'

'Yeah, and we don't kill innocent people.'

'Neither do we. I didn't murder anyone. I rescued Jemma. She came willingly. Neither I, nor any of my people, had anything to do with those murders.'

'I couldn't believe it when I heard. You would've changed dramatically to do something like that.' Tom stared into Sean's eyes as though trying to decide how much to say. 'There's dozens of extra police on the Gold Coast, and they've all got your photo. We'd better get inside.'

Although Sean still didn't trust Everson, he was confident Tom wouldn't be involved with murder. He checked the café and surrounding area, then sat with Tom, in a small booth at the back. 'Tell me about Everson.'

'What do you want to know?'

'Do you trust him?'

'Yeah,' replied Tom. 'I trust him, but he's not the one you have to worry about. It's my CO, Lieutenant-Colonel Williamson. He's doing his level best to make sure the murders stay pinned on you. I don't know why, presumed it was personal.'

'Don't believe I've ever met the man. Let me tell you our story, then we'll discuss what to do next.' Sean described how he'd rescued Jemma from the police safe house, and his belief that Everson knew more than he'd told them.

Tom sighed, 'SCARF is a legitimate army unit. None of my people would contemplate murder. If we'd been at that safe house, we'd have helped the police, not slaughtered them. Can you at least give me proof the scientist is alive and safe?' said Tom. 'I'll take it back to my people and have them back off. Although I'm not sure I'll be able to convince Williamson.'

'Okay, I'll take you to see Jemma and, if I can organise it, to speak to General Hunt. Is that enough?'

'You still work with the boss?'

'Yeah, you would too if you hadn't got yourself shot in Afghanistan.'

'Right, like that was intentional.'

Sean grinned, pleased to see Tom again, and impressed by how well he'd recovered. When he'd visited Tom in the spinal unit, Sean had doubted he'd ever walk properly again. But they didn't have time for a reunion. 'The boss won't be happy with any of this. I need to get to my rendezvous point and report in. Follow me. I'll take the lead on my bike.'

While in the café, Sean had continuously, but casually, surveyed his surroundings, checking every person in his visual range. He was pleased to see Tom do the same. Equally casually he paid their bill then, with Tom following, set off for the Nerang warehouse.

CHAPTER 7

It was now four hours since Dan had last heard from Sean and, each time he rang, his phone was answered by a recorded message. To make matters worse, the helicopter to retrieve Jemma hadn't yet left Brisbane airport. Early morning fog had backed up all air traffic and he'd been ordered to sit tight and wait. For the umpteenth time he checked the doors and windows in the old house, then returned to the kitchen table where Jemma sat with her head in her hands. He waited for her to look up. 'What's wrong?'

When she didn't respond he reached out his hand and, as gently as he could, prised her hands from her face. 'Tell me about it.'

'Don't know if I can.' She stared at him. 'I'm not sure I know.'

'Just talk. See if we can work it out together.'

'My parents were murdered.' Her voice hitched. 'Probably means my uncle was murdered too. I can't go home. Sean won't let me talk to Eric or Mary. A crazy man's chasing me because he says my mother had a title. Says he's got my sister.'

'Oh boy,' murmured Dan. 'Jemma, we'll find this fellow. If he's got your sister, we'll find her too. Sean's organised someone to talk to Eric and Mary this morning. They'll let them know you're okay.'

'But I need them.' She dabbed at a tear. 'I don't know how to fix this. One minute I'm crying, the next I'm arguing with Sean. I want to help. I know why he won't let me, but I'm not good at sitting on my hands. Now you're doing the same.'

'Understood. But you have to understand too, Sean gives the orders. I carry them out.'

She smiled. 'I doubt it's that simple. You two are peas in a pod. Aren't you both a bit senior to be babysitting me anyway?'

'Orders came directly from the chief.'

'Why?' She stared at him. 'Who's the chief'

'General Patrick Harris. I don't know why. He breathes rarefied air; doesn't usually talk to me directly.'

'Patrick Harris? I know that name,' said Jemma. 'My mother, he was my mother's friend. Came to dinner a few times.'

Dan slapped his forehead. 'Jesus, something just hit me too. What was your father's name?'

'Brad. Bradley Anderson. Why?'

'This is getting weird. My father's business partner was Bradley Anderson and he died in the 2011 floods. I should have put it together before. Dad was shattered by Brad's death. It's too much of a coincidence to think there could have been two Bradley Andersons killed in the same flood. What made me think of it was that I met General Harris through Brad when I was a kid. I don't think the General remembers me, though.'

'Dear God, Dan. This gets crazier by the minute.'

'Agreed.' The conversation had triggered unpleasant memories for Dan too. Memories he'd tried hard to forget. His parents had died in a car accident but, unlike Jemma, he'd never accepted the coroner's finding of an accidental death. They'd left home an hour before the accident, yet his perfectly healthy father had apparently fallen asleep behind the wheel of the car, drifted onto the wrong side of the road and ploughed into a truck. Both were killed instantly. The coroner had got it wrong for Jemma's parents, and he was damned sure they'd got it wrong for his parents. There had to be a link between their death and Jemma's parents, and now Patrick Harris. It might have been something to do with their business, but he had the uneasy feeling that there was more to it.

He sighed, he was keen to get out of there, but for now they had to sit tight. 'Go have a rest Jemma. I'll call you when the chopper's close.'

Minutes later the call came to get ready. He knocked on Jemma's door. 'Sorry mate, chopper's nearly here.' Even before he'd finished speaking, helicopter rotors sounded overhead. He led her to the front door and opened it just enough to look outside. 'Stand behind me.'

'But they're your people,' she said, without moving.

'We don't know that until they get out and we see them.'

She glared at him although she did as he asked, just as she was now used to doing for Sean.

Two people jumped out and ran towards the house. The first was a short, nuggety man dressed in jeans and a sloppy purple polo shirt. A female emerged next and Dan smiled when Jemma stared at her. She was the exact opposite of the man. Tall and leggy, she wore designer jeans and a perfectly cut white shirt which conformed to every curve, and ankle height boots with five-centimetre heels. A small pistol was nestled neatly into the back of her jeans. The woman was stunningly beautiful. She could have been a world class model.

'Don't be fooled,' muttered Dan. 'She's had me on the mat a few times.'

He wrapped an arm around Jemma and pushed her towards the helicopter, yelling at the other agents to follow. Once inside, he beckoned to the other two agents , then dragged the door shut. Relieved, he leaned back in his seat, and within seconds the helicopter was back in the air. But they'd barely cleared the treetops when he jerked forward again. A metal sphere appeared to their left, and not far away.

'Do you see that thing?' he yelled to the pilot.

'Already called it in. Air traffic control can't see it on radar. I've been instructed to keep going on my original flight path. The air force has launched some support for us. We're not far from their Amberley base.'

'Jesus.' The memory of one of those spheres shooting out a light, like the one that had chased him was still raw. If it tried that again, they'd be sitting ducks. The other agents both flicked a look at Dan as they leaned forward for a better view. They wanted direction, but he had no idea what to tell them. Suddenly, the thing vanished.

'Jets above us,' the pilot called.

He remained still, watching, but there was no further sign of the sphere and, half an hour later, they landed safely at Nerang. The jets peeled off once they were on the ground. Dan jumped out, helped Jemma down and pointed towards the warehouse. They'd only just cleared the rotors when someone yelled. 'Jesus, what the hell?'

Dan swung around, pushing Jemma behind him. The other agents, who'd moved out ahead of Dan and Jemma, charged back to the helicopter.

'Where's the pilot?' shouted Dan.

'They've got him,' the male agent yelled.

The female agent ran beside Dan. 'Damned sphere appeared out of nowhere. Beam of light shot down. Grabbed the pilot. Just sucked him up. Never seen anything like it. He's vanished, sir. And so has the sphere.'

'Jesus. Keep looking but don't put yourselves at risk.' Dan pulled Jemma towards the door of the warehouse.

*   *   *

Sean ripped the warehouse door open from the inside and charged out with Tom hot on his heels. He'd seen the chopper land on the security screens in the building, and the light shoot down. 'Stay with her and lock the door behind you,' he yelled to Dan as he ran towards the helicopter. There was no sign of the sphere until a soft whirring sound made him look up. The sphere had reappeared and a light, three metres in diameter, snapped on at its base. An intense beam flashed down to a spot beside the helicopter. Two figures floated down, one of them limp and not moving. The limp figure stayed on the ground, while the other slowly rose back up to the sphere. Tom raised his weapon. The top of it glowed red, but nothing happened. He shook it, said something and aimed again, but still nothing. The opening in the craft closed, and the sphere took off at astonishing speed.

'Damn thing failed,' said Tom, still shaking his weapon. 'That's never happened before.'

'Worry about that later,' said Sean, running to where the helicopter pilot lay, groaning. He tried to get up when he saw Sean.

'Relax mate,' said Sean. 'Help's on its way. Can you tell us what happened?'

'I couldn't fight that thing. It felt like a straight-jacket; I couldn't move. A man in there demanded I bring Dr Anderson out so he can rescue her. That was his word. *Rescue.*'

'Can you tell me what he looked like?' said Sean.

The pilot grimaced. 'I can do better than that. I had my phone. Got a photo. There were two of them.' He held up his phone for the men to see.

'Bloody good job,' said Sean. 'That's Pritchard. Who the hell's the other bastard?'

'No idea,' said Tom, leaning over his shoulder.

Sean grabbed the phone and sent the images to himself, then ordered the agents who'd accompanied Dan and Jemma in the helicopter to wait with the pilot until the medical team arrived. He strode back inside ready to snap at someone, although he didn't have anyone in particular in mind, but he held it back when he found Jemma wandering around the room checking the equipment.

The first time he saw this place he'd had the same reaction. It was a training venue for his team and he'd only ever known it as *the warehouse*, a reasonable description from the outside, but it was nothing like a warehouse inside. Twelve chairs surrounded a large table in the middle of the room and banks of computers lined three of the walls, each with multiple screens, the fourth wall painted a matte white. One set of screens showed images of the area around the complex, and two screens at the end of the row had multiple lines of data rolling across them to block outgoing, non-secured signals.

'What is this place?' Jemma shuddered at the sight of a chair bolted to the middle of the floor in a smaller room beside the main entry. It had shackles, all open, attached to the arms, legs and back of the chair, and to the floor.

Sean smiled. 'Relax, it's just a room. We're set up to hold a prisoner here temporarily, but we're not into torture. I'll explain it properly later, but for the moment I want you both to meet Tom Lambert. From SCARF.'

'SCARF? Jesus, Sean, it's time to tell us what this is about, mate,' said Dan.

'I wish I knew,' replied Sean. 'We all need to throw what we know into the ring and try to make sense of it.'

'Agreed,' said Dan and there's something else. 'Jemma and I discovered this morning that our fathers were friends ... and her mother knew General Harris.'

Tom's eyes narrowed as he looked at Jemma.

'What is it, Tom?' said Sean.

'I think we might have met before too. My father … oh, never mind. Probably imagining things.'

Sean's phone rang. 'Damn it, give me a minute.' He walked into the smaller room to take the call from his boss.

'Bellamy… where the hell are you?'

'Nerang. The warehouse.' He filled his boss in on the sphere before he went on.

'Christ almighty. Stay inside. I'll talk to the air force, see what they know. Everson claims you've now abducted one of his people.'

'No. Tom Lambert helped me out of a jam. He's here with me now. Willingly.'

'Our Tom Lambert?'

'Correct. The one who was under my command in Afghanistan.'

'And, therefore, my command. I know him as well as you do. Are you telling me he's associated with Everson?'

'Appears so. I'm about to question him now, but he reckons Everson's okay.'

'Work quickly,' said Hunt. 'We need to know what's going on up there. Everson knows more than he'll say, but the chief's demanding I co-operate.'

'Sir, they've got a warrant out for me. Reckon I murdered four police at that safe house. Can you get me more information?'

'Already on it. I was informed this morning. Stay low. If anything happens, I'll intervene, but I don't know how much influence I can exert. Everson has clout on his side, including the chief. I don't know why. There's something going on here, and I'm not privy.'

'Understood. I'll call as soon as I have anything.'

Sean tapped his phone against his chin and stared through a one-way mirror at the group in the large room. Could he trust Tom? He pocketed his phone and walked back in. 'Listen up everyone. That was the boss. Police channels are full of my murderous activities, and Jemma's disappearance. Tom, let's start with you. Tell us more about this bunch you're working with.'

'We're legitimate,' snapped Tom. 'Our project's above top secret, and you know what that means. I can't talk about it.'

He pulled up a chair opposite Tom. 'Did your people murder those police?' Sean knew from bitter experience that trauma could change people, but he and Tom had once had a close, if unspoken, bond.

'Back off,' growled Tom. 'You're the one wanted on the police and security channels. My guys were not involved.'

'I didn't kill anyone,' said Sean. 'You know that's not my style.'

'And,' interjected Jemma, 'I can vouch for that. I was there.'

'Tom, General Everson charged me to find an intruder to the SCARF site,' said Sean. 'Jemma also had an intruder, who we now know is Fredrick Pritchard. I suspect your intruder and Jemma's are the same person. We've got an image which I'll show you later, but I need some answers. What's SCARF's purpose, and why would you have an intruder?'

Tom looked at his feet before answering. 'Sean, if there was anyone I'd trust without question, it'd be you. But I'm sworn to secrecy. I'll tell you what I can, but it must remain in this room. Is that clear?'

'We're all clear,' replied Sean. Dan and Jemma both nodded.

'I was in rehab for three years,' said Tom. 'The doctors wouldn't clear me to go back to pre-injury duties. The SCARF job came up and they were prepared to accept me without a full clearance. I grabbed it with both hands. They've got amazing technology, and they helped me recover and get the clearance. They've given me my life back.'

Sean was impressed by the passion with which Tom spoke as he went on to describe SCARF's purpose. High-level research and development, part of a network of nine similar facilities across the planet, their main role to develop the capacity to communicate across long distances once missions began to Mars and beyond. They had a secondary role to develop effective treatments for viruses. There were other projects he didn't understand that involved strange elements, chemicals he'd never heard of, and metals stronger than titanium. The researchers, mostly civilian, scrupulously avoided bringing viruses into the facility. They wore the white robes he and Jemma both saw in the clearing that night, made from a material that resisted microbes. The blue light, released monthly, cleared the surrounding area of viruses, but Tom didn't know the technical side of it. Like Jemma, he and his colleagues had found dead animals in the previous few weeks, hence the stronger than normal burst of light that night. The thin light Jemma had seen at the end drew energy down, to power their communication source.

'Hang on,' said Jemma. 'You're saying it wasn't light shooting up, it was energy coming down?'

'That's right, and my understanding is sketchy. I can't tell you more because I don't know.'

'But where does the energy come down from?'

Tom shrugged. 'Satellites, as I understand it.'

'I've never heard of a satellite that can transmit energy down to Earth, or of light being used successfully to treat viruses,' said Jemma.

'No, I hadn't heard of light treating viruses either,' replied Tom, ignoring her comment about the satellites. 'But it works, I've seen it.'

Jemma persisted. 'I'd like to know more. Did your people identify the virus that killed the animals?'

'Don't believe so,' replied Tom.

'Dan and I found reports of people going missing around blue lights in other countries,' said Sean. 'Can you explain that?'

'We're aware of it, but we don't know any more than you do.'

'It would've helped if Everson had given us the whole story, from the beginning,' murmured Sean.

'Agreed,' replied Tom. 'But he tends to be secretive.'

Sean shoved his hand into his pocket as he stared at Tom. 'Shit, I forgot the note Pritchard gave the pilot.' He straightened it out on the table and read the top message which was addressed to him.

Return Dr Anderson to me or I will release the virus she found at Springbrook into the Gold Coast community.

The second message was addressed to Jemma.

If you wish to see your sister again, you must join me to develop the vaccine. Without that I cannot guarantee her safety.

A small plastic cylinder on Tom's belt, five centimetres long and a centimetre wide, suddenly unfurled and changed colour, shattering the shocked silence. 'Mr Lambert is telling you the truth, Mr Bellamy, Mr O'Leary, Dr Anderson.' Charles Everson's voice rang out through the room and a light shone on the wall opposite Tom. Everson's face appeared, as if on a giant television screen. 'I have been listening to your conversation, and I will take it from here.'

Sean walked towards the image. 'Then explain why you had those people murdered in the police safe house.'

'We were not present at that event,' responded Everson. 'However, you were, Bellamy, so I'm sure you understand why we believed you were involved. Having listened to Dr Anderson's account though, I accept you probably were not. I agree there must have been outsiders. We need to locate them and decide what to do about Dr Anderson who has now been far too heavily exposed to our operations.'

'You don't need to do anything,' snapped Sean. 'Jemma just wants to live her life in peace. But we do need to know who murdered those police.'

'As you say *we*, I take it you are now prepared to work

with Mr Lambert. It would certainly be more efficient, one would think.'

'We are, so long as you keep in mind, we have our own director and we answer only to him,' said Sean. Dan, standing behind him, nodded.

'Ah yes, Mr Hunt. He's a party to this call. I'll establish his link, so he can offer his perspective.'

Hunt's image appeared on a screen beside Everson. 'Gentlemen, I've heard your conversation and I'd be happier to work together. I will of course, be at your disposal any time you need assistance. Now, Mr Everson, do you have any idea what this sphere is that's followed my people'

'I have some ideas, but I'm not positive. For the moment we'll have to call it an unidentified flying object.'

'Oh, for Christ's sake,' said Sean. 'You're telling us we were followed by a UFO. By fucking aliens?'

'Do you have a better explanation?' replied Everson.

Sean walked off, shaking his head.

'Sir,' said Tom, looking at Everson. 'My weapon failed when I tried to use it to immobilise that fellow as he floated up. I couldn't get images of the sphere or the man.'

'That is odd,' replied Everson. 'It suggests very advanced technology. I'll check your weapon when you get back, but I doubt I'll find anything wrong with it. Now, Colonel Bellamy, would you repeat the messages from Pritchard please.'

*　*　*

Jemma listened to Sean read the messages again as she walked between him and the image of Everson. 'Are you going to hand me over?'

'Of course not,' Sean said.

'No, Dr Anderson, we will not acquiesce to his demands,' replied Everson. 'But I would like to know why he is so determined to get hold of you.'

Jemma leaned against Sean. 'I don't know. He says my mother had a title and it's now mine, but he didn't tell me what it was. And he claims to have my sister. I think the real issue is that he wants me to work on a vaccine for that virus. But given he's prepared to release it and kill both animals and people, I don't know why he wants a vaccine.'

'That would be self-preservation,' said Everson. 'He wants to release it, but he doesn't want to catch it. We need to find out about this title too. There's more to this than just developing a vaccine.'

Hunt's voice broke into the conversation. 'I agree. Bellamy, keep Dr Anderson inside. I'm on my way to you.' We'll talk more then. The light from Tom's gadget snapped off.

'Oops. Your boss didn't like that,' Jemma said to Tom, before turning to Sean. 'What now?'

Sean wrapped his arms around her shoulders. 'Are you okay?'

'Yeah, just a bit shocked. I need to do something.'

'I know,' he said with a sigh. 'We need a plan, and we'll get into that as soon as the boss gets here. He has to be part of it.'

'Alright.' She didn't pull away from Sean, his touch was

comforting, but she was puzzled why he always deferred to his boss. Sean was more capable of making his own decisions than anyone she'd ever met. 'I'd like to have a look at Tom's weapon while we wait.'

'Sure,' said Tom, placing his right palm on the side of the weapon. The square on top flashed bright blue.

Dan raised his pistol. 'What the bloody hell is that?'

'For Christ's sake, put your gun down and have a look. I'll explain it to you,' said Tom.

Jemma moved between them and glared at Dan until he re-holstered his gun.

'Alright,' said Sean. 'Settle down and listen to Tom.'

When Tom held the weapon up again, the light had gone dull. 'Track,' he commanded. The light strengthened and showed an image of the area in front of him, with a clear outline of Sean. 'Stand still, Sean. I won't hurt you. The track command shows an image of the quarry. The viewer can penetrate most things, even walls.'

'Prepare to stun,' commanded Tom. The light turned green.

To Jemma's amusement Sean flinched.

'It's okay mate, I won't discharge the weapon,' said Tom, with a big grin. 'If I were to use the operative word s-t-u-n again, it'd stop the target for a couple of minutes. It doesn't cause pain.' He held it up again. 'Prepare to immobilise.' The light turned red. He turned it around for the others to see. Two lines extended around Sean's image. 'If I used that word again, the target would be paralysed for about ten minutes. It does cause pain, because it shuts down the sympathetic nervous system and causes paralysis. Then it activates the parasympathetic system to protect the victim's organs, particularly the brain and heart. It allows us to get to the target and secure them without any long-term harm.'

Sean and Dan focused on how the weapon could be *used*, the technology leap years beyond tasers and capsicum spray. But Jemma was more curious about *how it worked*. She could see all sorts of non-military applications for the technology, including her own research, locating elusive, endangered animals.

'I've never seen anything like this before,' said Sean. 'Why isn't it available to all of us?'

'Don't know, probably because it doesn't belong to the military. We work in partnership with others, and they own the weapons.'

'What if someone overpowered you, turned it against you, do you have a backup?'

'It's programmed to work only for me. If it loses contact with my body, it turns off, no one else can use it. And no, we don't carry lethal weapons.'

Jemma touched Tom's arm. 'Who are these others, your partners?' Private contractors working with the military on advanced weapons made sense, so why the secrecy?

'I can't tell you. Don't look at me like that Sean. The identity of those partners would confuse everything.'

Everson appeared back on the screen and started to speak, unaware that Hunt had entered through the back of the room.

'Right, give us what you've found,' said Hunt.

Sean greeted his boss, but Everson's eyes narrowed in

Hunt's direction although he quickly regained his composure and began to describe the second person in the photo taken by the pilot. 'He is a biochemist and microbiologist. His specialty is the replication of viral genomes for the development of vaccines.

'Would you like to try that in English,' said Tom, then as an afterthought, 'sir?'

'I can explain,' said Jemma. 'Every person has a unique DNA combination. It's commonly used in criminal investigations. In the same way, every virus has its own DNA signature, which forms the basis of a genome. Scientists try to change viruses for lots of reasons, mostly to find new ways to treat disease. But there are some who look for ways to do harm, such as combining elements of harmless viruses that spread easily, like influenza, with lethal viruses that are less contagious. The swine flu pandemic of 2009 was thought to be one for a while.'

'I'm glad you mentioned swine flu,' interjected Everson. 'It was identified in April 2009, in Mexico, spread to the USA and within weeks at least thirty other countries, including Australia. Came out of the blue. It was clearly a manufactured virus.'

'No,' replied Jemma. 'You've made too many assumptions. It didn't come out of the blue. It was in the human population for months prior to the pandemic, and in the pig population much longer. There's a documented history of transmission of the influenza virus between pigs and people. No one's sure why, maybe because pig DNA is close to human DNA. Influenza A mutates easily and rapidly, so when a dramatic change occurs to the virus, people have limited immunity. Antibodies to other types of Influenza A are only partially effective against the new one. That's why a new virus can spread quickly and become a pandemic. That scientist may have followed the pandemic to document the nature of the spread.'

'Very interesting Dr Anderson,' said Everson, scowling. He insisted that many eminent scientists, including those in the security services, believed swine flu to be a manufactured virus.

'You need to listen,' said Jemma. 'There's another explanation, and as far as the scientific community is concerned, a more credible one.'

'Certainly,' replied Everson with a thin smile, as he put up the images taken by the pilot, of Pritchard and the other man.

His sarcasm was lost on Jemma as she rushed towards the wall on which the images had been projected. 'Oh Jesus. Oh no. No, it can't be.'

'Can't be who, Jemma?' Sean ran to her side.

'Dear God.' Tears ran down her cheeks. 'Increase the size. Oh God, oh God.' She wrapped her hands across her mouth, muffling a scream.

Sean grabbed her, forcing her around to look at him. 'Jemma, for God's sake, tell me what's wrong.'

'The man on the left,' she whispered. 'His name is Anthony Chang.'

'Who the hell is Anthony Chang?' He pushed her into a chair, squatted in front of her and gave her a small shake. 'Tell me.'

'You know about my Uncle Eric and Aunt Mary. Anthony's their son who disappeared five years ago. He's no criminal. Oh, dear God, he's alive. When he went missing everyone, state and federal police and even the Army, mounted a massive search, but couldn't find any trace. We all assumed he was dead.'

He held her hands until she settled. 'Jemma, this might be the break we need. We'll find him, I promise. Do you know why the army got involved in the search for him?'

'He was ex-army. Something to do with intelligence, but I don't know what. Somebody needs to tell Mary and Eric.'

'There'd have to be a file.' Sean stared at his boss who now stood on the other side of Jemma.

'Already thought of that,' replied Hunt. 'I'll get on to it as soon as we leave here.' He turned to Jemma. 'I will visit your guardians personally. Do I have your permission to ask them what they knew about your parents?'

'They're not my guardians, but we're close. They need to know about Anthony, and you can ask them anything you like. If they had information about my parents, they'd have told me.'

Hunt frowned as he stood and looked down at her. 'Not your guardians?'

'No. Why would you call them that? I do see them as my second family though.'

'Okay. You relax while I think about what to do next.' He looked up at Everson. 'If we're finished, I need a discussion with the men here.'

Everson's image disappeared immediately, and Sean cringed as he watched Hunt glare at himself, Dan and Tom. 'There's been sloppy work from all of you over the last few days. That's about to stop. Do I make myself clear?'

No one answered, but Sean stiffened, waiting for what was to follow – he knew the look so well.

'You let Dr Anderson's intruder get away from her apartment,' said Hunt. 'That's why those police are dead, and you've been tracked here.'

'Fair go, sir,' said Sean. 'I don't know how he got away, and we did everything in our power to avoid being tracked.' Hunt moved so close that Sean instinctively took a step back.

'Being puzzled is no excuse for letting your surveillance lapse. You're acting like a bunch of amateurs. Now that I'm questioning you, you're whining. When this is over, every bloody one of you will discuss the matter with me personally, including you, Lambert. You're in charge, Bellamy. Act like it. Lift your game, the bloody lot of you. I'm not interested in retrieving your bodies. Watch your backs and watch each other's backs. Is that clear?'

When Hunt shifted his attention to Jemma, Sean stiffened, ready to intervene until his boss lowered his voice. 'Dr Anderson, we must now work out how to manage your protection.'

'I need to help,' said Jemma. 'If Anthony's alive, I have to find him.'

'I understand, my dear, but you aren't trained, and we know these people are dangerous. I can move you to a secure safe house. Alternatively, Mr Everson has offered refuge on the mountain. I'm confident you'd be safe there.'

'Hang on a minute,' said Sean. 'Everson wanted Jemma delivered so he could place her somewhere out of the way. We can't trust him.'

'I have his measure,' he responded. 'He wouldn't move her. But I can understand your fears, given what's happened. So, I take it you want to find a safe house?'

'Damn it, I want to go home,' replied Jemma. 'I don't want any part of this.'

'Understood, but for the moment, I can't allow that. The risk is too great.'

Sean grimaced when Jemma stood up and glared at Hunt, arms folded in front of her chest, and demanded, 'Who the hell are you to tell me what I can, and can't, do?'

'I'm the person who'll take you into custody if you don't do as I say.' A humourless smile formed on Hunt's face. Sean, moving behind Hunt, drew his fingers across his mouth in a zipping motion. Finally, she seemed to get the message.

'Fine, but I'm not going anywhere near that blue light.'

'Fair enough,' replied Hunt. 'I will accept that for the moment.'

'What do you mean, *for the moment?*'

'If I come to consider that to be the safest place for you, that's where you'll go.' He stared at her; one eyebrow raised. Before she had a chance to respond, he excused himself to answer his phone.

She fronted Sean. 'This is garbage. I could be of use to

you. I have the scientific background that you don't. Why can't I help? Anthony's my adopted brother.'

'I will seek your help,' said Sean, 'but you can't come with us. It's too dangerous. I'm sorry Jemma, the decision is taken.'

'Listen up.' Silence was instant when Hunt spoke. 'O'Leary, you'll escort Dr Anderson to safe house five. Don't argue, I'll have you relieved as soon as I can, but for the moment, you're the best option. Bellamy, Lambert, with me.' He marched towards the door.

Sean smiled. Nobody would disobey Hunt's orders. He commanded respect, not blind obedience. He'd been in every major conflict, Afghanistan, Iraq and East Timor, and he'd held the lives of thousands in his hands. But it still worried Sean, the extent to which Everson had had him bluffed.

'Have you sorted Mr Everson, sir?' Sean walked with him. He wanted to get Hunt talking before they left, rather than wonder what would come next.

'Not really, but I've backed him off.' He'd gone up to the SCARF site at Everson's invitation. Shocked by the size of the facility, his real concern lay with the aspects that Everson didn't show him.

'Did you enter through that granite rock?'

'Yes, quite amazing. We walked around the place. It's got three levels, all underground.'

Sean whistled. 'How the hell have they hidden that?'

'Your guess is as good as mine. Some of the rooms were locked, and he steered me away from others. I'm damned sure he was hiding something. He wouldn't talk about the partners, muttered some rubbish about universities.'

'Sir, we've got to work it out. I'm trying to protect Jemma, and I have no idea what I'm protecting her from.'

'Agreed.'

'What was that about her guardians?'

'Not important, just something that the chief said. We'll sort out the safe house for Dr Anderson now, then I'm going to wring the truth out of Eric and Mary Chang, who I suspect do see themselves as her guardians.'

CHAPTER 8

Jemma glanced across at Dan. The intensity of his expression as they drove from the warehouse made her laugh.

'What?'

'You'll need a babysitting licence soon.'

'Yeah right,' he grimaced. '*The baby* can make me a nice cup of tea when we get there, then. Prove I've taught her something.'

'Yuck,' she retorted. 'Can we stop at a bottle shop? I'd rather a cold beer.'

'Only if you want me to face a firing squad, courtesy of General Hunt. We'll have to see what's in the fridge at the house. Your request is more than my life's worth, lady.'

'General Hunt sounds like the boss from hell.'

'No,' said Dan. 'He's not, but he is the boss, and his rules are clear. If I were ever sent back to a war zone, I'd want him as my commander.'

'You and Sean both speak about him like some kind of deity.'

'No, we don't worship him, but we do trust him, and we always know that whatever he says, he's got our backs.'

She stared at him but said nothing until he turned into the driveway of the safe house. 'Holy-moley.' The old beach-front fibro wedged between two high-rise Gold Coast ocean-front apartment blocks was itself, worthless. But the view… enough to make any self-respecting developer drool.

Dan led the way up the stairs, his hand on his pistol. Used to the drill now, she didn't argue, just followed behind until he waved her inside. She was greeted by two male and two female guards who stood aside for her to walk past. A narrow hallway opened out onto a balcony with a wooden staircase that ran down to a small grassed yard at the edge of the golden sandy beach.

'Sorry mate, we need to stay inside,' Dan called. 'You can look through the sliding doors, but you can't go out.'

'Right. Why doesn't that surprise me?'

Dan led her to the dining table. He gently went through a list of rules the length of a small novel which almost decreed she mustn't breathe without permission. Although he did his best to reassure her, and no locks or bars kept her in, she was, under any definition of the word, a prisoner.

When Dan finished, he suggested she move to the lounge to watch TV and wait for dinner to arrive.

'When did you order dinner?'

'I didn't. A whole team's in the background looking after you.'

'Oh, right. Do you think they might look after me with a beer, or a nice glass of wine?'

'I'll see what I can do.' He pulled out his phone, then

grinned at her before he made the call. 'You were going to make me a cuppa as I recall.'

'I would,' she replied, smiling, 'but we don't want to spoil your glass of wine, now do we?'

He patted the top of her head as he walked past. 'Never you mind. I'll make my own after I organise madam's wine.'

She poked her tongue out at him then lay back in her recliner chair to surf the television channels. When dinner arrived, Dan beckoned her out to the kitchen where he handed her a small bottle of light beer. 'Come on. You can join the civilised people to eat.'

'You got it for me,' she said, with a broad smile. 'Thank you.'

He bowed. 'My pleasure.' At the dinner table, six places had been set, but only one had a wine glass. She looked up at him.

'You can drink,' he said, 'but we're on duty.'

'Oh good, that means I get the whole bottle.'

'If you want,' he replied. 'And if you're too drunk to run, and we have to evacuate quickly, I'll throw you over my shoulder and dump you in the boot.'

'Before I met Sean, I'd have said you wouldn't dare.'

Dan laughed. 'But now we both know better, don't we?'

After a simple dinner of lightly grilled coral trout, and a fresh garden salad, they remained at the table chatting. Surprised when she checked her watch that a couple of hours had passed, she stifled a yawn.

'Better get some sleep,' said Dan, pushing his own chair back from the table. 'You obviously can't hold your liquor.'

'Oh, but it was so enjoyable. You should have tried it. Oops sorry, I forgot, you have to stay sober to look after me.'

He grabbed her upper arms, turned her around, and pushed her to her bedroom. 'Door stays open, please.'

As she walked into her room, she saw Dan place his side-arm on a small table within easy reach and curl up on a sofa just outside her door. Two of the other agents had positioned themselves inside the front and back doors, and she presumed the other two were resting. She turned off her light and did her best to sleep, but it was as elusive as Fredrick Pritchard, and when Dan's soft snores invaded her senses, she gave up and crept out to the lounge room, taking care not to wake him.

She scouted through some drawers in a small desk in the corner of the room for some paper and a pen, then settled on the sofa and started to make notes. She'd been at it for more than four hours when the orange glow of the morning sun spread across the water.

Dan rolled off the sofa. He stretched, yawned and stood behind her. 'What're you doing?'

'We've got to find Anthony, Dan. Eric and Mary believe he's dead. I thought he was dead. Even if he's turned bad, I want him back. I've written down everything I can remember about his army job and then the company that took him to America. Maybe it'll help.'

'Well done. It looks like it will,' said Dan, flicking through her notes.

Anthony had attended the Defence Force Academy and, with the Army's support, achieved two PhDs, one in

Microbiology, the other in Pharmacology, then served with an anti-terrorism unit for several years before he left. She reached up and flicked over a couple of pages. 'Anthony worked for Pritchard Pharmaceuticals in Sydney manipulating viruses to test anti-viral drugs. Surprise, surprise. They transferred him to New York with executive status. He was so excited. But we never heard from him again. Now it's looking like he's turned terrorist. I don't believe it. Pritchard has to be forcing him into it.'

'I'll call Sean, there's things here we didn't know. He can present it to the boss.' Dan frowned. 'I keep being struck by the number of coincidences and overlaps.'

'What do you mean?'

'Pritchard employed Anthony, then Anthony disappears. Your sister disappeared after the flood and now Pritchard claims to have her. From what he said, he had something to do with your mother's death. Now, he's after you.'

'Yeah, I've got that, but I don't get why,' said Jemma.

'No, and that's the problem. But there's something else.' Dan sat beside Jemma and took one of her hands in his. 'I don't even know if this makes sense but hear me out. We know that your parents died in the floods in January 2011 and I told you that my parents died in March 2011 in a car accident that I've never believed was an accident. General Hunt's parents died in June of the same year in a house fire. They were reported as being too frail to escape, but that was rubbish. They weren't even sixty and they were both fit and healthy. I know Sean's father died over ten years before that, but his death was suspicious too. I can't find the link, but there has to be one, and it's looking suspiciously like Pritchard.'

'Maybe. Your parents and mine were linked,' said Jemma, 'but I didn't know about the others. And Tom thought he'd met me before too. That was odd.'

'I agree. Plus, your mother was friends with the chief. Just too many coincidences. We've got to dig more.' Dan got up when another man entered the room. 'My replacement's here. Sit tight, Jemma. We'll find Anthony, and we'll get to the bottom of the rest of it.'

CHAPTER 9

The sun had barely lifted above the horizon when Sean arrived at his headquarters in the morning.

Hunt, already there, beckoned him in. 'Come with me. I'm going to tackle Dr Anderson's guardians.'

'Okay, but she insists they're not her guardians.'

'There's something you don't know,' replied Hunt. 'If my suspicions are at all confirmed, I'll fill you in. Otherwise, I'll accept I've been over-reacting and I'll put it to rest.'

'Sure.' He shrugged and, although Hunt's determined look made him uncomfortable, he put it aside so he could focus back on the investigation. 'There's three angles to follow. Everson and his blue light have to be top of the list. I accept he's legitimate, but he knows more than he's telling us, and he's gagged his staff. Even Tom knows more but he can't tell us. Secondly, there's Anthony Chang and whatever his role is. And thirdly, Pritchard clearly had something to do with those spheres. There's no doubt now that the spheres are tracking us.'

'And,' added Hunt, as they pulled into the driveway of the Chang's Sanctuary Cove home, 'the guardians.'

Sean waited for his boss to explain but when nothing was forthcoming, he walked up the stairs and knocked.

Mary opened the door with a smile, but it faded when she saw Sean and Hunt. 'Jemma?'

'No ma'am.' Hunt moved forward and extended his arm. 'May we come in? My name is Alexander Hunt, this is Sean Bellamy.'

'I know who you are,' she said, standing to the side to let them pass.

'Would your husband be here, ma'am?'

'No, he's at work. I'm perfectly capable of talking to you myself.'

'Yes ma'am, but I'd rather speak to you together,' said Hunt. 'It's not bad news.'

When she left the room, Sean murmured, 'How would she know who we are?'

'Don't know, but I plan to find out.'

Mary had lost colour from her face when she returned, but she politely offered tea or coffee and waved them to seats at the kitchen table which she stacked with biscuits and cake.

Several minutes later Eric, breathless and red-faced, flew into the kitchen. 'What's wrong? Where's Jemma?'

Sean held out the chair next to Mary's and waited until Eric was seated. 'Jemma's fine. She's at one of our safe houses because someone broke into her apartment.' He chose not to tell them about the police safe house as he placed the photo of Pritchard on the table between Eric and Mary.

'That's Drick,' exclaimed Mary. Eric looked up, his face now blank, but Sean hadn't missed the frown that flashed across it when Mary spoke.

'Who's Drick?' said Sean, looking directly at Mary.

Eric covered Mary's hand with his when she started to speak. She sighed and sat back in her chair, motioning Eric to take over.

'He caused us a lot of trouble years ago, but we haven't seen him for maybe twenty years,' said Eric. 'Not since your father died.'

Sean gripped the edge of the table. 'Did he have something to do with my father's death?'

Eric slumped back in his chair. 'We believed so. That's why he was removed.'

'Removed?'

'He had to be. Because of where we come from, of course. We couldn't risk antagonising our hosts.' Both Eric and Mary frowned. They clearly expected him to know something that he didn't.

'What do you mean?' said Sean. 'Where we come from?'

'Oh dear,' Eric sighed. 'You'd better speak to your chief.'

Hunt got up and stood behind Sean. 'Was it the chief who appointed you as Jemma's guardians?'

'No, that happened at her birth, but you'd better speak to him if you want to know more. Now, is there anything else?'

'Yes,' replied Sean. He put the photo of Anthony in front of them. 'Can you identify this person?'

Eric put his arm around Mary as she started to cry. 'When was this taken?'

'Who is he?' Sean pointed back to the photo.

'Anthony, our son,' said Eric. 'But you knew that.'

'Yes,' said Sean, measuring his words. 'But I needed your confirmation. One of our staff saw him and took this photo yesterday.'

'He's alive,' cried Mary. 'Oh, dear God. Why hasn't he come home?'

'We believe the man you call Drick has him, and is now after Jemma,' said Sean. 'Can you suggest anything that might help us find Drick?'

Eric shook his head. 'We haven't seen him in all these years. Please speak to your chief. If there's anything we can do to find Anthony or protect Jemma, we will.'

'Thank you,' said Hunt. 'We'll keep you informed.' He remained silent until they were back in the car. 'I'm calling the chief when we get back. He knows more. Everson knows more. Eric and Mary know more. One of them had better start talking.'

'Agreed,' said Sean. 'Whatever's going on is bigger than we'd thought. Do you want to tell me about the guardians now?'

'Oh yes, of course. Find a coffee place. I don't know how you'll cope with what I have to say.'

Sean pulled into a shopping centre and found a café. He eased into a booth nestled at the back and waited until the coffee had arrived and the waitress had moved back out of earshot. Once Hunt began his story, Sean sat motionless. He struggled to take it in, puzzled that he'd never been told of his father's rank and military history. But it was the conversation Hunt had overheard with his mother that bothered him most. 'Are you telling me I've got another sister or a brother out there somewhere?'

'That's how I interpreted what she said.'

'Jesus, what did your father say when you asked him about the guardians?'

Hunt shook his head. 'Denied everything. Couldn't get anything out of him and we're encountering the same brick walls again.'

'Why didn't you tell me before?'

'I was ordered not to,' Hunt said, rubbing his hand through his hair. 'I didn't understand any of it, presumed I'd misinterpreted the conversation. But with what we now know about Pritchard, or Drick, and the possibility he was linked with your father's death, plus the disappearance of Anthony Chang and Jemma's sister, it's time to investigate, particularly now that he's after Jemma.'

'I'd say it's a bit late,' replied Sean. His eyes narrowed as he stared back at Hunt.

'I'm sorry Sean. I realise now I should have ignored the orders and told you before.'

'No shit.'

'No, and I can't change the past, but we can try to do something now. Do you need more time to think about all this?'

Sean shook his head. 'I'm really pissed off that all these people know what's going on and won't give us the information we need.'

'As am I. Alright, time to go back and push them.'

When they arrived back at the office, Sean joined Hunt to

listen into the phone call with the chief. It started cordially, but when Hunt mentioned the guardians, and that they'd identified Drick, there was a long pause.

'Give me five,' replied the chief. 'I'll set up a secure video link.'

'I'll be ready, sir.' Hunt ordered Sean to stand behind him. 'We need to make it clear you're a party to this conversation.'

Sean instinctively stood straighter when the video came through and the chief stared intently at him.

'I have Colonel Bellamy, my 2IC with me,' said Hunt. 'He's cleared to my level.'

The chief nodded. 'Yes, I'm aware.'

'Sir, I have to ask how you are aware? And how is it that Eric and Mary knew both Bellamy and myself?'

It was a while before he responded, and Sean thought he was putting considerable effort into choosing his words carefully. 'Because you are part of our community. I won't explain over a video link. As soon as I'm able, I will fly up there and talk to you.'

'Who is Drick?'

'Our enemy. We had him incarcerated several years ago.'

'Mary identified him as Jemma's pursuer and we believe he has Anthony Chang, Mary's son.'

Sean looked away when he heard the chief swear.

'If he's back, we must find him,' replied the chief. 'He's more dangerous than you can imagine. Double your protection detail on Dr Anderson.' He looked away, then leaned closer to the camera. 'No, damn it. Take her to Everson. She'll be safer there.'

'I don't trust Everson,' Sean replied, then realised who he was speaking to. 'Sorry sir, but I don't.'

'Neither do I,' said Hunt.

'You mightn't, but that is an order.' He glared at Sean, then Hunt. 'Look, I know he has a difficult personality, but I give you my word that he's trustworthy. He can call on resources we may need, far greater than we can provide ourselves.'

Sean repeated Tom's statement about their partners.

'Yes. They're outside your current understanding, but they will help if we need them. I think we might move your whole operation there. Safer all around. I'll speak to Everson. Sort out your differences. Get him involved.'

Sean gaped at Hunt when he terminated the call. 'He wants us to move there.'

'Appears that way. And we don't have a choice when it comes to Jemma. We have to move her there.'

Sean groaned. 'I might let you tell her.'

'No, son.' Hunt slapped him on the back. 'It'll be good for your personal development. I plan to be as far away from that confrontation as I can get.'

'Thanks,' muttered Sean.

'We'll have to find out what we can from Tom,' said Hunt. 'Then I'm going to have to pin Everson down.'

'Right. Good luck with that.'

More confused than ever, Sean left Hunt's office. He was part of some community, along with the chief, Hunt, Dan and

Jemma. They had an enemy he'd never heard of, and Jemma had guardians. He had guardians himself, but they were appointed for him because he was a child at the time of his father's death. Surely to God, they weren't also a part of this.

He found Tom talking to Everson on a video link just outside Hunt's office and muttered a greeting. 'Sir, are you aware that Mary, Jemma's guardian, identified Fredrick Pritchard as someone she knows as Drick.'

Everson leaned forward and snapped. 'Was she sure?'

'Yes, and Eric confirmed it.'

'By all the stars,' said Everson. He stood, walked away from the screen, then came back and slammed his fist on the desk. 'You need to move Jemma right now. She's in grave danger.'

'But why?'

'If it is Drick, you must not underestimate him. I will explain later. First, we must concentrate on moving Jemma to safety.'

'We've already told the chief,' said Sean. 'He ordered us to bring her up to you but didn't explain why either. I'm about to head down to get her now.'

'Too slow,' replied Everson. 'I'll send a helicopter down from here. I'm closer to her safe house.'

It took a moment for Everson's words to sink in, but once they had, Sean tore back to Hunt's office and relayed Everson's fears. 'He's sending a chopper.'

'Okay,' said Hunt. 'I'll order ground back-up. Call her protection detail. Tell them to have her ready. Tom, you continue to liaise with Mr Everson. Bellamy, grab O'Leary if he's back and head down there. If Everson gets her before you arrive, follow them up to SCARF.'

Sean ran to his office to put his papers down but, as he turned to leave, his phone rang.

'Hi, I need to talk to you,' said Jemma.

'Hello. Me too. I'm about to come down to you.'

*   *   *

Jemma didn't hear Sean's response. Someone clamped her arm from behind and wrenched the phone from her hand. She screamed and swung around; her other arm raised to fight back but the man towered above her.

'Let me go. Who the hell are you?' She tried to pull away, but the fellow was so close that, as he smiled, the scars on his face made her shrink back. 'What do you want?'

At the same time, the agent who'd replaced Dan jumped up, aiming his revolver. A second intruder fired a bullet into his forehead. The guard's gun crashed to the floor and he stared at Jemma for a few seconds, before falling forward.

'Now, Dr Anderson, we must move quickly given you've spoken to your minder. We don't want to have to disable anyone else.'

'Disable?' She stared at the agent, then back to the intruders. 'You didn't disable him. You killed him.'

'Semantics. Let's go. I don't want to hurt you. You're valuable to us, so long as you stay alive.'

The man pushed her through the front room where several guards lay bound and gagged on the floor.

'The agent you shot. Is he dead?'

'Not your worry,' said the man. 'Keep moving please.'

'It is my worry. You just killed someone.' She tried to shake him off, to go back in case the man he'd shot wasn't dead, but he forced her forward. Sean would be on his way given how he'd been cut off, but he couldn't possibly get there in time. They'd be gone within minutes. The man locked the front door behind them, then dragged her down the stairs into the back of a dark four-wheel-drive station wagon with heavily tinted windows. He shackled her with chains attached to the floor. She sat, too scared to scream and the chains too tight for her to move.

From the floor she couldn't see out a window, but the vehicle accelerated, stopping twice, she thought at traffic lights, before driving into the garage of a house. A woman waved a hand-held device over her. It beeped on her wrist and the bracelet Sean had given her was torn off. The rear door slammed shut and the driver took off. Half an hour later, they entered a large metal building. A man unlocked her shackles, pulled her from the car, shoved her into the front seat of a small plane parked in the building and told her to fasten her seatbelt.

CHAPTER 10

Sean jumped up, smashing his chair against the back wall when he heard Jemma scream. 'Jemma. What's wrong?' He swung around, couldn't think past the fog that had overwhelmed his brain. 'Oh God. Jemma. Jemma,' he shouted.

'What's up?' yelled Dan, as he ran in with Tom on his heels.

'Jemma screamed. And I'm sure I heard a gunshot. Now I can't get her. I'm trying the sergeant in charge.' He leaned against his desk working hard to catch his breath as he waited. The phone rang out. He stared at Dan. 'Nothing. No one's answering.'

'I'll call his deputy,' said Dan.

Sean shook his head. 'She won't answer either. If the sergeant's the only one down, his partner would've called in. Jesus, all those guards were experienced, all capable.' He'd chosen them himself. No one could have gone past them if they were alive. He sank into his chair. 'Bloody hell. Dan, grab the general. Tom, call your boss. Divert the helicopter here. Quickest way for us to get to her.'

Tom spoke into the gadget clipped to his belt, then slipped into a chair beside Sean and logged into the CCTV viewer for the house. Sean moved aside but stayed close enough to watch over Tom's shoulder. There was no movement inside or outside the house. He slammed his fist onto the desk.

'Helicopter's about to land,' said Tom. 'Come on.'

'Dan, grab one of the emergency cars and follow us down, lights and sirens,' said Sean, as he prepared to follow Tom.

Hunt blocked them in the doorway. 'Bellamy, wait up. Did you get a tracking device on Jemma?'

'Yeah, a bracelet. The tech boys are checking it now. How the hell did they find her? That's the safest house we have. Not one of those agents would've let anyone past.'

'You know as well as I do,' said Hunt. 'It's not hard with the right equipment, and he obviously has it. He's been tracking her for some time. I'll notify the military police. I'll pull some other teams out to assist.'

Sean looked over his shoulder as Hunt stood aside to let him pass. 'Sir, can you get someone on to other CCTVs in the area?'

'Done.'

On their way to the helicopter, Everson notified Tom that the man who'd abducted Jemma had a lengthy police record, mainly aggravated assault. A thug for hire. Sean felt as if something had smashed him from behind.

'Breathe, mate,' said Tom.

But he couldn't register anything beyond the nature of the man who'd taken Jemma.

'Pull yourself together,' said Tom, tightening his grip on Sean's shoulder. 'You're no help to her like this. Mr Everson says the car that took her was stolen a week ago in Sydney. Dan's on the phone. He's got information. You need to focus.'

Sean took a deep breath and nodded. 'Thanks.'

'I've got the bracelet,' said Dan. 'It's in an empty house at Pimpama. Half an hour north of Jemma's safe house.'

'So, they're heading north,' Sean muttered.

'Yeah but they could have turned off anywhere. Doesn't help us much.'

'Tom, ask Mr Everson to inform the local police about Pimpama. Dan, proceed to the safe house,' said Sean, forcing himself to control his shattered thinking. 'We'll meet you there.'

'On it.'

The helicopter landed on a patch of firm sand behind the house. Pistol drawn, Sean ran to the back gate, flanked by Tom. He flicked the latch and pushed the old gate open, taking care not to let it squeak, then checked one side of the house, while Tom checked the other. Staying down, he made his way around to the front, then back to back with Tom, crept up the stairs. Sean positioned himself to the right of the doorway and signalled to Tom to use the master key to open the door. Someone groaned.

'Clear the house,' said Sean. 'Then check for injured.'

A few seconds later, Tom yelled, 'Man down.'

'Is he alive?'

'No pulse.'

Sean rolled him over and found the bullet wound in his forehead. Point blank. He hadn't stood a chance. A pool of blood on the floor surrounded the guard's head. 'Keep looking.' His voice cracked as he looked back at the guard, a man he knew well.

Four guards were on the floor in the next room, their wrists and ankles bound, duct tape covering their mouths. Two were sitting. Both had rope burns on their wrist and ankles where they'd tried to free themselves. Sean waved to Tom to help them, while he dropped down beside the other two who were prostrate on floor. The first was breathing and seemed stable but had clearly taken a heavy blow to the head. Sean tore the duct tape from her mouth, turned her on her side and signalled to Tom to watch her. The other wasn't breathing. He knelt beside him and ripped off the tape. It had covered the man's nostrils as well as his mouth, but he still had a pulse although it was weak and thready. He straightened the guard out on the floor, ready to resuscitate him, until the man gave a weak cough followed by a sharp intake of air.

Sean sat back on his heels. 'Everyone listen up. Help is on its way. Go down to the yard. Do not touch anything. Avoid that room.' He pointed to the one where the guard lay dead. 'Tom, I'll stay here until the ambulance arrives. Get the police tape from the car and secure the site.'

A female corporal demanded details on the dead man.

'I'm sorry, mate,' said Sean. 'There's nothing either of us can do.'

'Put me on the team to go after those bastards,' she snapped.

'You and me both,' replied Sean.

'I'll go tell his wife,' she said, choking back a sob.

'No. You're his deputy. The team here is your responsibility now. I'll go.' Sean knew the dead guard's wife and his four children. Even though he was relieved to have found four of his people alive, he couldn't stop thinking about the guard's family. The military police arrived at the same time as Dan. He filled them in, then left Dan to manage the scene and asked Tom to drive him to the guard's address. It took him a moment to collect himself when they arrived before he pulled himself from the car and walked to the gate. He stopped, his hand on the latch, then took a deep breath, opened it and walked up the path. An image crept into his mind of Hunt informing him that they'd found Jemma's body. With a shudder, he forced the thought away, walked up the stairs and knocked.

The guard's wife wiped her hands on a tea towel as she opened the door, but her smile vanished when she saw Sean and she slumped to the floor. He helped her up and led her to a sofa. From experience he knew that no words could really help in these situations. 'I have bad news,' he said, as gently as he could.

'He's dead, isn't he?' The pain in her eyes made Sean wish he was the one who'd been shot.

'I'm so sorry but yes, he is.'

She stared at him with vacant eyes and, when she spoke, her voice was flat. 'I tried to stop him going this morning. I had this terrible foreboding, not something I've ever felt before. I've been expecting a knock on the door ever since he left.' With a small choking sound, she buried her head against Sean's chest, and dissolved into tears.

He held her until the sobs subsided before asking who he should contact. Her mother arrived within minutes of his call. He slipped from the room, leaving them to cry, safe in each other's arms. All security people thought about the risks, but mostly pushed it to the back of their minds, and that's what he had to do now if he was to have any chance of stopping these bastards. They were always a step ahead of him, and he had no idea how they did it. Dan had scanned the vehicle he used to transport Jemma to the safe house for tracking devices. It had been clean. A chopper had followed Dan's car, and the pilot insisted there'd been no other aircraft of any kind anywhere near them, not even a drone, nor had any vehicles followed. Perhaps it was just that the sphere had tracked her, but an uncomfortable thought flitted through his mind. Was it possible that someone in his own organisation had leaked information?

Hunt had notified airports, shipping, train and bus terminals and sent photographs throughout Australia and, via Interpol, to every other country. There wasn't much else he could do. 'Alright Tom,' he sighed, 'we'll collect Dan, then go back to base. You can drive.'

'Which base, mine or yours?'

'Very funny. Until we know what your lot are up to, we won't go there.'

Tom sighed. 'It's all legitimate, mate. You know me well enough to know I wouldn't be involved if I had any doubts. And Mr Everson's done his best to help you.'

'Maybe but there's stuff he's not telling us, so I'll make my own judgement. It'll be up to General Hunt anyway, so no point in arguing about it.'

'Whatever,' responded Tom. 'I've asked Colonel Williamson to try to track Jemma too. He'll let me know.'

Sean rested his head back and closed his eyes. He'd only just managed to extract Jemma when he'd found her near SCARF. Now she'd been abducted from their most secure safe house, guarded by his best people.

*   *   *

Jemma fiddled with her seatbelt as she looked around the small plane. A large man standing in the front doorway held an automatic military-style shotgun and looked perfectly capable of using it. He jumped out as the engines quickened, slamming the door behind him, then the plane slowly taxied across the tarmac. Seconds later, it sped down the runway and commenced its lift off. Jemma rested her head on her knees and groaned. She didn't travel well.

A man, who must have been hidden somewhere at the rear of the plane, came forward and sat beside her. 'Just relax. It's not a long flight. You'll be okay.'

She recognised him instantly. Pritchard, this time minus his narrow-brimmed hat and the sunglasses. 'Who the hell are you?'

'Fredrick Pritchard, at your service, ma'am.'

'I know your name. What do you want?'

'I told you last time we met. I'm family, and I'm trying to get you to safety.'

'You're not family. I know you run Pritchard Pharmaceuticals, and I know you abducted Anthony Chang.'

'Abducted is a little harsh. But yes, he works with me.'

The aircraft hit a small air pocket, and she groaned again. Right now, she didn't care whether he was friend or foe, she wanted to be on the ground.

'We're almost there,' said Pritchard. 'We'll talk after we land.'

He leaned in close, and Jemma felt a sting on her arm. The next she knew the plane was parked on a small runway. She glared at him. 'What the hell did you do to me?'

'Just something to help you cope with the flight.' He held up a thin metal cylinder with a tiny green light on one end. It didn't appear to have a needle, but the sting had certainly felt like one. 'You'll be fine as soon as you move around.'

She stumbled getting out of the plane. Her legs felt like lead and she wasn't pleased that she had to accept Pritchard's help. She walked with him to the end of the airstrip and a large old well-maintained farmhouse surrounded by a neat and tidy garden. Brown grass crunched under their feet. She checked her watch. It had to be Central Queensland, they hadn't been in the air long enough for it to be further north.

As they neared the farmhouse, the scent of a roast wafted out, reminding her of her childhood visits to the family farm. A woman waiting for them inside the house showed Jemma to a room, offered her soap and towels to freshen up, and gently asked if she needed anything else. Jemma shook her head and walked into the bathroom where she held a cool washer to her face. She took her time to return to the kitchen. Pritchard sat chatting to the woman, and didn't seem to notice Jemma as she walked in, so she continued on past for a look around. She couldn't see any door locks or bars on the windows, and she hadn't noticed any fences outside.

'You're free to come and go as you please,' said Pritchard, smiling at her. 'Just don't go too far, too easy to get lost. It's only a few days, and so long as we get on, I'll take you to a safe environment.' The woman rose and left the room.

Jemma sat opposite him at the table. 'What is this place?'

Pritchard sighed, 'You don't need to know. I'm heading back to Brisbane shortly. I need to finish up some business there before we leave.'

'Why are we here?'

'Just a halfway place. I wanted us to be alone, to talk. My housekeeper's out with the pilot, so we can get started now if you like.'

'What have you done with Anthony Chang, and the others?'

'Ah yes, Anthony. Don't worry, he's well. You'll see him soon.' Pritchard sat back in his chair, a strange look on his face. 'He's one of us, you know.'

'What do you mean, one of us?'

'Surely your parents told you where you came from?'

'I told you before, I was born in Brisbane, grew up on the Gold Coast,' she snapped.

'Oh dear. I have a great deal I will have to tell you.'

She stared back at him. He had a genuinely surprised look on his face, as though she really ought to have known.

'Now Jemma, I need your help.'

'I doubt I can help you with anything,' she retorted.

'You're a scientist, and I know you're working on the DNA of the virus you found at Springbrook. I believe you've developed a vaccine.'

'No, I don't have a vaccine. I also told you that the other day. You could have emailed me if all you want is information.'

'No, I need you with me. You can help me, for the sake of the family.'

'You keep saying family, but I have no knowledge of you.'

'Your sister is my wife.'

'My sister?' She grabbed the edge of the table.

'That's right, your sister. It's taken me a long time to track you down. Your sister suffered a head injury in a car accident not long after she arrived in the US, lost her memory. She was employed in my company, but she used a false name and gave no next of kin details, so we had no idea who to contact and I felt obliged to help. As she recovered physically, I got to know her. We've been married five years now, but she still doesn't remember her name or where she came from. We have a three-year-old daughter and I figure I owe it to her as much as to Jenny to track down her past.'

'Jenny?'

'She used the name Jenny Sinclair. I know now that her name is Thera Anderson.'

'And she has a baby?' Jemma leaned forward on the table. A baby. Her niece. She wasn't sure if he didn't notice her distress or just didn't care, but he continued on.

'She had nightmares. She'd call out your name, mutter about floods and a car accident. One night she talked about Murphy's Creek which enabled me to pin it down. You see, I knew your mother died in the floods at Murphy's Creek. It was then that I realised she was talking about your parents … and you. I verified the DNA from a coffee cup you used in a restaurant. I believe if I reunite you with my wife, it might spark some memories for her. Then I can integrate you into the family business and look after both of you as your mother would have wanted.

Tears streamed down her face as she listened. 'If I'd had any idea, I'd have gone to her.'

'Of course. Let's get you started in the business and then I can get you there.'

She stared at him. *Getting started in the business* sounded like a condition to see her sister. Yet she had no proof that he was married to Thera, or that they had a baby. It wouldn't have been hard to discover Jemma had a sister, it'd been in all the newspapers at the time of the flood. 'Why did you want me to stay away from the mountain?'

'I didn't want you to come to harm. Have you heard of the SCARF project?'

'Yes,' replied Jemma.

'My company has researched cures for viruses for decades, without much success. I believe that these people have the technology to achieve where we've failed. We released a virus there to see what they'd do, but humans would be susceptible to it, not just the animals. I didn't want you to catch it.'

'So, all those dead animals were your doing?'

'Unfortunately. I thought SCARF would act quicker.'

'Why would you release a virus that could kill animals, or people?'

'Commercial viability, my dear. How else do I make them expose their cure? If I can use your vaccine, and get hold of their technology, all I have to do is release the virus somewhere, get a pandemic going, and governments will pay a fortune for my help. Believe me, if you come on board, I can make you wealthy beyond your wildest dreams.'

He went on, seemingly oblivious to Jemma's horror. Bio-terrorism was relatively new, from anthrax in the latter twentieth century to higher-tech viruses today, but Pritchard had taken it to another level. He had money and resources on an unstoppable scale and no qualms about abduction or murder. He told her of a lab in an abandoned military base in Costa Rica, and scientists who worked with him. When she asked how many of his people had caught the virus, he brushed her off.

'And there are other projects within SCARF that could be commercially viable, particularly the metal used to contain radiation in the blue light's power source.

'What radiation? They're experimenting with different sorts of metals, and methods of communication,' said Jemma.

'Oh, they have deceived you,' said Pritchard. 'They're not experimenting. They currently communicate with crafts outside our solar system. The people on those crafts provide everything they use. I want their core. I know it isn't uranium or plutonium.'

'That's just fanciful,' said Jemma. 'You're saying they're communicating with aliens.'

He laughed. 'Some of them *are* aliens, like their boss, Charles Everson.' He paused and became more serious. 'Like me.'

'That's ridiculous. Charles Everson and you are both human.'

'You're assuming humans are unique to planet Earth. Where do you think Earth's humans came from? You don't really believe people evolved from apes, do you?'

'In fact, I do. You're telling me we've got aliens on Earth; established communication with outer space; nuclear reactors that don't use uranium; and unknown metals,' said Jemma. 'Really?'

'The metal isn't unknown, although you won't see it listed on the periodic table. It's found in the Earth's core and identified as XP89E4 in scientific journals. Of course, it can't be commercially mined from the core.'

'You've seen my craft, the big sphere.'

'Yes.'

'Does it look like anything your air force owns?'

'No.' She thought back to everything that had happened over the last few weeks and the sphere that had followed her. But aliens? Whatever he was, she had to find a way to stop him from releasing that virus.

'I don't expect you to take everything in today,' he continued. 'When I come back, I'll take you to Costa Rica to show you our research. We have to work you through the business from the ground up.'

She did her best to smile. Although now convinced he was insane, she couldn't pass up the chance to find her sister. Trapped here, the only transport in or out light aircraft, she'd play along. The housekeeper would stay to cook her meals, but there was no capacity to communicate outside. When she asked what to do if either of them got into trouble and needed help, he advised her not to get into trouble.

Stunned after he left, she slid into a chair opposite the housekeeper and shared the roast meal she'd smelled on her way in, 'Has he really gone?'

The housekeeper nodded. 'Yes, thankfully.'

'Why do you work for him?'

'He has my son.'

Jemma froze, with her fork half-way to her mouth. Jesus, was there anything this man wouldn't do.

CHAPTER 11

Sean and Dan worked day and night to find Jemma, taking short naps on the sofa in the office tea-room when their bodies forced them to give in. Around midnight, on the second night after the abduction, the intruder alarm startled Sean awake, and he tore out to the office entry. All the high-tech security locks were in place, but a large brown envelope had been pushed under the door. Grabbing his pistol, he darted into the now empty hallway. He swung around in each direction until, in his peripheral vision, he noticed a flicker of movement at the far end of the corridor. He charged towards it, and only just avoided crashing into the stairwell door as it slammed shut. He reached for the handle, but it wouldn't budge. Turning side-on, he slammed his shoulder at the door, but his bodyweight alone wasn't enough to shift it. When Dan caught up, it took a few tries, but they finally managed to force it open between them. Sean swore as he fell through, and he had to grab the railing to steady himself. Taking the stairs two and three at a time, he raced down with Dan close behind, stopping on the bottom step.

He looked over his shoulder at Dan, 'Ready?'

'Damn right.'

Sean cracked the door into the foyer open. It looked clear,

so he pushed it the rest of the way. A man ran towards the building's exit.

'Stop,' yelled Sean.

The man swung around, raising his pistol.

Sean leapt behind the security desk and shouted, 'Dan. Get down.'

As Dan leapt for cover, a red stain appeared on his upper arm. A security guard jumped from behind the desk and forced him down.

Knowing someone else had stepped in to help Dan, Sean pulled himself up to return the shot but, in the instant that he'd looked away, the man had streaked down the front stairs to a waiting vehicle. Sean charged after him but, before he could get there, the car had accelerated off. It didn't have a number plate. He dropped his gun down by his side. Despite all the work he and Dan had done over the last forty-eight hours, he had nothing substantial to go on, and now this. He bent forward, resting his hands on his knees and heaving for breath. What the hell did he do now?

A security guard ran up behind him. 'Are you alright, mate?'

He holstered his pistol. 'Yeah, I'm fine. Dan?'

'Just a graze,' replied the guard. 'I've dressed it, but your mate's hopping mad.'

'Not surprised. I need to check your cameras. Did that fellow show you any ID?'

'Yeah, he did.'Spect it's fake, but I've printed a copy. Cameras got him, but don't think they'll be useful. Leather jacket, balaclava. He removed the balaclava when he came in and appeared to be acting normally, but there's static on every picture, so you can't see his face. The bastard knew what he was doing.'

'Figures. Must have used some kind of electronic interference. Are you okay, Sergeant ...?'

'Szabo, sir.'

'You know who I am?'

'Of course. I was General Hunt's drill sergeant long ago. Too old now for anything active, but we chat.'

'Okay,' said Sean, making a mental note to ask the General about this fellow, given he'd never seen Sergeant Szabo before. 'I'll get you to work with a police artist in the morning.'

'Okay, no worries. Whatever we can do.'

Sean trudged slowly back up the stairs. Dan ran ahead, cursing and punching the wall every few steps. By the time Sean reached him, the note was in a plastic sheath and he was pacing the room. He read out the list of demands, growling after each one. They wanted blue-prints for the virus treatment, blue-prints for the long-range communicator, and samples of the metals used on the mountain, Jemma to be released once their demands had been met.

Although they had no proof of the note's validity, Sean wasn't prepared to wait for business hours to act. He expected an icy response from the general at three in the morning, but he braced himself and picked up the phone.

Hunt listened to the story in silence. 'Do you think the note's legitimate?'

'Yeah, I do. Sir, it's more than forty-eight hours now. The

trail's cold. It's a long shot, but we're out of leads, and we're running out of time. The chief said Everson had access to resources we might need. I'm still not comfortable with him, but I've got nothing else. Everson's hiding something. We need to know what it is. Maybe he's got something we can offer in exchange for Jemma.'

'Agreed. We'll head up and tackle him. It's time he told us the truth.'

'Right, I'll have a car waiting when you get here.' Sean slumped into his chair and stared at the ceiling. What if she was already dead? He shook his head; he didn't dare allow himself to think that way. After ordering Dan to organise a couple of cars, he grabbed a notepad and wrote some instructions for his staff, more to distract himself than to organise them. Hunt and Tom could go with him to the SCARF facility. That'd leave Dan to follow through with the airstrips. He left a message on Everson's phone to advise they were coming, then took the lift down to the basement carpark to wait. Someone had to start telling the truth. He didn't care who; Everson, the chief, the guardians.

As soon as Hunt and Tom arrived, he took off, his anger increasing with every kilometre he drove up the mountain. He parked as close as he could to the SCARF site, then ran the two kilometres through the scrub to the clearing. Not waiting for Hunt and Tom to catch up, he strode directly to the boulder. Everson should have his message by now and be waiting, but there was no sign of him which was odd, given the level of surveillance around the entry and the clearing.

He whirled around to Tom. 'How do we get in?'

'Can't on foot. Unless they roll the boulder back, we'll have to wait.'

Sean called again, leaving another message. 'We're not going. Kindly let us in.' He walked around the rock as he waited, but still no response.

Tom called someone on his gadget and was told that no one inside could be interrupted. He shrugged as he relayed the message, adding that things like this occasionally happened. Hunt called the chief, requesting his intervention but got much the same answer.

An hour after they arrived, the boulder moved, and a dishevelled, weary-looking Everson emerged. Another man behind him also looked like he hadn't slept in days.

Sean gasped, 'What the hell?'

Tom stepped next to Hunt. 'Sir, this is Lieutenant-Colonel Williamson.'

Hunt nodded, then turned his attention to Everson. 'We need to meet.'

Everson raised his hand. 'I'm sorry, we've had some technical problems. I can't let you go in. We'll meet out here.' Unshaven, his clothes unkempt, his hair in wild disarray, he stammered as he spoke, very different from the self-possessed, arrogant individual Sean had come to expect.

'I think you'd better fill us in,' said Hunt. 'Jemma's still missing. You failed to acknowledge our presence for an hour. You're clearly in trouble. And you're denying us entry.'

Williamson, still behind Everson, had a smirk on his face

and Tom moved closer, his hand firmly on his newly acquired pistol. Sean looked at Tom and shook his head, then turned back to Everson, 'Well?'

Everson hesitated before answering. 'I offered her sanctuary here, but you insisted you could do better.'

'Cut the crap. By the look of you, she wouldn't have been particularly safe here. What the hell's going on?' Sean, his hand on his weapon, stood centimetres from Everson, past intimidation by this man. He wasn't surprised when Williamson's hand moved to his own weapon. But he hadn't expected Tom, his pistol out of its holster, to close in on Williamson.

'Stop that, all of you,' growled Everson. 'Lambert, you know what's here. Tell them, it'll shock them to the core.'

Hunt moved forward. 'Why don't you let us judge that? You've sworn your people to secrecy, which has put Lambert in an untenable position. We've seen most things. I doubt you can shock us.'

'Not this,' said Everson.

'We can decide that,' growled Sean. It was too late for any more cock and bull stories. Whatever Everson said, they were going in.

Everson's normal façade had slipped, and his voice was strained. 'The last forty-eight hours have been particularly trying, although I believe we are close to a solution. You have no idea what I'm dealing with. It'd be better if you'd leave it that way. What I have in there will make you question every belief you've ever held. You'll lose respect for your system, and your leaders. Lambert can verify that. So, the question is, what do I do?' He slumped back against the boulder; his fatigue undeniable.

Sean took a deep breath. It wouldn't pay to get Everson too far off side, but one way or another they had to get in, unravel his subterfuge, and find out if what he was doing here had anything to do with Jemma's disappearance. 'Why hasn't it shocked and changed you, or Lambert, or Williamson?'

'It has affected all the staff, but my situation is different,' responded Everson. 'If I let you in, I'll end up explaining why.'

'What you're doing here is the reason Dr Anderson is missing,' said Hunt.

'No, it isn't. My only interest is her protection.'

Hunt continued. 'We need information, and I believe the chief has ordered you to co-operate with us.'

'Yes, he has.' Everson sighed. 'Alright, on your own heads. I have warned you. You will have difficulty coping. First, you must agree you will never divulge anything you see here. Not to anyone. That includes your military superiors. And if you need counselling to cope, it will be with my counsellors.'

'Those are ridiculous terms,' said Hunt. 'They're equally your superiors.'

'Not really. You'll understand shortly. But you must agree before I let you in. If, at the end of the day, you still think I'm bullshitting, you can renege. But I assure you, that will not happen.'

Sean went first, down a steep flight of stairs into a large vestibule that had numerous hallways extending from it. Furniture was stacked along the walls. A large screen directly in front of him showed images rather than traditional radar blips. A female army captain stood next to it, recording something.

'Gentlemen, may I introduce Captain Nikola Denis. She's watching for any aircraft in the vicinity,' said Everson. 'She is also waiting for one particular aircraft that will bring the help we need.'

Sean nodded to her as he moved closer. The screen showed the outline of an odd-looking craft that moved towards them at great speed. Flight co-ordinates and ETA appeared on the screen beside the craft.

'Don't worry about the computer, I'll explain later,' snapped Everson. 'First, I will tell you about our activities. We treat viruses that others can't manage. Only the highest military personnel know about us. They send through patients who would otherwise die.'

Sean wanted to shake this fellow. 'Why haven't we heard about it before?'

'I said top levels, way above any of us. Forty-eight hours ago, they sent us twenty-six people, some so low we couldn't do anything. Three have died. The rest are at varying stages of illness and consciousness.'

'How about you just get to the point, and tell us the whole story this time? The one you should have told us months ago,' said Hunt.

'It's on a need-to-know basis. You didn't need to know at that point.' Everson sighed, 'I'm not sure you need to know now.'

'Try us,' Sean snarled.

Everson rubbed his eyes. 'It's best if I show you. You must

be treated for viruses before we go further. Lambert, tell them there's nothing to fear.'

Sean thumped his fist on the table under the screen. 'Let's get on with it.'

Everson paused, but the fight was gone as he began to explain. While his team could cure ninety-nine percent of viruses, a small percentage that he termed anaviruses, were resistant to their treatments. Conventional medicine didn't recognise these viruses, but the patients currently in treatment all had anaviruses. They stimulated the body to produce anti-nuclear antibodies, which attacked the nuclei of otherwise normal cells, particularly within connective tissue. They had to act quickly to prevent permanent damage. The security guards who Sean had seen that first night with the awkward gait had all suffered from anaviruses in the past, which had damaged their motor systems. Everson had requested urgent help from elsewhere for the latest patients, in the hope he could avoid long-term damage.

Sean exploded. 'What does elsewhere mean?'

With a shrug, Everson led them down a long corridor, into an ante-room with a central column and a faint blue light. 'The column emits the treatment. It will take five minutes once I activate it. If you have the good sense to believe me you shouldn't go further, take the door directly ahead, and go back up the stairs through which you entered. Alternatively, we can go through the other door.'

'No more crap,' said Hunt. 'You can take us to whatever it is you're hiding.'

'Fine. Put on these eye protectors.' Once they'd covered their eyes, he rested his hand on a small metal plate on the wall. The light instantly intensified and, even with the eye covers, Sean couldn't look directly at it.

When the light faded, Everson got up, opened the door and led them to a room with a large window, through which they could see ten patients in beds. All looked settled. Three screens on the wall, beside where they stood, showed similar setups in other rooms. The attendants all wore Hazmat suits, as they'd been warned. The scene looked much like any ICU in an infectious diseases outbreak, until one of the staff stood tall, and turned around towards the viewing screen.

Sean jumped. 'Holy shit. The attendants, who are they? What are they? They're enormous. I can't see their faces with those suits on, but they look big.'

'I said we'd had to call in outside help.'

'That's not outside help,' said Sean. 'What the hell are they?'

'Not what. Who?' The arrogance had now melted away from Everson. His statements were matter of fact, and he no longer seemed to care how they reacted.

'Who?' Sean moved closer to the window. 'That one's fifty or sixty centimetres taller than the nurse standing beside him, and she's not short. Is that what you're doing here, hiding mutants?'

'No,' Everson sighed. 'I told you not to come here. They're not human, and they're not from Earth.'

'Perhaps I can help,' said a deep, melodic voice from behind them. 'Mr Everson called us yesterday and asked for assistance. His technology is insufficient to treat these people. He needed our help.'

Sean swung around, hand on his side-arm, ready to react. 'Jesus, who the hell are you?'

Everson's hand slid across Sean's wrist. He tried to shake free, but Everson's grip continued to increase until he had to release his weapon.

'Stand down colonel,' said Everson. His hand remained on Sean's wrist although he reduced his pressure. 'I would like you to meet Supreme Commander Zadrus.'

Sean had to crane his neck to look at this being's face. The head was large, out of proportion to his size, and his hands were easily twice the size of Sean's. Otherwise, he wasn't much different; brown hair, fair skin, two eyes, two ears, mouth, nose. He was dressed in a loose-fitting black uniform, like a pilot's jumpsuit, with a gold crest on the right shoulder. Two palm-like branches bordered the crest, and a bar underneath contained ten stars. The centre of the crest had two swords that were pointed downwards. They were intertwined at the tip of the blades. Two hands clasped in a handshake completed the top of the shield. Zadrus, unarmed, stood quietly, his hands held together in front of his chest.

Tom and Nikola, the captain they'd met on the way in, had quietly moved next to Zadrus, both holding weapons like the one Tom had used at the warehouse.

'You'd fire that thing at me?' Sean snarled at Tom.

'It would not be my preference,' replied Tom. 'But yes, I

most definitely would. I've been working with Zadrus for almost two years and I trust him. Without him, I would still be crippled, so please listen to him, and don't make me use this.'

Hunt stepped forward to stand beside Sean. 'Is this one of your partners, Lambert?'

'Yes, sir. He's their commander, and he's genuinely here to help us.'

'What does that mean? Here to help us?' growled Sean.

'Let me explain,' said Zadrus. 'I am from the planet Sidlow, and a Trustee of the Interplanetary League. We have been in orbit around your planet for two years. When I received Mr Everson's call, my medical people came down to assess the situation, and let me know what was needed. We have just arrived with the necessary equipment.'

'Bullshit, all major governments have constant surveillance of space surrounding Earth. You'd have been seen. And intercepted.'

'We have been sitting just outside your observable zone. We can make ourselves hard to see. Numerous crafts out there are doing the same thing. Your governments know that we are there.'

'That's crap,' said Sean.

'No Sean, it isn't. I've been up there on their spaceship. It's beyond anything we can imagine until you see it. And even then...' Tom shrugged as he looked between Sean and Hunt.

'I've been there too, sir,' said Nikola.

Sean looked at her, then back to Zadrus. 'Where's Sidlow?'

'It is on the other side of the region we call the universe, many millions of light years from here.'

'No. No.' Sean threw his hands in the air, and turned to Hunt, then Everson, then back to Zadrus. 'So, you're telling me you just popped over from the other side of the universe to give us a hand?'

For the first time Zadrus smiled. 'Not quite. Earth is part of our routine patrol.'

'Jesus wept. Now you're on patrol. No one can travel that sort of distance.'

'Our crafts are different from anything you have on Earth. We can cover very large distances, by utilising the folds between galaxies, and galaxy clusters, to reduce those distances. Centuries ago we discovered what we call transport zones that use those folds to connect us from one side of the universe to the other. We also travel at very fast speeds and once we cross the speed of light, everything changes. The space-time continuum becomes distorted, and distances change. If you wish I will organise one of my scientists to explain it in depth later.'

'So, is Earth part of this League?'

'Earth has been invited, but so far has not accepted. The invitation remains open. We exist to support our member planets, but we also help other planets. Our intervention here is not unusual. May I show you the transporter we used to get here today? That might help.'

Hunt turned to Sean, 'You go. Captain Denis, go with him please. Lambert and I will remain here and talk more to Mr Everson.'

Sean hesitated when he saw Williamson scowl because Hunt had overridden him and taken charge, but he figured that wasn't his fight, so he turned and followed Zadrus, barely aware of the captain by his side. They'd gone down another flight of stairs and along at least a kilometre of corridor when he felt a tug on his sleeve.

The captain held out her hand. 'I'm Nik.'

'Sean,' he replied absently, then looked back at her. 'What's going on here?'

She grinned. 'Zadrus is who he says he is. I had a hard time accepting them at first too, but some of the things they can do are amazing.'

'Them? How many are there?'

'They're an entire civilisation, Sean.' She pulled up, her tone serious as she spoke. 'I suppose I've met twenty or thirty, but there's millions out there.'

'I don't buy it. It's got to be a scam.'

'No.' She held onto his arm. 'Listen to me. They're real. Open your mind. Once you understand who they are, and what you can learn from them, your life will never be the same.'

'So why has my military training always been that aliens are a myth?'

'You know why. Mass hysteria. Bureaucrats and politicians who fear losing power. Scientists having to admit that all our beliefs on our origins are baseless crap.'

Shaking his head, he continued behind Zadrus to an enormous open space carved into the mountainside. Several small aircrafts were parked around the edge, but it was the craft in the middle of the central runway that caught his attention. It was round, easily fifty metres in diameter, and fifteen to twenty metres in height. The skin of the thing was dark grey and it had a smooth metal texture. Four fine supports balanced the craft, each surrounded by a bright light.

'They use that to get to their mothership,' said Nik. 'It's called a transporter.'

Sean stared at her. He couldn't find words to respond, but he could see similarities with the metal balls he and Dan had glimpsed, although there were differences too. The top three metres of these crafts shaped up to a dome. A middle section, about ten metres in height, extended horizontally outwards below the dome. Three rims of an opaque material ran right around the craft in that section. Another dome shaped smoothly down a further three metres, mirroring the top, and making the whole thing look like a squashed-in ball. Numerous people worked around the craft, preparing equipment and sorting items, some of them the same size as Zadrus, and others, human. Sean couldn't see how the equipment had been unloaded until someone, who looked like Zadrus, walked to the middle of the base. A bright blue light surrounded him, much like the one that had shot down from Pritchard's sphere. It took him up into the craft, like an elevator, although Sean couldn't see a platform.

'Please come with me,' said Zadrus. 'I will show you inside, that should give you your proof.'

Sean hesitated, not quite ready to trust either Zadrus or the method of entry.

'It's okay,' said Nik. 'I've done it heaps of times.'

He tentatively put his hand into the light, but quickly withdrew it.

Zadrus smiled. 'It is safe. I will go in first, then come back for you.' He was taken up into the craft and came down again, then held out his hand. 'Follow me.'

Sean cautiously accepted the proffered hand and floated with Zadrus and Nik through the blue light and into the interior of the vessel. At one end, a structure rather like a curved island kitchen bench appeared to house the controls for the craft, and three empty chairs were fixed in position behind it, presumably for the crew. Rows of comfortable-looking, lounge-style chairs graced either side of the area through which he'd entered. The three-metre ceiling height suggested there'd be a couple of levels above the one in which he stood. A circle remained on the floor where the elevator light had been. It felt like solid floor when he walked across it, but Nik grabbed his arm, pulling him away when an alarm sounded. The blue light snapped back on and someone came up through it.

'You are fascinated by our entry portal,' said Zadrus, startling Sean. 'All our crafts have this type of entry. It is practical and easily reversible if we land somewhere and do not like what we see. While the light is on, we are fully protected from anything outside.'

'Sure,' replied Sean. He had no idea what to say, so he

walked towards what he thought must have been the controls, although there didn't appear to be any instruments.

Zadrus again explained. 'We advise the co-ordinates we require, and when to take off. The craft does the rest. A manual panel underneath allows for failure of the automated system, but it is rarely required. Your craft will use this sort of driving system soon enough. Technology can only advance so quickly. The people of your planet would not have coped if we had pushed you into it too fast.'

The light dimmed slightly, and the craft shook. Sean still hadn't dismissed the possibility of an elaborate hoax, but he couldn't see what would motivate Everson to do such a thing.

'Good, my second transporter has arrived,' said Zadrus.

'Look out the window,' said Nik. 'You'll see another transporter, a smaller one. Zadrus has started teaching me to fly them. They're keen to teach us everything they can, Sean. We just have to let them. The opportunities are mind-boggling.'

A smaller version of the craft in which Sean stood flew through the opening at the end of the runway, and hovered for a minute, before someone on the ground gave a signal to land.

'Jesus Christ,' he muttered, as he whirled around to face Zadrus and Nik. 'These really are flying crafts. Who the hell are you?'

'I have not lied to you,' said Zadrus. 'If I had time, I would take you to my mothership, but that must wait, we have a more urgent issue.'

When Sean hesitated, Zadrus urged him to ask whatever he wanted to know.

'Several of us have seen a large metal sphere. It seems to be following us, and it's a bit like your smaller craft but it's shaped like a ball. Is it yours?'

'No,' replied Zadrus. 'It is not ours. Some people here have seen them also but unfortunately, I have not. I have a few ideas, but I must see one to be sure.' Crew members bowed their heads towards Zadrus as they passed.

'It appears you're an important person,' said Sean.

'We have rank in our society, although it is not as rigid as your military. My role is probably equivalent to someone above your Mr Everson. Have you seen enough? I must return to direct operations.'

As they left the craft, two aliens carried a stretcher past them. 'Is that one of our people?' said Sean.

'Yes,' replied Nik. 'Some of the patients are too ill to treat here. They have more extensive facilities on their mothership.'

Sean's initial fear had morphed into curiosity, more than a little due to Nik's enthusiasm. He'd steeled himself for the unexpected, but not this. Zadrus, and those with him, were obviously not human. Given all the stars out there, he'd always reasoned there had to be other intelligent life forms in the universe, maybe more intelligent, but he'd doubted any beings could develop the capacity to bridge the distance between their planet and Earth. It appeared Zadrus's people had solved that.

He looked up at Zadrus. 'Sir, for someone who's only been here a couple of years, your English is fluent.'

'I was required to learn your major languages before I came

here. It is a matter of necessity. I speak English, French, German, Spanish, Mandarin and Arabic. I also wear this.' He pointed to a credit card-sized device attached to the left side of his shirt. 'It translates if I have any difficulty with language. And I can use it to magnify my voice in an emergency.'

Advanced enough to travel across space, and to cure diseases that baffled human doctors, it seemed logical that they'd have developed something as straight-forward as a translator, and he'd already seen Everson use a card to amplify his voice. Sean stopped and stared at Zadrus. Jesus, Everson used one of those translators.

He strode into the office and grabbed the front of Everson's shirt pointing to the translator. 'Who the hell are you? Are you one of them?'

Everson steadied himself against the edge of his desk. 'No, I belong in this galaxy, but I am not from Earth. I did tell you this would make you question everything you believe. Before you accuse me of anything, I am here at your government's request. We have not invaded.'

'Can you prove that?'

Everson took a few seconds to compose himself and when he spoke again, some of his arrogance had returned. 'Of course, I can, but enough of that for the moment. Now we all know who we are, we need to get on the same page.'

'All we needed was the truth out of you in the first place,' growled Hunt, who'd been in the room talking to Everson when Sean interrupted.

'You've got it now.'

'Getting back to the point,' said Sean, 'Commander Zadrus seems to have the treatment of the virus under control. We need help to find Jemma.'

'I'll work with you once this crisis is over,' said Everson. 'Zadrus may be able to get better information than your CCTV cameras. Get any information you can, and then we'll meet again.'

Nik had walked in behind Sean. 'I can get started on it straightaway. How do I contact you?'

Sean gave her his phone number, then turned towards the doorway, but three armed guards blocked his way. 'What the hell?'

'I can't let you leave until I have your agreement you will not discuss anything you've seen here with anyone else. I did warn you of that,' said Everson.

'And we agreed,' snapped Sean.

Everson looked to Hunt who nodded, and then Tom who smiled and looked towards the guards. 'Stand down,' said Tom. 'They're safe.'

The guards responded immediately, and Sean heard the boulder rumble back. It hadn't occurred to him before, these guards had to be Tom's staff. But walking back to the carpark gave him time to think, and he snapped at Tom before he got in the car. 'You could have warned us. We'd have sought their help a lot sooner, and we probably wouldn't have lost Jemma.'

'You can't kick me any harder than I've been kicking myself, but Sean I was sworn to secrecy. Would you trust me now if I'd broken that oath?'

Sean grunted a response, but couldn't argue and, as he drove down the mountain, he realised that somehow everything had changed, although it was nothing he could quantify. So many questions. If Everson came from another planet, did Earth's humans come from the same place? Could evolution be just another flat Earth theory? He shook his head. A spaceship and a major alien facility right under their noses, and no one knew.

'Bellamy, slow down,' roared Hunt.

Sean's foot had leaned heavily on the accelerator. 'Sorry. Bloody Everson's been hiding this from us. If we'd known, we'd have handled everything differently. And, while we're all wondering if there's something out there, and whether they'll ever make contact, he's got them fully integrated, working with our government. And apparently other governments.'

'Whoa, settle,' said Hunt. 'Yes, we'd have acted differently. It may, or may not, have stopped the abduction. Everson coming from another planet does explain a lot though. I've met most Brigadiers in the Australian Army, somewhere along the line. Some, I know well, others I've just met in passing. But I have met them. The first time I met Everson was when he approached us to identify his intruders. It'd take someone at very high levels to assimilate him into that position.'

'Yeah, but who?'

'The chief obviously knows, but beyond that, no idea,' replied Hunt.

'Something else worries me,' said Sean. 'When we agreed to help him, I did my own research. I wasn't conning Jemma when I told her people had disappeared around these blue lights. There were multiple reports. That's why I suspected Everson had something to do with Jemma's disappearance.'

Tom leant forward from the back seat. 'Sir, it's not us. We've heard the same reports. That's why we needed your help.'

'Understood,' said Sean. 'And I guess that explains some of his attitude. He's been protecting Zadrus and his people.'

'I'd say so,' replied Hunt. 'Your intruders, Tom, the metal balls, Jemma's abductors are probably all one and the same.'

'Agreed,' replied Sean.

'Good, drop us off at front entrance, then head straight up as soon as you've parked.'

Still fuming as he parked the car, Sean swore when his phone rang.

'Time to get your head out of the clouds,' said Hunt. 'Everson just called. Captain Denis checked back over their surveillance and believes she's seen something.' Zadrus is heading up to his spaceship to verify. You need to be here when he calls back.'

CHAPTER 12

Desperate for a decent lead, a sighting, a person of interest, anything he could follow through, Sean made his way to Hunt's office.

'We're ready,' said Hunt, as he swivelled his chair towards the wall behind his desk.

The gadget on Tom's belt lit up and images appeared on the wall. Nik and Zadrus had searched through their surveillance records from the time of the abduction. They'd followed the car that had taken Jemma but, less than a block from the safe house, static obliterated the image.

'It's like the security tapes when we chased that intruder from our building,' said Sean. 'Some kind of electrical interference.'

'Probably used the same tool,' replied Zadrus.

'So, another dead end?' Sean walked to the wall, hoping he'd see something behind the static.

'Yes, and no,' said Zadrus. 'Nikola suggested they would have wanted to get Jemma a good distance away from the safe house, and that would probably require an aircraft, so we shifted our attention to small airfields. There are two in the region, from which aircraft left at the time in question, one military, one civilian. Two training flights left the local Air Force base. Both returned without incident. Four aircraft left from Archerfield, the private airport. Three followed their flight plan, but the fourth disappeared from radar five minutes after it lifted off.'

'Took off,' said Sean, absently. 'I'll check with air traffic control.' He picked up the phone on Hunt's desk. Reports of the missing plane had been logged, but so far nothing found. He questioned how a plane could vanish from radar without triggering a major disaster recovery operation. The operator assured him it wasn't uncommon with small aircrafts, and given they had no reason to suspect a crash, the search would be low priority.

'It's a lead, and it makes sense,' said Hunt. 'Given where they dropped Jemma's tracking bracelet, they drove north from the safe house, so Archerfield is a strong possibility. But, if the authorities don't know where the damn plane landed, I'm not sure how much that helps us. We don't even know if she was on it.'

Zadrus interrupted. 'The interference with our surveillance convinces me they have access to advanced technology. If so, they could easily mask their aircraft against radar.'

'Oh, come on,' said Sean, walking closer to Zadrus's image. 'Are you telling me they're aliens too?'

'I do not know,' replied Zadrus. 'But you must be careful. I will watch you from here, but they may shut me out. Keep in mind they may also be tracking you.'

Tom stepped between Sean and Zadrus's image. 'Take the warning seriously, Sean. Zadrus knows how these things work.'

Sean nodded. 'Fine. I'll be careful. Come on, Dan, let's go.'

Dan had edged in close to Sean and now stared at the wall.

'Oh hell, I'd forgotten you hadn't seen this.' Sean dragged Dan from the room, hoping Hunt wouldn't call them back. He didn't let go until the lift door had shut.

'The boss told me about the little green men and the spaceships,' said Dan, in a voice that was more curious than frightened. 'I checked. It isn't April Fools' day. So, what's going on? And who was that dude on the screen? He wasn't little, or green. Is he one of them?'

'Sorry, mate. I clean forgot you weren't with us on the mountain,' said Sean when the lift opened to the carpark. 'Come on, get in the car. We can stop at a pub, have some lunch, and I'll fill you in as much as I can. It's pretty weird.'

Tucked away in a booth with their meals, Sean recounted his experience on the mountain, and his tour of the spaceship. 'I think Zadrus is for real. Tom's convinced he is, and Tom's no fool.'

'Zadrus,' said Dan, shaking his head. 'That's the one on the screen?'

'Yep.'

'I'm kind of glad I wasn't there. Don't think I could have taken it as calmly as you lot have.'

'No,' Sean chuckled. 'I definitely wasn't calm, but Tom and a captain up there, Nikola, were so relaxed with him that I started to accept him too. And if they can help us find Jemma, I don't care who they are.'

'Yeah, I guess. But they're aliens, and they claim to have been here for centuries. You really believe they're for real.'

'Can't see any other explanation,' replied Sean. 'Have you finished your lunch?'

'Yeah, I have.'

'Okay, let's go.' On the way out, Sean had the same sensation he'd had on the mountain. Everything looked normal, the people, the place, even the weather, yet somehow everything had changed. He wondered if Dan felt the same. 'Right, time to get our act into gear. I'll drive. You look for anything out of place.' He parked the car at the airport and strode inside, Dan close behind, and asked for the manager introducing himself as military security. Not quite accurate but it usually worked. He wasn't impersonating military police, security could come from anywhere.

The manager, a small man, rushed out, his hands shaking as he greeted them. He answered all their questions, spreading papers on the relevant flights over the counter. But when Sean asked to look at the plane, he declined, explaining that it was a private hangar.

'Understood,' said Sean. 'Please ring the plane's owner. We'll look outside the plane while we wait.'

'I'd prefer you stayed here,' replied the manager.

'Let me explain again.' Sean kept his voice low and measured. 'Our victim was abducted. She is an important person, which is why it hasn't hit the press. She's been gone forty-eight hours. We don't have time for unnecessary delays. Do you understand the urgency?'

'I do understand, I do. But even so, you can't wander around the airport.'

Sean lowered his voice and spoke slowly. 'The owner of this aircraft may, or may not, be a party to the kidnapping; may, or may not, be associated with terrorism. Here is what you will do. Call him. Tell him to come here. Do not explain why. Tell him Defence Force Personnel are waiting at his aircraft.' He paused to assess the impact of his statement, then raised his voice. 'Now, go.'

The manager scuttled away.

'Okay, mate, we've got a plane to look at,' said Sean.

Mindful not to disrupt traffic Sean stuck to the edge of the tarmac but when he found the door of the hangar locked, he thumped the wall beside it.

Dan took a small tool from his pocket. Within seconds they were inside. 'You didn't see that. A little token of my misspent youth.'

'Didn't see what?'

'Precisely,' replied Dan, with a broad grin.

Inside was a near new, well-maintained Lear jet 75 which didn't look like it'd been off the ground. Dan whistled, 'Jesus, these guys've got money.'

'Can we get inside?'

The plane door was locked. Dan reached for his tool, but a loud voice from the hangar door stopped him.

'I'd rather you didn't do that.' A man in overalls walked in. 'I've worked hard to get this jet in the condition you see it.'

Sean introduced himself and Dan. 'And you are?'

'I'm Mr Crockett's mechanic. Ted's the name.'

'Sir, we believe this plane may have been used by terrorists.'

'Not this aircraft, son. We've been waiting on a part to come from Europe. The plane was flown here, but we couldn't start it again. Bloody shame. They paid a fortune and can't use the damn thing.'

Sean walked around it, ducking under the wings. 'Could someone have fixed it, even in a temporary way?'

'No, mate. This thing hasn't moved. Won't move, without the right part.'

Dan had double checked the call sign for the submitted flight plans before they arrived. This was the plane. 'Would you check the motor, make sure no one's fiddled with it? We need to exclude it from the investigation.'

'What investigation would that be?' The voice belonged to William Crockett, a well-known Queensland television journalist and producer. 'This is my hangar. I don't believe you have any right to be here. I'd like to know how you got in. I left all doors locked.'

'It wasn't locked as I came in, sir,' Sean responded, truthfully. 'We're investigating a terrorist abduction. Your plane was registered for a flight two days ago. We believe our people were forced onto that flight.'

'Wasn't this plane. It's a white elephant. Show him the motor, Ted. Then they can leave us alone.'

The mechanic exposed the motor bay. Carefully placed loose connections waited ready to attach once the part arrived for the repair.

'There you are,' Crockett continued. 'You can't fly with wires all over the place. I'm sorry to hear about your person, but it's nothing to do with us.'

Sean had to agree, this plane wouldn't fly, but it wouldn't be hard to lodge a flight plan with erroneous information. Crockett's attitude was too indignant. Hunt had impressed on him from the time he started this work, to listen to his instincts. 'Do you own any other aircraft, Mr Crockett?'

'Are you serious? I'm not your man.' He sighed. 'All right, if it'll get you off my back, I have two others, both in the hangar next door. One stays, the other's waiting for its new owner to come and get it. Satisfied.'

'I'm sure I will be, sir. Can we have a look at those planes?'

'Where's your search warrant?'

'I don't require one. A plane using your call sign has been involved in terrorist activity. I can look at your equipment. I can also arrest you and hold you without charge for seven days.'

'Not once I get my phone call.'

'No, sir. No phone calls. You've been watching too many movies. But a little co-operation can prevent any further distress to you.' A staring war played out between the men, Sean determined to maintain his ground.

Crockett looked away. 'Fine, so long as you then leave us alone. We've got nothing to do with your terrorist activity.'

'I'll need you to join us, sir.'

Crockett marched to the next hangar, unlocked and opened the door, and with his back to the interior of the hangar, and an over-extravagant wave of the arm, ushered Sean and Dan inside. 'You will see two small jets side by side, which clearly haven't been moved.'

'No sir, there's only one,' said Sean.

'What?' Crockett pushed Sean out of his way and stood where the second plane should have been, as though his presence would make it re-appear. He tore outside and ran towards planes parked on the edge of the runway, ducking under wings and checking call-signs.

Sean waited for him to calm down. 'Sir, we need to go back inside, and discuss this.'

Crockett gave him a blank look, and for the first time since he'd arrived, meekly complied.

Sean breathed a sigh of relief; he didn't want to tackle this man. Physically it would be an easy task, but Crockett's television network would have a field day.

Inside, Dan had the mechanic comparing logbooks with the mileage registered on the instruments. Both the new Learjet and the old ones showed consistent figures. Aside from the manufacturer's delivery notes, the same hand had written in all three logbooks, William Crockett.

Crockett's shock seemed genuine as he grabbed the flight documents. Sean looked over his shoulder at the signature.

'I've never seen this before,' said Crockett. 'It's not a bad forgery, but it's definitely not my signature.' His aggression vanished as reality began to dawn on him.

'We'll have a handwriting expert look at it, but I agree it's different from your other signatures,' said Sean. 'You must now realise you are involved, no matter how inadvertently. We need your co-operation.'

Crockett looked towards his mechanic, shaking his head. The mechanic smiled and shrugged his shoulders and Sean didn't miss the frown that crossed Crockett's face. He noted the mechanic for further investigation.

'Dan, call in a forensic team. I want every inch of this place searched.'

'You can't do that,' snapped the airport manager, who'd walked in behind them. 'We can't have police crawling all over the airport. There's training crews and commercial operations here.'

'That's easy,' responded Sean, shrugging. 'Dan, close the airport.'

Crockett gave a deep sigh. 'That'll do. Your team has full access to my hangars. If anyone complains, send them to me. I'll deal with them.'

'I need everything you have on the missing aircraft. We might find something to help us track it,' said Sean, relieved by Crockett's change of heart.

'Can you track an iPad?'

'If it has a GPS chip, we can.'

'I believe I had an iPad on board last time I used the plane,' said Crockett. 'I've been meaning to come back and get it for a couple of weeks. I'll find the number for you.'

Sean waited for the forensic team to arrive, then called the techs to get them working on the iPad, after which he left to return to his office.

'Could we really hold him without charges for seven days?' Dan ducked into the car and stared across at Sean.

'Doubt it. But it sounded good.'

'And what about closing the airport. We couldn't do that,' said Dan. 'Could we?'

'Suspect I'd have to bury you in paperwork for a month to get away with that. But the fact that you're asking tells me it sounded credible.'

Hunt greeted them as they walked into the office with the news that the tablet had been located. He stressed it may no longer be with the aircraft.

'I've asked Everson if his spaceship mates can use the co-ordinates of the iPad, and get a good look at the area,' said Hunt. 'We need to know if a helicopter can land there.'

'And of course, she might not be anywhere near the iPad now,' said Sean. 'But I don't have any better ideas at this stage, so I think it's worth pursuing. Might at least lead us to whoever stole the plane.'

*   *   *

When Jemma woke, the farmhouse was quiet, and the rich aroma of coffee to which she'd become accustomed over the last couple of days, was missing. She jumped out of bed, pulled on jeans and a t-shirt and stood in the doorway, peering up and down the hall, and listening. Thinking that she heard a faint groan from the kitchen, she ran towards it, crying out when she saw the housekeeper on the floor, next to the table, and unable to move.

'Oh, my God, what happened?' cried Jemma.

'Fell,' she moaned. 'Can't get up.' The woman's left leg was twisted at a peculiar angle. It seemed shorter than the other leg, and the woman whimpered each time she tried to move.

'I'll get help,' said Jemma.

'There's no one close enough to help. I need some painkillers.'

'I'll get you those, but I'm also going to try to find help.' Pritchard had promised to be back in a couple of days, but there'd been no sign of him, and she couldn't wait on the off chance he might reappear. The housekeeper needed medical attention straight away. She arranged pillows and blankets around the woman and placed food, water and painkillers within reach then pulled on her boots, found a small back-pack, and packed enough water bottles and food to tackle the mountain range that formed the northern boundary of the property. On her first day in the farmhouse she'd tried climb-ing down into a wide and deep ravine that circled the rest of the property, and only just avoided falling into an abyss. Getting to the top of the mountain though, would be more than a Sunday hike, but she had to try. With a deep breath, she started out, aiming for the highest peak. If she could find another house, or a road to flag down a passing motorist, the woman lying injured inside the farmhouse might have a chance.

Sweating under the intense tropical sun, the hill grew taller with every step. It took all day to reach the top, and the sun had dropped down to the western horizon by the time she got there, but it was still blisteringly hot. All her previous experience had been in the lush green rainforests of the Gold Coast hinterland and that didn't help her get through this harsh, dry scrub with its thick stands of huge, ancient iron-barks, black wattles and bloodwoods wrapped around macrozamias, occasional patches of spinifex, and a smattering of solitary grasstrees, with their peculiar spear-like spikes. Slippery, rotting leaves and dead branches from the long drought covered the forest floor offering ample cover for taipans and the other deadly snakes of Central Queensland.

She suspected that a cluster of twinkling lights, around twenty kilometres away, had to be a town, but there was a farmhouse with a thin line of smoke rising from its chimney nestled in the foothills, and it was closer. Hugging the tree line, she made her way along a track that wound down towards the house. Given the shabby state of the place, and the neglected bush around it, she'd have judged the place deserted if it hadn't been for the smoke. Squatters were a possibility, but she couldn't rule out Pritchard.

A full moon helped her dash from tree to tree, but the gaps between them left her exposed and vulnerable. When she got closer, she dropped down behind the scrub and crawled to the edge of a twenty-metre stretch of lawn that surrounded the house. Suddenly, light flooded the yard. Two men walked out onto the porch flashing portable spotlights in her direction. She pulled back into thicker scrub.

The larger of the two dropped his flashlight. 'Forget it.

Probably a roo, same as last night. Boss's almost here. Take the truck to the other house, over the hill.'

The smaller man nodded. 'Do you want me to bring the women here?'

'Nah. Get rid of them. We'll tell him she ran away. Fell down the ravine. He won't care about the housekeeper. Torch the house. We'll do this one too before we take off.'

'What if I can't find the girl?'

'Head back. The boss can track 'er from that airship of his.'

Jemma crawled deeper into the bush and curled herself into a tight ball. She'd never felt so alone. Had she really just heard an order to kill her? Last time she'd been trapped like this, Sean had come from behind and rescued her. This time she'd have to find her own solution. When the lights went out, she raised her head to look for the best escape route, but the whirring sound of a sphere made her drop back down. She pulled the top of her shirt over her head, and lay face down. It zigzagged down the hillside and the beam of light it had used on Dan and the helicopter pilot came within centimetres of where she lay. The light flicked off as the sphere flew forward to land beside the house. She clasped her hand across her mouth to avoid making any sound when Pritchard jumped out.

Ignoring her aching muscles, she waited for him to go inside, then crawled back into the thicker bush and retraced her path. At the top of her hill, she stopped to look around. A firebreak, that looked like it had been maintained by a grader, curled through the bush, behind the house. She scooted down to it and along the track, using the cover of a thick patch of saplings until she was level with the back porch. Peering through the trees, she saw someone move inside a rear window.

Someone yelled her name. Pritchard. But there was another voice and it was also familiar. A tall man with long, straight, black hair looked out the window. 'Anthony,' she whispered.

He turned and stood with his back to the window blocking Pritchard's view. Had he seen her? She sprinted to the window, praying there were no motion sensors, and dropped down below the sill.

'Leave Jemma out of the research,' yelled Anthony. 'We've almost got a vaccine ourselves. We don't need her.'

'It's not just about the vaccine,' roared Pritchard. 'You can protect your little princess when I get hold of her.'

After Pritchard marched out, Anthony looked anxiously around. He called to someone inside the house, 'Bloody hot. I'm going to open a window.' Two other people closed in behind him, blocking the view from other rooms. He turned to her and whispered, 'What the hell are you doing here? I thought you got away.'

'I did.'

'Okay. Now you need to keep running. For God's sake, don't let him catch you.'

'I can't run and leave you here.'

'We're prisoners, sweetheart. You can't get us out. I want you to get as far from here as your legs will take you.'

'I'll go for help.'

'It'll be too late. They plan to head us out tonight. Go to the police. Tell them he's taking us to an abandoned military base in Costa Rica. They've set up a lab there.'

'I'll tell them. Oh God, Anthony. I don't want to leave you.'

'You have to, honey. Now go. And tell my parents I'm alive.'

'They already know. Our pilot took your photo inside that metal sphere over Nerang.'

'Right. I didn't know he did that.'

A woman's voice called, 'Someone coming.'

'Go, Jemma,' urged Anthony. 'Get the hell out of here. The future of our community depends on you.'

'What?'

'Go. Go now.'

She flew back into the scrub when someone appeared in the doorway and, even after she saw Anthony leave the room and the lights go out, she remained still. *The future of their community? What community?* Voices at the side of the house jerked her back. She picked herself up and bolted. Half an hour later, she had to stop. Gym fit, but not used to running through thick scrub, she perched against a gum tree heaving for breath, then grabbed her water bottle and took several large gulps. Dropping her backpack, she sat and pulled out some of the food she'd packed before leaving the first house and contemplated her situation. She had to find that road and get help, not just for the housekeeper now, but to get Anthony away from Pritchard. Too exhausted to keep running, she paced herself into a brusque walking rhythm.

She'd gone another kilometre when smoke began to invade her lungs. Within minutes, the acrid smell had her gasping for breath, and the crackle of burning leaves raced towards her at fearsome speed. She tore off her shirt, doused it with water from one of the drink bottles and held it across her nose and mouth, then took off again, sticking as much as she could to the track, but she couldn't see beyond the tall trees. She hoped the track would lead to a road.

Sharp twigs cut into her arms and, in the limited visibility she failed to see many of the trees until she slammed into them. Her lungs burned, her legs were ready to collapse, but she couldn't die here where she wouldn't be found. She planted an image in her mind of Sean plucking her from the fire, and prayed it'd get her through. Someone had to be told what had happened to Anthony, and no one else knew.

A couple of hundred metres ahead, a greyish cloud rose from the path. Surely, they hadn't lit a second fire. But it was dust, not smoke. A police car was almost on top of her when it skidded to a stop.

The driver jumped out. 'Are you okay, ma'am? We heard about a lady lost out here somewhere. So, we came looking.' Another man got out of the car and stared at her.

'Who told you that?' Nobody knew she was here. Her captors wouldn't have contacted police. Neither of these men wore a uniform, and both had guns tucked into the back of their belts. One of them extended his hand and invited her to get into the car. Somewhere, she found the energy to pick up her backpack and, holding onto the straps, flung it with all her might at the head of the nearer man. She whirled around and ran through a small gap in the trees. Bullets flew past her head, but the man she'd hit with her bag yelled at the other to cease fire. Apparently, they wanted her alive. She put aside any thought of pain or fear and ran.

CHAPTER 13

In the middle of his search for Jemma, the order came through for Sean to commence moving his unit to SCARF. He stormed out of Hunt's office, threw a few personal items, including the only photo he had of her, into a backpack, then slammed the rest of his belongings into boxes to be sent up separately.

'Feel better?' Hunt leaned against Sean's office door, a broad smile on his face.

'Why the hell are we doing this when we should be searching for Jemma?'

'Because Everson has technology that will improve your capacity to search for her, and he's keen to help.'

'Yeah, right. He's been real helpful.' He pushed past Hunt and looked around for Dan and Tom.

'What's that? Did I hear yes, sir? Thank you, sir?'

Sean whipped around to retort, but Dan had positioned himself between the two men, preventing further interaction.

'All's good, sir,' said Dan. 'We'll go to the helipad and wait for Mr Everson's chopper.'

Sean felt Tom on his other side. He shook them both off and marched to the lift, then stood with his back to Hunt.

'Drop it,' said Dan, walking up beside him. 'You're about to get yourself into hot water and that won't help at all.'

'I know.' He sighed. 'But for God's sake, we need to concentrate on the search.'

'Agreed. Like you always tell me, roll with the punches. This is a detour. We'll throw our bags down and get back to it.'

'Yeah, fine. See if Everson really can do anything useful.'

'I've spoken to Nik,' said Dan. 'She's already working on it, and she says she's got stuff for us when we get there.'

'Nik?'

'You know, the captain you met up there.'

'The captain? But you haven't met her.'

'Yeah, I have. She dropped some stuff down for the boss. We had a good chat. She told me a bit about the aliens.'

'The aliens. How many times have you spoken to her?'

'A few. She's a whiz with the alien technology.'

'Technology?'

'Are you going to repeat everything I say?'

'Hell no. So, you only talk technology?'

'Spent a bit of time talking about the aliens and how they can help us. She's excited about what they can offer.'

'Sure. Good looking too, as I recall.'

Dan glared back at him. 'Helicopter's here. C'mon.'

'Yep, let's go meet the aliens… and Nik.' He ran behind Dan to the helicopter. As they approached the SCARF clearing, Tom spoke to the pilot. The chopper suddenly veered away and dropped down into the surrounding valley, before it turned and flew directly towards the cliff face. Sean gripped his seat to stop himself sliding on top of Dan and, when the exposed rock slid back to reveal the runway on which he'd previously seen the transporter, both men gasped.

'Bloody hell,' exclaimed Dan. 'It's another façade.'

Sean leaned forward to stare at the runway. 'Holy shit.'

Tom laughed. 'Thought you'd enjoy it. You've got a lot to get used to.'

'Not sure I'm ready,' muttered Sean.

'Jeez, I am,' said Dan. 'This is fantastic.'

Sean greeted Nik, amused by the slight frown on her face as Dan, with his back to her, pretended to be deep in conversation with Tom. But he forgot all about Dan when Nik said she'd located the iPad. He followed her to the aliens' control room. She walked to the back wall and murmured a few words. The wall seemed to morph into a bush scene.

'What's this?' Sean took a few steps towards her. The scene was so life-like that he expected to find himself moving between the trees. It had substance. It wasn't semi-transparent like a hologram. Just like the images Zadrus had projected into Hunt's room.

'Alien technology,' she said, smiling. 'You'll get used to it. It's kind of a computer… but kind of not.'

'That clears up everything … but kind of not,' he retorted. 'There has to be some kind of control box.'

'No, it's all around us,' she replied. 'I call it Artie. You know, for artificial intelligence. I don't think Zadrus approves.'

'No, and neither do I, Humie. You know, that's short for human.'

Sean stared around the room. 'Who, or what, said that?'

'Artie. He's quite cheeky,' replied Nik, with a grin.

'Bloody hell.' He shook his head. 'Alright, I'll have to accept I don't understand any of this yet, particularly a moody computer, or whatever it is. But forget about that, what have you found on Jemma?'

'Zone back,' she said, facing the wall. The image changed to two houses, one on either side of a steep hill, each with an airstrip alongside. She told it to return to the first house and go inside. 'We found a body.' Her eyes flicked up to Sean's face and she quickly added, 'No, not Jemma. A woman, late fifties, grey hair, Asian features. The angle of her leg suggested a fractured hip.'

'You can see in that much detail?'

'Yes, we can.'

'Was it the hip that killed her?'

'Sadly, no,' replied Nik. 'She had a bullet wound to her head.'

'Jesus,' said Sean. 'What kind of arseholes are we dealing with?'

'The worst kind,' Zadrus replied, as he walked in.

Sean took a couple of steps back.

Tom stepped beside him, 'He's okay Sean, and he's our best hope for finding Jemma.'

Zadrus paused a moment, waited for Sean to steady himself, then continued without commenting. 'We found no sign of anyone else there, living or dead. Colonel Williamson has requested local police attend the scene.'

'Oh, my God,' Nik yelled. 'Look at this.' Fire erupted

from the second house and spread at an alarming speed along nearby treetops.

Sean made a noise, somewhere between a howl and a scream. 'If by some miracle Jemma escaped, she could be in that fire. Can the computer look for her?'

'Primitive. I'm not a computer.'

'Be quiet, control,' said Zadrus. 'Look for a lone woman, anywhere in the fire zone.'

As Artie muttered and mumbled, Sean looked between Nik and Zadrus, his eyebrows raised.

'Ignore it,' said Zadrus. 'It's doing the job, just likes to grumble.'

Sean shook his head.

'I have just spoken to Mr Everson,' said Zadrus. 'The helicopter that brought you here will be refuelled in ten minutes. Colonel Williamson will show you to temporary offices. Put your goods down, then return to the landing bay. I will meet you there to update you if we find anything.'

Williamson looked irritated when he arrived, snapping at both Dan and Tom but polite to Sean, which irritated Sean more than anything that was said. He dropped his bags in the allocated office and waited while Dan dropped his in a smaller office next door, then went looking for Tom who'd retreated when Williamson arrived. 'What's the story with your boss?'

'Nothing,' Tom sighed. 'I just don't like him.'

'Nobody does,' said Nik, joining them. 'The helicopter's ready. We haven't found anything yet, but Zadrus is still looking.'

'Thanks.' It concerned Sean that Williamson's two most senior officers detested him. But he didn't have time for that now. With Dan, he followed Tom back to the helicopter and had one foot on the boarding step when he heard Everson yell. Sean dropped back onto the tarmac.

'I'm coming with you,' said Everson.

'Weren't you liaising with Zadrus?'

'I am, and Nikola will assist him here.' Everson produced a device which fitted into the palm of his hand and unfurled as he stretched out his fingers. When he closed his hand, it rolled back into a small cylinder, slightly larger than the one Tom wore on his belt. 'Zadrus will send us co-ordinates when he locates Jemma.'

The helicopter rotors quickened as they took their seats, then abruptly slowed. 'Sorry folks,' said the pilot. 'We've been denied a flight path. Massive bushfire at the requested co-ordinates.'

'I know there's a bushfire there. That's why we're going,' Sean growled.

'Sorry, sir. I've been denied permission to take off.'

Before Sean could ask, Everson had called Zadrus. The fire had spread quickly, and the house at the heart of it was well alight. Zadrus couldn't see any aircraft but could see a vehicle heading in the direction of the fire along an internal bush track. The amount of smoke obscured his vision and he had Nik working to clear it.

'Shit. We've got to get there. That country's tinder-box dry.' Sean called to the pilot, 'What's the nearest town? See if we can get permission to land there.'

'Springsure, by the look of it. I'll get onto it.'

Sean searched for Springsure on his phone. It was north-east of the fire ravaged area, and fifteen minutes away by road. The nearest large town was Emerald, over an hour by road. The pilot yelled to buckle up and Sean felt the chopper move before he'd managed to fasten his seatbelt. Half an hour into their flight, he saw smoke billowing above the horizon. Another half hour and the extent of the fire as they flew directly over the top, left Sean gasping for breath.

'About to land, sir,' said the pilot, a few minutes later. 'Police car near the runway. Your lift, I imagine.'

Sean nodded. 'Thanks, mate.' The dust and dirt stirred up by the rotors, stuck to his clothes and skin in the intense Central Queensland heat as they ran to the car, but he ignored it, focussed only on his need to find Jemma. The driver, a police sergeant, took off as soon as their doors were shut. Sean already knew that fire units were on their way from every nearby town but, in the outback, *nearby* could mean hundreds of kilometres away and the sergeant didn't hold much hope for anybody caught up in the fire.

Sean closed his eyes and took in a deep breath. *This couldn't be happening.* Sirens on and lights flashing, the driver ignored speed limits, although he did slow for crossroads and took a careful look. Limited traffic on isolated rural roads made it easy to forget about other vehicles. Even so, they reached the highway within minutes. The sergeant informed them a police car had been stolen from the Springsure station earlier that morning by two armed men, and to be wary if stopped by a police car.

While Everson asked Zadrus to focus on the vehicle he'd seen earlier, Sean spoke to the police officer. 'We'll head south, refine our direction when we get better co-ordinates.'

The car slowed to a crawl in the thick smoke haze. At one point, the driver had to slam on the brakes to avoid a slow-moving tractor. 'Give me five minutes with the arsehole who lit this,' he growled.

'Me first,' said Sean. 'Do you know if Firies, or Forest Rangers, have any tracks through the bush?'

'Yeah, there's at least one. I came here with rangers on an animal cruelty case two years ago. Christ, it's going to be hard to find. I've got less than twenty metres visibility.'

'Understood. Did anything mark the entrance?'

'No, just a track through the trees. There was one of those *authorised vehicles only* type signs. I can't remember how close it was to the road, though.'

'Right, gives us something to look for.'

Everson sat forward and stared out. 'Satellite says we're ten kilometres from the stolen car. Entry to the road is one and a half kilometres from here, on the right. A house just before it, almost on the edge of the road.'

'There's the house,' yelled Sean, a few minutes later. 'And a break in the trees. Might be the track. I can see a sign. Pull in there.' Although Sean understood the driver's lack of visibility forced him to slow on the rough track, he was on the edge of his seat waiting to get close enough to start the search for Jemma.

'Actual fire's still a distance away. This is all smoke.'

Everson remained focused on his communicator. 'A car about a kilometre ahead. Might be the stolen police car.'

The driver swore at a large tree as he swerved to miss it. He had to back up to see where the road went without hitting any other trees.

'To your right,' called Sean.

'Stop,' Tom yelled. 'Any further back you'll hit that rock.'

The driver pulled the car back onto the track but could now only inch forward and, despite the air-conditioning, fumes filtered inside.

'I see something,' called Tom. 'Looks like a car.'

Sean and Dan jumped out and edged towards it. Close up he could see it was the police vehicle. No one in it or anywhere nearby, although with the worsening visibility, someone could have been two or three metres away and not be seen. Sean called the others to join them, then spread out to search.

'No more talking unless you find something,' said Sean. 'I don't want voices being used as targets.' He motioned to fan out, but it was just minutes before Dan yelled for help.

'Keep calling, mate. We're heading towards you.' Dan held someone whose arms and legs hung down, limp and not moving.

'Jemma.' Sean was afraid to breathe. 'Is she alive?'

'Yeah, just,' replied Dan.

'Get her back to the car,' said Sean. 'Everyone else cover us. Don't let down your guard. The bastards could still be here.'

Dan gently placed her on the back seat. He turned the air conditioning up while Sean sponged her face, dribbling water into the side of her mouth. She groaned, and tears rolled down her cheeks as she stared at Sean.

'Anthony was there,' she whispered. 'He's gone.'

Sean felt himself go cold. 'What do you mean, gone?'

'They took him with them.' Closing her eyes again, she continued sobbing, her face slightly swollen, her breathing harsh.

Everson put his hand on Sean's shoulder. 'She needs a hospital.'

'Yeah, I'll take her back,' Sean replied.

'He told me …' She stopped, working hard to get a breath.

'Don't talk, Jemma,' said Sean. 'We're taking you to hospital.'

'Have to … Anthony said … told me to get away … said for the future of our community.' She closed her eyes, her breathing now shallow and rasping.

'We'll all go back,' said Everson. 'Let me just check if the other police car's driveable. You stay with Jemma. I'll organise the rest.' The engine turned over easily and Everson waved back to the driver of Sean's car. It turned around, lights and sirens activated.

The sergeant picked up his radio handpiece. 'Springsure car to base. I have an emergency. I'm coming in code one.'

A voice came back on the receiver, but it was patchy. Sean could make out the words, 'What is your emergency?' The rest broke up.

'I need a helicopter on the road. Patient is ambulance category one. Severe smoke inhalation. Will need ventilation.'

The crackly voice returned. 'Royal Flying Doctor Service has a chopper and Intensivist standing by in Emerald. What is your location?'

The sergeant provided directions, and landmarks. 'We're surrounded by smoke. You'll have to land north of us.'

'On the way. Keep driving north. I will advise when chopper close.'

Although they were going as fast as the driver dared, Sean noticed the sergeant steal a few looks back at Jemma's swollen face.

'Get back on the radio. Tell them she's deteriorating.'

'That's what category one means. I have no doubt they're in the air now, but I'll tell them.'

The operator assured him the chopper was close and roadblocks were in place from both directions. Finally, the smoke cleared, and Sean saw the helicopter flanked by two ambulance vehicles, both with lights flashing.

The sergeant pulled in as close as he dared, then orders were yelled, and Sean was pulled out of the car to let the emergency doctor in. He was too dazed to do anything other than comply. The sergeant, and a paramedic, gently steered him to the side of the road, where he sank to the ground.

The paramedic pulled out a stethoscope. 'No,' said Sean, 'focus on her.'

'She's in good hands. You've also inhaled a fair amount of smoke. We're taking you in too.'

'If that's the case, you'll have to check the rest of my crew.

They should be here soon. We didn't think about the smoke, just needed to find Jemma.'

Everson squatted beside him. 'Zadrus can't find any sign of life near either house.'

'Jemma was sure they took Anthony with them. We need to get on with the search, catch those bastards,' said Sean.

'No,' said the paramedic, 'you're going to hospital to be thoroughly checked.'

Sean opened his mouth to respond, but Everson smiled and raised his hand. 'I think you've met your match, Bellamy.'

'No, we have to find Anthony before they kill him. I can't waste time here.'

'Well, gee Bellamy. I believe I'm still the ranking officer. You will get into that chopper. You will do what this paramedic tells you to do. And you will leave the chase to me. Is that clear?'

'Fine,' Sean replied, looking away then, still puzzled by Jemma's words, he turned back. 'Do you know anything about Jemma belonging to some community?'

'No.' Everson frowned then clasped Sean's shoulder. 'I heard what she said but don't worry about it now. I'll speak to Zadrus. We are working hard to get to the bottom of it.'

At the sight of Jemma, Sean forgot about Everson, and Zadrus, and their alien world. A tube snaked through her mouth. A bag of clear fluid was attached to a tube in her left arm. Still another tube, from her right arm, was fed by a smaller bag with a cloudy fluid. A machine rested on the end of the trolley. Someone shouted that the ventilator was ready to go. A person with a stethoscope around his neck, and DOCTOR written across his back, stood back from the trolley, then nodded to Sean on the side of the road.

'She's doing okay, mate. We'll keep her unconscious until the swelling goes down. Probably a few days.'

'Where are you taking her?' Sean struggled to stay focused on his role in her protection.

'We need a tertiary hospital with a serious burns unit. The nearest is Brisbane. A plane's heading for Springsure now, with a retrieval team on board.'

'I have to go with her.'

The doctor's eyes narrowed, 'Are you related?'

'No. I'm her bodyguard, but I need to stay with her.'

'Alright. The police car can get you to Springsure. We should be able to fit you in the plane, but you must stay out of our way.'

'I can do that,' replied Sean.

Everson organised a paramedic to take Dan, who'd suffered more smoke inhalation than any of them, to the nearest hospital.

CHAPTER 14

Sean strapped himself into a small seat at the head of Jemma's stretcher and stared down at her face, now swollen beyond recognition. She stirred as the plane lifted off from the runway but when he leaned forward to check on her, a nurse waved him back. He pushed his fist into the edge of his seat, swallowing a growl, but he sat back as directed and stared out the window. None of this was the nurse's fault. A knot formed in his stomach as they flew over the fire. How Jemma must have felt, trapped in the dense smoke and undoubtedly aware that death beckoned.

The doctor must have seen his shudder. He leaned across. 'Hang in there, she's doing well given what she's been through.'

'Thanks,' said Sean. 'She's … Holy hell.' A sphere skimmed across the top of the flames, flying towards them at tremendous speed. It stopped within metres of the small plane. He couldn't see inside but had no doubt Pritchard would be in there and looking at him. Without warning, the sphere shot upwards and, seconds later, blue light swirled around and through the small plane.

'Jesus,' yelled the pilot. 'What the hell is that?'

'Get onto the controller. Tell them we need help,' the doctor shouted at her.

'Won't do any good,' said Sean, edging his way around the medical team to stand behind the pilot. 'Air traffic control can't see them. They're invisible to radar.'

'They have to see it.' The pilot grabbed her radio. 'It's big and it's metal.'

Sean pulled a small gadget from his pocket that Everson had pushed into his hand when they parted, shaking his head when the thing unfurled to line his palm. 'Mr Everson?'

Everson's face appeared on the screen within seconds of Sean uttering his name. 'Problem?'

'A sphere. We're under attack. We need an escort.' He held the gadget where the pilot could hear the instructions.

'On its way. Whatever you do, do not act scared. Tell your pilot to stick to her flight plan.'

'I have to do something,' she said.

'No, we wait. Air Force will be here soon.' Sean moved back to his seat and did his best to re-assure the others, but when that didn't work, he sat back, stared at his watch and waited. Finally, two Air Force jets raced towards them and settled into formation on either side of the plane. The blue light vanished, and the sphere disappeared.

Shortly after, the pilot announced she'd gained priority clearance at Brisbane airport. Cruising across the bay seemed interminable to Sean, although once they were over land the plane zipped quickly down. He expected a flurry of activity when it stopped, but the pilot had to complete protocols before the door opened, then respond to a series of safety checks from outside. Once the stairs had been lowered, and all the boxes and monitors were secured and checked, Jemma was first to be moved.

When he finally got permission to disembark, he jumped down the small flight of stairs and ran to a group of armed men in military uniform standing beside two SUVs. They pulled out in convoy, an SUV, the ambulance, then the second SUV with Sean on board, and all with lights flashing. At the base of the hospital's emergency ramp, the front car peeled off allowing the ambulance to move forward and bypass others on the ramp. Sean, followed by the military police officers from both cars, ran to the back of the ambulance.

The doctor held up his hand. 'You can't come inside.'

'I not only can, I am,' replied Sean. 'Understand we are armed. We will not disrupt you. But we are your shadows while Dr Anderson is here.'

'I'm calling the police.'

'Please do,' said Sean. 'You should tell them my colleagues are military police. That way they can investigate what's happening before they get here.'

Sean followed the procession to the ICU, not satisfied until he saw her surrounded by doctors and nurses. Then he called to inform his boss that he planned to stay by her side until she recovered. Surprised that Hunt agreed, he finally gave in to his own exhaustion and allowed a nurse to direct him to a chair close to Jemma's bed but out of the way of those working on her.

Despite his exhaustion, when an alarm sounded in one of Jemma's machines, he was immediately alert. It seemed that the entire hospital descended on her bedside. He'd never felt so helpless as he listened to questions and orders flying back and forth, while nurses fiddled with machines and called out numbers from screens. His chest hurt as he fought his panic. It felt like someone had reached in and pulled his heart from his body. He'd hardly got to know her yet, but he knew now, she was much more than a subject to be protected. All he wanted was to be close to her. When the staff pulled back from her bed and their voices sounded calmer, the pain in his chest settled to a dull ache and he sat beside her, willing her to get better.

Over the next three days, Jemma continued to improve and, on the morning of the fourth day, the doctors decided to remove the breathing tubes, describing it as a trial of life. What the hell did that mean? *A trial of life?* What if she failed? The doctor, who must have seen the look on his face, gently explained the importance of having her breathe on her own as soon as possible. The tube could go back in if necessary.

Sean realised he hadn't breathed himself through the whole process and when the tube was out, he gulped in some air. Jemma seemed to heave a breath in response.

The doctor smiled at Sean, 'She's more than a VIP to you, isn't she?'

'Yeah, but don't tell anyone else that.'

'Okay. She still has some light sedation onboard. We'll reduce that slowly and see how she responds. You need to get some rest.'

'I can rest sitting here.'

As the doctor walked away, Sean rested his head on the edge of her bed and dozed. Several hours later he sat up, and holding her hand, began to speak to her as the nurses had instructed him. 'I'm still here, and I'm not going anywhere until you talk to me.'

He noticed her eyes flicker and she squeezed his hand, only a little but enough to convince him she meant to do it. Leaning closer, he whispered again. 'I know you're in there. Squeeze my hand again if you can hear me.'

She squeezed again, but it was several more minutes before she managed to open her eyes and look at him. 'Hello,' she said, softly.

'You're back,' he said, waving to the nearest nurse.

'How big was the truck that hit me?' she whispered, smiling.

'Pretty big.' He kept hold of her hand as she drifted back to sleep, afraid she mightn't wake again.

Next day, the doctor said he was so pleased with her progress that she could be transferred to a private room. The nurses organised the shift and brought in a trundle bed, telling Sean to get some sleep, but most of the time he sat on the edge of the trundle, resting his head on Jemma's bed and watching. She slept fitfully, occasionally crying out, at other times thrashing around in the bed. But it was the quiet times that worried him most, and he frequently checked her breathing. Each day she improved a little and on the tenth day from when she'd been rushed to the hospital, her doctor agreed she could go. Sean was worried it was too soon as she still became short of breath walking the short distance between the bed and the bathroom.

Then he had another problem. Hunt had made it clear they'd be heading directly to SCARF, so he'd have to explain the facility and its purpose to Jemma and, even worse, introduce the aliens, the spaceships, and the Interplanetary League.

'Jemma, we need to talk before we go.' He eased her onto the edge of the bed and squatted in front of her. 'General Hunt has organised a chopper to land here at the hospital.' His heart took a dive as she looked back at him, her eyes full of trust. He had to tell her, but he expected that as soon as he filled her in, she'd feel he'd betrayed that trust.

'Okay,' she replied. 'When?'

'Soon. We're going directly from here to SCARF.'

'You've got to be joking,' she exclaimed.

'I need you to trust me. Without Everson, we wouldn't have found you, at least not in time.'

She drummed her fingers on the side of her bed. 'Will you be with me?'

'I will, and so will Dan and General Hunt.' He left her to think about it and opened the door to advise the MPs, and the nurse in charge of the ward, of the move. Then he waited with her for the signal to go.

A nurse delivering Jemma's discharge medications smiled at Sean. 'I'm sorry, but I have to say I'm glad your MPs have gone. I understand you needed them, but they made us all nervous.'

Sean stuttered slightly as he reassured her that he understood but, as soon as she left, he locked the door. If the MPs had been pulled off the job, he'd have been notified and given time to make alternative arrangements. He hit Hunt's number, checked windows and cupboards, investigated the bathroom and fiddled with the door's lock. Those bastards were everywhere. How the hell did they do it?

Hunt answered quickly. 'Problem?'

'I think we've been breached, sir. MPs have gone.'

'Shit. Where the hell could they've gone?'

'They were here just after I spoke to you. A nurse came in. She told me they'd left.'

'Head down to the front entrance. I'll redirect the chopper. O'Leary will pick you up.'

'Jemma, we have to go. Dan'll be waiting at the front door. Your stuff can be collected later. Walk in front of me. If I tell you to do something, don't argue.'

'How much danger are we in?'

'That's just it, Jem, I don't know, but I'm not taking risks. Leave the worry to me. You focus on getting to the front door. If anything bothers you on the way, tell me. Otherwise do exactly as I say.'

Relieved she didn't argue, he checked his sidearm, opened the door and looked both ways then steered her towards the lift but as he pressed the close button, someone yelled, 'Hold it.'

'Get behind me, Jemma. Sorry, mate, can't take anyone else. Psych patient.'

'I'm good with that,' said the man.

'No, sir. You can't join us.'

The man put his hand between the doors as they started to close. Sean reached out and bent his hand back at the wrist. 'There is no room in this lift, sir. Back up.'

As the doors began to close again, Sean grabbed both the man's wrists, and shoved him away. The strength of his push sent the fellow sprawling backwards onto the floor. A man and a woman, both dressed as nurses, and both sporting side-arms, rushed towards them, but Sean got the doors closed and pressed the bypass button.

'Stay by my side and keep your hand on my arm,' said Sean when the doors opened, stepping out with one foot. He scanned both directions, then beckoned her to follow and walked as fast as he dared, given her shortness of breath. The few minutes it took to reach the front door felt more like an hour. As they stepped outside, the passenger window of a black SUV, parked just outside the front door, rolled down and Tom poked his head out. Sean pushed Jemma in the back, scrambled in after her and closed the door. 'We're in. Go.'

Dan accelerated down the ramp. 'Were you followed?'

'No, but I'm sure we were observed,' replied Sean.

'We're heading to the showground across the road,' said Dan. 'The helicopter's hovering above the hospital. It'll head over to us when I give the signal. Zadrus wants us on board quickly so they can take off, before your intruders realise that we're gone.'

Jemma interrupted. 'Who's Zadrus?'

'He works with Mr Everson,' said Tom, who held a

gadget like the one he'd used at Nerang to communicate with Everson.

A tense silence followed, with Jemma glaring at each of them, but Sean didn't waste time explaining.

'I have your vehicle,' said Zadrus, through Tom's gadget. 'No one is following. Your helicopter is about to land.'

Once the car had stopped, Sean jumped out and helped Jemma to the helicopter. Hunt assisted her in, then yelled to the men to join them but, before Sean had shut the door, three black wagons skidded around its base.

'Take off,' yelled Hunt, grabbing his phone. The chopper rose into the air, then banked sharply, but not before a couple of shots pinged its outer shell.

'Deja vu,' Jemma muttered, as Sean leaned over to hold her upright.

'I know.'

The pilot aimed for the grassy stretch around the granite boulder. 'No, go to the landing bay the others use,' said Hunt.

'There's a lot here we have to explain,' said Sean. 'But wait until we're safely inside.' Her body tensed when the helicopter headed directly for the side of the mountain. Ignoring his own fear, he assured her that the ancient volcanic rock would slide open, although he wasn't sure it was wide enough when the helicopter raced through. By the time they'd touched down, the rocky opening had already started to close. With a shudder he helped Jemma out and headed her towards the facility's entry doing his best to block her view of Zadrus's transporter, but she saw it and demanded an explanation.

'It's a secret military aircraft,' said Hunt from behind. 'Inside quickly.'

Jemma raised her eyebrows.

'Sir, I think you need to explain what's going on here,' said Sean.

'Agreed. Settle her into her room. I'll send a nurse to help you, Jemma.'

'No need, sir. I've organised a two-bedroom apartment, so I can be nearby,' replied Sean, keeping his gaze firmly on Hunt. He wasn't going to back down on this one.

Hunt's eyes narrowed, and he shook his head. 'Fine. Just make sure Jemma understands the seriousness of the situation.'

She glared at him. 'Are you mad? I've been chased through the forest, shot at, kidnapped, damn near died in a bush fire, and found I was in danger in a hospital. I doubt you could have any better understanding of the seriousness of the situation.'

Sean steered her away from Hunt, keeping going until they reached their new apartment. A shouting match wouldn't help right now. He stood outside and waited for the door to open, smiling when Jemma jumped back. Not so different from his own reaction a few days ago. 'It's alright. I'll explain everything later. I'm sorry I didn't tell you that I'd organised a share apartment, but I didn't think you should be alone. If you're not happy with it, I can get it changed.'

'No, it's fine. I'd be a bit nervous on my own as yet.'

'Good. Now, let's try and be as normal as possible,' he said. 'It's been a big morning. I suggest you rest for a while.'

'I'd appreciate that,' she replied. 'Are we really safe here?'

'Safer than anywhere else I know,' he said, walking towards her bedroom. 'I'll leave the door slightly open, so if you need me, I'll hear.' She was already lying down, her eyes shut. He gently brushed the hair away from her forehead, then backed out and headed for the coffee pot. The stronger, the better. It'd help him think. He sat on the sofa and propped his feet on the coffee table. The spacious, well-furnished apartment had a lounge, a dining area and kitchen, and two large bedrooms, both with ensuites and walk-in wardrobes. When he'd arrived here, he'd found a full set of uniforms in his robe; dress, work and cams, shoes, runners and boots, jeans, T-shirts, shorts and even underwear. Some basics had been added to Jemma's wardrobe while he'd been away. She'd need more but it'd do for the moment.

The last couple of weeks had been close to the most difficult of his life. He'd clung to the belief he'd find Jemma, and she'd be just fine. She wasn't fine, but she did survive, and now no one would get in the way of her recovery, not even Hunt, his boss of over ten years, and someone he respected more than anyone else on the planet.

Jemma stirred. He sat up, wide awake and ready for anything. Years of training himself to be alert meant the slightest noise roused him. She made another small noise in her sleep and he opened the door to her room to check. The blanket had been thrown off and he gently pulled it back over her. He struggled to breathe as he looked down. How had he stuffed up so badly? He should've done so much more to protect her, right from the beginning. Yet, he had no idea what else he could have done. He hadn't come across terrorists like these before, ahead of him every step of the way, even down to knowing the location of the safe houses.

He sat on a chair beside her bed, transfixed by the rise and fall of her chest as she slept, and he could no longer deny how he felt. That, of course, brought his objectivity into question, and he suspected Hunt had recognised that. She groaned and let out a small cry, settling back into a deep sleep as he stroked her face. A few minutes later, she groaned again but this time she opened her eyes and smiled up at him.

'Are you okay?' He continued to run his fingers through her hair. She was beautiful, intelligent and brave and he knew how he felt but would she feel the same way? What could she possibly see in him?

'I'm okay now.'

It was more than compassion. His body tingled as he leant down and kissed her on the forehead. 'I'm so glad we found you in time.'

'So am I,' she said. 'I wondered if I'd ever see you again. I thought about you all the time, even dreamed about you, and not just that you'd save me.' She raised her arm and touched the side of his face.

He leaned forward and kissed her tentatively on the lips, relieved she didn't push him away.

'I heard you stayed with me the whole time I was unconscious, wouldn't leave my side, made the doctors uncomfortable,' she said.

'Yep, I probably did do that. No way I was going to leave you once I'd found you.'

She smiled up at him and drew him back down towards her. 'Not a chance. Now kiss me properly.'

This time his lips met hers with a hunger that surprised him. She responded by pulling him closer, and he slid down the bed beside her. The warmth of her body, and the faintest whiff of perfume, excited his senses. He wanted her so badly, but not just for now, he wanted her forever. There was no way he'd rush it and scare her off.

Propping his head up on his arm, he lay on his side to look at her. 'I was so afraid we wouldn't find you. When Dan carried you out of the forest and you couldn't breathe, I thought I'd die if you didn't make it.'

She smiled. Such a beautiful smile. And it was all for him.

'Just as well I did then,' she said. She paused, as if trying to formulate something in her mind. No hurry. As he waited his hand caressed her arm, and slowly travelled down the side of her hip and leg, until it found its way back up to her breasts.

When she spoke, she looked directly into his eyes, as though speaking to his soul. 'I knew the first day I met you that I wanted to be close to you. I kept dismissing it, because of the situation, and you're so professional, I didn't think you'd feel the same way. Then with everything else that happened, I didn't believe it'd come to anything. Now, I can't imagine going on without you.'

He lowered himself putting one arm around her shoulders while the other explored under her blouse and deftly reached behind to unclip her top. Just as quickly, he rolled her blouse over her head, then tore off his shirt and curled in close, her skin so soft and warm and comforting. He kissed her, this time a long, passionate kiss. But still not quite sure of himself, he gazed into her eyes, 'Do you want me to stop?'

She curled her legs around his. 'I've dreamed about this moment since we first met,' she said. 'The last thing I'd want to do is stop.'

Rolling over, he covered her with his body. He'd had plenty of lovers in his time, but he'd never felt this way before. Not just sex, and no longer just about him. This was about joining her, loving her, protecting her.

CHAPTER 15

Jemma slept for several hours, her first relaxed sleep since the fire. Alone now in the bed, she wondered if she'd imagined the whole thing, but her body told her otherwise. An enticing smell wafted through, accompanied by faint humming, so she pulled on a T-shirt and pair of shorts she'd found in the cupboard, and made her way to the kitchen.

'Are you hungry?' Sean looked decidedly pleased with himself.

'I'm hungry in lots of ways,' she said, putting her arms around his neck.

He smiled as he ran his fingers through her hair. 'I managed to get an apartment with a proper kitchen. Didn't have anything else to do, so I cooked us some dinner.'

'Smells good.'

A white tablecloth covered the dining table and two places had been set, each with enough cutlery for three courses. He placed a large ceramic bowl on the middle of the table. Soup, aromatic, a touch of chilli, garlic and lemon grass. A variation on a Lhaksa. Nice.

Next, a beautifully stuffed and roasted cut of beef with a mix of vegetables. This man could cook, the beef pink, not red, not brown. Perfect. Matched with a rich red wine, maybe a Shiraz. She thought she'd eaten enough until the strawberry shortcake came out. A sweet white wine to wash it down. More than everything she'd eaten since the fire. She wondered if she'd be able to get out of the chair without waddling after all that food.

'Up you get.' He smiled, as if he knew what she was thinking. 'Coffee's in the lounge.'

She picked up two coffee cups and held them out for Sean to pour the coffee. He sat beside her on the lounge, and she snuggled into him.

'So, what now, Sean?'

'General Hunt's working out what to do. I'll be talking to him later this evening.'

'You trust him?'

'I do. He's the only person I trust without question. Except you, of course.'

She smiled, 'Of course.'

'We don't always agree, but I always trust him. He was my first CO when I graduated from Duntroon. I got into more trouble than I'd care to admit to. The boss roared at me so often, I considered setting up my own spot in his office. It would have been more efficient.' The memory of his early years made him blush, and he wondered if Jemma thought him an idiot. Most of the young officers found themselves in trouble with Hunt at one time or another. He usually got rid of officers who didn't perform, although they'd often already applied for transfers to get away from him. Sometimes he'd get them booted right out of the Army. 'For some reason he stuck with me, and I don't really know why.'

Jemma laughed. 'I know why.'

'Yeah, but you're biased.'

'Yes, I am, but he'd have valued your intelligence. You're a thinker. You consider your options and find an answer without having to rely on someone to tell you what to do. And you think outside the box. You got into trouble because you don't go by the rules, you look for your own solutions.'

'Haven't changed much, have I? Suspect I'm in a bit of trouble again now.'

Hunt's voice boomed through a small box sitting on the coffee table. 'That'd be the understatement of the day. May I come in please?' A flap on the front of the box shot upwards and showed an image of Hunt. Sean stiffened then strode to the door which again opened automatically.

Hunt walked in and sat on a chair opposite the sofa. There was something about the man. He looked relaxed, had a smile on his face, yet he seemed to exude authority. She didn't know much about military ways, but his presence changed Sean. Her relaxed companion was now tense and ready to respond.

Hunt greeted Jemma warmly, asking her to stay while he questioned Sean about the hospital, and why he hadn't noticed the MPs missing. Puzzled by how someone could so easily change their demeanour, she was relieved that he accepted Sean's explanation that the MPs had been there a few minutes earlier, and neither he, nor Jemma, had heard anything. The relationship between the two men puzzled her.

They clearly respected each other, but the power discrepancy made her wonder how Sean managed to maintain his independent streak. Perhaps she'd understand in time.

Once they'd exhausted their discussion of how things had gone so wrong, Hunt turned his attention to her. He wanted to know everything that'd happened after the safe house, who she met, where she went, how she escaped. Her own muscles tensed, and she gripped Sean's hand but answered Hunt as clearly as she could, given she had to stop every few words to catch her breath. She described being bundled into the station wagon, the flight in the Lear Jet, the house where she'd been dropped, and the housekeeper. He demanded minute details. She recounted Anthony's statement that he was a prisoner and was about to be taken somewhere that night.

'Do you remember where?' said Hunt.

Trembling, Jemma leaned back on the lounge and stared at the ceiling. 'Central America. I think.'

'It's okay, Jemma,' said Sean. 'You're safe now. If you can remember where in Central America, it might help us find him.'

She slapped her hand against her forehead then suddenly sat forward. 'Oh, I remember. Costa Rica. He said, an old military camp.'

'I'll get Captain Denis and Mr Everson on to it,' said Hunt.

She sighed. 'I know Everson was there when you rescued me from the fire, but I still can't see any good reason to trust him.'

'It was Mr Everson who found you,' replied Hunt. 'We

now work with him and have access to everything on the mountain. He will help us protect you until we sort this out. I'm afraid that means keeping you with us. I am sorry this has happened to you.'

'Yeah,' she said. 'So am I.'

'I really am sorry. Now, may I speak to Bellamy on his own?'

With Sean's help she got up and walked to the bathroom. A hot, soaking bath sounded like heaven. They'd thought of everything when they set this place up. She ran the bath, throwing in a lavender bath-bomb she'd found in the cupboard, then put a big fluffy towel next to her, and relaxed into the tub, the warmth so comforting.

*   *   *

Sean braced himself as he returned to Hunt.

'That's a beautiful young lady you're caring for, Bellamy. I take it the interest is more than professional?'

Sean sighed, 'A lot more.'

'Well, that changes things. Look, I understand these things happen, but I'm disappointed you didn't tell me.'

'Sir, I think that's a bit unfair. It only just happened. Until we got here, I was totally focused on her safety. I still am, probably even more.'

'I'm sure you are, but your judgement is gone.'

'Jemma told me something else before we flew her to Brisbane.' Keen to distract Hunt's attention, Sean relayed

Anthony's statement to Jemma that she had to survive *for the sake of the community*.

'Yes, Mr Everson said something about that. I spoke to the chief. He claimed he didn't know but I'm sure he did. I'll tackle him again, but I have another pressing issue to discuss with you in the meantime. Those SUVs that met us at the show grounds. Mr Everson heard one of the staff here, on the phone, tell someone that a helicopter was on its way to pick Jemma up this morning.'

'Jesus, who?'

'Lieutenant-Colonel Williamson.'

'Are you serious?' said Sean, jumping up and pacing across the room. 'I know his staff hate him, but are you telling me he's a traitor?'

'Appears that way. I've spoken to him, and while he wouldn't tell me who he spoke to, he hasn't denied leaking information.'

'Let me at him,' said Sean.

'No,' replied Hunt. 'I want him charged, tried and convicted.'

'I can do all that,' said Sean.

'Not going to happen,' replied Hunt, although there was a smile on his face. 'Let me give you something else to occupy your mind. I've spent the last hour talking to the chief. Well listening to him growling rather than actually being able to say anything.'

'About?'

'Grab a chair.' Hunt paused. He didn't look happy. 'We're

to stay here. The rest of our team will join us. You'll take over as CO. I'll have a broader role.' He held up his hand as Sean went to respond. 'We don't have a choice. Ironically, I think the chief had planned to move Williamson on anyway, which is why he moved us here in the first place.'

'But why?'

'That's the million-dollar question,' replied Hunt with a sigh. 'The only thing I know for certain is that the chief wants a full protection and investigation unit operating from here. Our purpose will be to protect Jemma and this facility against Pritchard and his people. From there it's all sketchy. He sees Jemma as a very important person, speaks about her as though she's royalty, but won't tell me why. He describes Pritchard, or should I say Drick, as one of the worst criminals ever seen on this planet.'

'Then why doesn't Jemma know anything about it if she's so important.'

'I don't know.' Hunt sighed, 'He just won't divulge his reasons. He also says that Mr Everson's considered crucial to our new purpose. They want him supported, which I'm happy to do. In return, he's to include us with his extra-terrestrial role, and that's where a lot of my focus will be.'

'Will he include us?'

'Yeah, I think he's relieved to have someone he can trust to work with.'

'Is that why he's been such a prick?'

'Suspect so. Probably thought all of Earth's military were like Williamson.'

'Sir, I don't mean to be rude, but I'm surprised he's leaving someone with your rank to head up a simple investigation and protection unit.'

'Yeah. That was my first thought but, as he went on, I realised he didn't see our task as simple. And I think he's right. When I arrested Williamson he said, and I quote, *fine you've got me, but my people will wipe out your community. The guardians can't stop us.*'

'Shit, what's the chief got to say about that?'

'So far nothing. Just said again, he'll get up here and talk to us as soon as he can get away.'

'Okay, if we don't have a choice, we'll get on with it,' said Sean. 'But I want to talk to you about Jemma. I don't know what you plan to do to protect her, but her lung function is still compromised, and she fatigues after very little effort. I don't want to see her pushed too far.'

Hunt smiled. 'Understood. But she must come to grips with her situation and learn to do exactly as I say. It will be hard for her, but if I need her to do something quickly, I can't have her questioning my authority. She will have to learn that. Normally, someone much lower down would take charge of her, probably not even an officer, but under the circumstances I'm stepping in.'

'I've seen you push female officers. I know you don't give them any quarter because they're female, and I accept that, but you often push them harder than the men. Jemma can't take it at this stage.'

'I'm hearing you, Bellamy, but listen hard to what I have

to say. I'm taking charge of her. There is something about her that we may have to protect with our very lives. I have no idea what that is, and so no way of ensuring watertight protection. We've found one traitor; we could have more. Jemma must recover her health and learn to look after herself. I'm best placed to deal with that. You will not interfere. Is that clear?'

They stared at each other until Sean muttered, 'Sir.'

'Bring her to my office at 09:00 tomorrow.'

Sean's head buzzed after Hunt left. He'd have to get Jemma scanned tonight. The aliens called it printing, not just fingerprints, a whole-body print. They'd identified twenty-five unique features on the body which could be used to identify an individual. Doing his best to sound cheerful, he headed to the bathroom. 'Jemma, we need to talk.'

'Uh-oh, sounds ominous.'

He helped her out of the bath, waited for her to dress, then led her to the lounge. 'You're tired, and I want you to rest, but I need to prepare you for your meeting with General Hunt. He's going to tell you that you're now in protective custody.'

'You mean I'm a prisoner. Again. I'm getting used to that, Sean.'

'I know, but this time you really are a prisoner in every sense of the word. Agree to whatever General Hunt says. He can withdraw privileges, have you locked up, or transferred to another secure facility. I know how determined you can be. And I know how determined he can be. I'll do everything I can to protect you, but he's the boss, and I can only argue so far.'

She glared at him. 'Alright, I've got the message. Be a good girl, do as I'm told, and don't argue. Trouble is Sean, I'm not a girl, I'm a woman. I'm not used to being told what to do, and I don't want to be here.'

'I know. But we have a problem that I can't solve. It's not safe for you to go home, so the powers that be, and they're a lot higher than General Hunt, have decided you will stay here. They can keep you here as long as they choose. General Hunt is now your boss, whether we like it or not, and I don't particularly. What he says, goes. You can't walk away. The MPs would come after you. You can fight him and be miserable, or go along with him and be the sweet, obedient little thing I know and love, and stay happy.'

She threw a cushion at him. 'I'll go along with him, so long as he doesn't demand something outrageous.'

Maybe she had got the message. He caught the cushion and threw it gently back. 'We have to head upstairs to get you scanned. Come on, I'll explain as we go.'

She took his hand, resting her head on his shoulder as they walked. Hopefully, her tiredness would keep her a bit subdued when she met with the general in the morning. Jemma could be feisty, and that wouldn't serve her well now.

*   *   *

Next morning Hunt dismissed Sean before ushering Jemma into his office. He shut the door and moved the chairs away from the front of his desk. Leaning back into a half sit on the desk, he looked up at her, and no longer had the smiling, friendly look on his face. Not nasty, business-like, determined.

'Has Bellamy explain protective custody to you?'

She nodded.

'Did you understand him?'

'I think so. It means I can't leave here.'

'Good, but there is more. You're right, you cannot leave here without my permission, and an armed escort. It must be my permission, nobody else's, not Sean's, not even Mr Everson's. I must know where you are at all times.'

'Understood.'

'Our doctor will set up a recovery program, which may involve rest or exercise. Whichever it is, you will follow it. My fitness instructor will help you.'

'Okay, but I don't think I'll need help. I want to get well.'

'While under my protection, your health and wellbeing are my responsibility. I will be monitoring your progress. And I will push. Is that clear?'

'Quite clear,' she replied. 'But I don't understand your attitude. I won't try to leave; I want to be with Sean. And I want to get well, so if your doctor gives me good advice, I'll follow it. Is that clear?'

Hunt's eyes narrowed, and he stood before speaking again. Not as tall as Sean but definitely more intimidating. His face rested centimetres from hers and his voice was cold and hard. 'While you are in my custody, you will follow my rules. Your welfare is my concern, whether you like it or not.'

Jemma took a deliberate step back and glared up at him. 'I

understand what you are saying. I don't understand why you feel you need to say it.'

'This is a military facility. I give the orders. You, like everybody else, will obey them.'

She shook her head. 'I'm not military, and you know that I've never refused to co-operate with Sean or Dan.'

'That's not entirely true. Have you been printed?'

'Yes.' She crossed her arms in front of her chest and waited for him to continue.

'Then think hard. Your happiness here will depend entirely on yourself. Now stay here, we have another meeting scheduled. I'll send Bellamy in as soon as I find him.'

CHAPTER 16

Sean waited outside the office door and wasn't at all pleased to see Hunt's grim look when he emerged.

'Leave her be,' said Hunt. 'She's got a lot to think about. Our visitors are scheduled to arrive in half an hour. It won't hurt her to sit and stew until then.'

'For God's sake, can't you just let her recover. She's not going anywhere.'

'No, she's not and I will organise the best medical and psychological help I can find to ensure her recovery. In the meantime, she can learn that there are rules and she must abide by them. Find something else to do for the next thirty minutes and give her the time she needs.'

Sean strode back to his office, but his anger at Hunt rose with every paper he tried to look at on his desk. Giving up, he made his way to the control room where Nik continued her search for Pritchard's lab and Anthony. Amused to find Dan deep in conversation with Nik, he cleared his throat, just loud enough to make her look up. She'd be a good match for Dan, not just attractive with her blonde hair and blue eyes, but capable of matching him, probably outclassing him, intellectually.

She pulled away from Dan and pointed to her screen. 'I lost the plane that took Anthony sir, but I've found an old army camp in Costa Rica that would be perfect for Pritchard and seems to fit with what Anthony said to Jemma. It's just a hunch at this stage. It's still night there, and it looks deserted, so I'm going back through yesterday's footage.'

'Good thinking.' He nudged Dan. 'Learning about the alien technology, were you?'

'Smart arse,' growled Dan. 'And yes, I was learning about the technology and I'm keen to learn more.'

'Pleased to hear it,' replied Sean, grinning.

'Look at this,' called Nik. She grabbed Sean's shirt sleeve and pointed to the screen. 'That's Anthony, isn't it? And Pritchard's with him.'

'It is,' said Sean, easing her grip from his arm. 'Well done.'

'Sorry, sir.' She quickly withdrew her hand and shoved it in her pocket.

'It's fine,' said Sean. 'I was just avoiding a bruise. Relax. You've got good instincts, Nik. I'm impressed. Can you steady that thing?'

'I'm trying,' she muttered. 'Come on Artie, you can do it.'

'Perhaps I can help.' Zadrus walked in and, pointing to Anthony's image, said, 'Behave yourself, control. Highlight that image.'

The picture and the audio cleared immediately, Anthony's voice now loud and clear, saying, 'What is that thing?'

'Show me what he's looking at,' said Zadrus. The image moved to the metal sphere. 'Oh,' he said. 'It's a Norellian

Sphere. I couldn't see the thing that chased your plane after the bushfire, it was masked, but I suspect it was the same thing.'

'Yes, it was,' said Sean, moving closer. 'So, what's a Norellian Sphere?'

'A transporter,' replied Zadrus. 'Much like ours but they're intended for intra-planetary travel.'

'You mean they can't go out of the atmosphere?'

'They can, but not far. They are not strong enough for repeated trips.'

'So,' said Sean, 'Pritchard's claim to come from another planet is true.'

Zadrus nodded. 'It would appear so. Another planet, possibly another galaxy. I do not know which one.' He went on to explain that every IPL aligned planet used the type of transporter he had shown Sean, and the same motherships. Other planets used a variety of different crafts, the Norellian Sphere was quite common. He knew of two planets within the Milky Way galaxy that used them and suggested there would be hundreds more within Laniakea, the surrounding super cluster of galaxies. He'd already transmitted the image of Pritchard, to find out if he had a history somewhere else.

'You'd better talk to the chief,' replied Sean. 'He knows more about Pritchard than he's telling us. Calls him Drick. Mr Everson knows about him too.'

'I have heard that name. It sounds familiar, but I can't bring it too mind. I'll speak to my partner, Werrimen. She may remember something.'

'Okay,' said Sean. 'Can we focus on Anthony? I'll get on to the Costa Rican military and organise flights to head over there.'

'May I suggest I fly you there,' said Zadrus. 'I intend to leave this afternoon. Costa Rica is sixteen hours behind us, so it will still be dark there when we arrive. But we will get there before your aeroplane flight.'

'In a transporter?' muttered Sean, taking a deep breath.

'Yes, of course.'

The last thing he wanted was to go anywhere in one of those things, but if it'd get him there quicker, he'd have to deal with it.

'Zadrus, we've seen that sphere multiple times now. It's felt like it was tracking us,' said Dan.

'That is the most logical conclusion.'

'Probably, not *us* though,' said Sean. 'He's after Jemma.'

'I agree,' replied Zadrus. 'He seems to be focussed on her and if they have been masking their craft, she would not have known. It is possible she has something implanted within her body that they have used to track her. Has she ever mentioned anything to you?'

'No,' replied Sean. 'Could there be something she doesn't know about?'

'Possibly. I will seek more information. If we can identify Pritchard's planet, and if she comes from the same planet, we might be able to work out what she has and neutralise it. And we can't exclude the possibility that he is also tracking you.'

Nik scanned back to hear the rest of Anthony's

conversation. A chill ran down Sean's spine when Pritchard assured Anthony that he planned to get Jemma back.

*   *   *

Hunt was aware that he'd sounded like an uncaring arsehole, but sobeit. If she hated him now, fine. Her physical weakness made her vulnerable and if she found herself at the mercy of those terrorists again, he'd most likely lose her, unless he could teach her to stand up for herself. He'd already failed her multiple times. With no idea what Pritchard might do next, he had to prepare her for anything, and he had to do it quickly.

He walked into his office, waving Sean to a chair beside Jemma. 'Have you thought more about our conversation, Jemma?' said Hunt, struggling to contain a smile as she lifted her head and looked directly at him.

'I don't respond well to bullying.'

'I'm not bullying you. I'm setting the rules.'

'A positive explanation and sensible discussion would be far more helpful than abstract threats.'

'Should an emergency arise, I must know you will obey me without argument. You must recognise I am in charge.' He waited through a prolonged pause during which Sean squeezed her shoulder, and her defiant look faded.

'Alright,' she sighed. 'I'll go along with you but I have to be in control of my own recovery.'

'No,' replied Hunt.

'What do you mean, no?'

'Exactly that. You just agreed to recognise that I'm in charge. Now you're saying you won't obey me when it comes to your health. You're the scientist. You tell me. Isn't your argument contradictory?'

She looked down at her feet again then raised her head and glared at him.

'Good,' he said quietly. 'I want you to spend time thinking. You will not leave your apartment for the next twenty-four hours. Now I'm expecting some visitors. Wait here while I look for them.

As Hunt left, she threw herself into Sean's arms. 'Arsehole,' she muttered.

Still in the doorway, Hunt sighed. 'I heard that. Your twenty-four hours just became forty-eight.'

*   *   *

Sean took hold of her shoulders and eased her around, so she had to look at him. 'Are you crazy? I told you he'll keep upping the ante.'

She snuggled into him. 'I know, but I feel better.'

He shook his head and laughed.

'I love you,' she said. 'I'll try for your sake as well as mine, but I don't promise I'll like him.'

'Fair enough,' he replied. 'In the end, I think you will. I know he likes you.'

'Funny way of showing it.'

Sean grinned. Part of what he loved about her was her

feistiness, but it wouldn't serve her well now. He had to get through to her. 'Sweetheart, we have to talk.'

'Your boss is a bully.'

'No, he's not, but he is the boss and he does expect you to recognise that. You mightn't believe me now, but he cares what happens to you, that's what's motivating him.'

'I'm not a child.'

He sighed. 'No, you're not a child, but he has the authority and he won't budge. I know him too well.'

'Then I'll have to convince him.'

'No, you won't. His troops, including me, would follow him anywhere. You think I'm tough, but I'm nothing compared to him.'

She glared at him. 'I'm not one of *his troops.*'

'No, but you are his prisoner. He's tough, and he's hard, and he'll demand more and more until you do what he wants. I don't want you to suffer, but you will if you don't give in. All he's asked is that you do as he says.'

'He didn't ask, he demanded. And what if I find myself in a situation where I can't do as he says.'

'You're backing up over his attitude. He hasn't actually told you to do anything, yet. It's time to grow up and face reality. You're stuck with him.'

'Fine, I'll just ignore him then if he does tell me to do something.'

'No, you can't. Do you want to spend the next few months, or even years, in a cell?'

'I've got rights. He can't do that.'

He sighed. 'No. You don't have rights. Damn it, don't you realise that if I could take you to a deserted island, fan you with a palm as we basked in the sun and drank cocktails until you'd recovered, I would? But that can't happen, and we have to make the best of where we are.'

'But you could do more to help me,' she snapped back.

A fist in the chest would have stung less. How could she fail to realise how hard he was working to help? 'Is that all you think of me? I'm looking after myself, and to hell with you?'

'No, of course not.' She looked down and fiddled with her shirt. 'But you have to be able to do something.'

'Will you please co-operate with him, even if it's just for me? I want to help you cope, not pick up the pieces after he chews you up and spits you out. And believe me, that will happen.' What else could he say? Whatever was going to happen, would. She was a big girl; he couldn't make her decisions for her.

CHAPTER 17

Jemma stared at her feet not wanting anything more to do with Hunt, but when he returned with Everson, and spoke directly to her, she had to look up. 'Jemma, I have some people joining us shortly, but I need to fill you in first, to explain why SCARF exists, how General Everson fits in, and why I think the terrorists are chasing you.'

'Okay.' she replied. 'I'd appreciate some information.'

Hunt ignored the jibe. 'I had difficulty accepting what I am about to tell you at first, and I suspect you will too, so I need you to open your mind and listen. Can you do that?'

'I always keep an open mind.'

'I'm afraid I'd have to disagree with that,' replied Hunt, smiling, but he went on without allowing her to retort. 'I'm told that around four hundred years ago, a group of beings from planets other than Earth decided to build facilities here. They chose places that were, at the time, relatively uninhabited. There was a small tribe of Aborigines on the mountain who, by all accounts, befriended the aliens.'

'Aliens? Really?'

Sean leaned across. 'It's true, Jemma.'

She shrugged. It wasn't impossible. There were plenty of

uninhabited places aliens could hide, and plenty of people claimed to have seen them, but she'd make up her own mind.

Hunt continued. 'The SCARF facility was built as a kind of transmitter station for long distance communication. By that, I mean signals across many light years. Do you understand that sort of distance?'

'I understand the definition. It's the distance light would travel in one year in a vacuum, but I don't think anyone really has a concept of how far that is.'

'You can if you've travelled across that distance,' said Everson.

'You're telling me you've travelled in space?' Her eyes widened as she looked at him.

'There are all sorts of intelligent beings throughout the universe,' he replied. 'Some look just like you and me.'

She shrugged, that was possible.

'I am not from Earth,' said Everson. 'My planet is in this galaxy but a long way from here. There are many here on Earth just like me. We walk among you, but as we are here to help, it is better we don't make ourselves known.'

'Fredrick Pritchard told me that. He also said he wasn't from Earth, but can you prove it?'

'I both can and will, and I suspect Pritchard told you the truth. There are many humans like you and me throughout the universe, but some aliens do look different. You are about to meet two of them who, like me, belong to the Interplanetary League. They come from a planet called Sidlow, which is millions of light years from here. They are tall and have some different proportions to our bodies. Otherwise they're not much different from us. Would you like to meet one of them?'

When she looked around and saw Zadrus standing in the doorway she jumped up, knocking her chair over, and bolted in front of Sean. 'What the hell?'

Everson picked up the chair and motioned to her to sit down again but she didn't respond, still clinging to Sean. He held her hand and gently pushed her back into the seat continuing to reassure her.

'You're telling me this fellow is from another planet. What's going on?'

'It's okay, Jemma,' said Sean. 'Do you remember Tom mentioned Zadrus in the car as we left the hospital? This is who he was talking to. Zadrus helped us find you in the fire, narrowed down the area where you might be. Without him, you wouldn't be alive.'

'Why didn't you tell me? If he's from outer space, the whole planet needs to know. There's another species out there. Don't you realise how important this is?'

'Our governments have known that for centuries,' said Hunt. 'The IPL have helped us from time to time, but Earth is expected to look after itself. The rest of the planet doesn't need to know, at least not yet.'

Zadrus bowed his head and walked into the room, followed by a female alien who he introduced as Werrimen. She was shorter than Zadrus, her hair longer and slightly darker, and she had finer features.

Jemma heard Everson start to explain that the craft she'd seen as she came in belonged to Zadrus, but the room began to spin. She gasped for breath. Hunt jumped across his desk and the female alien, Werrimen, rushed to her side. She made Jemma look at her, told her to breathe slowly, to take deep breaths, and hold each one for a few seconds. Jemma tried hard to do as the woman said and her breathing slowly improved.

'My dear,' said Werrimen. 'Would you let me take you to the medical centre and run some tests? I may be able to help your recovery. I've been told about everything that has happened to you.'

Jemma looked towards Sean and gripped his hand harder.

'Yes,' Hunt said to Werrimen, 'we'll do that. Bellamy, stay here. Bring O'Leary and Lambert in. Zadrus and Mr Everson will catch you up on their findings. I'll take Jemma to the medical centre.'

Jemma had no idea what to make of General Hunt. He had his arms around her and wasn't at all perturbed that she gripped onto him. Werrimen had a bed organised when they arrived and attached an oxygen mask as Jemma lay down. Hunt hadn't taken his eyes off her the entire time. He sat beside her and she closed her eyes, the bed so comfortable she felt herself starting to doze until the alien woman sat on the other side of the bed.

Werrimen spoke in a soft, melodic voice. 'I am just going to put this bar against your arm for a few seconds. It will sting a little as I put it on, but that is all. It will tell me everything I need to know from your blood.'

When the bar first touched her skin, Jemma winced.

Hunt edged closer to her on the bed and put his hand on her shoulder. 'Shh, she won't hurt you.'

Werrimen moved back to a desk that looked like a nurses' station. A broad smile crossed her face. 'Yes, I do believe I can help you. I can't immediately cure you, but I believe I can speed your recovery. Are you able to stand up, my dear, and come look at my screens?'

Hunt helped Jemma up. 'Is it okay if I look as well?'

She stared at him. The caring version of the man had returned. But would it last? 'Of course,' she replied.

Werrimen pointed to two images, the first of which showed everything from the trachea through to the bronchioles.

'Your airways on both sides are uneven. Patches are so narrow that the protective mucous your body is putting out can block the tubes, making it hard for you to breathe. You should recover naturally in a few months, although I suspect you will have some scarring.'

Jemma slumped backwards towards Hunt who still had a firm grip on her.

Werrimen pointed to the second image. 'I do have some good news though, my dear. There does not seem to be any significant damage to the lung tissue, so with the right treatment I believe you can recover fully. If you will let me help, I believe I can have you fully functional within three to four weeks.'

Jemma didn't know how to respond. Of course, she'd like help, but she had no idea if she should trust these alien beings.

Without her realising, Hunt had steered her onto the bed propping up the back, so she could continue talking.

He seemed to have read her thoughts. 'Exactly what would that involve?'

Werrimen described a plant, found on another planet hundreds of years earlier, that had been shown to help with burns to the skin. They'd developed a cream which her people now used routinely. But someone had wondered whether it could help with internal burns to lungs such as Jemma had experienced, and trials of an inhaled form worked well. Eventually, they'd developed a synthetic version of the substance, which they'd use with Jemma. 'It would be best if we transferred her to our ship for treatment.'

Jemma felt herself go cold. She grabbed Hunt's arm. 'No! No, no, no. Please don't let them take me away from Sean again.'

He eased his arm out and put it around her shoulders. Then he looked back to Werrimen. 'Is there any way the equipment could be brought down here? She's been through too much. I don't want to traumatise her any further.'

Werrimen tinkered with some devices behind the bed. 'It might be. I will send down one of my medical team later in the day to see if they can set it up. I do understand.'

'I'd rather not have to send her away again,' said Hunt.

*   *   *

'Send who away again?' Sean glared in turn at Hunt and Werrimen as he entered the room.

'I would like to start Jemma's treatment as soon as possible,' said Werrimen. 'I doubt I can organise the equipment down here today. Jemma, would you consider coming up with me for one treatment, then straight back? I am sure someone from here could come with you.'

'If that's necessary, I'll go with her,' said Sean.

'I agree someone should go with her, but it does not have to be you,' said Werrimen. 'I know how busy you are.'

'Jemma's my priority and I don't want her to suffer any more.'

'That is not something we can ever guarantee, no matter how much we care. You must also show her that you trust her, and that you believe in her.'

Sean sighed. He'd failed to protect Jemma before, he wouldn't do that again.

Hunt walked to the door. 'My office before you go, Bellamy.'

Sean settled Jemma, then followed Hunt. Whatever it was, he needed to get it done, so he could get her moving and start the treatment.

Hunt motioned to him to sit. 'Is Jemma okay?'

'Yeah, still upset, but she'll be alright.'

'Right, we still have to find the core of Pritchard's activities, and retrieve Anthony. Any progress?'

'Zadrus intended to head to Costa Rica this morning but he'll wait until after Jemma's treatment. We'll still get there before dawn. If we're finished here, I need to get her some lunch.' When Hunt growled, he snarled back. 'You're the one who's confined her to her room.'

'You're an insolent bastard. This situation is bloody hard for everyone, we've got to work through it together. Your job is to find Anthony and the lab. Jemma's my job. You can go with her this afternoon, then I take over. Accept it.'

'I've got that message … sir.' He bolted for the door, before Hunt could retort.

*   *   *

Jemma held onto Sean's hand as they floated up in the blue light to the transporter, fascinated despite her nerves. The machine that would take them out of the Earth's atmosphere, to an orbiting spaceship, was no more than the size of a small plane. Comfortable lounge-style chairs graced the interior, but no seatbelts, no oxygen, no spacesuits and she wondered if they'd float once they got out of the atmosphere.

One of the Sidlowns sat beside her. 'I believe this is the first journey for either of you on a transporter.'

Jemma nodded, surprised as she followed the Sidlown's gaze at how nervous Sean looked. She hoped she wouldn't get sick like she did on small planes, but her excitement had taken over and she asked if she could move closer to the window. The Sidlown held out his hand and assisted her to move.

'God, Sean, come and look at this.' Planet Earth slowly receded beneath them and looking up she caught her first glimpse of the mothership. Bigger than an average city block and just hanging there, stationary. She had so many questions. How did this thing work? How did they take off without rocket propulsion? How did they travel those distances? How did they maintain food and water supplies? How did they control their oxygen?

'Bloody scientists,' muttered Sean. 'I'd rather have my feet planted on solid ground.'

'Sean, think about what this means for us. Their knowledge. Their experience. Aren't you excited?'

'Of course, I'm excited, I've already thought about all of that. But right now, we're out here in space in a tin can that's fifteen metres in diameter. I want to know everything. I just want to hear it on Earth.'

She shook her head and turned to the Sidlown. 'So, how do we land on this thing?'

'We dock directly into the landing bay. The door closes behind us, then we are safe to disembark into the ship.'

'Damn,' said Sean. 'I should've let Werrimen take you up there. You could've driven her mad with your questions.'

'Love you too.' Reaching out to pinch his cheek she laughed but she couldn't ignore his misery and once safely docked she helped him out of the transporter to the landing bay where Werrimen and Zadrus waited to take them to a lounge. Werrimen sat beside Jemma, Sean and Zadrus on single chairs opposite.

'We have something we wish to discuss with you both,' said Werrimen.

It again surprised Jemma how comfortable she felt sitting and chatting to Werrimen, just as she would with another human being, despite having collapsed when she'd first met her only a few hours ago.

'We found something in your blood which surprised us, Jemma,' said Werrimen. 'Do you know where your parents were born?'

'Dad was born in Sydney, Mum County Tyrone in Ireland, a town called Omagh.'

'Pardon me for pushing this. Did you ever see birth certificates for them, or for yourself?'

'Well no, I never saw theirs, but I had one. Had to use it at school. I was born in Brisbane. At the Mater Hospital.'

The two aliens exchanged looks.

'You're scaring me,' said Jemma. 'What's this all about?'

Werrimen described her DNA as unusual for someone born on Earth. Nothing unusual about the four types of amines but when they analysed the sub-types that were as yet unknown to Earth scientists, their combinations revealed a problem. They hadn't expected what they found.

She stared back at the aliens. 'What are you trying to tell me?'

'Jemma, every Earth-born human has at least ten percent Neanderthal genes in the DNA. You blood has less than one percent.'

'But that doesn't make sense. Humans and Neanderthals existed in different time frames.'

'No, that is not quite right,' said Werrimen. 'They not only co-existed, they co-habited.'

'Then why did Neanderthals disappear?'

Again, Werrimen shook her head. 'They didn't disappear. As they crossed more and more with humans, who were the stronger of the two species, their offspring took on human characteristics until eventually the characteristic Neanderthal features faded and finally disappeared. You see it today with the weakening of many indigenous people in every country. As other countries invade and intermingle, defining characteristics are weakened.'

'I guess that's true, but I can't believe you're telling me I wasn't born on Earth because I don't have Neanderthal blood.'

'No, not just that. It is the DNA combinations and, there is one other thing. We found minerals in your blood that do not exist on Earth. Do you recall any long-distance flights, even as a small child?'

'No, we flew to Sydney a few times, but I've never even been overseas. Please tell me what your findings mean.' Abnormal DNA for a human born on Earth, and extraterrestrial minerals. What else were they going to come up with?

'Those two things in combination make us think that you were not born on Earth.'

'She has a birth certificate,' said Sean. 'I've seen it and it looks just like mine. None of this makes any sense. Where do you think she comes from?'

'Birth certificates are easy to forge and I'm afraid there are numerous possibilities for her origin. I would like to check your blood too, Sean. We both sensed immediately there was something different about each of you. This might explain it.'

Jemma took a deep breath. 'I can't believe any of this. It

doesn't make sense. Pritchard kept talking about mum having some title. Are you telling me she came from another planet? That she was hiding out here?'

'All possible. We do not have answers. But we will keep working on it.'

Sean frowned. 'Could it have something to do with the community Anthony spoke about, or the guardians?'

Werrimen turned her attention to Sean. 'I don't know yet, but we are seeking information. Now Sean, you fear me.'

To Jemma's surprise, he gripped the base of his chair. 'No,' he replied. 'But you seem to look right through me, ignore my words and tell me what I mean, or why I'm wrong. It's unnerving.'

'You are easy to read.'

'I'm used to keeping my thoughts to myself.'

Jemma watched Zadrus as this conversation unfolded. Werrimen had a plan. She'd thought at first it was for her, but it obviously included Sean, and Zadrus was a party to it. He leaned back in his chair, smiling.

Werrimen smiled too. 'You have more talent than you know, Sean. Part of the reason we were sent to Earth was to find, and develop, human talent. That is my plan for you. In time, we will also work with Jemma, but her health is our first priority.'

Her voice bore no threat, only fact, but her words deepened the mystery, and Jemma wanted much more explanation. 'Why are you here? Please don't misunderstand. I am grateful beyond anything I can express for your help in finding me, and your help now. But we need to know more before we can fully trust you.'

'I intend to be your guide, Jemma, so let me answer,' said Zadrus. He pulled his chair between Jemma and Sean and took one of each of their hands in his. Jemma felt a surge of something rip through her body. It wasn't painful, or frightening. On the contrary, it felt good. Sean jumped. He must have felt it too.

Zadrus sat without speaking for a few moments. 'Jemma, please describe what you felt.'

'I don't know if I can. Warm, calm. Better than I've felt for weeks. What did you do?'

He turned his hands over, both of their hands now resting palm down on his palms. 'I transferred some of my energy to you, because I feel you both need it.'

She frowned. 'When I first met Sean, he touched me, and I felt like an electric shock go through my body. Is that the same thing?'

'I remember that,' said Sean. 'I felt it too.'

'It is similar,' said Zadrus. 'I'd say that's the point where you made a connection. You did not need to feel it again. I have learned to harness my energy and that is what you felt from me. Your experience is encouraging though. You have nothing to fear from us. Mr Everson told you about the Interplanetary League. Our role is to protect our member planets, and primitive planets which can't protect themselves.'

'I take it we're a primitive planet,' said Jemma.

He smiled, 'Yes, my dear, you are, although with our help, you have started to move ahead over the last century. And that is the problem. We have often seen it before. Planets accept our training and agree to our rules, but as they develop their technology, they tend to become overconfident and withdraw the controls that we put in place. The result can be wars, violence, environmental damage, criminal fraud. We have tried to warn your governments, but they won't work with us. We believe Earth is at risk of destroying itself.'

'We all believe that, but what can you do about it?'

'Our mission here is to determine that,' said Zadrus. 'We will talk much more about this over the next few months. But for now, you must start your treatment.'

*   *   *

Sean had intended to sit with Jemma, and talk about their conversation with Zadrus and Werrimen, but she drifted off as soon as the treatment began. So peaceful, he could have sat there for hours watching, but Zadrus had other ideas and invited Sean back to his office.

'We will leave tonight,' said Zadrus. 'It should still be dark enough in Costa Rica for us to go in without being seen.'

They spoke for a considerable time and, once Zadrus had firmed his plans, and Sean had collected Jemma to return to the mountain, it was after 19:00 hours. He sat rigidly beside her on the journey back to Earth, holding her hand. She seemed content resting against his shoulder and dozing. Hunt met the craft and led them to the dining room, where he had dinner set out.

Sean reported his arrangements with Zadrus to take a transporter to Costa Rica that night.

Jemma glared at him. 'Do you know where Anthony is?'

'Sorry Jem, I haven't had a chance to fill you in yet,' said Sean. 'Nik's defining the exact location as we speak.'

'I'd like to go with you,' said Jemma.

'No,' replied Hunt. 'You need daily treatments.'

'What I need is to find Anthony, and you bastards won't let me be involved.'

Sean squeezed her shoulder. 'Steady.'

'We'll ignore the outburst,' said Hunt. 'You need my permission to leave here, and you don't have it.'

'Why?'

'Your lungs are still compromised. If you caught the virus they are playing with, you would die.'

She slumped back in her chair. 'You said you tracked him, and Nik's working on the co-ordinates.'

'Yes,' replied Sean. 'Nik's in the control room and she'll be there throughout the operation. Werrimen will help if she needs it.'

'Then can I work with Nik? At least that way, I might be of some help and I'll know what's happening instead of sitting by myself and worrying.'

Hunt leaned forward towards her. 'Fair enough. Your treatments are a priority as are any tests Werrimen recommends.'

'Okay.'

'I'll be checking on you regularly, and if I tell you to rest or do something else, you'll do so without question.'

'Of course,' she retorted. 'I'm far too immature to take care of myself.'

Sean quickly steered her out of the dining room, and away from Hunt. She was so tired; she'd get herself into hot water if he allowed her to continue.

CHAPTER 18

Sean left Jemma to rest in their apartment, then headed back to the dining room for coffee and to prepare himself for the flight ahead. He didn't realise he'd tightened his fist around the paper cup until coffee shot out, burning his hand and he hadn't recovered when his phone rang. 'Bellamy,' he snapped.

A short silence was followed by an irritated female voice. 'Good morning. I am Dr Therese Morgan from San Jose Hospital in Costa Rica. A patient asked me to call you.'

He flicked the loudspeaker button on the phone and modified his tone. 'Yes, ma'am. What can I do for you?'

'Someone I believe you know, presented here this afternoon. Anthony Chang. He is exhausted but okay. He had another person with him. She has bilateral pneumonia.'

'Yes, I do know him. You must listen to me and do exactly as I say. I am Lieutenant-Colonel Sean Bellamy. They have been held by terrorists and forced to work on a dangerous project. Their illness is highly contagious. Isolate Anthony, the other person and anyone, including yourself and your nurses, who have had contact. If I'm right, their infection is deadly. Can you do that?'

'Yes, I can, but it appears to be an influenza that's deteriorated into pneumonia. We can manage it.'

'Ma'am, I don't mean to tell you how to do your job, but I know what I'm dealing with. How long did it take her to develop that pneumonia from the onset of symptoms?'

'From Dr Chang's description, less than twenty-four hours.'

'I'm on my way. Please isolate them. This infection could escalate to a global catastrophe. You're in the key position to prevent that.'

Sean ran into Hunt's office. 'Just took a call from a hospital in Costa Rica. Anthony's somehow got himself there. He's unwell but he brought another scientist with him who's seriously ill. I'm on my way to meet with Zadrus. We're heading over there.'

Hunt took the details. 'Go. I'll notify my counterpart in Costa Rica. Take O'Leary.'

'Sir.' He ran from Hunt's office and, as he charged past Dan's room, he yelled, 'Dan. With me.' He wasn't even sure if Dan would be there given the time of night, but when he heard a chair scrape, he kept going.

Everson arrived at the landing bay just after them. 'General Hunt filled me in. You need my help.'

Sean nodded. 'Will we bring patients here, or to an American hospital?'

'Neither,' Everson replied. 'Zadrus's ship is their best chance of survival. We can be screened and treated there too.'

The craft entered the landing bay at high speed, slowing

less than ten metres from where they stood. 'Follow me,' called Everson. 'Run underneath, the blue light will draw you up.'

Sean's legs refused to move. Dan grabbed his arm, forcing him to move forward.

'Bloody hell. I don't think I'll ever get used to this,' muttered Sean, as he floated up within the blue light.

'Toughen up,' said Dan. 'At least you've experienced it. It's my first time.'

Sean glared at him but didn't bother answering.

'Seats quickly,' said Everson. 'I don't want anyone standing.' The craft shot out from the runway and lifted vertically at speed.

'Are you okay?' Everson leaned close to Sean, forcing eye contact.

Sean said nothing, but Dan grinned, 'This is awesome.'

'You sound like Jemma.' Sean took in a deep breath before turning to Everson. 'How are we going to land in Costa Rica where no one sees us?'

'That is organised,' said Zadrus, leaving the controls to sit beside Sean. 'Our people in Florida have given me the co-ordinates for a place to land and transport will be waiting.'

Sean groaned as the transporter zipped down, leaving his stomach somewhere in the stratosphere. He kept his focus firmly on the floor until the craft had stabilised on the ground. When he finally looked up, he was shocked to see thick jungle in every direction. If their vehicle didn't arrive, he doubted they'd find their way through it.

Everson pointed to the blue light exit. 'Quickest way. Zadrus and I cannot go with you.'

An ambulance, big enough to carry at least four patients and paramedics, pulled in close and its rear door shot open. Sean and Dan jumped into the back, and were greeted by four soldiers, all armed with automatic weapons.

One of the men held his hand out to Sean. 'We've got a team heading down to the military field. Should know within the hour what's happening there. I haven't notified Costa Rican police or military, but don't know what the hospital's done.'

'I believe my people have notified the appropriate authorities,' replied Sean, shaking the man's hand. 'You're from Florida?'

'Yeah. Just got here.'

The ambulance sped up a rough mountain track that made the Springbrook road seem like a modern highway. Sean welcomed the sight of a bitumen road after the dirt, but it was just as rough. The driver skirted animals in his path, and repeatedly honked at other cars and people walking in the middle of the road.

Relieved, after an hour of rough travel, to see the outskirts of San Jose, he asked the driver to slow. He wanted to see the carpark, gardens and perimeter before going in, and was surprised when the communicator he now carried, lit up, but pleased to see Jemma's face.

'Sean, can you hear me?'

'Loud and clear. Hello Jem.'

'Hello. This feels a bit strange.' She gave a nervous laugh. 'Listen, we've scanned all around the hospital. We can't see Pritchard or any other threat, but Werrimen said be careful, there could be a Norellian sphere around and we might not be able to see it.'

'Thanks sweetheart. Tell her we'll be careful.' He closed the communicator and jumped out at the hospital's front door, then strode to the reception desk. The security manager waited to take them to the doctor's office, a small room at the back of the Emergency Department.

'What the hell is she doing here? I told her everyone who had contact with Anthony or his mate was to be isolated,' growled Sean.

A female voice responded. 'I have stayed away but decided to finish some paperwork. Dr Chang is isolated. His friend is in ICU. I do know how to manage a medical emergency.' Her voice was cool, irritated.

'I doubt you know how to manage this one, ma'am.' He turned to the security manager. 'You need to find a large room, a ward or common room, that can be sealed off. Everyone, including the good doctor here, the nurses, Dr Chang and any guards, including yourself, are to go to that room and stay there. I'll join you once I've organised reinforcements. This hospital is quarantined. Nobody in or out. Notify your ambulance and emergency services you're on bypass.'

'I can't do that without management approval.' The security manager, almost as big as Sean and with the physique of a heavy-weight boxer, stepped forward. Sean signalled to the team from Florida. They immediately aimed their weapons at the man.

'Looks like the boss has spoken,' said Sean, his voice tense. 'I will explain this only once. If this virus gets out, it could wipe out Costa Rica. If it spreads further, it could create a global crisis. Local police are on their way, and I've spoken to the general from your counter-terrorism force. He confirmed this hospital is to be shut down. Anybody who has left here since Anthony and the person he brought in arrived is to be detained by local police. They have been advised.'

'You can't do that. This is a civilian hospital,' said the doctor.

'We've done it, ma'am. This is potentially catastrophic. My name is Sean. I spoke to you on the phone, I believe. This is Dan.'

'What? You can't have spoken to me on the phone. That was only a couple of hours ago. The man I spoke to was in Australia.'

'I didn't say I was in Australia,' he replied, without allowing her time to question him further. 'Many of you will become ill over the next twenty-four hours. It should be a short quarantine, but we must do it.' He turned back to the security manager who still stared at the weapons. 'Do you have a room?'

'Use the staff dining room,' said the doctor. 'Clear everybody out. It's the only place that's big enough. You and your men need to wear protective masks and gowns before you go there. I'll show you where to find them.'

'That was a bit dicey,' said Dan, after she walked away with the manager.

'You're telling me. Police are here. Would have preferred Counterterrorism first, but we'll work with what we get. Just hope they speak English.' He turned to the US contingent. 'Weapons down. We've got reinforcements.'

Sean showed his credentials to the Costa Rican police chief. Fortunately, the woman did speak English. He asked her to secure the building until the military arrived, and to start tracing anyone who'd left. One of the US crew informed Sean the old military base had been raided. Eleven people had been rescued. None of them were associated with the terrorist organisation. They were on their way to the hospital to be isolated. As they spoke two truckloads of Costa Rican soldiers arrived, and their commander walked into the hospital, looking ready to throw his weight around.

'Here we go,' Sean muttered.

Dan responded under his breath, 'We've dealt with worse. Just bluff him.'

The man held out his hand. 'Major Martinez.'

His rank was clearly important to him, and Sean suspected if he stressed his own rank, although not official in this country, he might be able to intimidate the fellow. 'Good afternoon, Major. I am Lieutenant-Colonel Bellamy, and this is Major O'Leary. Pleased to meet you.'

When Sean explained the problem, Martinez, without so much as a blink, ordered his people to station themselves at every hospital entrance, and all the gates. He asked to accompany Sean in case of language difficulties, although Sean suspected it was to keep an eye on him.

Now early morning in Costa Rica, the morning-shift staff had started to arrive, but the police turned them away, and stopped current staff from leaving. With Martinez, securing the perimeter, Sean was satisfied that the hospital was now under control, and he made his way to the isolation room. The noise accelerated when he called for order and someone yelled that she had children at home alone, others had appointments to keep. He acknowledged their concerns and offered assistance but confirmed they would not be permitted to leave until they'd all been cleared of infection, at least forty-eight hours. Sean spotted Anthony sitting alone in a corner. As he made his way over to him, he noticed Martinez scatter his people around the room and motioned to Dan to keep his eyes peeled.

'Are you okay?' said Sean, pulling a chair next to Anthony's.

'Think so. Bit of a headache. Nothing else. Have you heard how Petra is?'

'That's the woman you brought in?'

Anthony nodded.

'She's holding her own,' said the doctor, walking up behind them.

'Thanks,' replied Sean. 'Anthony, were there any other Australians at the base?'

He nodded. 'Two other scientists, a doctor and a nurse. Can't think of their names, sorry. This headache's getting worse.'

'Alright, you've questioned him enough,' said Dr Morgan. 'Ask your men to have some beds brought in here. Anthony needs to lie down. Go on, don't just stare at me, do it.'

'I'll sort that,' said Dan, grinning.

The communicator distracted Sean, stopping him from snapping back.

'Sean, another truck just pulled up,' said Jemma. 'We've checked with police, military and CT. It doesn't belong to any of them.'

'Thanks, sweetheart, I'll get Everson's US team onto it.'

'Good. Do you call all your colleagues, sweetheart … honey?'

'No, ma'am. I'll be much more formal in the future.' Sean handed the communicator to Anthony, mildly surprised when he accepted it without questioning what it was. Presumably, he'd seen Pritchard using one. Sean sat back to think through his next move, and to allow Anthony to chat to Jemma.

*   *   *

Hunt had leaned on the back wall behind Jemma and Nik, during Jemma's exchange with Sean, impressed that their focus on the task had made them oblivious to his presence. He also liked the way they worked together making decisions, deciding which sightings mattered and where to shift their attention. Both women had potential for extraordinary futures but when Jemma gently chided Sean, he couldn't hold back the laugh.

She waited until she'd ensured Anthony was okay then, hands on hips, glared at Hunt. 'Can I help you? As you can see, I'm quite busy.'

'Good to see. Perhaps you could fill me in.' Hunt replied, working hard to control his amusement when she whirled back to Nik and told her to keep scanning while she brought the general up to speed. Even though Nik had greater technical expertise with the alien technology he'd thought Jemma might emerge as the leader, but he hadn't expected it quite this quickly.

'What would you like to know, General?' She drew out the word, General.

He stood a little closer, his hands behind his back, invading her space just enough to make her step back although her defiant look made it clear she hadn't accepted yet that he was the boss. She had to learn to respond to him quickly, without resentment, but he didn't want to dampen any of her enthusiasm or to stop her from questioning and making her own decisions. His problem was that he had to bring her around quickly in case something else happened that he couldn't control.

'Well,' he replied. 'Perhaps you could tell me what you're trying to achieve, how you're going about it, and any progress you've made.' She started to say something until she looked into his eyes. Then she stopped and her eyes flicked away from his, just for a second, but that was enough for him to know that he was getting through. In response, he sat and pointed to a chair opposite.

'Werrimen said to look for Norellian spheres and anyone hiding, acting suspiciously or making trouble for the police,' said Jemma. 'We searched the clearing where the transporter landed, and the hospital, and a wide circumference around each.'

'Good.' He was impressed by her capacity to tell the story succinctly yet with all the necessary information. 'And what have you found?'

'We haven't seen a sphere anywhere near the hospital, but there has been one hovering near the transporter. Werrimen notified Zadrus, and Nik spoke to Everson.'

'Just a minute. Do you mean to tell me two of my most senior agents are at risk and you didn't consider including me in the loop?' Now Jemma looked flustered and he had to remind himself that she wasn't one of his staff and, as yet, probably didn't understand the chain of command.

'I'm sorry,' she stuttered.

'No, I apologise. I should have given better instructions on how I wanted you to operate.'

She glanced at Nik, and then, the screen. 'Dear God, Anthony's getting worse.'

When she looked back at him, her glistening eyes drove home her vulnerability and he put his arm around her shoulders. 'I'm sorry, Jemma. In the heat of the moment I forgot your situation. Are you sure you're okay to be here?'

'I'm best here,' she replied. 'At least this way I know what's going on.'

'Right, what can I do to help you?'

Jemma stared back at him. 'Umm, I'm not sure. Perhaps

you could establish a link with Zadrus. That way we'd know what's happening at both locations in Costa Rica.'

'Good idea. You go back to your tasks. I'll contact him.'

*   *   *

An irritated US team leader told Sean the truck that had just arrived was his, but it had a couple of Homeland Security agents on board, which clearly didn't please him. Sean bristled too, even though he'd expected that to happen at some point. They'd have to ensure that Homeland didn't get even the slightest hint of the aliens or their craft. Political reaction in the US was currently too volatile and unpredictable. He couldn't do much from the isolation room, so he reported to Hunt then settled in to wait along with everyone else for the others to arrive from the camp.

Anthony's fellow prisoners all appeared well on arrival and given they'd have been exposed at the same time as him, Sean hoped that meant they'd escaped the virus. But Anthony was now clearly deteriorating, as was the doctor.

'Change of plan,' he said to Dan. 'We can't wait. Tell Everson we're on our way. I'll get the patient in ICU. You organise Anthony and the doctor. The Florida team can help.'

He grabbed his communicator and headed for the door. 'Jemma.'

'Yes,' she replied. 'Something wrong?'

'We're heading out. Can you scan around for threats again please?'

'We haven't stopped. Is there anything in particular that you're worried about?'

'No, I want to be aware of any threats. Can you notify Everson we're coming?'

'Okay, I'll let you know if we see any problems.'

'Thanks.' He paused. 'Sweetheart.' But he shut down the connection before she could respond.

The military commander followed him to ICU. Sean didn't know if he planned to help or intended to stop him. Several staff tried to intervene but, to his surprise, the commander held them back. One of the nurses, who must have realised he would take Petra regardless of their protests, helped him secure the fluids and remove unnecessary apparatus. Within minutes, he had Petra on a gurney, and he raced her out of the ICU, down in the lift, and out through the ambulance entry. Two of the US contingent waiting inside the ambulance helped him load her. The other two patients were already on board.

He gave the signal to go, then watched helplessly as all three patients deteriorated on the long journey back over the rough, winding mountain road. He'd have preferred to have the alien craft come in closer, but given the Homeland presence at the hospital, he didn't dare suggest it. Even now, he couldn't be absolutely sure they hadn't been followed, although the Florida contingent didn't seem to think so, and he knew Jemma and Nik would be watching.

When they reached the transporter, Everson waited underneath, and Sean glimpsed Zadrus inside. Petra, unconscious, went first. Anthony, now delirious, next, then the doctor, who was still semi-conscious. She had to be restrained by Dan until Zadrus could administer a sedative.

Zadrus and Everson worked hard to stabilise the patients until darkness descended and the craft could safely leave. To Sean's dismay, it again shot vertically up. Although he trusted Zadrus, his transition from no idea of aliens on Earth, to working directly with them, seemed to have happened at the same breathtaking speed as the spaceship now hurtling up beyond Earth's atmosphere

He sat back in his seat and attempted to clear his mind, to think of other things and shut everything else out, including Everson's stare. Since he'd started working with the man, their relationship had warmed. Everson had been more helpful than Sean could ever repay in finding Jemma, but that didn't make him feel any better in this damned alien craft.

'Sean,' said Everson. He leaned across and placed his hand on Sean's knee. 'Look at me.' He waited a moment but when Sean didn't respond his voice and his grip hardened. 'Look at me, Colonel Bellamy.'

Sean forced himself to turn; he didn't want to be bothered, but Everson would pull rank if he ignored him.

'Keep looking at me. I have travelled on these craft, and even smaller ones, thousands of times. You are safe. Stop thinking about it. Focus on something else.'

Other heads turned in their direction when Everson raised his voice, and Dan moved away from the window to join them. They kept him talking for the rest of the flight, forcing him to respond, although he doubted anything that he said made sense. They didn't seem to care so long as he answered them. When he finally stepped onto the mothership's landing bay floor, he found Everson and thanked him.

'Happy to help. Don't worry, you'll get used to it.'

Sean doubted that. Being in the transporter reminded him of his ninth birthday. His father had taken him up in an experimental aircraft, well above normal commercial flight levels. Something had happened and they'd dropped thousands of feet. Sean had passed out and vomited into his helmet. He spent almost a week in hospital after the episode. They said he'd aspirated, and that had caused pneumonia. He'd coped since by avoiding jets, didn't even like commercial flights although he managed them, but this transporter was a whole different ball game.

CHAPTER 19

Sidlown medical teams whisked each of the patients from the transporter. Sean's stomach clenched when he saw the tube running from Anthony's mouth, just like the one that had helped Jemma breathe after the fire. Yet, apart from that, almost everything was different in this highly advanced world. Metal bars, the size of ballpoint pens, sat on both Anthony's arms, although Sean couldn't see how they were attached. A fluid-filled tube ran from a spherical device that floated above the stretcher to the bar on his left arm. A small screen showed a single line that moved rhythmically up and down.

Suddenly, Anthony gasped for air. He pulled at the tube in his mouth, which triggered an alarm. An attendant clamped Anthony's arms while another attached a tiny cylinder to the top of the bar on his right arm. Within seconds, the smooth rhythm of his breathing resumed.

'He is good now,' said Zadrus.

Sean let out a breath he hadn't realised he'd been holding and moved closer to the unconscious Anthony. He dreaded how he would tell Jemma if Anthony didn't survive. Zadrus directed him to the disc that would take them to the medical centre and Anthony's stretcher floated alongside. It had no legs or wheels and he couldn't see how it operated. Even though he'd experienced the disc before, he stiffened when their surroundings faded. Zadrus touched his arm and the warm, calm sensation he'd felt the previous day flooded his body.

When everything cleared, he recognised the medical floor where Jemma had had her treatment. There'd been no sense of movement on the disc, yet they were clearly on a different floor. He was still shaking his head when Dan arrived with Everson beside Petra's stretcher. Together, they followed each of the stretchers into their separate treatment rooms and waited until the Sidlown attendants reported that their patients were stable.

Everson, who until that point had been hovering, now moved in front of Sean. 'You must come with me now. I don't want you developing symptoms.'

'Just a bit longer,' said Sean. 'I need to know more about the condition of the patients.'

'Two minutes, no more. You have done all you can.'

Dan tapped his shoulder, 'Come on, mate. Mr Everson's clear we're at risk too. There's nothing we can do here.'

'We must leave them with the crew now,' Everson said gently. 'You and O'Leary have had more exposure to the virus, over a longer time, than either Zadrus or myself. Your treatment is urgent.'

Sean took one last look at each of the patients then reluctantly followed Everson. He threw himself on a lounge chair, attached the eye protection Everson handed him and sat quietly throughout the antivirus treatment. When it was finished, and he'd removed his eye protectors, Zadrus leaned towards him.

'There is something else I must tell you. My scientists are working to determine the nature of this virus. This area of the ship is now isolated, and you must wait here until we are cleared. Use your communicator to contact General Hunt if you wish.'

After he'd spoken to his boss, Sean sighed and leaned back, so exhausted his eyes drooped shut but he didn't realise he'd dozed off until Dan shook him.

'No further viruses detected,' said Zadrus, with a smile. 'Please join me now. I will take you back to the landing bay and your transport home.' He led them back to the disc.

Each other time Sean had been in the landing bay he'd been too pre-occupied to take much notice, but this time he looked around. The large transporter Zadrus had used the day they met took up almost a quarter of the floor. Parked on each side were three smaller transporters but, it was the area closest to where they stood, that captured Sean's attention. Twelve tiny crafts, around five metres in length and two metres wide, each of which would hold one or two people, were parked in rows. Zadrus described them as fighters, rarely used, but available if needed. He started to move on.

Sean didn't follow. He gripped Dan's arm and gaped at the fighters. 'Could one of these have been on Earth ... around twenty years ago?'

'Most ships have them,' replied Zadrus. 'It is possible one might have been down there for some reason.'

'I think I've been on one.'

'Tell me about it,' said Zadrus.

'My father took me up in an aircraft on my ninth birthday. I'd always thought it was a jet, but it wasn't. It was one of these. Something happened. I don't know what, but I got sick, aspirated and spent a week in hospital with pneumonia.'

'That explains your fear of the transporters.'

'But how the hell did he get it?'

'We must find that out. It may give us the information we need.'

Sean walked along the line of fighter craft. 'There's more. I've had this vague sense of familiarity in the transporters and on this ship. When I thought I was in hospital, could I have been here? As a child?'

'Not this ship, but most of our ships have a similar design. Your recognition, even though vague, tends to verify our findings. Let me investigate and see what I can find.

Sean did his best to appear confident as he floated up in the blue light to the transporter. Everson ordered him to sit close to the middle of the craft and kept him talking as they began their journey.

'Zadrus told me about the fighter craft,' said Everson.

'Yeah, I don't understand how my father had access, but I know it was one of them.'

'We will try to find out. Knowing about it helps and probably explains your fear.'

'Hey, come here. Look at this,' yelled Dan.

Sean gritted his teeth and walked with Everson to the

window, stunned to see a Norellian sphere travelling alongside their transporter. Too far out of his comfort zone to know what to do, he looked for Everson who was speaking to someone on his communicator. His free hand punched the air as he spoke. Within minutes, six of the small IPL fighter craft had fallen into a formation and surrounded the sphere.

An image of Pritchard suddenly replaced their view outside the craft. 'Mr Bellamy, Mr O'Leary, I'm sure you know by now that I am Fredrick Pritchard. It is my intention to liberate you, Dr Anderson, and the rest of our community from the IPL. They may pretend they are here to help but will attack and destroy this planet just as they did ours.'

Everson stood close to the image of Pritchard. 'What is your planet?'

'Silence,' yelled Pritchard. 'I do not speak to the enemies of my people. Now Mr Bellamy, I suggest if you value the safety of your community, that you lead your people out of SCARF. We will rescue you as soon as you are clear.'

Sean kept his tone polite, his fear of space temporarily forgotten as he focused on Pritchard. 'It is important to me, if I come from another planet, to know which one. Could you please tell me?'

Pritchard smiled. 'As soon as you are free of our enemies, I will explain everything. You must save your people, Mr Bellamy. I will be waiting for you outside SCARF tomorrow morning.'

'Shut it down,' growled Everson to his pilot.

'I'll be waiting,' yelled Pritchard, before his image disappeared.

'Gentleman,' said Everson, pointing to the chairs in the middle of the floor. 'What did you think of that?'

Dan spoke first. 'Are you going to deny destroying his planet?'

Everson's head dropped forward, and he sighed. 'Unfortunately, I don't know which is his planet, so I have no idea of the history but, even if I did, and I were to deny his allegations, why would you believe me? I suggest you get together as a group, with General Hunt, and draw your own conclusions.'

Sean watched Everson's body language and eye movements during this exchange. All he saw was exhaustion and frustration, no subterfuge. Everson, Zadrus and Werrimen had all worked hard to help him find both Jemma and Anthony and they were still helping. 'Sir, I have no reason to believe anything Pritchard says. I don't know what else to say.'

When they landed, Hunt stood in the entry. 'I've heard.' He directed them to a small conference room. Jemma, Tom and Nik were already there. Jemma flew to Sean, launching herself into his arms.

'I'd tell you to get a room, but I need both of you here now,' said Hunt, smiling. 'Zadrus said that you retrieved those people just in time. I'd planned this to be a celebration.' He held up a bottle of champagne and pointed to six glasses on the table. 'I guess that's changed but I think we could all use a drink.'

Sean accepted a glass and took a sip, but then put it down.

He couldn't relax yet. They'd rescued three young, fit people from Costa Rica who'd succumbed to the virus within hours. How would the elderly or young children fare? It had to be stopped, and no matter how long it took, Pritchard would pay for what he'd done to Jemma. Sean repeated Pritchard's message for those who hadn't heard.

'I need your views on whether to trust Everson and the IPL,' said Sean.

'You can't trust Pritchard,' Jemma said quietly. 'I don't care what planet he comes from, he's a criminal. He's happy to abduct people and doesn't care who he kills.'

'I agree,' said Dan. 'I'm as shocked as anyone to find aliens here on Earth, but Sean, we both know that without Zadrus, Jemma and Anthony would be dead. The virus is clearly ready to be released, so we have to stop him, and our only hope to do that is with the aliens' help.'

Hunt nodded. 'I agree. None of us have any reason not to trust the IPL, but we do have ample evidence against Pritchard.'

'Alright, we're all on the same page,' said Sean. 'My problem is I don't have much to go on. Counterterrorism in Costa Rica didn't get much from the other captives. Pritchard hasn't been seen in the US since he came to our attention and he's got everyone from the FBI to Homeland Security after him. They've questioned all the vice-presidents of Pritchard Pharmaceuticals and got nothing. Several of them remembered Anthony but none of them knew he was still working with Pritchard. We've had no luck finding the mechanic from

Archerfield, even though I've got the local police onto him as well.'

'They're a bloody elusive lot,' said Hunt. 'I think we may just have to wait for Pritchard to show his hand. I have no doubt he will. We'll ask Zadrus to help with surveillance in case he does show up in the morning.'

Sean sat back in his chair and sighed. Dan was right, they'd need help from the aliens, but other than that, all they could do was wait.

'Sir,' said Nik, looking at Sean, but keeping an eye on Hunt. 'I'm keen to be actively involved, to be part of the bigger picture, not just the tech stuff.'

'Okay.' Sean had scrutinised both Nik's and Tom's reactions during the discussion, confident now that both were loyal. Nik's request helped him decide his first course of action. If he did find a way to go after Pritchard, he'd need all his staff to be fit and ready, and even Tom looked well below his top form. 'Alright,' he said. 'Let's start with fitness.'

Hunt nodded, then stood, 'Jemma, come with me. We have a few things to discuss.'

'But I want to be part of this investigation. Maybe I could take over the *tech stuff*.'

'Absolutely, but I want to talk to you first.'

'Go on, Jem,' said Sean. 'We'll talk later.' He smiled when she glared at him, but he had to get back to working with his staff and he knew Hunt had recognised that. He'd sort it out with her later. He waved Dan, Tom and Nik to chairs, then stood in front of them. 'Nik, I know Dan and

Tom well, but I don't really know you yet, or your capacity. Are you prepared to prove yourself to me while we wait for something to happen with Pritchard?' That was the kind of thing Hunt would say, and he couldn't believe it had just come out of his mouth.

'Anything you say.' She sounded excited.

He liked her attitude. 'Right, I need to do something physical to clear my head. I like to run. How fit are you?'

'Haven't done much for a while, but I'll do my best to keep up.'

'Alright, let's go for a ten-kilometre run down the mountain tomorrow.'

'I'm sure I can do that.'

'Then the same ten kilometres back up.'

She grimaced slightly. 'I think I can manage that.'

'Fair go. It's bloody hot out there,' said Dan.

Sean snapped, far too tired to deal with backchat, even though he knew Dan's outburst was about protecting Nik. 'That'll be fair go, sir, and you just made it fifteen kilometres each way. You can show her how to do it, given you're so concerned. I'm told this whole bloody unit's slack and that includes you, Lambert, so you can join them too.'

Tom glared at Dan. 'Thanks,' he mouthed.

Dan obviously hadn't got the message. 'Are you serious?' There was a pause. 'Sir.' His eyes narrowed as he stared back at Sean.

'I'm deadly serious. Would anyone else like to grumble? I'm happy to make it twenty kilometres each way.'

There was a chorus of, 'No, sir,' but Dan still looked savage.

'Clean skin, first up. Shorts, t-shirt, runners and at least two water bottles each. Meet at the stairs, 0600 tomorrow morning, ready to go.'

He walked out of the room, unaware Hunt had returned until he spoke, the last person Sean wanted to deal with now.

'Bellamy wait up. I've ordered a meal, and a stiff cup of coffee to be brought up to you. My office in half an hour. Sharp.'

Christ, he needed sleep, not another meeting, but he couldn't growl at Hunt. He had his meal, then knocked on Hunt's door at the allotted time. 'You wanted to see me.'

'Come in. Shut the door. Grab a seat. What was that all about, with O'Leary?'

'I told Nik she'd have to prove herself if she wanted to be more involved, and set up a run for tomorrow morning,' said Sean. 'Dan objected, so I squashed him. Then I thought a bit more and told them they could all do it.'

'So, what do you plan to do? You'll need a support vehicle. Will you be in it?'

'No, the PE Sergeant can do that. Assess how they're going. I'll lead them in the run. I genuinely do need some exercise to clear my head. My only concern is what to do if Pritchard does show up. I'm too far out of my league with the aliens.'

'Agreed. I've spoken to Zadrus and he plans to be closeby tomorrow morning in a transporter. He has plans on how to deal with Pritchard, but he hasn't explained them to me.'

'Okay, I guess we have to leave that to him.'

'Yes, I think we do,' said Hunt. 'You need some sleep now though.'

'Yes, I do.'

'Take one of the visitor's rooms. I've already informed Jemma that's what you'll be doing.'

'Yeah, okay.'

'I'm not surprised Denis wants to work with you,' said Hunt, smiling. 'Williamson gave her a difficult time. He was a plodding misogynist fool.'

'And I thought it was my innate charm,' Sean muttered.

With a shake of his head, Hunt continued, 'You lost your temper with O'Leary. Not ideal, but it won't hurt him. Push them all. Find out what they're made of. God knows what skills we're going to need in the next few months. Make your peace with O'Leary but be clear he's to lift his game. He can be to Denis, and maybe Lambert, like you've been to him. Now, go and get some sleep.'

'Sir.' Sean's head swam, desperate to hit the sack but he knew it'd be better to sort it out with Dan straight away rather than let it fester overnight. He laughed to himself when he thought about the language they'd be using, to describe him. Probably the same as he'd have used about Hunt but, when he found them, they weren't swearing, they weren't saying much at all, just staring at each other.

'O'Leary, my office,' he said, turning on his heel. Dan followed quickly looking worried, which Sean didn't enjoy seeing. Dan shouldn't have interfered, but normally he'd have handled it very differently. 'Pull up a chair.'

Dan said nothing but did as he was told.

'I owe you an apology, I overreacted,' said Sean. 'Don't relax. It's your role to support me with junior officers, not question what I tell them to do. At least not in front of them.'

Dan nodded. 'Okay, you're right, but Tom's not actually junior to me. I apologise too. I knew you were tired. I should have sought you out later.'

'Yes, you should, and from here on, that's what you'll do. You might be the same rank as Tom, but you are definitely my 2IC. I don't object to you questioning me, so long as you do it privately. I value your judgement, we've been mates for a long time, but we have to play it differently now. We both have to start behaving like senior officers even if we relax when it's just us. Do you understand me?'

'I do.' There was a long pause, and a big grin on Dan's face, 'Sir.'

'Get out of here. Tomorrow morning, I want to push Nik. And I need you to beat Tom. Don't let me down. Okay?'

'Sure, now would you please go and get some sleep. Lock yourself in. Your mood's dangerous.'

Sean ran after him, pretending to throw a punch. 'Let's just see this as officer training. We've got to work with these buggers, might as well start pushing them now. Tell Nik and Tom to have their junior officers join us. They've got four lieutenants between them.'

Sean arrived fifteen minutes early the next morning, pleased to see Dan, Nik and Tom already there, stretching and checking on their staff.

'Alright, everyone outside,' said Sean. 'The support car will start following us once we get to the road. Go.'

Sean and Dan led out, and the pack stayed close together for the downhill run, but when they turned to head back up the mountain, he noticed Dan had dropped behind although he didn't appear distressed. He smiled when he saw that Dan was helping Nik struggle up the hill and he dropped back beside them. 'Something wrong?'

'Nik isn't coping. I'm helping her.'

'I'm sure you'd enjoy that but leave her to me. You manage the rest of them.'

Dan scowled, but Sean waved him away then dropped back beside Nik. 'Problem, captain?'

'No. I fell back, and I'm trying to catch up.'

Good answer, but she obviously was in difficulty. 'Pace yourself against me, and forget the pack for the moment?'

'Okay.'

About five kilometres up the mountain, she fell, her face scarlet. Sean called for the support car. 'How much water have you had to drink?'

'Some.'

'Show me your water bottle.'

She pulled it off her belt. It was still around three quarters full.

'You should have completed your first bottle by now. Are you unwell?'

She shook her head. 'I'm less fit than I thought I was.'

Sean perched against a fence to wait for her to recover. As

he stretched his neck and back to stay loose, he spotted the Norellian sphere, moving slowly across the top of the mountain. He grabbed Nik's arm, 'Up there.'

She followed his gaze and nodded, still struggling to catch her breath. 'Pritchard?'

'I'd say. He said he'd be here this morning.' Sean notified Hunt, then returned his focus to getting his team safely up that hill.

He called Dan to take charge from the front and once Nik's face had returned to a more normal colour, he put the aliens out of his mind.

'Right. On your feet, Denis. You're not getting a free ride.' She wobbled as she stood, but he was confident she could keep going and he didn't consider it in her best interests to let her give in. The sergeant agreed, but stayed with them, in case Sean needed help.

'Alright, take off. Keep up with me.' He ran beside her at half pace, aiming to stay just slightly faster, and every few minutes he told her to drink some water. She seemed to get into a rhythm beside him, and her pace improved.

At the top, as they started to head through the carpark, the Norellian sphere re-appeared. The base of the sphere lit up with the now familiar blue light.

'Nik, run.' They still had a couple of kilometres to get to safety. He grabbed her arm and propelled her forward. Seconds later, the sergeant ran from behind and took her other arm. Nik tripped when a beam of light hit the track in front of them. The men lifted her up and zig-zagged around the beam. They continued the same way until they reached the granite boulder. Sean pushed Nik down the stairs then sat her down. Her face was bright red, and she was heaving for air.

Once her breathing slowed, he told her to hit the showers. Now nearly an hour late to meet with Hunt, he asked a female sergeant to check on her, then ran in for a quick shower himself before heading to Hunt's office.

CHAPTER 20

Jemma waited on the edge of her seat in Hunt's office, with Everson and Werrimen, for Sean to return. He was long overdue.

'The chief's late,' said Hunt, when he joined them. 'Just as well, given Bellamy's been held up.'

Jemma jerked forward. 'Is something wrong?'

'No, no, nothing like that. He's been delayed, but that gives us a chance to talk. Mr Everson would like to discuss something with you.'

'Jemma,' said Everson, 'I believe Sean told you about Pritchard's statement to us yesterday on our way back here?'

'Yes.'

Everson exchanged a look with Werrimen. An entire conversation seemed to pass between them although neither spoke. Finally, Werrimen nodded.

'Are you aware that, like Zadrus and Werrimen, I have sworn allegiance to the Interplanetary League?'

'Yes,' replied Jemma.

'Therein lies our problem,' said Everson. 'Many of the alien humans here on Earth do not have any such allegiance. I believe Pritchard to be one of them.'

'I'd already gathered that.'

Hunt stood and walked around the desk to her. 'But, do you understand the implications of that, Jemma, particularly in terms of working out who we can trust?'

'I think so. If we all look the same, there's no way to determine who's friend and who's foe.'

'Exactly. We identified a traitor here the day you arrived. Were you aware of that?'

She nodded. 'That's why Sean's now the commanding officer.'

'We have some more information on that person that I believe may be important to you.' Hunt nodded to Werrimen to continue the story.

'Sean gave me a cup Williamson had used, that he thought might hold the man's DNA,' said Werrimen. 'Our analysis shows that Williamson is not from Earth, and his origins might be the same as yours. He has similar minerals in his blood. General Hunt and I plan to question him later.'

Jemma shuddered. 'So, if Pritchard was telling the truth about coming from another planet, he might also have been telling the truth about my parents' death.'

'I'm afraid so,' replied Werrimen.

'Has Sean explained to you that, with our old team joining us here at SCARF, we will have an integrated army unit that will be devoted to your safety,' said Hunt.

Jemma gaped at him, 'Why?'

'I don't have answers Jemma. I hope the chief is about to explain.'

'So, do I. This is crazy.'

'I understand, but if Williamson is linked with Pritchard, we don't know how many of them have infiltrated and it's now even more imperative that we teach you to defend yourself,' said Hunt.

'Not yet though,' exclaimed Sean, walking through the door. 'She's not up to it.' He pulled his chair next to Jemma's.

'I disagree,' said Hunt. 'Werrimen has determined she is ready to start.'

Before either of them responded, another man walked into the room, dressed the same as Sean and Hunt. Both men stood straight and stiff as they greeted him. She hadn't yet worked out their ranks, but Hunt's shoulder sported a sword and scabbard and a pip. This man also had a sword and scabbard, plus a crown and two pips. Must have been something higher than Hunt.

'As you were,' the man said, then he greeted Everson and Werrimen before turning towards Jemma.

'Jemma,' said Hunt. 'I'd like you to meet General Harris, chief of the Australian Defence Force,' said Hunt. 'Sir, this is Dr Jemma Anderson.'

'I'm very pleased to meet you again, Dr Anderson. Alex, I'd like Major O'Leary and Captain Denis to join us please, and my son.'

'Certainly sir,' replied Hunt, and left to get them.

'Again?' said Jemma.

'Yes, we met when you were quite young. You may not remember.'

'I think I do. Vaguely.'

Both looked up as Hunt returned, 'They're on their way, sir.'

Harris nodded, then continued. 'Werrimen, you and Mr Everson know me as your liaison here on Earth but there is another layer. Those of us who know about it have maintained a strict silence on the orders of our Ruler, but I will now fill you in and would have done so sooner if I'd known that Pritchard, who I know as Drick, was still around.'

'I have heard that name before,' said Werrimen. 'I just cannot place it.'

'I'll explain as soon as the others arrive.'

Dan and Nik walked in, both looking stiff and formal and greeted the chief, then quickly moved to the other side of Sean, Nik doing her best to hide behind the two men. But Tom looked annoyed as he walked up to the chief and, standing directly in front of him, said, 'Hello, Dad.'

Beside her, Jemma felt Sean stiffen again. 'Dad?'

'Yeah, yeah. I took my mother's name when I joined the army. I didn't want to just be my father's son, but that's wrecked now, isn't it?' said Tom, glaring at his father.

'Alright Tom, your sensitivities can't be our priority now,' interjected the chief.

'Thanks,' muttered Tom.

The chief ignored him. 'A decision was taken when most of you were still children to withhold information regarding your origin until each of you turned thirty.' The chief turned to Hunt, 'In your case Alex, we were also waiting for Sean to reach the appropriate age which he now has. Let me tell you the story from the beginning. None of you in this room are from Earth.'

Jemma held Sean's hand as the chief launched into a story of turmoil on his home planet. Our Supreme Ruler made the decision to evacuate the most important members of the planet's ruling houses to a safe planet until the trouble passed.

'Ruling houses?' said Jemma.

'We have three ruling houses. Kilkinan is the upper house and rules over all of our planet. Bellear is the security house and Xander, the house of the guardians. There are a couple of lesser houses, but they don't affect us.'

'I knew the guardians were important,' muttered Hunt.

'Yes,' replied the chief. 'It's best if I tell you what happened in chronological order. That way the purpose of each house will become clear.'

'A security party from Bellear, led by General Bellamy, your father Sean, came here first. I was his deputy. We arrived in 1990, when you and your sister were almost two years old. General Bellamy approached the government of the day, and we were eased into army positions. That gave us legitimate power here.'

'Just a minute,' snapped Sean. 'You're telling us that you just walked into the Prime Minister and said g'day, we're here, give us a job in your army, but it's got to be a top one.'

The chief laughed. 'Not quite. We'd been in touch with Earth's governments for several months. There are open channels between governments of various planets for regular communication.'

'Oh, come on,' said Sean. 'We've never even had an official radio signal arrive on Earth from another planet. Now you're saying they chat regularly.'

'You've met Zadrus and Werrimen,' said that chief. 'I think you accept Mr Everson is from another planet. All the while your government denies any knowledge of life on other planets. Do you really believe that's all they're denying?'

'I guess.' Sean leaned back in his chair. 'So, my father really was a general.'

'Oh yes. And he was military long before we came here. I'm surprised you didn't know. I suppose you were so young when he died.'

'Yes, I was. But why here? Why didn't you go to one of the superpower countries if you were after protection?'

'We weren't after protection. We provided our own security. Australia was considered a safe haven, as well as a very pleasant destination.'

When Sean trembled, Jemma saw anger not fear. She squeezed his hand. The chief described the attack on Sean's father in East Timor in 1998. They'd identified Drick as the perpetrator and removed him to a technologically primitive planet.

'Like Earth,' muttered Jemma.

The chief smiled. 'No, much less advanced.'

But Jemma didn't hear. Pritchard had murdered Sean's father as well as her parents. Who else? She felt Sean's arm come around her and looked up at him. He pulled her in close and rested his head on hers. Nobody spoke.

'We believed Drick was safely contained on a planet, in another sector, and ceased surveillance on him in 2010.'

Jemma couldn't quite read the look on Werrimen's face as she stepped forward, but her voice sounded angry. 'What is your planet?'

'Anders Major.'

'Oh, I see,' replied Werrimen. 'And to what sector did you send Drick?'

He dropped his eyes and sighed. 'Sector two. We thought it was far enough. Clearly not.'

'No, clearly not. I am familiar with Anders history and this explains a great deal. But I have one more question. You said you belong to the security house?'

The chief nodded, and at the same time averted his gaze from Werrimen's glare.

'You must be a Trustee and, I suspect given your seniority, a Supreme Trustee?'

'Yes, ma'am.'

Jemma eased closer to Sean, as Werrimen's voice took on a more menacing tone. 'Then can you explain to me why the IPL was not notified of this situation?'

'Ma'am, I have no excuse. We believed we had it covered. Clearly, we didn't.'

'Again, clearly not,' snarled Werrimen. 'The IPL is already searching for Drick. What else do we not know?'

The contorted expression on Werrimen's face left Jemma with no doubt that the chief's failure to notify the IPL wouldn't end there. Harris took a moment to compose himself, then confirmed that Sean had been fast-tracked through the ranks so that he could eventually assume his father's position, as was his birthright.

Werrimen exploded. 'Don't you think if that was to be his role, he should have been introduced to us much earlier for Trustee training?'

'Yes, but we felt he'd suffered so much we didn't move in that direction.' Harris paused and stared at the ceiling. 'I realise now that we made a mistake. Sean, there is something else, and I don't know how to tell you this, other than to say it directly. Your father was ordered by our Ruler to hand his second son over to his cousin to raise. It was intended to ensure that one of the children would survive if your family was ever attacked.'

Sean stood, knocking papers off the general's desk as he moved towards the chief. 'So, the conversation General Hunt overheard was true. I do have a brother, and you stole him from my mother?'

'Yes,' replied the chief, unable to maintain eye contact with Sean. 'We did as we were ordered. Your brother is standing behind you. Ironically, it was my son's injury and evacuation from Afghanistan which allowed me to bring you together.'

Sean whirled around to Dan who stared back at him. Neither of them moved.

It was eventually Jemma who broke the silence. 'I always thought you two looked like brothers. Sean, we can't change what these people did to you and Dan, but now that you know, you can at least greet each other.'

Sean's stare was blank when he looked at her, and he still didn't move.

'Damn it,' said Dan, and he reached out to Sean and forced him into an embrace.

'We should have been told. Hell, we should have grown up together,' growled Sean, once they'd parted.

'Looking back, I agree,' sighed the chief. 'We were so well indoctrinated, and I include your father in this, we always obeyed our Ruler.'

'And to hell with our needs,' shouted Sean. 'Or our mother's needs.'

'I know.' The chief went on to explain that the people of Anders Major saw the people of Earth, including Sean's mother, as a useful gene pool, so primitive that they'd welcome the offer to come to a much better way of life on Anders. He presented his society as arrogant rather than evil.

Jemma rejected his interpretation when she heard that Sean and Dan's mother had been abducted from Earth a year before Sean was born and forced to marry his father. She was pregnant with Dan when they came to Earth together. Her views were considered primitive and irrelevant. 'Why didn't they take Sean's sister?'

'You're asking if they were sexist. No, Sean's sister was considered, but in the turmoil of the move the twins were left together too long, and by the time they'd settled here, there was another baby on the way.'

Stunned by their cold, calculated thinking, Jemma sat back, waiting for whatever else was to come. Her hand remained on Sean's arm and she could feel his tension rising, coiling, ready to spring.

'I have no doubt my mother loved my father,' said Sean. 'We were a happy family until dad was injured. But all my life I've seen pain in her eyes. Now I know why.'

The chief sighed, 'Your father was a decent man, Sean. He courted your mother. It was her choice to marry him and they were devoted to each other. When your father died, she knew that she, and you and your sister, would be next. She demanded intervention from the guardians, then removed herself to ensure your safety. After that she suffered a breakdown. Your mother loves you dearly, but she lost the capacity to deal with it. She is still in therapy.'

'For Christ's sake,' snarled Sean. 'If I'd known any of this, I could have helped her as I got older. I thought she didn't care about us, so I left her to contact us when she wanted.' He looked at both Jemma and Dan. 'Even worse, Dan's mother is alive, and he's never had the opportunity to meet her. I could have brought them together. What you've done to us is unpardonable.'

'We thought that too dangerous,' said the chief.

'So, who the hell are you to play God like that?' Sean reeled around to Hunt. 'And you're not innocent either. If you'd told me what you knew earlier, I could have talked to her, maybe helped her.'

The chief started to admonish Sean, but Hunt raised his hand. 'No, we've all held back believing we were protecting others, but if we'd spoken up and been open with each other, we might have prevented the current situation.'

Jemma did her best to comfort Sean and saw Nik doing the same for Dan. Both women jumped when Werrimen thumped her fist on a filing cabinet behind Hunt's desk.

'Why were we not informed? Your manipulation of these people has been unimaginably cruel. I should strip you of your trustee status right now. You know that I am Supreme Commander in Chief and the most senior IPL leader in this sector. You were required to make yourself known to me, and to my predecessor.'

'I know, and I apologise. I acted on the orders of my Ruler. With Drick gone, I thought we were safe. All the deaths in 2011, Jemma's parents, Alex's parents, Dan's guardians and Nik's father genuinely appeared to be accidents.'

'How many interrelated deaths do you need before you get suspicious?' Sean shouted.

Jemma grabbed Sean and pushed him towards the door. He jerked himself free and strode out of the room muttering, 'What a bloody fool,' as he went.

She heard the chief say, 'We need some disciplinary action here.'

Hunt turned to Jemma. 'Follow him.' Before she left, she heard him bark at the chief, 'Back off. There'll be no action. You could have prevented this.'

*   *   *

Those left in the room stood staring at each other before Hunt broke the silence. 'We need a break.'

'I agree,' said Werrimen. 'General Harris will remain here with me.'

'Alright,' growled the chief. 'But we still have more to discuss.'

Hunt nodded. 'We'll reconvene here in one hour. O'Leary, Denis, Lambert with me.' He turned on his heel and marched out of the room, convinced that Harris hadn't recognised the emotional punch he'd slammed into either Sean or Dan. He kept going until he reached the dining room where he ordered everyone in there to get out, then sat with the three officers at one of the tables. 'Alright, we all need to settle down. When you're ready, I need your thoughts.'

Tom recovered first. 'My father never told me any of this. Obviously if he's from Anders, so am I. Why didn't he tell me?'

'Good question,' replied Hunt. 'And there's more to come which may well involve you Lambert. Stay here with Denis and talk about what you've just heard. O'Leary, you and I need to check on Bellamy.' He watched Dan as they walked quietly to Sean and Jemma's apartment. Composed, yet he had to be in turmoil. He'd just discovered his parents weren't his parents and that these people had treated his biological mother like a slave, separating her not just from him but also from Sean and his sister. And Sean's sister, who he'd never met, was now also his sister.

Hunt put his hand on the communicator outside Sean's door, but didn't press it. If Sean's mother had been right, his own father must have played a role in separating the children and bullying their mother. They'd all have to come to grips with the damage of their parents' generation and now was as good a time as any to get that started. He raised his hand and this time pressed it on the communicator.

The door slid open. Jemma and Sean stood just inside holding onto each other as though afraid to let go. 'Sean,' he said quietly. 'Dan needs to talk to you.'

Sean looked up. 'I know, I just had to clear my head.' He released Jemma and stood looking at Dan. 'I don't know how to act. What to do.'

'Me either. We need to talk.'

Hunt put his arm around Jemma. He could bring the men together, but he couldn't sort this one for them. 'You okay?' he said to Jemma.

'Yeah, I guess. Whatever else he's hiding; it has to involve me.'

'Agreed. Dan and Sean need time. Let's go back and see how Lambert and Denis are faring.'

*   *   *

At the end of the hour, Hunt collected Sean and Dan and together with Jemma, Tom and Nik, they returned to his office where Werrimen still glared ferociously at the chief.

Jemma spoke first. She wanted the full story before Werrimen killed General Harris. 'We keep hearing about the guardians. Who are they?'

'Ah yes. The guardians,' he replied, as though it was a relief to be able to focus on something other than Werrimen.

'Alex, your father came from the house of Xander and was the manager of the guardians. Like Sean, you were fast-tracked to take over that role. I knew that your memories had been altered so that you did not remember your childhood, and when he died, I realised you knew nothing of your history. I temporarily took over the role myself.'

Werrimen moved forward again. 'Is this true? You lost your memory?'

'It is,' said Hunt. 'I was told I'd had an accident and lost all my memories up to the age of fifteen. I had to learn to read and write again. I spoke a language that seemed normal to me, but my parents and doctors said it was gibberish. Thinking back now, I wonder if it was the language of Anders Major. I have to accept now that the whole thing was calculated to deceive me.'

'By all the stars,' snapped Werrimen.

The chief ignored her. 'Not to deceive, Alex, to protect you. Jemma, to answer your question, every child born to a ruling house has an official guardian, their role similar to a godparent on Earth, but more formal. Sean's neighbours were his guardians. Eric and Mary were yours.'

'Just a minute.' Jemma stood directly in front of the chief. 'Do you mean Eric and Mary only looked after me out of duty?'

'How dare you even consider such a thing?' Mary stood in the doorway, hands on hips, and glared at Jemma. 'How could you doubt how much we love you?'

Jemma stared at Mary, then, tears streaming down her face, ran to Mary's outstretched arms and buried her face against her guardian's shoulder.

Sean walked across to them, shaking his head. 'I guess I should have picked it.' He pointed to her uniform. 'I take it you're a Trustee. I was impressed by how hard you made it for me to get to Jemma. Annoyed but impressed. Now I understand.'

Jemma took a step back and looked Mary up and down. 'I've never seen that before.' Mary wore a black uniform, the same as Werrimen's but she only had five stars in the box underneath her crest, unlike Werrimen's eighteen.

Werrimen stepped forward. 'We have not met.'

Mary bowed her head. 'Your servant, ma'am. I am Mary of Kilkinan. My husband Eric, also of Kilkinan, will be here shortly. He is talking to Zadrus about our son, Anthony.'

'Kilkinan.' Werrimen nodded. 'I see. It is my pleasure to meet you. Anthony is doing well. We will take you to see him later.'

'Your reputation precedes you, and I apologise too that you were not notified, however our leaders here on Earth advised us to keep our secret hidden, and we were so fearful at the time that we didn't know who to trust,' said Mary.

'Thank you,' replied Werrimen. 'I do understand. However, fear is not an adequate excuse. You must accept that I am now involved and will decide later what action I will take with all the Anders Trustees. I will expect a list of names before this day is out.'

'Ma'am,' said Mary, with a bow of her head. 'Now, Patrick Harris, have you explained Jemma's background, or have you botched that too, the same as your failure to find Drick.'

Jemma felt Sean cringe behind her. It had been his job to find Pritchard, who they obviously knew well.

Mary must have noticed Sean's reaction too. 'I don't blame you, young man. Patrick has clearly failed you too.'

'That's a bit harsh, Mary,' said the chief, shuffling his feet.

'No, it was your job above all else to ensure Jemma's safety. It is only due to the dogged determination of young Sean here, and the help of Werrimen and Zadrus, that she is still alive.'

Jemma watched both their faces as Mary spoke. Mary had always been special to her, but her curiosity piqued when she saw this man who was top of the army tree, defer to Mary.

'Would you please sit down, Jemma.' said the chief. 'As you have probably realised from Mary's … statement, you are from Kilkinan. Your grandfather, the Supreme Ruler of Kilkinan and therefore of all Anders Major, ordered your mother's evacuation from Anders when the hostilities increased. He was killed in late 2010, Earth time, and your mother was asked to return to Anders to take over as Ruler. Arrangements had already begun when she died.'

Jemma jumped up. 'Did Pritchard kill him, too?'

'We believe now that it was Pritchard, or his people,' replied the chief.

Mary interrupted, 'When your mother died, even though we thought it was an accident, Eric and I believed you were too young to take on that role. We were going to explain it all to you on your thirtieth birthday and let you make your own choice. Obviously now, we can't wait. Jemma, you are now your grandfather's heir.' When Jemma didn't respond,

Mary spoke again. 'If you wish to claim your title, you will become the Supreme Ruler of Anders Major. I believe that is why Pritchard is after you and has taken your sister.'

'Bloody hell,' said Sean, when Jemma still didn't respond.

'But that can't be,' said Jemma. 'I know Pritchard said mum had a title, but she'd have told me something as important as that.'

'No dear,' said Mary. 'We all thought it too dangerous for you to know as a child. You could have inadvertently let something slip to the wrong person. Then, as I said, your parent's death changed everything.'

'I don't believe any of this. I'm just a normal person, born and bred in the suburbs of the Gold Coast.' She slumped forward in her chair and Werrimen squatted beside her as Mary and Sean both tried to comfort her.

'I wish that were true,' said Mary.

'Pritchard wanted my mother to renounce her title. Would all this end if I renounced the title?'

'Unfortunately, I don't think so,' said Werrimen. 'Now that this part of your community has come together, I believe Pritchard will see you as an even bigger threat. We must prepare you to deal with him.' Werrimen stood but didn't remove her hand from Jemma's shoulder. 'Are you finished, Mr Harris?'

'No. There is one more thing,' said the chief. 'Captain Denis, would you come out from behind O'Leary? I understand this situation is intimidating but you also need to know your origin, in the house of Kilkinan. You are Jemma's cousin.

The people you called your parents were, in fact, your guardians. I'm afraid your parents were both killed in the conflict. Your guardians whisked you away and brought you here.'

Dan put his arm around her. 'Okay?'

She looked up at him, shaking. 'My parents told me I was adopted, but they were always wonderful to me, and I couldn't have had a better life. They told me my biological parents were killed in an accident. I never questioned them.'

'You will all need to talk together,' said Werrimen. 'It will take time to comprehend this information and I would like to be part of your discussions. General Harris you will organise a Trustee meeting by tomorrow, at the latest. You should all be prepared to present to an IPL council hearing and expect disciplinary action. General Hunt, Dan, Nik, Tom, you will need to consider your futures, and under the circumstances, I would like each of you to consider the same Trustee training that we have offered to Jemma and Sean. I will talk to each of you over the next few days.'

'Sir,' said Sean, staring at Harris. 'How many of us are there? And how many others are in the army?'

Harris sighed. 'Just under a thousand Anders people are on Earth. Around two hundred are Trustees and many of them are in military positions in the country in which they reside.'

'Two hundred,' yelled Werrimen.

'Yes, ma'am,' replied Harris, quietly.

'Get me that list before the end of this day. And it had better be complete.' She took a deep breath and turned away from him. 'Jemma, I would like you to come with me so we can talk more about what you wish to do. Pritchard is not gone, and now that I know why he is after you, I have no doubt he will increase his efforts. We must be ready.'

Jemma nodded. She rose unsteadily and, with Werrimen's support, walked in silence to the medical centre. Werrimen produced a small bar and placed it on Jemma's arm. 'I just want to check the effect of that meeting on your stress. Have a seat.'

She didn't see Hunt until he sat beside her. 'Penny for them,' he said.

'I don't think I know myself.' She hated the idea that she needed Hunt and his protection, but she did, so there was no point in fighting him.

Werrimen interrupted them. 'All your observations are good,' she said. 'Better than I'd expected.'

Hunt looked pleased. 'So, we can jump right in?'

'No, Jemma's injuries have seriously damaged her immune system. We must start slowly and test every day to make sure we are not worsening her condition. If you are worried about ensuring her safety here, I can take her to the spaceship and ensure it.'

Jemma looked up at her. 'No. I understand why you'd say that, but I'm not going anywhere. I need to stay with Sean.' Once Werrimen had finished, Jemma left the Medical Centre to return to her apartment, so absorbed in her thoughts that she didn't see Sean and Dan until she almost ran into them. And they were so deep in conversation that Sean only just managed to extend his arm in time to catch her.

Grinning, and with a mock bow, Dan said, 'Good afternoon, your majesty.'

She slapped his arm. 'Stop it. If any of that were true, why didn't my mother tell me? I just don't believe it.'

'I think it is true, Jem,' said Sean. 'After you left, Everson and the chief had a long, ferocious talk. Everson said he had to get hold of some machine that would help him prove, or disprove, the whole story. He was pretty cranky that they'd kept him in the dark, too.'

'I still don't buy it,' she said. 'When's he going to have this machine?'

'Depends on whether he has one in his kit. He's taking Eric and Mary up to see Anthony now. He'll let us know as soon as he can.'

She left the men to talk. They also had to make sense of their lives. Dan might, on the surface, have been making light of it all, but she knew he'd be deeply hurt at the subterfuge that had robbed him of his parents and his brother and sister. She also wanted to talk to Nik but had to sort out her own head first. If any of Harris's story proved to be true, she'd have to decide whether to stay on Earth or return to the planet of her birth, a planet she didn't know at all.

All afternoon, she tossed the information around in her head until Sean suggested she focus on what she could do rather than what might happen, or what she might have to do. By the time she'd collapsed into bed that night, she'd decided that she'd put her heart and soul into Hunt's training now that she understood the need for it. Hopefully, he'd let her stay involved with the alien tech and wouldn't object to Zadrus teaching her to fly a transporter, so she could start to feel useful again. Her mind made up, she fell into a deep sleep, not stirring when Sean got up.

When she did wake at 08:30 she shot out of bed, showered quickly, grabbed a coffee and ran to Hunt's office. He'd asked her to be there at 09:00 but she didn't quite make it.

'Morning Jemma, I'm waiting for Werrimen to join us.' He looked up. 'Ah, here she is now.'

'Mr Everson has something which might help us,' said Werrimen, her voice still clipped.

Everson's gadget looked like the instrument doctors used to check ears, only the top was bigger, and it had a small screen at the back. 'This is an electrometer. If I find what I'm seeking, it will emit a high-pitched noise. Be ready, it can hurt the ears.' He asked Jemma to stand away from the others, then turned it on. The deafening sound intensified as he ran it, from a distance, up and down her body, worst at the top of her right hip. Then he turned it off. 'Do you have any skin abnormality there? Or a tattoo?'

She stared at him in disbelief. 'I have a tattoo. My mother said it was a family tradition. She said the words were Gaelic, but I've never got around to checking. Sean's got one too.'

'So do I,' said Hunt.

'I'm sorry to ask this, Jemma,' said Everson, 'but could you loosen the top of your pants so I can see it.'

She released the button at the front of her jeans and rolled them down over her right hip at the back.

Everson turned the machine back on and held it over the tattoo. 'Just as I thought,' he muttered.

'Explain please,' said Werrimen.

'This machine is in my language,' replied Everson. 'So no point in showing you, although I'm happy to give you a copy so you can have it translated to verify what I'm about to say. The words on the tattoo are not Gaelic, they translate to *Jemma, daughter of Thera of Kilkinan.* Harris spoke the truth. General, may I see your tattoo?'

He rolled down the back of his trousers.

Everson sighed. 'This one too. It says *Alend, son of Braimard of Xander, leader of the guardians.* We thought Braimard had been killed in the Anders conflict. But this does explain how Pritchard has been tracking you. He'd have a more sophisticated version of this device on his Norellian sphere.'

'Let's remove the tattoos then,' said Jemma, staring at Everson.

'Not that easy, I'm afraid,' said Werrimen. 'The ink used for these tattoos contains tiny reactive spheres. Over time, they migrate through the body. It isn't possible to remove them.'

Hunt stared at Everson and Werrimen then refastened his trousers. 'If we can't do anything, we'll have to work out how to live with them.'

'I guess,' responded Jemma.

Everson touched her arm. 'I suspect you need to go and think about this. I'll check Sean, Dan, Tom and Nik later, but please call me if I can help you. I do know quite a lot about the Anders conflict.'

'Thank you,' she replied as she left the room, taking her time to walk back to her apartment. She settled on the sofa and stared at the ceiling. She knew how hard they'd all tried to help but first, she'd have to accept all this as her reality, and she had no idea how to do that.

CHAPTER 21

Sean had just completed a gruelling workout in the gym and started on the track when he heard footsteps closing in behind. 'Hello Dan.' He didn't bother slowing down. No one else on the mountain could catch him.

'Hello.' Dan ran past. 'Bit slow this morning, are we, big brother?'

'I'll show you slow,' Sean muttered, picking up his speed, but Dan proved harder to catch than he'd expected. Not sure where he found the strength for a final spurt, he pushed forward and beat Dan, but only by a couple of centimetres. 'You've been practising. .'

'Nah, just naturally better.' Dan ducked out of the way as Sean threw a playful punch. 'Any idea why we're meeting with the general again this afternoon?'

'No. Maybe to tell my staff they should show me due respect.' He waited for a retort, but Dan just stood there grinning.

'What?'

'I like the idea of having a big brother,' said Dan. 'I just don't understand why they did it to us.'

'No, I don't either. My whole life I've seen something in

mum's eyes, although I've never understood it. I knew she missed dad, but always something else. Maybe now I can get her to open up. We'd better have dinner before we see the boss.'

He groaned when he heard, 'Bellamy, O'Leary, my office, 10 minutes.'

'Apparently not,' he muttered.

'I've organised food, you won't starve. Dress uniform, please. They're waiting for you in the change room.' Hunt turned on his heel and marched off.

'Shit,' muttered Sean. 'What now?'

'I have news for you both,' said Hunt, as they walked in. 'I won't stuff around. Bellamy, I have another pip for you. You're now a full colonel.'

'Bloody hell. Thank you, sir. I did the courses, but I didn't think you considered me ready. Is this something to do with the chief's visit?'

'You'd better be ready, and yes, he gave me the go ahead yesterday. When the staff from Brisbane arrive, you'll have both units under your control. This will give you a bit more authority.'

'Thank you, sir,' said Sean, staring at him.

'Problem is that's left a gap. There's no one between you and the majors.' He turned to Dan. 'Are you up to filling that gap, major?'

Dan stuttered. 'I'd like to think so, sir. But that's for you to judge.'

'And me,' said Sean. 'He's not only up to it, it's about time he got it.'

'Well, thank you for your vote of confidence, Bellamy,' replied Hunt. 'So, O'Leary, I suppose I'd better give you this pip to add to your crown. Congratulations, Lieutenant-Colonel O'Leary. Don't get too excited, you've got a hell of a job ahead of you. Eventually, you will take over one of the units, but for the moment you'll work with Bellamy and cover both. Work it out between you. It's back to the military game now. You will set the example. No more backchat to Bellamy, or to me for that matter, when others are around.'

'Yes, sir, I figured that. I've already apologised to Sean.'

'Good, pleased to hear it. It has to be obvious you're in charge. We'll adjourn to your office Bellamy. SCARF's officers should already be there.'

Without another word they followed Hunt. With all the officers packed in, there was barely enough room for Sean to squeeze around to the front of the assembly. He jumped when Nik squealed, throwing her arms around Dan, and rubbing the extra brass on his shoulder. Aware that Hunt wanted him to play a strict CO role, he growled at Nik and ordered everyone to sit, then laid out a program of fitness and military training. He informed them if he saw any sign of individuals going about their tasks without enthusiasm, they could expect to answer to him. He assured the senior officers they would be held responsible for the behaviour of everyone below them, and if he had to discipline a junior officer or an NCO, the senior officers would also be disciplined. Nik and Tom looked worried, but ironically, Dan looked more worried – probably because he knew how hard both he and Hunt could be. Hunt stood behind him looking like he'd swallowed a saucer of cream which made Sean groan inwardly. He supposed it was inevitable he'd end up being like his boss.

He dismissed the junior officers and asked the senior officers if they had any questions.

'Sir, there's something I need to say,' said Tom, directing his gaze to Hunt.

'Go on,' Hunt replied.

'I think I might inadvertently have been the leak from here. I requested Williamson's help when we were searching for Jemma. I answered all his questions. He was my boss, and I didn't know he was dirty, but he did get some of his information from me. I'm sorry.'

Hunt sighed. 'No. You couldn't have known. We all need to learn from this experience. If you're suspicious of someone, there's probably good reason, but I don't think you could have picked this one.'

After everyone, including Hunt, had left, Sean, painfully aware that he hadn't checked on Jemma all day, ran back to their apartment.

She threw her arms around his neck then pulled back a little and looked him up and down. 'I haven't seen you in full uniform before. It's pretty.'

'Pretty. Give me a break. Handsome, masculine, dashing, debonair, official even. But, pretty?'

'Yep. I always enjoy tearing the pretty wrapping off a package.'

'So, I'm a package?'

'Oh, you're a real package.'

'You're a wanton woman,' he replied, laughing.

'No, just a woman in love.'

'So, what's new?'

'Well, just one small thing, I've been promoted. Full colonel.'

She squealed and hugged him again. 'Congratulations.'

He eased her back slightly. 'How are you holding up?'

'Yeah I'm alright. Obviously, everything's changed but, so long as you're with me, I'll get through it.'

'I'll most definitely be with you.' He brushed a light kiss on her forehead.

She yawned and, taking hold of his hand, started towards the bedroom, but he steered her back to the sofa. If he didn't talk to her now, he'd lose the nerve.

'I have something I want to ask you.' He wiped the sweat from his forehead. For a moment, all words left him but, now he'd started, he had to say something. *God, just spit it out.*

'Okay, shoot,' said Jemma, frowning slightly as she looked back at him.

'Jemma, I know we haven't been together long, but I've never been more certain of anything in my life.' He took a deep breath and closed his eyes for a moment. 'When you were taken, I missed you more than I thought I could ever miss anyone.' He dropped down onto his knee. 'Would you consider marrying me?'

She didn't move, didn't utter a sound, her hand went limp in his. He'd been terrified she might say no, but she said nothing. It seemed a long time, but it was probably only seconds before she snapped out of it, smiled, and put her arms around him.

'Oh, my God Sean, I didn't expect that. I've never been more certain either. Yes.'

He sat up, pulled her in to him, and held her as tightly as he dared.

'You goose,' she said. 'I thought you were annoyed with me, and you were about to tell me off again.'

'I've never really been annoyed with you. But sometimes it is hard to make you see reason.'

'Is it now? Then, let me help *you* see reason.' She grabbed his tie, and pretended to pull him up with it, to which he readily succumbed, holding up his hands in mock surrender. 'I believe I still have a package to unwrap.'

Sean slipped out of bed to his alarm at 05:00, crept to the shower, dressed, and was ready to leave, when he heard, 'Aren't you going to say goodbye?'

He bent down and kissed her, then sat on the side of the bed. 'You stay in bed. I'll come back around eight and take you to breakfast. No need for you to get up yet.'

With two minutes to spare, he joined the others at the gym. Dan had them set up for unarmed combat training. Nik had teamed herself with a female sergeant, so Sean leaned over her and said, 'Not a tinker's chance in hell that's going to happen.' He directed the sergeant to work with Dan and took Nik to work with him.

He laughed at her worried expression. At a hundred and ninety-two centimetres, and nearly a hundred kilograms, he was an accomplished fighter. Nik knew that, and she was slightly shorter than Jemma, maybe a hundred and seventy-five centimetres, and at best seventy kilograms. The sergeant had a similarly dismayed look on her face. Dan was his size and she was a bit smaller than Nik. But he needed them to develop skills to handle men the size of himself and Dan. It wasn't in their interests to go easy on them, although he thought in the past that's probably what had happened.

When they'd finished, and Nik had walked off with Liam, he sensed movement behind him. Jemma must had decided to make use of her new-found freedom.

'You cruel bastard,' she said.

'Morning Jem. You look good.'

'I am, but I still think you're a bastard.'

'Mm, possibly. But I'm having fun.'

'At Nik's expense.'

'True, and one day she'll thank me for it. Think about all the situations over the last few weeks we've encountered. If it'd been Nik, do you think she could've got by with any less capacity than I have? She's doesn't have my height and weight, she's not as strong, but she still has to succeed, no matter what. She has to have more skills than me. Her life will almost certainly one day depend on it.'

'You could be nicer.'

'Do you think someone trying to attack her will be nicer? Perhaps you'd like to get in the ring with her.'

'No, I wouldn't. She's told me several times that you're a good boss. I can't see why.'

'I am a good boss.'

'And an arrogant toad.' She pretended to hit him in the stomach, to which he playfully doubled up.

Feigning agony, as he leaned on her, he whimpered, 'How about we go to breakfast, and you can tell me how much you love me?'

*   *   *

After breakfast, Sean had a meeting with Hunt, which left Jemma with three quarters of an hour before her own meeting about starting her training, so she went in search of Nik. When they'd worked together to find Anthony, they'd formed a close bond and she trusted Nik. She found her in the control room, sitting on the floor and leaning back against a wall, her head bent forward.

Jemma ran to her, and dropped down, 'What's wrong?'

'Hard to explain,' she replied, with a sigh. 'It's Colonel Bellamy.'

'What's he done to you?'

'Nothing. He's the most switched on boss I've ever had, but everything I do with him, I end up looking like an idiot.'

'No, no,' said Jemma. 'I can say for sure, and I'm not conning you, he doesn't see it that way.'

'Thanks.' Nik managed a smile. 'I think you are conning me, at least a bit, but that makes me feel better.'

'Hey, I've just had an idea. Could we use Artie to look at where my hide used to be?' She could probably do it herself, but she wanted to get Nik off the floor and doing something.

'Sure.' Nik got up and walked towards the back wall, 'Focus south of the mound.'

The wall morphed into the area just outside. A wallaby hopped across a few metres into the forest and, without thinking, Jemma started to run towards it until Nik shouted, 'Stop.'

Jemma pulled up and spun around.

'You were about to hit the wall. Reach your hand out, you'll see. I know how real it seems, but the wall's still there, and I've hit it a few times myself.'

'Yeah, so have I, but this is incredible,' whispered Jemma. 'The detail here's amazing.'

'I know.' Nik gave some rough co-ordinates to the machine, and the image shifted around until she found Jemma's research area.

'Oh Nik, if I can use this, it would let me have a go at doing some of my research.' She mightn't be able to disseminate her findings for the moment, but they had to release her eventually, and it'd get her brain working again. 'I'd like to know how this thing works.'

Nik smiled. 'Me too. Zadrus says it's all around us, that

it's part of the fabric of the walls, and doesn't need any kind of engine to run it.'

'Why won't he explain it to you?'

'He says he will, but he wants all of us to experience their technology, and then choose where we want to focus. They're keen to teach us, but we have to show the right aptitude and motivation.'

'Makes sense, I guess.'

'I've got an idea,' said Nik, grinning. 'We've still got a bit of time before your meeting. How would you like a walk on the beach?'

'If only,' sighed Jemma.

'Then, I've got a surprise for you. You have to follow my instructions. If you're worried at any point, just say stop. Okay with that?'

Jemma hesitated, 'Don't know what you're up to, but sure.'

'Take my hand.' Nik didn't give Jemma time to question but reached out and took her hand. 'If you lose my hand, say *Stop*, straight away.' She waited for Jemma to agree, then said, 'Transfer to Surfers Paradise beach.'

As the room around them faded, Jemma again heard, 'Don't let go of my hand.'

When the surrounds cleared, they stood, hand in hand, on the beach, on the dry side of the high tide line. Jemma threw off her shoes and was stunned to feel the sand under her toes, and a soft breeze against her skin. She murmured, 'Is this real?'

'Yes, and no,' replied Nik. 'It's a real place. If you touched someone, you'd feel them. If you spoke to them, you'd get a reply. But if you were to ask them later, they wouldn't remember you. I can't explain it, but I like to enjoy it every now and then. When I've asked Zadrus about it, he just smiles and says, *in time*. Now would you like to get your feet wet?'

She picked up her shoes and ran, with Nik, down to the water's edge. She was sure she could smell the saltwater, but that was nothing to the way it felt. She wanted to dive in, but Nik pulled her back. They'd have to leave if Jemma was to get back in time for her meeting.

In a clear voice, Nik said, 'Stop.'

When the surroundings cleared, they were back in the control room, Jemma's shoes still in her hand, and her feet wet, with sand wedged between her toes. She hugged Nik, and giggled. 'I feel like I should ask for a pinkie promise not to tell mum.'

'Or, in our case, the boss,' grinned Nik.

'Okay.' They linked their little fingers, and in a solemn voice Jemma said, 'I swear I will not tell General Hunt our secret.'

'What secret would that be?' Hunt stood in the doorway.

'It'd hardly be a secret if I told you,' retorted Jemma.

'I'm here because you're late. How much worse do you plan to make it?'

She pulled herself up, 'No worse.' She turned back and winked at Nik, then walked through the door and waited for the general to follow her. She expected a rebuke, but he changed the subject.

'What did you think of the training session you saw this morning?'

'I thought you and Sean were downright cruel to Nik. He tells me I don't understand.'

'Bellamy's right. Your training starts today. We'll take twenty minutes after your gym session, nothing strenuous, starting with the basics. When you're at least as good as him, I'll ask you the same question again, and I won't be satisfied until you can take me down.'

'But nobody can take you down, not even Sean.'

'That's right, he can't. I'm pleased to see you spending time with Captain Denis. What do you think of her?'

'I like her. Her biggest worry is how to improve herself enough to impress Sean. I told her she's already impressed him, but she's not satisfied.'

'Good, I like that attitude. Enjoy her company, but don't turn into a pair of giggling schoolgirls.'

Jemma groaned; he had to growl about something. She looked him in the eye. 'Sometimes it pays to find your inner child.'

'Let's go, we don't want to be late for Werrimen.' He turned on his heel and walked off, but Jemma didn't miss the smile that he'd tried to hide. Perhaps he'd eventually relax with her. She walked quietly by his side to the gym.

After the session, Werrimen sat beside her on the bench, and while her words were directed at Jemma, her gaze fixed on Hunt. She described a treatment that would help Jemma's immune system but wasn't sure whether to go ahead. The treatment would improve her energy, but Werrimen was concerned that if she then pushed too hard because she felt better, it could delay her long-term recovery. If she agreed to Werrimen's boundaries, the treatments could begin.

Jemma shrugged and asked when she could start, but Werrimen clearly wanted Hunt's agreement first. Even then, Werrimen didn't appear convinced.

Not prepared to be held back, Jemma reiterated, 'When can I start?'

'That is up to General Hunt,' said Werrimen. 'You will need to come up to the spaceship each day for a week.'

Hunt didn't answer. He led Jemma from the medical centre and turned towards the runway. Half the middle floor of the facility was taken up with accommodation, forty apartments in all, and two dining rooms. The other half contained the gym, with its full-sized running track, and enough exercise machines to be the envy or any commercial enterprise. At the back of the gym, a doorway opened onto an Olympic-sized swimming pool. To the front of the pool was the well-equipped medical centre with its consulting rooms and six-bed ward. A corridor, which ran between the accommodation side and the gym side, opened onto the alien's landing pad, but just before it, on the gym side, was a locked room that Jemma had assumed was a storeroom. When they entered it, she gasped at the fifteen-metre-wide, twenty-metre-long room with padded floor and walls.

Hunt smiled at her expression. 'Relax, it's a serious training room. Only the most senior officers know about it, and now you. I don't want anyone other than you, me and Bellamy to know I'm training you. I think that's safest. If Pritchard, or any of his people trouble you, they won't expect you to be able to retaliate, and that gives you an advantage.'

In there alone, with someone who no one else on the mountain could take down, and no way out, she did precisely as she was told, no cheek, no backchat. He had her stand facing him and showed her different stances which would give her the best balance if she found herself in a combat situation. Remarkably gentle, with none of the bullying she'd encountered at the beginning, he made her stand for the last five minutes with feet apart and knees slightly bent. Relieved to be allowed to move her burning legs when he told her to relax, he instructed her to repeat the exercise several times a day until it felt natural for her, then sat her on the floor to recover before marching her back to Werrimen.

As he left, he said to Werrimen, 'Would Monday be alright for you to take her up and start your treatments?'

'Certainly,' replied Werrimen.

Once he'd gone, Werrimen took her hand. 'I doubt this is the best moment to discuss it, but Zadrus and I are keen to start working with you too, when you are well enough.'

'You know I think the world of you,' said Jemma. 'It's the general I wish would leave me alone and let me recover.'

'I understand, my dear. Our work will be nothing like his, but you must realise that we are all, including General Hunt, committed to your welfare. You are special, that much we know. We want to explore that, but we will never force you to do anything. I would like to start your trustee training. Will you talk to me more about it on Monday?'

Jemma nodded. She already knew of Werrimen's plans but, when Hunt pushed her too hard, she sometimes wished she'd died in that fire. It didn't last, but it was the first time in her life she'd ever had that kind of thought.

CHAPTER 22

Sean had shut himself in his office to wait for Jemma and had just fired up his computer when Nik ran in. He almost waved her away until he looked up and saw her face. She leant over his desk, heaving for breath.

'You've got to see this,' she gasped.

'Okay, calm down.' He pointed to a chair. 'What is it?'

'General Hunt sent me down to head office with a package. When I went to leave, a man was leaning on my car. I didn't recognise him until he introduced himself, I guess because I've never actually met him. It was Fredrick Pritchard. I ran back to security, but he was gone when they came out. So I came straight back here. He gave me this.' She handed Sean a large padded envelope.

He cautiously opened it, checking for powder or other substances. Satisfied it was clear, he pulled out a medium-sized photograph album. On the first page, a teenage Jemma stood on a veranda. A younger girl, who looked very much like Jemma, straddled the veranda rail and looked up at her. The rest of the photos, which appeared to span around ten years, were of the other girl. In the last photo, she stood with Pritchard, and a Norellian sphere hovered in the background.

'Jesus Nik, that has to be Jemma's sister,' said Sean. 'We'd better get her in here. General Hunt will want to see this too.'

She nodded. 'Pritchard said he'd be waiting in the carpark of the Southport shopping centre at 6pm today. She's to come alone. I told him that wouldn't happen. He shrugged. Said when she sees these, she'll come.'

'Jemma and the general are in the gym. I'm expecting him here shortly. While we wait, I'd like to suggest something to you. Have you got time for that now?'

'Yes, sir.'

'No need to be formal.' He smiled, she'd immediately tensed as he always did with Hunt, but he wanted her to relax. 'We need to move forward, and I plan to push everyone in this unit. Hard. Your Anders background, and your relationship to Jemma, has changed your position within this unit. Adding the knowledge that you've gained with the alien tech; you really are central to our new role. Are you willing to work with me, to go the extra mile, so I can get you up to speed?'

She smiled. 'Yes, sir. I want to work with you. I'm not sure I'll always be happy about it, but I'll do my best.'

'You probably won't be happy a lot of the time, and I'm going to demand better than your best. Are you still up for it?'

'Oh boy.' She looked directly at him. 'Yes sir, I am.'

Smiling, he went on. 'Good. Now, I'm still trying to come to grips with the extent of Williamson's interference. Please understand that I'm not accusing you of anything.'

'Okay,' she murmured.

'Did you ever have anything to do with Williamson outside SCARF?'

'Not really. Initially we got on well. He organised flying lessons for me with a training school at Archerfield. I wanted to try out for helicopter pilot in the Army's flight wing, but I had to learn to fly a plane before I could take helicopter lessons.'

'Did you ever meet William Preston?' Sean leaned forward.

'No, but his hangar was next to the flying school, and his mechanic often came in for smoko. He was really chatty and interested in what we do up here.' The shocked look returned. 'God almighty, was he grilling me for information?'

'Almost certainly. Did you give him any?'

'No, I swear to you. Oh my God, the only way he could have known I worked up here was if Williamson told him. That mongrel set me up.'

'Sounds like it,' said Sean. 'Is that when your relationship with him deteriorated?'

'No, it was when I talked about wanting to fly helicopters, because that's what my father did.'

Hunt walked in at the tail end of their conversation. 'I knew a Colonel Denis in Afghanistan. He flew choppers, but he was killed, enemy fire downed his chopper. Six or seven people died. Was that your father?'

Her lip trembled slightly, and she had to take a deep breath before continuing. 'Yes sir, and Colonel Williamson's brother was on board that aircraft. He blamed my father for his brother's death. After he made the connection with my father, he treated me like an enemy.'

'Weak prick,' said Hunt. 'I recall an allegation of sabotage to his helicopter.'

'Yes,' she replied. 'But the records were sealed, and we couldn't get an investigation.'

'After the chief's visit, we'd have to assume those allegations were true,' said Hunt. 'Your father was most likely in General Harris's camp and Williamson was clearly on Pritchard's side, whatever that is. It's very hard to judge which side is right, given we know nothing of Anders, but having said that, we do know that Pritchard is a murdering, conniving criminal.'

'Nik, find Jemma and bring her here,' said Sean. 'I'll fill the general in on the photos while we wait.'

Hunt waited for the door to shut. 'What's up?'

Sean passed the photo album over without saying anything.

Hunt whistled as he looked at the pictures. 'Has to be the sister.'

'That's my guess. I haven't seen a photo of her. Jemma didn't have time to get anything from her unit when she was moved by the police. But they're so alike, it has to be.'

When Jemma walked through the door, Sean pulled a chair next to his and sat her down, his arm around her shoulders. He set the album in front of her.

She looked up after she'd leafed through.

'First,' said Hunt, 'is it your sister?'

'Yes, it is, and that's Pritchard beside her.' Nik had told her the story including his demand that they meet. 'I have to go, of course,' said Jemma.

'No.' Hunt rested against Sean's desk. 'I understand you'd want to go, but this fellow can't be trusted. He wants you to work on his virus. Meeting your sister is the bait. It's not the end game.'

'I still don't understand why he's so determined to perfect that virus. It can't be about the money. He's way beyond wealthy. And I don't understand why he's so keen to get me to develop a vaccine, or to get the aliens' cure. I know Mr Everson said he wants it for his self-protection, but he's working with it now and hasn't caught it. He's probably already immune.'

Hunt nodded. 'I discussed all that with the chief yesterday after you left. He believes that Pritchard's intention is to wipe out anyone still alive from the ruling houses, which is why he's trying to combine a virus that he brought with him with a more transmissible virus. The vaccine and cure are to protect his own people, in case any of them aren't immune. It has nothing to do with money or releasing it on Earth, unless he decides to do that as a test run.'

'Jesus,' said Jemma, 'and he's got my sister. Does he plan to kill her too? We have to find her.'

'Yes, we do,' said Hunt. 'Denis, get on to Zadrus, see if we can get his help to lure Pritchard out. Jemma go have some lunch. Give me some time to develop a plan.'

After they'd left, Hunt turned back to Sean. 'I've got

someone in mind we could dress up to look like her. Stay with Jemma this afternoon. She might be tempted to try to leave to find her sister. We can't let Pritchard get access to her again.'

Just before 18:00, Hunt's decoy approached the shopping centre. Zadrus, with Jemma beside him in the control room, had the decoy under surveillance. Sean had his people strategically placed around the centre, while he and Nik also watched with Zadrus, but no one approached the decoy.

After an hour of waiting, Sean notified Hunt that he thought they'd been made.

'I agree,' said Hunt. 'Tell everyone to stand down.'

*   *   *

Torn between disappointment that Pritchard and her sister hadn't shown, and relief that he hadn't attempted to abduct Hunt's decoy, Jemma watched Sean leave to join his people in a search of the shopping centre. She didn't expect he'd find anything. Pritchard had been so damned good at eluding them. She made her way back to the control room where Nik had Artie searching for the site where Jemma had had her hide.

'I thought this might take your mind off Pritchard,' said Nik. 'I'll sit and watch with you for a while 'til you're confident you can manage my boy yourself.'

Jemma laughed. 'What makes you think Artie's a male?'

'That's easy. He's rude, arrogant and 'ornery.'

'Fair enough,' replied Jemma. She sat on the floor, Nik beside her, and settled in to watch.

Nik kept talking, explaining how to focus in on an image to get better detail, and how to set up two images at the same time, from different directions. Jemma knew Nik was doing it to distract her from the events of the afternoon, and she appreciated it.

'Oh my God, look at that,' said Jemma, as Nik twisted the direction of the image once again. 'It's a latrine mound.'

'What? You're excited by some kind of toilet?

'No,' cried Jemma. 'Well yes, I suppose. It's something that's unique to quolls. They always do their business in the same spot, and it builds up to form a mound, so if you find a latrine mound you know there's a quoll somewhere close. It may not be the quoll I'm looking for, but it's definitely a quoll.'

'Sure.' Nik stared at her as though she'd finally gone mad.

'I can see one.' Jemma, up now on hands and knees, crawled towards the image. 'Look. Over there. At the base of that tree. It's the one I'm after, the spotted-tail quoll. Just standing there. It's staring at us. Oh Nik, this is fantastic. It almost makes me feel normal.' Nik stayed with her and they both squatted on the floor, watching, for two hours but didn't see any others. By the time they'd finished, Nik was as involved with the hunt for the animals as Jemma, pointing out every movement she saw. Jemma wrote copious notes on the quoll she'd identified, its condition and appearance, and the size and shape of the latrine mound. When she lamented that she couldn't get measurements, Artie gave her a height and length and estimated the animal's weight. Delighted, she completed her notes, then headed for the runway to meet Sean.

Early the following Monday, Hunt stood beside Jemma to wait for the transporter that would take her up to the spaceship for the first of her new treatments.

'I'd hoped Sean might join me,' she said.

'Nope. He's busy.'

She stared at him, no way would Sean be too busy to join her for this. She never knew whether to confront Hunt or leave it be, but she was tired of someone else running her life. Damn it, too bad if he yelled. 'Why are you keeping Sean away from me?'

'Do you want the truth, or do you want me to make you feel better?'

'I'm not a child. Give me the truth.'

'You just answered your own question.'

'Not to my satisfaction. I'd like you to clarify.' She clenched her fists behind her back. Pummelling him wouldn't get her anywhere, but she'd have liked to.

With a smile, he reached out and held her shoulders, turning her to face him. 'I do not see you as a child. I see you as a capable person, and I intend to make you more capable. In fact, I have to make you more capable if I'm to keep you safe. Sean has lingering memories of seeing you pulled unconscious from a fire and struggling to survive. I want you to grow, and believe you are well enough to start doing that. He wants to cocoon you. It's not that I don't understand how he feels, but I don't think it's in your best interests. Satisfied?'

'No, I'm not satisfied. He loves me. Part of my recovery is his recovery. I think you need to understand that.'

Still holding her shoulders, he looked down before meeting her gaze, and sighed. 'I believe the day will come when you will both appreciate what I'm doing. It's not today.'

She opened her mouth to retort, but what could she say? Whatever she thought, she was stuck here on the mountain, and fighting with him wouldn't do much good.

'Here's your ride. Relax and have your treatment up there today. Tomorrow, we work.' He threw a pretend punch at her arm. She responded, but hers connected. He grabbed her arm, pushing it gently behind her back. 'Careful. You're not ready to beat me up yet.'

As he pushed her towards the transporter, she turned to face him, 'No, but the day will come.' The blue light took her into the craft before he could retaliate.

Werrimen waited for her in the landing bay on the mothership and took her straight to the medical floor for her treatment. It took less than half an hour, after which Werrimen took her to Zadrus's office to talk. They found him pacing at the back of his room.

'By the stars Werrimen, these Earth governments have no compassion,' said Zadrus. 'They have rejected these young people with no thought about their futures. They just do not care.'

'They are afraid. They have denied our existence for

centuries and would lose face to admit it now. Politicians are the same everywhere.'

'That is no excuse,' he replied. 'They say ridiculous things, like it is for the greater good. How could that be? We are talking about the lives of innocent young people. They should be rushing us with ideas about how to help them. Jemma, at least, has people with her on the mountain, but although Anthony's parents have visited him here, he is not permitted to leave. The young doctor, Therese, and the scientist, Petra, do not have visitors. They are utterly alone.'

'There is no excuse. We must ensure their future. If it can't be on Earth, then somewhere else. Anthony's parents are still with him and may choose to stay.'

He glared at her. 'Are you saying we should just accept it?' He picked up items from his desk and threw them down.

'No, I am saying if you plan to do battle, you must first be sure there is a chance you can win.'

He growled. 'And you believe we cannot win?'

'No, but I believe it is unlikely.' She stood firm, and barely blinked as he fumed.

He flopped on his chair, his head falling onto his hand. 'Perhaps, but we cannot leave it at that.'

She shrugged. 'Agreed, and you must continue trying. Just be prepared for rejection.'

'I have organised a meeting on Wake Island with the appropriate government leaders. I have to leave in a few minutes.'

Jemma coughed. She was suspicious they'd forgotten she was there. 'I'd like to go with you.'

Werrimen took both her hands and paused before she spoke. 'I am not sure you are well enough yet, my dear.'

'Timing's bad, but I'm much better than I was. General Hunt wants me to make my own decisions, and that's what I'm doing.' Neither of the aliens replied for some time, but if there was any chance that she could influence what happened to Anthony and Therese, she had to try.

'You must agree to follow my instructions,' said Zadrus.

She laughed. 'I'm used to taking orders. General Hunt? Remember?'

Another look passed between the two aliens. Finally, they agreed she could go.

'We must leave straight away,' said Zadrus. As they walked to the transporter, he explained to her that Wake Island, in the Pacific, was a regular meeting place. It'd been an important US military base in World War II but was now uninhabited, and so served their purpose. He advised her to expect a hostile reception, given the conversations he'd had with several of the leaders. Although he controlled his anger on the way down, his demeanour changed when they landed on the island. He was more determined now than angry, but clearly not prepared to tolerate bad behaviour.

A high level, military presence was in place. Most of the leaders had already arrived, and most were polite to Jemma but didn't welcome Zadrus. The chair of the meeting, the German Chancellor's representative, waved them to chairs. 'I believe we are here to change the future of Earth.' His smirk annoyed Jemma.

In a booming voice, Zadrus responded, 'Yes, you do need to make decisions. You are destroying your planet, and the level of violence on Earth has increased markedly. We have seen this before on other planets. If you do not make changes, your world will cease to exist.'

'Bollocks,' said the British Prime Minister. 'How many times have we heard the doom and gloom message? But look at us. We're doing better than ever. We just have to be vigilant.'

Zadrus stood his ground, although his hands were clenched into fists behind his back. 'What about the terrorist threats? Do you really believe no other country offers any threat to you?'

'All controllable,' responded the US representative. 'Is that why we were brought here? My time's valuable. I don't appreciate having it wasted.'

Zadrus's voice, although now icy, remained firm. 'I have with me a young scientist who has been a victim of the same terrorists.' He introduced Jemma and asked her to tell them the story of her abduction. There were several murmurs and gasps as she spoke, and some of the delegates looked less sure about their decision.

'The other young people we have on board our ship are not different from Jemma, and you know there are others on other spaceships, all of whom found themselves in the wrong place at the wrong time. They should be returned to Earth and their families, but we are being stopped from doing that. Why?'

'The new ones are ours,' responded the Australian Prime Minister. 'You know why they can't be returned. They might talk. Then everything gets out of control.'

'How can that be relevant?' Zadrus thumped the desk in front of him. 'They are wonderful young people. You should be doing everything in your power to ensure they have a future.'

'It's not within my power,' said the Australian Prime Minister, softly.

'You give him a future,' said someone else. 'You rescued him. You deal with him.'

'Do you not care at all, about your own people?'

The Australian Prime Minister responded, 'You should have let nature take its course. We are grateful you helped us identify the terrorist camp. It is unfortunate, but innocent people often do die in these circumstances.'

'But he did not die. We were able to save him.'

'As far as the community is concerned, he did die. Now, is that it? Are we done here?'

Zadrus's voice increased in volume. 'So, you are happy to have us develop our communication stations on Earth, which will help you, so long as they remain hidden. And you will accept our help to rescue people, if we discard them somewhere else. But you will not listen to our advice, our experience that you need to change what you are doing. I will say it again. We have seen it before on other planets.'

'I'm not listening to any more of this rubbish,' shouted the German. 'This meeting is closed.'

'You know how to contact us,' boomed Zadrus. 'We will remain here to help however we can. I can only hope you do not do too much more damage, before you accept our help. There will be little we can do if you destroy your species.' He marched out to his transporter and instructed his pilot to take off immediately.

Jemma ran behind him. She'd read about conspiracy theories and politicians acting in their own self-interest, but if this was the calibre of people leading government on Earth, then Earth's future was anything but assured. They didn't care about people. They'd happily abandoned Anthony, Petra and Therese and, from what she'd just heard, others too. She stood behind the pilot, gripped the back of his seat, and rocked back and forth.

Zadrus took her in his arms, held her close to him. 'Relax, my dear. You do not want to challenge your health.'

'I can't believe what I just heard. They don't care at all. Just cast us off. Abandoned us. No remorse. How can they do that? Do they know we come from Anders? Is that it?'

'I don't know if they are aware, but you are still citizens of this country, so that is no excuse and I am not happy with my people either. My orders are to sit back and watch it happen. The IPL's failure to act is just as bad as this stupidity. I must find a way to make them intervene. Before it is too late.'

Jemma called Sean on the communicator, that he now always carried with him, to say she was on her way back. Zadrus had his pilot fly into the SCARF landing bay, stopping just long enough to drop her off, then quickly left. She walked towards the entry hoping Sean would be waiting for her.

'What's wrong?' he said, running from the doorway as soon as she stepped down from the transporter.

Without answering, she snuggled into him, burying her head in his shoulder.

Still supporting her, he gently eased back and started to walk. 'Come on, let's get some food into you, then you can tell me all about it.'

Given the late hour, the dining room was close to deserted, but he rustled up a sandwich and some coffee. She toyed with it, too churned to eat not knowing how he'd react to what she had to tell him.

He took hold of her hands. 'Tell me what happened.'

She started tentatively but, with his encouragement, everything poured out.

'I'm not surprised by the behaviour of the politicians, but I'm shocked that Zadrus took you to Wake Island with him.'

'I insisted. If they were prepared to be so cruel, I had to know why. It's not just Anthony, or Therese, or Petra, or me. There are others, being taken care of by other IPL members on different spaceships. They don't care. God help us, Sean. They just don't care.'

'I know.'

She sat up and gripped his hands hard. 'We have to change their approach. We can't sit back and allow them to cast people off this way.'

'I doubt we've got much hope of changing them.'

She leaned forward, more determined than she'd ever been. 'We have to do something, Sean.'

'Yes, we do,' he replied. 'I haven't worked out what yet, though.'

Next morning, Jemma decided it was time to take a risk and to confront the general. She desperately needed to use her brain, and to be part of the investigation to find Pritchard. After all, if she really was the supreme ruler of her people, she had an obligation to them. Treating her like a delicate princess who had to be told what to do, just wasn't working. By the end of the day she'd either be in a cell, or on a better footing. Whichever it was, she had to try. She knocked on his door, took a deep breath and strode into his room.

'Good morning. I need you to allocate some time to have a discussion with me during which we won't be interrupted.' She'd spoken so quickly she hadn't exhaled at all. Now she had to, and it came out as a loud sigh.

'Good morning. How much time would you like?'

He had a habit of raising one eyebrow which always felt like a challenge. Usually she crumbled, but today she was determined to rise to it. 'At least half an hour.'

'Now's good.'

She pulled up a chair without being invited and hoped his curiosity would get the better of him, so he wouldn't yell or threaten her. She sat back in the chair, and crossed her legs, mostly to control the shaking, but hoped it made her look confident.

'Okay, shoot.'

'Yesterday you said you saw me as a capable person, yet you persist in treating me like a child. It's time to renegotiate the way you and I interact.'

He raised one eyebrow. 'You're still weak. I don't intend to risk either your health, or your safety.'

'I'm not fully recovered, but I'm much stronger than I was, and I'm not mentally deranged.'

This time he laughed. 'You are most definitely not mentally deranged.' He walked around his desk and dragged a chair close to her but turned it around, so he leaned on the back of the chair as he spoke. 'What changes do you propose?'

The worst he could do was say no, then she'd be back to square one, but at least she'd have tried. 'Whenever I come in here, or report to you, I'm worried. I want that to stop. I want us to start interacting like two adults. I know I can't leave, I need to regain my health, and you want me to learn to defend myself. Given that, I want you to stop bullying me. You say you want me to make my own decisions, yet you won't give me the room to do that.'

Now, with both eyebrows raised, his chin rested on his hands as they clasped the top of the chair. 'You may not believe me, but I do understand. Problem is I have to be in control, because I have legal requirements regarding your custody here.'

She slapped her knee. 'No, you don't have to be in control. You set the rules, I accept that. But I control my own actions, and I know that I'll answer to you if I fail.'

'So, how's that different from now?' The slight frown on his face told her he genuinely didn't understand.

'It's in your attitude, the way you speak to me, the demands you make. Try this. I promise you I will not make any attempt to leave this facility without your knowledge.'

'I already trust you to do that, and you have the full run of this facility. What change do you want?'

'I don't have the full run. I'd like access to the scientists who are working with the aliens on their research. And I'd like internet access so I can do some research, and I can use my brain again. I'm prepared to promise that I won't use email, and I won't contact anyone outside here without your consent.'

For several minutes, he stared at her, and she had to work hard to maintain her determined look. 'Right. Internet I'm okay with. If you promise you won't contact anyone, I'll accept that. Contact with the scientists, I'm not sure. Their research is on viruses. I don't know what risk there might be. I'll think about that one and talk to Werrimen. Now, your health issues and self-defence. There can't be much negotiation there.'

She sighed. He still didn't seem to get it. 'You have to stop treating me like I'm delicate. I promise you that I will do everything Werrimen tells me to do. I will also work hard with you on the self-defence training. But I want to be able to tell you when I don't feel I can cope, or even if I'd like to pick it up and do more. Now I'm too worried about the response, and it's holding my recovery back.'

'Ah. I accept your promises, and I do trust you, but can I tell you the story from my perspective?'

'Of course.'

'There was this young, stubborn, difficult and determined scientist who stumbled across an alien facility. We all agreed she had to run from it, because we didn't understand it at the time. My people had to rescue her, but then my protection failed her, and she nearly died at the hands of terrorists. We failed to protect her at the safest safe house we have. Worse, we discovered terrorists had infiltrated where we have her under our protection, and even though we know why they're after her now, we still can't entirely guarantee her safety. I have the resources of the entire Australian Army at my disposal and I've still failed. So, I decided to be strict with her, and she's cranky about that.'

Now it was her turn to stare. 'So your attitude to me is motivated by your fear, and your sense of failure?'

'In a word, yes. And I'm not negotiable on your need to get fit and learn to protect yourself.'

'I'm prepared to work with you, and you know I'll work hard. I just want you to treat me like an adult, not a battering ram. And I accept you're in charge.'

'Okay, I think I get it. You want me to bark less and listen to you. That I can do. You want to be allowed to do something useful. Fair enough on that too. I'll chat to Werrimen about it, perhaps you can do more with Captain Denis and the alien technology. You've made promises and I know you'll keep them, so I'll organise a computer and internet for you. But I am not going to back off your fitness or your training.

In fact, once Werrimen clears you, hopefully today, that will all increase significantly. It's about your safety.'

It felt like two steps forward and one back, but it was better than nothing. She felt so lost in his world. Still, if she could use her brain, that might help her feel semi-human again. He remained sitting, as though waiting for what he'd said to sink in. Then he stood, put his hands on her shoulders, and drew her up and into a hug.

'I know this is hard for you, and I'd like you be as happy as it's possible for you to feel here. I'll keep everything you've said in mind, and so long as you keep up your end of the bargain, we'll get along just fine. Now it's time for your big test. Let's go.'

Not sure if she'd achieved anything at all, she followed Hunt to the Medical Centre. Now several weeks since her rescue from the fire, and a full month of alien treatments, she expected Werrimen would probably clear her, but had no idea what to then expect from Hunt. He sat beside her, his hand resting gently on her arm as Werrimen offered her findings. Her test results were all back to normal, but Werrimen, staring at Hunt, added that she planned to keep testing every week to ensure Jemma didn't go backwards.

'Are you happy with that, Jemma?' The question sounded genuine. Maybe she had got through to him. When she nodded, he pointed to the door.

'Right, let me outline your new program.'

She grimaced.

'I told you it'd get harder. You promised me you'd do your

best. And you also said you understood you'd answer to me if you failed.'

'And I meant it, but that doesn't mean I have to be happy about it.'

'Fair enough. From today you will do one hour in the gym, then one hour of combat training. You will have two hour's rest, then return for a second combat session, then one hour of weapons training. For the rest of this week, you will go up with Werrimen for your treatments in the evening.'

She gaped at him.

'Problem with that?'

'No, but you're going to spend four hours a day with me?' She couldn't believe he'd waste that kind of time on her.

'We'll train one on one, and I may have to change times if I get caught up. Your gym work will be with the PE Sergeant, and your range work with either myself or O'Leary. Don't mention to anyone else what we're doing.'

'What about Sean?'

'Bellamy knows, but he's not involved.'

She followed him into the gym where Liam, the fitness instructor, and Dan lurked in the background.

'You know the sergeant,' Hunt pointed to Liam. 'He'll set up your training program. He'll push you, and you will comply. Colonel O'Leary is here to ensure that. Don't let me down.' He turned on his heel and marched out of the room.

Jemma sighed. So much for making her own decisions. She turned to Liam. 'Right, what do you want me to do?'

Dan came up behind her, although she hadn't heard him.

'Atta girl. Do your best. I don't want Sean kicking my butt if you get into trouble.'

'Fine, but if I get into trouble, I'll make sure he knows it's your fault.'

He laughed. 'Right, the challenge is on. You need to remember I'm just as mean as they are.'

'Christ is there anyone in this army who isn't a bastard?' she muttered to Dan's retreating back as he walked away, a broad grin on his face.

'Ignore him,' said Liam. 'He's just playing silly buggers. He's one of the better ones.'

She sighed, 'I know, I've just got to forget everyone else, and do my own thing.'

'Spot on. Whatever the old man says, I'm here to help. Don't go slack on me though, or I'll get into you too. You've got to remember I'm under orders, just like everyone else.'

'Of course. Bastard: selection-criteria number one to enable you to work here.'

He chuckled and gave her a quick shoulder rub. 'Come on mate, cheer up. We'll warm up with the treadmill. I'm leaving it at five clicks today. The boss has more than doubled your exercise program. We'll see how you cope, change it tomorrow if it's too easy today. Don't push yourself too hard, let me work out when you're ready to change up.'

Once she found her rhythm walking, Jemma looked up to see Dan streaking around the athletics track. Liam had a stopwatch on him. Probably training to beat Sean. They were best of mates even before they discovered they were brothers, but Christ they were competitive. Liam returned and shifted her to a weights machine, then a short track workout with Dan running alongside, then push-ups, sit-ups and stretches. Next thing she knew Hunt was in the doorway, waiting for her to join him for her combat session. By the time she was released for her two-hour break, all she wanted to do was hit the sack, although first she'd set her alarm, so she wouldn't be late back and get herself into trouble.

When she returned to her apartment, she was pleased to see that true to his word, Hunt had a computer installed, with instructions on how to access the internet. But right now, she needed sleep.

CHAPTER 23

After two months of intensive training, Jemma was fitter than she'd ever been. She enjoyed her gym sessions, but the combat training with Hunt was hard. Most nights she'd return to her apartment, exhausted. One night, after a particularly gruelling training session, she walked into the apartment, ready to put her feet up, and saw Sean's full-dress uniform laid out on the bed. Her body slumped.

'Come on,' he said, putting his arms around her. 'Put on your Sunday best. I want to pretend we're going somewhere special to dinner.'

She clung to him, too tired to argue. Looking pleased with himself, he gently eased her back and pointed to the walk-in robe, but there was no way she was going anywhere without a long hot shower. She ordered it on full blast, allowing the water to flow over her and murmured, 'Control, muscle therapy.' The water streamed harder. It felt like fingers pushing along each of her aching muscles. A perfume wafted around her, floral, soft, relaxing.

'I need to stay awake,' she said to herself, as she struggled to keep her eyes open. The scent changed to something sharper, forcing her eyes open and making her blink. The water now slapped her skin, rather than the pleasant massage it had been.

'Water off.' She picked up a large, fluffy towel, wrapped it around herself and buried her face in the end. They were encouraged to use the air dryer because it also treated the skin for bacteria and protected against dryness, but she wanted the softness of the towel against her skin.

'Do you require medication to stay awake?' said Artie.

'No.' She sighed. 'I'm fine, even if I am talking to a computer.'

'Not a computer,' she heard Artie mutter before it went silent.

She headed back to the walk-in robe. An outfit had been supplied for formal occasions when she first arrived that she'd never bothered to look at. It was still in its wrapping in the wardrobe. A long black skirt, with an embroidered lace top, and a pair of shiny, black, heeled pumps. Probably not something she'd have bought herself but looked alright in the mirror once she'd dressed.

Sean held her at arm's length and looked her up and down. 'Wow. You scrub up well.'

'Well thank you, kind sir. You're not so bad yourself.' She hooked her hand into the crook of his arm and followed him from the apartment. In the dining room, Hunt, Dan, and Liam, all dressed the same as Sean, waited. Another man stood at a table which was covered in a white tablecloth and Nik waited on the far side of the table from Hunt. With a shake of her head, Jemma looked up at Sean.

'Do you still want to marry me?' he said, shifting from foot to foot as he waited for her answer.

She wasn't sure whether to laugh or cry. 'I've never had any doubt about that. Of course, I do.'

'Let's go. I have a surprise for you.'

Almost everyone she knew on the mountain, including Zadrus and Werrimen, even Eric and Mary with a gaunt-looking Anthony beside them, waited in the officers' dining room. Nik handed her a bouquet of flowers and fussed over her until a minister, also dressed in military uniform walked into the room and stood in front of them.

'Are you both ready?' said the minister.

Jemma met Sean's rather worried gaze and laughed. 'I am absolutely ready.'

The ceremony began, and she saw several people dab their eyes as they both said, 'I do.' At the end, the minister guided them to a book he'd set up on a side table. Then Hunt and Nik signed as witnesses. A lavish dinner followed. She couldn't say she wanted to be here on the mountain, yet all these people treated her like family, and every one of them would protect her with their lives.

Sean's arm slipped around her shoulders. 'I know things aren't ideal, but you've made my life whole, and I'm confident whatever happens now, we'll get through it together.'

'I love you so much, Sean. I just wish we could have our honeymoon somewhere other than a huge cave cut out of a mountain top by aliens.'

He laughed. 'Maybe we should say thank you to everyone, then go and get started on that honeymoon.'

'Hang on.' Hunt wheeled in an enormous three-tier wedding cake.

Tears flowed down Jemma's cheeks and both Hunt and Sean rushed to comfort her. 'It's alright,' she said between sobs. 'I'm overwhelmed by what you've all done for me. For us.'

After they'd thanked each person individually, they made their way back to their apartment where they talked well into the night. As she snuggled close to him, she knew Sean was right, so long as they were together, nothing else mattered.

Next morning, the honeymoon was clearly over. Hunt informed her that Sean's old team would arrive around mid-morning and he might be late for their combat session. He said to wait for him in the medical centre. She sighed, and started towards the gym, irritated when Dan, cheerful as ever, ran up behind her.

'C'mon, Mrs Bellamy, let's jog down.'

'Let's not.' That was the first time anyone had called her *Mrs Bellamy*, but she didn't have time to process it and wasn't in the mood to act like Hunt's demands were all a bit of fun. She wanted time alone with Sean, just the two of them, no interference from anyone else.

Dan stopped abruptly, a metre in front of her. 'You can't get out of this. The boss has spoken. Liam and I have to enforce his orders. You know that. Why don't you try to enjoy yourself? If it'll help, I'll do everything alongside you. Come on, can we be friends?' He pouted as he crossed his arms in front of his chest and waited for a response.

She couldn't get past him, and try as she might, she couldn't stop the smile from forming. He was so like Sean, right down to the mischievous grin. In the end, she slipped her arm through his and as he picked up his pace, she jogged alongside.

'Well done,' he said. 'Let's do this together, and I'll do my best to make it fun for you.'

If only he knew. She'd have loved to tell him about the combat training, but she'd been told to tell no one.

Dan placed himself on a treadmill beside her and set himself at a walking speed, chatting to her as she went. There was nothing pretentious about Dan, he could have been a smart alec, and run at twice her speed to show her up, but he genuinely wanted to help. He even had her laughing with some push-ups, which he did alongside, and pretended to find difficult. The supremely fit Dan. Yeah, right. She'd always liked Dan, but her opinion of him now soared.

Before she knew it, her session with Dan was finished, and she was into her combat training with Hunt. When that was over, she headed to the dining room for some lunch. Nik was already there with some of the scientists and called her over.

'We've been talking about the animals outside,' said Nik. 'Joe has been checking around for any more dead animals. Tell her, Joe.'

'I've found only two in the last week, and both died from

natural causes. Either the virus is gone, or the animals have developed immunity. Do you see what I'm getting at?'

'You're saying it's now safe out there. No more dead animals.'

'You've got it. So, I've asked General Hunt if you could join me one night. We could look for your quolls. He's agreed, so long as he's with you.'

'Seriously? He's going to let me go outside. When?'

'We didn't get that far, but I'm going back to see him now.'

Nik was smiling at her. 'Does that make you feel a bit better?'

'You bet.' The prospect of standing outside and breathing fresh air was exciting. 'Do you think …' She hesitated.

'Spit it out,' said Nik.

'Could someone take some samples from those latrine mounds? Maybe I could help analyse them in the lab.'

'Great idea,' replied Joe. 'I'll put that to the general too when I see him.'

Three months after arriving at SCARF, Jemma still worked hard with Dan and Hunt. Both seemed pleased with her, and Hunt had kept up his end of the bargain, being much less aggressive. Joe had brought in some of the samples she'd requested, and Hunt had agreed to her working in the lab. Although she had yet to go outside, her day-to-day life had fallen into a pattern, so she was surprised when, one morning, Hunt ushered her away from his office until, as she turned, she saw Sean and Dan talking to two armed soldiers, both with so much body armour, she couldn't determine if they were male or female.

'The police have found the mechanic from Archerfield,' said Hunt. 'He'll arrive here mid-morning. I'll need you and Denis to identify him. We'll get to your combat session as soon after that as we can. I know how devastated you'd be if we couldn't.'

'Shattered.' Only someone exceptionally hard of hearing could have missed her sarcasm.

'Pleased to hear you enjoy it so much. Tell Denis what I've said. O'Leary already knows. If I possibly can, we might go for that walk outside this afternoon. Your scientist mate is demanding your presence.'

'Do you mean that?' Ignoring his raised eyebrows, she ran down the stairs to the gym, thrilled at the possibility of walking even a few metres in the fresh air.

Late morning, after both she and Nik had identified the mechanic, Hunt told her to wait for him in the medical centre. It was after midday when he arrived, but he still insisted on conducting her session, finishing around 13:30 hours. He told her to have lunch and be waiting for him again at 14:00, although he wasn't sure what time he'd get back.

14:30 came and went, but Jemma waited. At 14:45, one of the scientists ran in. She looked up and smiled at him, 'Where's Joe?'

'With the general. He sent me down to bring you up to the top of the stairs. They've rolled the boulder back and they're waiting for you.'

'That's odd. General Hunt's always said I'm not allowed to go out by myself.'

'No, I'm to go with you. You won't be alone, and you'll see them as soon as you get to the top of the stairs. Joe's been asking for weeks. You don't want to blow it.'

He was right, she didn't want to *blow it*. It did sound like a direction from Hunt, and he had said he'd try for this afternoon. She followed the scientist, but hesitated at the bottom of the stairs.

'C'mon, the general's waiting.'

Neither of them noticed Nik pull herself into a doorway as they approached.

Jemma followed the scientist up the stairs but hung back at the top, hesitant to leave the protection of the stairwell. She looked out, but couldn't see Hunt, or Joe.

'Stay there, I'll look for them,' said the scientist, walking out of sight around the boulder. 'Here they are,' the man called back. 'Around here.'

She edged out. It still didn't feel right and when she saw Joe stretched out unconscious on the ground, she knew it wasn't, but it was too late.

The scientist, although she now doubted that's what he was, swung around and aimed his pistol at her. 'Don't make me use this. Come with me, I'll get you away from this place, and you won't have to deal with these bastards ever again.'

'What are you doing? Who are you?' Jemma stared at the weapon. The stairs weren't too far behind her, but her legs wouldn't move.

'I'm trying to help you. Your brother-in-law sent me for you. I'll take you back to your family, your sister.'

Despite the photograph album of her sister, she still had no real proof that her sister was with Pritchard and even if he was her brother-in-law, she could never work with him. But there was no point debating any of that with this fellow. She had to get away. One of Hunt's first instructions had been, 'Centre yourself and clear your head. Then keep the person talking and convince them to come into your space.' She stood straight and pushed every other thought from her mind as she stared back at him. 'I don't understand. How can we get away, so we won't be found?'

'Mr Pritchard's got the transport lined up, we just have to get away from here and he'll pick us up in his sphere. You only think that insufferable Colonel Bellamy cares about you because you're stuck with him. Your family really does care about you.'

Jemma edged within kicking distance. 'I'd like to get away, but I'm afraid they'd catch me. Then I'd be locked in the cells, probably tried for treason. I don't think I can do it.'

The man lowered his weapon and stepped forward. 'No, no. Mr Pritchard can fix all of that. He'll look after you.'

Now almost close enough to touch, Jemma raised her leg and, with all her might, slammed her foot into his crutch. She pulled back as he started to fall forward and punched her fist into his jaw, then smashed the other fist into the side of his face. He dropped to the ground and, from behind, she pushed her knee into his spine and dragged both his arms behind his back. He groaned but didn't move. Still pumped, she reached for her communicator to call Hunt.

*   *   *

After seeing Jemma on the stairs, Nik had run into Hunt's office praying he wouldn't yell at her for interrupting. 'Sir,' she said, looking directly at Hunt. 'I need you out here. It can't wait.'

With only the slightest hesitation, Hunt followed.

'I just saw a man take Jemma outside. He was dressed like one of the scientists. I heard him tell Jemma you were out there waiting for her.'

'How long ago?'

'A minute. Less.'

'Follow her.' Hunt strode back to his room. 'O'Leary, with me. The rest of you continue questioning the prisoner.' Nik ran for the entrance.

*   *   *

Jemma started to shake as the realisation of what she had just done began to register, so she forced herself to focus on keeping her knee wedged on the man's back and steadying her hands enough to use the communicator. She heard movement behind.

'Jemma, it's me,' said Nik. 'General Hunt's on his way.'

Jemma's mind whirled as she felt Nik's hand on her shoulder. She couldn't be sure of anyone. It was Nik who'd introduced her to the scientists. Then again, she'd seen Joe unconscious, a few metres away. She had no idea what to do until she heard the general's voice. Then she knew it was over.

'Well done, Jemma,' said Hunt. 'Stand up and come to me. O'Leary, Denis, take charge of this fellow.'

Nik helped Jemma up, while Dan dragged the man to his feet. She'd never seen Dan look so fierce.

'I've got a gun to your back, mate, not an alien weapon,' said Dan. 'Any stunts and I'll use it.'

Jemma stumbled towards Hunt. He pulled her close to him and she buried her head into his shoulder.

'Take him to the cells. You go too Denis, back O'Leary up. I'm taking Jemma to the nurse. Head back and meet us there once you've got him locked up.'

'You've got to help Joe.' Jemma pointed to where she'd last seen him, but he'd gone. All sorts of scenarios rushed through her head, the worst that he'd set this attack up, but they found him clinging to the back of the boulder. Hunt called for help.

Once Joe had been shifted to a stretcher, Hunt eased his hold on Jemma. 'What possessed you to go out there with that fellow?' She could tell from the tone of his voice, he wasn't annoyed, but was keen to understand what had happened.

'He was dressed like a scientist and said you were waiting for me. I believed him.'

'What did your instinct tell you?'

'I didn't want to go. I hung back, but he went around the rock out of my sight, and it sounded like he was speaking to you. I thought you were there.'

'And what then?'

'He pulled that gun on me. I kept him talking like you always said, and edged closer to him, until I was within range. Then I seemed to go into autopilot.'

'I'd rather you'd listened to your instincts, but I'm proud of you. You handled yourself well. Aren't you glad I made you do all that training?'

She glared at him but didn't have the strength to bite back. It annoyed her to admit it, even to herself, that she'd be long gone if it weren't for Hunt's twice-daily torture. He eased himself back but kept his arm around her shoulders as they walked down to the nurse.

Jemma sat with Joe while the nurse bandaged his head, then waited with him until the helicopter arrived to take him down to a Gold Coast hospital.

When Dan and Nik returned, Hunt had them stay with Jemma so he could check that both the mechanic and the fake scientist were locked in the cells, and that section was sealed off, before he brought Sean down. 'Bellamy might just try to strangle him.'

'I want to strangle him,' muttered Dan.

'We both do, but neither of us will. Bellamy just might.'

Less than five minutes later, Sean tore into the medical centre. 'What the hell happened?' he yelled at Dan, as he ran to her side.

Aware Hunt needed time to isolate the prisoners, Jemma told Sean to calm down, but once she'd completed her story he jumped up, his face tight and red and his fists clenched so hard the knuckles were white.

'Where the hell is that bastard?'

Dan stood eye to eye with Sean. 'Where you can't get to him,' he said, keeping his voice low and even.

'Get out of my way,' snarled Sean.

'No mate, I'm not going to let you do it.'

'You think you can stop me?'

Nik sat beside Jemma. 'Christ, I don't want to see this play out.'

'Stand down, both of you,' Hunt growled as he walked in.

Sean whirled around to Hunt. 'I'll kill him,' he snarled.

'No, you're not going to get that opportunity. Back off.' Hunt turned his attention to Jemma. 'Are you okay, Jemma?'

She nodded.

'Good. O'Leary take her up to my office and wait for me there. Denis, you join them.'

'I want to stay with Sean,' said Jemma.

'No. Head out, O'Leary.'

Sean jumped when Hunt slammed the door.

'Alright,' said Hunt. 'We're both angry. Time to settle down and decide what to do.'

'That bastard could have killed her.'

'Yes, and now that he's safely tucked away, we have to start thinking strategically and use him to find Pritchard. That's the only way we'll ever make her safe.'

'Alright,' snapped Sean. 'I'll go interview him.'

'Not in your current mood,' returned Hunt. 'We'll let him stew for a while, then I'll go down. They'll all be up there waiting for us now.' Hunt turned on his heel and strode to the door, 'With me.'

They were greeted with startled looks as they entered Hunt's office, but no one spoke, and when Jemma started to get up, a low 'No,' from Hunt made her sit again.

'We need to know how these arseholes are getting access. And whether there are any more of them here,' said Hunt.

'Sir, may I say something?' Nik appeared nervous, not surprising given she was surrounded by a general, a brigadier, a colonel, the colonel's wife, a lieutenant-colonel, all of whom looked like thunder, and several majors.

'Of course, Denis, if it's relevant.'

'You've probably read about alien abductions. People say they were taken into spaceships, and had their memories altered.'

Hunt looked like he was about to eat the young woman. 'Your point is?'

'Sir, if you'll bear with me. I don't know about alien abductions, but I've seen Werrimen alter someone's memory. She told me it works like hypnosis but, with her method, the person can't resist. About a year ago, someone tried to break in here, and Werrimen was on site. She touched him on the neck, and the fellow answered every question, couldn't lie. So they don't just use it to alter memories, they use it to make people tell the truth.'

'Oh, damn,' said Everson. 'She's right. Why didn't I think of that? Werrimen has tried to teach me, but I've never quite got it. I'm sure she'd come down and help us.'

'Right, can you organise that?' When Everson left, Hunt dismissed everyone except Jemma and Sean.

Jemma spoke first. 'I'd like to be part of the investigation. It's me they're after and I'm sure I can do more.' She expected a negative response and lines formed on his forehead. He prevaricated but didn't say no. She felt his eyes bore into her as Everson returned to say Werrimen had readily agreed to help and would start in the morning.

'Captain Denis has volunteered to be your first subject,' said Hunt, when he joined Werrimen and Jemma in the conference room the next morning.

'Very good,' replied Werrimen. 'Nik, do you understand what I plan to do. You will not be able to lie to me after we begin.'

'Yes, ma'am. I'm happy for you to question me.'

'You are one of the original SCARF team,' added Hunt. 'So our questions will be about your loyalty although, after yesterday, I have every confidence in you.'

'Understood sir, and if it will help you trust me, I'm happy with that.'

Werrimen closed her eyes and moved behind Nik. She touched Nik's neck and declared her ready. Sean took over and started the questions he'd worked on with Hunt.

'What is your name, date of birth, rank and army identification number,' said Sean.

She rattled them off. Sean went on, 'Have you ever gone by any other name?'

'Yes, my birth name was Nikola Denisov.'

'When was it changed to Nikola Denis, and was it official?'

'My parents changed it by deed poll, before I was five.'

'Where were you born? Are you an Australian citizen?'

'My adoptive parents, who were Australian, or so I thought, told me I was born in Moscow, Russia and that we came here after my parents were killed in a car accident. But that's clearly not right. I gained citizenship through my adoptive parents when I was a child.'

'Have you ever provided any information to anyone outside this unit, about your role here?'

'No.'

'Have you ever accepted money in exchange for information, at any time, or anywhere, since you have been in the army?'

'No.'

Sean nodded to Werrimen that he was finished. She again touched Nik's neck, checked and cleared her. He asked Nik if she could remember everything she'd said.

'Very clearly.'

'Did you try to say anything that wasn't truthful at any point?'

'Yeah, I really wanted to lie about my Russian connection. I don't see myself as Russian, I can't remember anything about Russia. As far as I'm concerned, I'm Australian.'

Sean smiled and gently reminded her she actually came from Anders Major. His only interest was where her loyalties lay now. 'What happened when you tried to lie?'

'Nothing really. I'd formulate the wrong answer in my head, but the truthful one came out, no matter how hard I tried. I wouldn't want to have done something wrong. You wouldn't stand a chance.'

Hunt punched his fist in the air, and declared he'd stay with Werrimen to hear if anyone admitted disloyalty, but Sean was keen to crack the mechanic from Archerfield, so he went in search of Dan and then headed to the cells.

CHAPTER 24

The basement level of SCARF housed generators, water tanks and stores as well as the cells. It reminded Sean of a medieval dungeon. Its walls were hewn from the surrounding rock and there was a vague smell of moisture and mildew. He'd only visited the basement twice since he'd moved to the mountain and, on each occasion, he'd been sure that he'd heard someone speak. The second time he'd frozen to the sensation of someone taking hold of his arm. There'd been no one there on either occasion. So many stories had to be hidden within these walls, and a quick look behind told him he wasn't the only one affected by the place. Dan looked quite pale.

He signed in with the on-duty guard, waited for Dan to do the same, then proceeded to the cells. The mechanic sat on a stretcher bed which had been fixed to the wall with large bolts pushed into age-old holes which Sean suspected had once held chains. While that would seem to fly in the face of the alien attitude, he knew that they worked with the attitudes of the people at the time.

The man stood as they entered and held out his hand. 'Ted's the name. And you are?'

'Colonel Bellamy and Colonel O'Leary,' Sean replied.

He'd expected the fellow to demand his release or protest his innocence, but Ted sat back on his bed and chatted as though they were old buddies knocking off a couple of beers in the local pub on a Friday night. He freely told them he'd been offered money to keep Crockett's Lear jets in flight ready condition, laughing that Crockett had never guessed what he was up to. Crockett's pay was miniscule compared with the money Pritchard's people had paid him for information on Williamson and his team. After a few beers, Williamson had leaked like a sieve and Ted had recorded the conversation. It'd then been simple to get Williamson on the payroll after he threatened to release the tapes.

'Fucking idiot,' growled Sean. 'Alright, what about the captain you saw yesterday?'

He'd tried Nik too, disgusted that all she wanted was to learn to fly. He offered names, the phone number of his contact, and the location of his contact's headquarters, but he couldn't say where the terrorists had gone after Costa Rica.

'That was too easy,' said Sean after they left him. 'Was he checked for tracking devices when he came in?'

'Don't know, the whole thing with Jemma got in the way,' replied Dan. 'Maybe the attack on her was timed to make us miss things. I'll get it organised now.'

'Yeah, okay, but strip him down to his underwear, then scan him. Remove his clothes from the room, and take your time replacing them. Make him uncomfortable. Then check if anyone's outside looking for him. Get Nik to help.'

Nobody should be able to get in, but he'd thought that

before and been wrong. Even so, the mechanic's attitude bothered Sean. The man should expect jail time, yet he showed no concern. His contact, Giovanni, obviously expected a call, but Sean wanted to know more before he made that call. Neither he nor Dan would be perturbed if the questioning got rough and the cells didn't have cameras, so no one would know. When they returned, Sean began, 'Do you understand you're looking at multiple years in jail?'

The mechanic shook his head. 'You still don't get it. I won't go to jail. I won't even get to court.'

Dan moved closer and lowered his voice. 'How do you figure that?'

'See all that brass on your mate's shoulder? The one who's looking after us has different stuff, a sword and scabbard, then a crown.'

'Who? Why would a lieutenant-general bother with a low-life like you?'

'I don't have his name, but there can't be too many of them and we've got a Federal minister on board. And heaps of police.'

Sean grabbed the man and pushed him against the wall, his forearm pressed against the fellow's throat. 'Give me names.'

'No point attacking me, mate,' gasped Ted. 'I don't have names. I gave you a number. Use it. You'll get your answers from him. Probably be on the payroll before dark. That's how they've got the others.'

'So, what's their game?' said Sean, releasing some of his pressure.

'Are you really that innocent? Every government will buy their virus. Big dollars.'

Sean couldn't believe anyone could be so calculating, so evil. They might get the money, but they could die from the virus. 'What do they want from us?'

'Your leaders know how to cure viruses. Nobody else does. And it's quite specifically you they want to talk to, Bellamy, and your lady.'

Sean stared at him in disgust, contemplating the number of ways he could drop the fellow where he stood. 'As far as I'm concerned you can rot in here. Your mates won't get access to you.'

He marched out but said nothing until they reached his office. Then he slammed his fist on the desk. 'We've got to use this idiot to find Pritchard.'

'I think we're going to have to try his contact,' replied Dan.

'Better discuss it with the general. If they really have got top brass, it's way out of my league. I'm not sure it isn't out of his.'

Hunt reacted angrily when it dawned on him that one of his superiors might be dirty. Everson stared at Sean until Hunt had finished, then he thumped the wall, smashing a hole in the fascia.

'I'll bet I even know who it is,' said Everson.

Sean jumped. 'Who?'

'No, I won't drop a name. I could be wrong. Give me a while. After everything we've done to make this facility work, I'm not about to let Drick destroy it.'

It could have been a damned good act from Everson, but Sean didn't think so. 'How do we stop them?'

'So long as we can identify them, we have ways,' said Everson. 'They're not necessarily conventional ways, so I won't tell you at this stage. The most important thing is to identify them.'

'Sir, we're not murderers,' said Sean.

'No, neither am I, and that's not what I'm suggesting. Find them. Then I'll tell you the options. You can be part of the decision.'

The mechanic's confidence he'd get away with everything left Sean uneasy. 'I'll need Nik to set up a trace before I call the contact.'

'Can't have her, she's gone down to the hospital to visit Joe, the scientist. She left straight after her session with Werrimen, said she had to be alone for a while. You'll have to put up with me,' said Jemma, tucking her hand under his arm.

'But you're not up to speed with the alien equipment.'

'Well, that's not quite right,' said Hunt. 'She asked to be more involved and she's been working with Nik and Zadrus. She wanted to surprise you, although we didn't expect it'd be like this.'

'Surprise.' Jemma grinned at him. 'Now, down to business, I've got everything ready to set up your trace. Zadrus is on his way down, so if you need anything more complicated, he'll help me.'

Sean shook his head as he keyed in the phone number.

Not in the mood to waste words, he snarled when the phone answered, 'We have your mechanic, what do you want?'

'Good,' replied the man. 'The direct approach. First, you should know I have someone of yours.' There was a pause. 'Captain Nikola Denis.'

Sean felt all the air escape from his lungs. He struggled to keep his voice steady. They had high level officials in their pockets, no qualms about kidnapping scientists and forcing them to work, and didn't care if they lived or died. Now Nik. The look on Dan's face was pure shock, and Everson had moved in to steady him.

'What do you want?' Sean repeated. His voice was terse, but he managed to hold it firm.

'Once you've shown me your viral cure and given my scientists enough information to replicate it, we'll let her go. I'll also have my mechanic back. And you can return Dr Anderson to us. Today, if you please.'

Aware of Hunt easing in behind him, ready to back him up, Sean struggled to think of anything other than Nik, and how to get her back. They obviously didn't know about the fellow who'd lured Jemma outside, or they'd have demanded his release too which confirmed Werrimen's belief she'd cleared everyone on the mountain.

He took a deep breath, determined to sound composed. 'Who the hell are you?'

'You don't know me, and it doesn't matter. Do as I say, and no one else need be hurt. Otherwise you will receive Captain

Denis back, piece by piece. I do not threaten, I act. You have two hours to decide what you will do.'

The short call hadn't allowed Jemma to define the contact's location. He'd have to find another way.

'I've tried several times to call her,' said Tom. 'She hasn't answered, so I just contacted the hospital. She left there more than an hour ago.'

Hunt, who had slipped out of the room, returned with Werrimen and Zadrus.

'Jemma?' said Sean, breathing hard and propping himself against a desk.

'Lambert's with her in the control room,' said Hunt. 'We have to see this through.'

'I know,' said Sean. 'Jemma won't be safe if we don't stop them, and now Nik. Jesus.'

'Yes,' said Hunt. 'Remember they're cousins. Nik was the obvious target. We should've seen it sooner.'

Werrimen took Sean's hands in hers. 'You need my energy.' She looked into his eyes and waited a moment before she spoke again. 'I would like to take Jemma up to our ship. Zadrus will stay here to continue tracking. That is the only way we can be sure Jemma is secure.'

'I agree,' said Hunt. 'Lambert can go with her.'

'She won't want to leave under the circumstances.' Sean didn't want to let go of Werrimen's hands. Even under her calming influence, he struggled to stay focused.

Jemma eased into the back of the room, Tom by her side. 'I'm not leaving. I'm the reason they've taken Nik. It's my responsibility to see this through. If the facility becomes compromised, I will go then, but not before.'

Hunt stared at her. 'If at any time I or Zadrus or Werrimen tell you to go, you will do so. Lambert stay with her.'

'No,' Jemma replied. 'That is a decision I will make. Would you like me to set up the traces now for the next call?'

Sean jumped in before Hunt could reply, although Jemma's determination pleased him. 'Yes, I'm ready.' Now one hour and fifty minutes after the first call, Sean called again. 'We have to meet. You need to convince me Nik's alive and well.'

'I take it you've checked she's missing.'

Sean said nothing.

'Fine,' said the man. 'I'll take that for an agreement. The shopping centre at the bottom of your mountain road. I'll be in the carpark in a grey van. Don't think you can storm us. My people are more than a match for you. Captain Denis will be in the van. You have one hour to get there.'

He stood after terminating the call, to allow Zadrus to implant a tracking device under the skin on his shoulder, and a tiny earpiece in his right ear with a highly sensitive embedded microphone. Jemma, standing beside Zadrus, checked all the devices on a small screen. On her okay, Zadrus cleared him to go.

'Take the station wagon from the carpark,' said Hunt. 'Use the ATV to get to it. O'Leary and his team will be close behind you.'

It took Sean just over half an hour to reach the van that held

Nik. Her captors had cordoned off the carpark with police tape. He glimpsed Dan jog past and a female soldier drop off behind the van, presumably to check for explosives and to find somewhere to plant a tracking device. Hopefully she'd also make contact with Nik.

Sean casually submitted to the terrorists' checks for weapons and wires, doing his best to slow them down and give Dan the time he needed. Relieved Zadrus's devices weren't detected, he looked at the contact, and waited.

'Thank you for joining us, Colonel Bellamy. You can see Captain Denis in the van. She is alive and well, but I'm happy to change that if you don't co-operate.'

Sean growled, 'I'm here, aren't I?'

'Easy, Bellamy,' said Hunt in his ear.

'Yes, you are,' responded the man. 'Let me make it clear, my people will intervene should you attempt to stop us. The van will leave shortly, and I will accompany you to your facility. My men are already there. They are armed and capable, so your people should co-operate with them. I will advise you when we get there what information we require.'

Sean suspected the fellow must have at least suspected he had Zadrus's microphone on him and was sending a message to co-operate. 'I'll check with my superiors.'

'No, you won't. You'll do as I say.'

'Go ahead, Bellamy,' said Hunt. 'Zadrus has a fix on the van and is tracking it from the spaceship. There aren't any explosives. We've disarmed the people who landed here. They had alien weapons. We don't know where they got them, so be careful.'

Sean did his best to appear confused. 'Alright, get in the car. How are you so confident you'll get what you want?'

The man smiled. 'If you fail, I dispose of Captain Denis, and you'll be ordered from above to do as I say anyway. We need what you have. Our operations are sanctioned by your government, partly funded by your government.'

'That's ridiculous,' said Sean. 'Why would they fund terrorists?'

'Simple. Your government wants what we've developed. It's a quid pro quo thing. Please don't tell me you believe your people wouldn't use biological warfare.'

'Our government has always been antagonistic to biological warfare. So, no I don't believe they'd be supporting you.'

'Oh dear.' He laughed as he looked over at Sean. 'There's a world of difference between public statements and private actions.'

Hunt spoke into his earpiece. 'Cool it, Bellamy. Don't make him suspicious.'

Sean wasn't prepared to let it go. 'So, who's this politician you're in bed with?'

'Bellamy, shut the fuck up.' The man was looking the other way and didn't see Sean jump in response to Hunt's bellow.

'That's on a need-to-know basis. And if you co-operate, you don't need to know.'

Sean remained silent until they reached the top of the mountain and transferred to the ATV.

'What the hell have you done with my people?' said the man, when they reached the clearing.

Sean shrugged, 'How would I know, I've been with you.'

Hunt, Everson and several staff emerged, all armed with alien weapons. 'Follow me,' said Hunt. 'Or I will immobilise you.'

The man smirked and dragged out his own weapon.

Hunt fired. The man arched his back, then fell.

'God, I love these weapons,' said Hunt grinning.

Sean ran to the granite boulder and down the stairs to find Jemma. She was focused on an array of images and in deep conversation with Zadrus. They'd tracked the van to an old disused pub ten minutes from the shopping centre. Dan's team was already there. Jemma turned to Sean and told him that Dan and his crew had captured the perimeter guards and were about to move inside.

Dan swore. 'Got them, but Nik's not here. We've had the premises surrounded. They can't have got her out. We're starting an internal search.'

'We are looking too,' called Zadrus, zooming inside the building. He scanned from room to room. A red haze appeared around each of the people. Suddenly, a section of the floor glowed red.

Jemma called to Dan. 'Look for something under there, a metre in front of you.'

'Got it. There's a trapdoor.' A tense few moments followed. 'Found her. At least twenty others, most of them pretty low. I'll need multiple ambulances.'

Sean continued to watch until all were out, and the ambulances had left. 'Dan, you can leave the others to finish. Bring Nik back here, so we can check her.'

When there was no reply, Jemma continued scanning until she found them, holding onto each other.

Sean put his arm around Jemma, 'Interesting.'

'Bellamy, you can leave Colonel O'Leary to sort that now,' said Everson, marching into the room, his face scarlet. 'Come with me.'

Sean had to run to catch up with Everson's stride, and was stunned when Everson hurled a bundle of papers on his desk.

'They don't waste any time,' said Everson. 'Lieutenant-General Johansson has ordered me to release all prisoners to that creep you brought in. I'm to take them to the airport. Someone will meet us there and take over. He pointedly reminded me I'm a visitor on this planet.'

Sean's eyes narrowed. He'd never worked with Johansson, but he knew people who had. All of them had left the army after their experience with him.

Hunt swept in, equally angry, saying that he'd just had a similar phone call.

Everson remained silent until the door was secured. 'Before you react, Bellamy, I have organised a solution. Zadrus will take Johannsen to the spaceship, erase his memory, then shift him to another planet. Plenty of planets will help.'

'That'll take some serious planning,' said Hunt, 'and first we have to capture him.'

'Agreed, but I'm sensing neither of you are opposed to making him disappear, just the mechanism of how to do it.'

'I don't want to sound like the devil's advocate here,' said

Hunt, 'but the civilian police and MPs will put two and two together and point the finger at us.'

'Already thought of that,' replied Everson. 'No one knows we've captured his people. The general won't admit he's in bed with terrorists.'

Hunt answered his phone, then swore as he hung up. 'We're about to have visitors. Lieutenant-General Johansson and he has someone with him.'

'He's told you what he wants,' said Sean. 'Is he coming here to enforce his orders? Shouldn't we notify the chief?'

'I've spoken to the chief. He's already forgotten my call. He did suggest that if the good general's companion is the politician, that we could tidy up.'

Sean gaped at him. 'Tidy up. You're talking about knocking off a general, and a senior politician. It feels like treason to me. Are you sure we're not getting in over our heads?'

Everson was surprisingly calm. 'I understand your concern, Bellamy.

'Sir, you have visitors.' Nik looked nervous as she poked her head through the door.

'Thank you, Denis. Have you been cleared?'

'Yes, sir.'

'Head to the control room. We'll meet you there.'

Sean stood straight; he wasn't giving these fellows any room to criticise.

'And this is?' said the general, looking at Sean.

'Colonel Bellamy,' replied Hunt. 'Bellamy, this is General Johansson.'

The general extended his hand. 'Pleased to meet you, Bellamy.'

'Likewise, sir.'

'Now, I'd like you to meet my colleague. I'm sure you all recognise him, Terry Yeung.' Yeung was a senior Federal Cabinet Minister, well known for his anti-military views. Johansson went on to acknowledge Sean's skill in capturing the terrorists but insisted his concerns were misguided. Their project could potentially stamp out war.

Sean struggled to maintain his calm. 'Stop wars by wiping out the rest of the population, you mean?'

'That'll do, Bellamy,' said Hunt.

'No, no, it's a fair comment,' replied Johansson. 'You see, if we find a radical government or a terrorist group controlling a country or a province, we could introduce the virus and stop them in their tracks.'

'But what about the civilians who'd die in the process?' said Sean.

'There may be collateral damage, but if it saves the rest of the world from some monstrous regime, then it'd be worth it. Do you understand where I'm coming from?'

Aware of the need for caution, Sean took his time to respond. This fellow was as insane as Pritchard. Hunt was right, play along. In the end, he muttered an agreement, then stood back.

'Now perhaps you could take me to my people, and we can organise their release.'

'Afraid not,' said Everson. 'We've taken them back to where we picked them up. There's no one left here.'

Everson and Hunt remained impassive and it was clear to Sean they knew something he didn't.

'I'm sorry if this has been a wasted journey,' said Everson, extending his hand towards the door. 'Would you like a tour of the facility while you're here?'

'Yes,' replied the general. 'That would be a good idea.'

'Do you have a driver or anyone waiting for you? I can organise some refreshments for them while we go around,' said Hunt.

'No, it was such a nice day, I decided to drive myself. Gave us a good opportunity for a chat, and the walk through the bush from the carpark was most pleasant.'

Yeung didn't look at all happy to Sean. Perhaps he'd picked up on Everson's plan.

As they left the office Everson turned back and winked at Sean. 'I'd like to show you one of the transporters we use to get to the mothership. If you have the time, we could take a short trip out, and you can get a feel for them.'

Sean had been called audacious in his time, but this topped all. He walked back to the stairs hoping some fresh air might clear his mind. Supporting himself against the granite rock, he saw a transporter hovering a couple of kilometres to the East. 'Jesus Christ,' he muttered, as the general's car slowly rose in the blue light. He rubbed his eyes to make sure he wasn't hallucinating, and saw Hunt approaching. 'That's got to come back to haunt us. I can't believe no one will suspect us of their disappearance.'

'Possibly,' replied Hunt. 'I've just called General

Johansson's office to enquire when they expect the good general to arrive. They were quite surprised; thought he'd already be here. Strange we haven't seen him yet, isn't it?'

'Yeah, sure,' replied Sean.

'Cheer up. The last time I saw them they were safely tucked away in the big transporter with Werrimen explaining how it works. They'll be well out into the atmosphere before they realise that they're trapped.'

'God, I hope you're right.'

'Have faith. Johansson and Yeung won't bother us again. I've sent two records of interview to the chief, one from your discussion with the mechanic, the other my chat with Williamson.

'Why?'

'Both mentioned Johansson, suggested he's dirty. Don't you remember?'

Sean shook his head and turned to go back inside until he felt Hunt's hand on his chest.

'Don't speak of this to anyone, not O'Leary, not Jemma, no one. We are innocent of any wrongdoing, if none of us know what is going on.'

'What about Nik?'

'I'll swear her to secrecy. I'm not worried. She's loyal to us.'

Sean could only shake his head. 'Yes, she is. Now what about the prisoners?'

'Set up that arsehole who kidnapped Nik to call his controllers. Once you've got all the information you can out of him, hand all the prisoners over to the counterterrorism squad.'

Knowing Zadrus had set up the equipment needed to track any calls and listen in, Sean returned the kidnapper's phone and told him he had the right to make a couple of calls. He expected the man to call the general first, then the politician, but it was the next call that should be most interesting. That should be to one of the terrorist leaders.

The man did just that, staring at Sean after his second attempt. 'No one's answering.'

Sean advised him that two high-level people, suspected of links to Pritchard, had disappeared. He casually dropped the names and suggested that others might also be involved.

'Someone up there in your organisation might be picking off weak links,' said Sean, doing his best to sound disinterested. 'You'd now be the weakest link of all, of course. I'm happy for you to keep trying until you get someone.'

The man slumped in his chair, sweat dripping from his forehead. He claimed he hadn't been outside Brisbane. His only other contact had been a mobile phone number, a throwaway that changed every three to four weeks.

Sean told him to call that number and Dan explained, in a pleasant voice, that if he said anything untoward, he'd swallow a bullet.

'Those things don't kill,' the man growled.

'No, but this does,' said Sean, with a smile. He pulled out his trusted 9mm Glock 19, and pointed it at the man. 'And don't doubt my capacity to use it. I can't see any reason to keep scum like you alive.'

The man's armpits were soaked, and his palms left a mark

on the table where he'd been resting, but he picked up his mobile phone and dialled the number.

'Be very careful,' growled Sean. 'Put it on loudspeaker, and once you get them, keep them talking.'

When the phone answered, the man told his contact that the police channels were full of the disappearance of the general and politician. He asked them to get him out of the country. After a protracted silence on the other end, the contact asked how long it would take to get to the Gold Coast airport. He could have him on an international plane in about five hours. They'd pick him up from there. Sean gave him a signal to keep talking, so he asked what they wanted him to do with the local operation. The other end told him to abandon it, then cut off. Dan announced they had a trace to a warehouse in Munich, and Everson already had Interpol on it. They both believed the man when he said he had no knowledge of that part of the operation and had never been there.

All the other prisoners proved to be dead ends. It seemed to Sean that every small cog in the wheel knew something, but no one had enough to put it all together. He notified the Federal counterterrorism agency to expect the terrorists, and news slowly trickled in that Interpol, and the Munich police, had captured several terrorists, and searched their premises.

CHAPTER 25

Jemma trembled as she followed a grim-faced Hunt to his office. He pointed to a chair and waited until she sat. 'I've spoken to General Harris. My request for your release was denied. With Pritchard still at large, he said it was premature.' Hunt's upper lip quivered, and he looked away. 'I know you want to leave here, but we can't achieve that yet. I promise you I won't stop trying.' His voice was soft, gentler than she'd ever heard, and when she raised her eyes to meet his, she saw him dab his eyes.

'Will they ever let me go home?'

'I don't know Jemma, but we mustn't lose hope.' He leaned forward until his head gently touched hers and rubbed her back, just as her father had done when she was a child.

She tried to laugh but it sounded false, even to her. 'I'm a pariah as far as the government's concerned. They think I'm important so they can't risk my safety. Yet they won't let me take responsibility for myself or give me any freedom. Looks like you're stuck with me.' Her resolve evaporated when, as he wrapped his arms around her, she saw tears roll down his cheeks.

'I'm happy to be stuck with you,' he said, once they'd both settled. 'Now, I've got something to suggest to you. We've got on so much better since our heart to heart, I'd like you to consider working more with me. Maybe we can find a way to give more meaning to your life here? Would you consider that? I'd like to see you as part of this team.'

'I can't be part of your team, I'm not military.'

'Yes, you can. We're an oddball group. It's my job to make the best of our situation, and I can integrate you into some of our activities.'

'Do I have a choice?'

'Yes, and I'm confident you'll make the right one.'

She laughed. He was so damned sure of himself. 'What's your plan?'

'I knew you'd see it my way.' Now more serious, he went on. 'I have a suggestion for you, and I want you to hear me out before you reject it. Bellamy, O'Leary, and all the officers you know here went through the Military College for their training to get their commissions. But there are other ways. Sometimes professional people, like Anthony Chang for example, are granted a commission to do a specific job. I'm wondering about that for you because I think if you were a sworn officer, I might be able to achieve more freedom for you. The government might then see you as more connected to Earth than Anders.'

Her jaw dropped, and she gaped at him, unable to formulate words to respond.

'Talk to Bellamy about it. Don't dismiss the idea out of hand. It might just work for you. And if it does, we might be able to resurrect Dr Chang's commission and help him too.'

'Jesus,' she muttered. If she refused, it'd look like she didn't care about Anthony. If she agreed, Hunt would be her boss in every sense of the word.

With a smile, he continued, 'I was very pleased with the way you handled yourself in the search for Nik. As an officer, I could put you in charge of the alien technical work and liaison with Zadrus and Werrimen.'

'But that's Nik's job. I can't just push her out of the way to give me something to do. I won't push her out of the way.'

'No, she'll stay involved but I have other plans for her. Let me tell you what I want to do here. Then you might understand better what I'm suggesting. Okay?'

Jemma shrugged and waited.

He went on. 'I've been ordered to turn the SCARF team into a cohesive military unit. Do you understand why?'

'Kind of. Sean's told me that everybody's training is about to be lifted.'

'Yes, but there's more to it than that.' Hunt shifted uneasily in his chair. 'After the chief identified you as the heir to Anders Major's ruling house, he informed me that the main role of this unit is now your protection.'

'What rot.'

'No, not rot. We nearly lost you when you were lured out of here. And we could have lost Captain Denis. Your cousin. You and Captain Denis are to be protected at all costs. Neither the chief, nor I, consider our performance acceptable.'

'We can both look after ourselves.'

'That's not right. Your capacity has improved since you've

been here, but Denis has a long way to go. Which brings me to the next point. Denis has real talent and it's time to push her to another level. You've been working with her and she trusts you, so I think you can help.'

Jemma groaned. 'You mean you want me to get her to accept the same sort of treatment I've had?'

'Now you're getting the idea. I can't ignore the problems she had with Williamson, but I don't think she was the cause. Even so, the way she handled him was less than ideal. She buried her head in the technology. I have to know now that she can manage those around her, including those she sees as her superiors.'

Jemma frowned at his roguish smile until she realised Nik's superiors were himself, Sean and Dan. 'Oh no. No one could handle you lot.' She was also impressed at how Nik had accepted the situation and knuckled down, but she considered Nik to be a friend and didn't want to see her mistreated. 'Of course, I'll help. Maybe I can shield her from your bullying.'

Hunt grinned as he called Sean on his communicator and told him to bring O'Leary and Denis to his office. His smile was downright mischievous as he looked from Jemma to Sean.

'Hello sweetheart,' said Sean.

'Don't ask me. I guess it'll become clear soon.'

Hunt looked pleased with himself. 'Right, terrorists are gone, but we can't be sure they won't return. We will all now be on Pritchard's radar, so it's time to focus on sorting this unit. Here's my plan. Captain Denis, you will now be attached to Colonel Bellamy as his adjutant. O'Leary, all the majors, including our old team, will report to you. Dr Anderson will take over Denis's tech work. She'll need your ongoing help, Denis.'

'Of course, sir,' stuttered Nik.

Jemma wondered if Nik had any idea what Hunt was up to. It'd be much more than a normal administrative adjutant job. Nik would suffer before she got to her goals.

'Jemma successfully defended herself against that man because I've been training her for months. Those training sessions will now include the four of you. I may later include Tom, but that will depend on his father.'

Dan and Sean both shrugged, and Jemma groaned, but Nik stood mute, her mouth hanging open. She probably recognised the compliment, but Jemma wondered if she realised she'd have to work harder than she'd ever worked before.

Hunt closed the meeting after ordering Dan to commence organising his teams.

Next morning, when Jemma arrived at Hunt's office, she was surprised to see Dan and Nik already there.

Dan shrugged his shoulders, 'I dunno, I just do as I'm told.'

'Changed your ways then have you, O'Leary?' Hunt stood in the doorway with an amused look on his face. 'You might as well all come in together.'

Dan grinned, 'Always happy to oblige, sir.' Hunt pretended to clip him under the ear as he walked past, but Dan ducked, and scooted into the room.

'Right, you're all going to want your program. O'Leary,

your role will be to develop the training program here. Starting with the group in this room, we will require two combat training sessions every day. We are also to be included in the training for the rest of this unit, which brings me to my plan. With the combination of SCARF, and the Brisbane staff, we have four neat and tidy teams, each with a major, a lieutenant and five or six others. You can see us as another team O'Leary, which gives you five teams who can rotate between five programs of fitness and military skills each morning. We have to come together as a cohesive unit. Bellamy and I will have a major role there, but the training is very much part of that.'

'Okay.' Dan glanced at everyone else in the room, probably hoping for more explanation.

Jemma stared at Hunt. What he'd just outlined shouldn't involve her at all, so why was she there?

'And O'Leary,' continued Hunt, sneaking a look at Jemma, 'you can include Jemma in your morning training. She's up to it now, so long as you don't team her with Bellamy. Just leave her out of the direct military skills, but she can do everything else. Mind you, I wouldn't be distressed if she did want to learn some military skills. I've already proposed a professional commission for her. And a good run down the mountain will do her good.'

He never let up.

'Not sure I'm up to that,' muttered Jemma.

'Yes, you are,' said Dan, but he was careful not to look at her.

'I thought I wasn't allowed to go outside.'

'I'll be with you and I'll be armed, as will O'Leary,' said Hunt. 'You agreed yesterday to be part of the team and I note that while you objected to the run, you didn't reject the military skills.'

Cunning bastard. If she'd refused yesterday, he'd have found a way around it. And if she argued now, he'd up the demands; she'd find herself running to Brisbane and back. Dan pushed her out of the office in front of him. Just like Sean, trying to stop her from putting her foot in it.

*   *   *

Sean encouraged Jemma to apply for the proposed officer commission and once she did, Hunt set a gruelling pace for her. He insisted she participate in the military skills training run by Dan. When the day came for her to be sworn in, Hunt demanded she wear a uniform. Sean had taught her how to salute and he watched on, with an overwhelming sense of pride, when Hunt handed over the crown and she saluted. They'd classified her as an eminent scientist, and appointed her to the rank of major, with a bit of help from General Harris.

'I know,' said Dan, as Sean rubbed his eye. 'She's quite special, our Jemma.'

Sean laughed. 'Our Jemma? What about *our* Nik?'

'Her too,' said Dan, with a grin.

Both men laughed when, after the ceremony, Jemma flew from the room and back to their apartment to change out of the uniform. Sean returned to his office to wait for her but was interrupted by Nik.

'Pritchard's been spotted.' Nik and Jemma had set up an automatic surveillance of police channels for any mention of him. 'He walked into a police station and asked about SCARF. Claimed he's been searching for his sister-in-law, Jemma. Said he thinks SCARF's got something to do with her disappearance.'

Sean whistled. 'Jesus. I'm not surprised the bastard's still around, but that pretty much takes the cake. Let's go see the boss.' He presumed Pritchard would be gone but thought he should head down to the police station and nose around.

'Alright, find what you can,' said Hunt. 'Take O'Leary. Denis, track them. Are we due to run outside tomorrow?'

Sean's face was grim. 'Yep.'

'Good. We all go out heavily armed, side-arms and alien weapons on everyone, including Jemma.'

'Shouldn't we leave her behind? She is the one we're supposed to be protecting and she's never used a weapon.'

'I've been training her for months.' Hunt sat back in his chair; his hands clasped behind his head. 'You've never got it, Bellamy. That girl is exceptionally capable. I'm not leaving her out.'

'I'm tired of putting her at risk. She's not really military.'

Jemma walked in as he spoke. 'Must be, I've got the uniform. Don't bother arguing, I'm not waiting back here wondering if you're alright. I'll be there with you.'

'She's part of our team, Bellamy. We'll all be armed. If anything happens, I have confidence in her to handle herself.'

Sean looked down. In his book, just because Jemma wanted to be involved didn't mean she should be.

'And,' said Jemma, 'given I'm part of the team, permission to join Colonel Bellamy to investigate the police station, sir.'

Although Sean had told her she should call General Hunt sir, with any formal request, he almost choked when he heard it.

Hunt leaned back in his chair and rubbed his chin. 'I'd like to let you go, but don't think that would be wise.'

Jemma leaned across his desk. 'I understood that's why I had to apply for the damned commission.'

'Yes, and if it were anyone other than Pritchard, I'd approve. I'm sorry Jemma, permission denied.'

She pushed herself off the desk and flounced out of the room.

'Oops,' said Sean.

'Yeah, I know. She's just going to have to deal with it,' said Hunt. 'Brief Lambert about tomorrow. He can stand by in case we don't return. And notify Zadrus.'

Sean's trip to the police station was fruitless. The police on duty hadn't recognised Pritchard until the report went online and then they were inundated with notifications from other stations.

*   *   *

When Jemma woke in the morning Sean, who looked like he'd been up for some time, had her clothes laid out, water bottles filled, and her weapons organised into her belt. She reached out and touched his arm. 'You okay?'

'Yeah, yeah. You get in the shower. I want to go through everything, make sure you know how to use it all before we leave.'

Taking hold of both his arms, she gently pulled him around to look at her. 'Sean, I know how to use the weapons, and I know what to do. I need you to focus on leading the team, not panicking about me.'

'I can't. Would you reconsider and stay behind?'

'No, and I don't think General Hunt would accept that anyway. You have to treat me the same as Tom and Nik. I didn't choose to be part of this team, but it's happened and wherever the team goes, I go.'

He pulled her into a tight hug. 'I love you and I won't forgive myself if something happens to you.'

'Nothing's going to happen. Go meet with the general. I'll join Nik and Dan and wait for you.' She left him and headed outside hoping the fresh air might clear her head. Dan and Nik were in the clearing with two armed sergeants.

Hunt gave the order to go as soon as he joined them. As they jogged through the rainforest she gazed at the area where her hide had once been. She still missed her animals, but she'd never before had the sense of belonging that she'd found with the people running alongside her. Sean stuck to her side as they ran, insisting she drink and telling her to pace herself. She didn't need his instructions, but she let him fuss, hoping it would help him calm down. They all wore bullet proof vests, and the webbing belt that usually only held two water bottles was now weighed down with a semi-automatic pistol in a holster, and an alien stun weapon.

Ten minutes into their run four people, in police uniform, ran onto the road, their guns pointed at the SCARF team. Jemma's hand flicked down to her pistol when one of them yelled, 'Drop your weapons.'

Hunt stood his ground. 'State your business.'

The police officer repeated his demand. 'Drop your weapons. You are all under arrest.'

They didn't respond immediately and a young constable, more anxious than the others, fired off a shot that hit one of the army sergeants. Jemma suspected the shot was accidental, but it began a cascade of events. As the sergeant went down, he shot and killed the constable, then he also shot at a more senior police officer, killing him. Before the policeman succumbed, he fired off a round, and that hit the army sergeant in the head. Nik tried to help the sergeant, but it was too late. She stood with her weapon pointed at the superintendent until a dozen more people jumped out from the scrub. One of them slammed something into the back of Nik's head, and she fell to the ground, not moving.

Jemma ran to her, praying that Tom would realise something had happened and come looking. She barely heard Hunt give the order to cease fire. Within seconds, two mini vans appeared. She fought the man who tried to pull her away from Nik but failed and was pushed into a seat beside Dan. Nik, still unconscious, was dumped opposite them. Dan shifted across to her and cradled her head in his lap.

Nik groaned, then slowly opened her eyes. 'What happened?' She grimaced. 'My head hurts.'

'Shhh. Just rest,' Dan murmured softly, but his face reflected his anger.

Jemma rested her hand over his clenched fist, waiting until she got eye contact. 'We'll get our chance.'

He nodded but didn't answer.

Jemma sat back on her seat and looked over to the other vehicle which had Sean, Hunt and the rest of their team packed into it. She tried to open the door next to her as the vehicle started off, but it wouldn't budge and there was nothing she could do until the vans drove in to the back of a dilapidated building. The van doors were flung open and they were dragged out and pushed into a large room, probably an old storeroom, going by the shelving on the walls, then shoved onto a row of chairs in the middle of the floor. When one of her captors dragged her arms behind her back, and started to tie them, Jemma separated her hands as far as she dared and, with a bit of wriggling, managed to loosen the knot on the rope that bound her feet. She looked at Nik who, although still groggy, had also loosened her bindings.

Pritchard walked through the door with his bodyguard who Jemma recognised as the bastard who'd abducted her from the safe house and nearly cost her life. He wouldn't get away with it again. But she'd learnt well from Hunt. Bide your time. Wait for the opportunity. Pritchard sauntered over to them as if they were about to have a friendly chat. He offered them money for the alien virus cure, then ranted about their freedom in exchange for the cure. Clearly irritated by their silence, he changed his tack. 'Jemma, it is my very great pleasure to see you again. I'll have my men untie you, if you'll agree to join me in the business. Your sister is very keen to see you.'

She didn't move, or speak, or return his smile. He turned on his heel, and said to his bodyguard, 'Dr Anderson is not to be harmed. She can see how you treat the others, then bring her to me.' He left the room.

The bodyguard dragged Hunt, chair and all, to the front of the room threatening to kill him if he didn't co-operate. Then he'd start on each of the others. When Hunt refused, he undid Hunt's vest, exposing his chest and shot him in the right shoulder, too high to damage his lungs, but enough to shatter bone and cause excruciating pain. Hunt slumped forward, breathing hard, but otherwise made no sound. The bodyguard waved something under his nose, and he jerked back upright. After another refusal, the terrorist shot him in the left knee. Hunt's head slumped again. Jemma thought he'd passed out, until he raised himself up. He remained mute and stared at his tormentor.

Too much now for Jemma, she struggled with her tethers, finally freeing herself just as the bodyguard raised his gun again. Jumping up, she grabbed her chair and charged at the man. She smashed the heavy metal frame into the back of his head, shattering the wood on the seat. Then she swung around to punch his left temple, quickly following with a kick to his right kidney. As he went down, he punched her in the abdomen.

She doubled up but managed to grab his gun. Forcing herself to stand, she ran to Nik and freed her just in time to take on another of Pritchard's men who'd run in to check on the commotion. Then she ran to Sean and grabbed the knife hidden in a pocket in his boot. Once she'd cut his and Dan's ties, she shrank to the floor clutching her stomach. At almost the same time Tom, and his team, stormed the building.

Jemma forgot her own pain when one of Pritchard's men aimed his gun. 'Tom, look out.' She heard a shot. Tom stared at her and, without a word, crumpled and fell. She ran around the edge of the room, taking care to stay out of sight of the shooters, to where Tom lay. His sightless eyes stared up at her. He didn't move. She dropped down next to him. No pulse. His chest still. Blood surrounded a small, neat hole in the middle of his forehead.

Nik howled, aiming her gun at the man who'd shot Tom, 'Try this, arsehole.' She fired off three rounds in quick succession, mortally wounding the shooter, but he fired back, hitting Nik in the left shoulder and the right side of the chest. Jemma stared at her. She should have been wearing a bullet proof vest, but the blood pouring from the gaping wounds in her shoulder and right side suggested she wasn't. She fell on top of Tom and, even when the remainder of Pritchard's men were overpowered, Nik didn't move.

'No, no,' cried Jemma. She begged Nik to hang on until help arrived. Tom was gone, but Nik still had a pulse and her chest moved, although her breathing sounded harsh and gurgly.

Everson charged into the room followed by military paramedics and soldiers in tactical uniform. While Hunt and Nik were loaded onto the stretchers, he pulled Jemma away from Tom. 'Come with me. You can't help him now. He's gone.'

She stared at him. 'Why? This is all my fault. It's me Pritchard wants. I should have gone to him.'

'No. It wouldn't have stopped him. We must go now. I want to be away before the counterterrorism squad arrives and delays our departure.'

When Jemma reached the helicopter, Nik and Hunt were already on board. She sat next to Nik whose every breath sounded like it might be her last. Despite his injuries, Hunt, his stretcher on the other side of Jemma's seat, reached out and took her hand.

The pilot took off as soon as the door was shut. It only took a few minutes to reach the back entrance of SCARF and the helicopter flew fast and low through the opening into the mountain runway. There was nothing gentle about the landing. He was on the ground as fast as he could manoeuvre the craft. Everson held her back until the stretchers had been removed. She ran to Zadrus who stood between the helicopter and the transporter and was already assessing the patients. One of his staff handed him something that looked like a plastic tube. He placed it in the wound in Nik's chest and attached a small gadget to it. Nik's breathing instantly relaxed. As Jemma helped Zadrus pull up a blanket, she confirmed that Nik wasn't wearing a vest. God help her when she was well enough to debrief. Hunt would kill her. Jemma allowed herself a weak laugh. No, he wouldn't kill her, but she'd feel his fury.

When the transporter took off, Jemma stood on the runway staring after it. She looked up at Everson as she felt his arm around her shoulders, and didn't resist as he gently steered her inside to wait for Sean and Dan.

*　　*　　*

Once the counterterrorism team had taken over, Sean was told to stand down. He gave his report then reluctantly grabbed Dan and headed out to wait for the SCARF helicopter to return. He sighed. Jemma had survived but she shouldn't have been there in the first place. Even though none of them would be alive without her, he still believed that the risk of putting her in that situation was unacceptable. As he stared back at Tom, he slumped. Tom's body had to be left behind until both the civilian and military police had completed their investigations. He'd been Tom's first boss, when Tom graduated from Duntroon, right through until he was shot in Afghanistan. He'd been his boss again now and got him shot again. And he'd known the sergeant who was shot on the mountain road for five or six years. A great bloke. He didn't know how to deal with any of this.

When the helicopter touched down on the SCARF runway, he jumped out. Before he'd turned around, Jemma flew into his arms. They stood together for several minutes before he eased back to look at her, his face drawn.

She stared up at him. 'Tom?'

'Yeah. Where's Dan?'

'I took him inside,' said Everson, joining them. 'I've established a link with the spaceship, so he can talk to Zadrus. He's devastated about Nik.'

'He would be,' said Sean. 'Do we know how Nik and the general are?'

'Both doing well,' said Everson. 'There are people waiting inside to talk to you. I want to let you know before you get there that your government has taken the decision to close this facility temporarily.'

Sean gaped at him. After all they'd been through trying to protect it, they'd decided to shut it down. Just like that. 'Who are the people?'

'Your Prime Minister and four other members of Earth's Council of Leaders.'

'I've never heard of Earth's Council of Leaders,' said Sean.

Everson nodded. 'It is not well known that such a group exists. Jemma met with them when she accompanied Zadrus to Wake Island.'

'What about the staff?' Too many decisions had been made in his absence.

'They will go to the West Australian facility, or back to ordinary military units once their memories have been altered. Please come with me.'

*   *   *

Seeing Sean falter, Jemma took his hand and urged him to follow Everson. When Dan walked up behind, his face ashen, she held out her other hand. 'How's Nik?'

'Alive. Unconscious. Zadrus says she'll pull through. Same with the general. Jesus Jem, I don't want to waste time here, I want to be with her.'

'I know. Let's just deal with this, then we'll ask Mr Everson to take us there.'

Four people rose from their chairs when they entered the conference room, the Australian Prime Minister, a representative of the US President, the German Chancellor and someone she didn't know, but a quick look at his place card told her he was from Costa Rica.

'Please be seated,' said the Australian Prime Minister. As soon as they'd settled into chairs, she continued, although she didn't look happy. 'I am aware that around thirty years ago this Council's predecessors granted a request from the Supreme Ruler of Anders Major to provide you with refuge here on Earth. We were pleased to help. However, your presence has now placed the citizens of Earth at risk. I am afraid that we must withdraw our support. The IPL will ensure your safe passage from Earth. If the terrorist action continues, then all Anders people will be located and removed. I am sorry this has happened.'

Jemma was first to speak. 'Are you aware that none of us have known any home other than Earth and that all of us are genetically more than fifty percent of Earth origin.'

'Yes, I am. But you are now the Supreme Ruler of Anders Major, Dr Anderson and clearly the central target of the terrorist's actions. Again, I am sorry, but you must leave.'

Jemma stood, mute, then turned and indicated to the men to follow her.

'IPL transport is on its way,' said Everson, following them out. 'I will do what I can here to turn this around, but I suspect I will be next on the eviction list. Take care. I may not see you again once you leave.'

CHAPTER 26

Jemma grabbed two suitcases from a shelf in the walk-in robe and flung them on the bed. She ordered Sean to pack his clothes in one, while she threw some of her own clothes into the other. Then she found Dan and sent him to pack for himself and Nik. Once she had Dan occupied, she told Sean to pack a bag for Hunt. Amused that both men followed her orders without question, she waited for them to finish, then shepherded them to the landing bay. She sighed as they neared the transporter and Sean tightened his grip on her hand. She'd hoped he'd get used to the alien craft, but clearly that wasn't going to be. Once she'd pushed Sean and Dan into the blue light and watched them drift up, she turned back to Everson, 'You know Pritchard got away?'

'I do indeed,' said Everson. 'He's number one on the international most wanted list. Every agency has joined the hunt for him. They'll find him, and I doubt he'll survive the encounter.'

'Thank you for all your help,' she said, kissing his cheek. She walked into the blue light, then found Sean and sat close, comforting him as the transporter slid out from the runway before shooting up.

'Do you think they'll ever let us return?' Dan stared at the ceiling. He didn't seem to be speaking to anyone in particular.

'Doubt it,' replied Sean.

'We don't know that,' said Jemma. 'Come on. We need to keep our minds open.'

'Don't much care what they decide so long as Nik pulls through and I can be with her. But there is one thing I need.' Dan walked to the window and stared up at the mothership as they approached.

Jemma joined him and gently rubbed his back. 'What, Dan? What do you need?'

He looked back at Sean. 'I need to meet my mother.'

Sean inhaled sharply. 'Mate, I've asked for that repeatedly. I need to see her too, now I know what they did to her. The chief keeps saying he'll organise it, but he hasn't so far. Maybe Zadrus can help.'

'I'd like to meet her too,' said Jemma, as the transporter eased into the ship's docking bay. 'She is, after all, my mother-in-law, and it sounds to me like she needs our support, just as much as we need hers.'

In the docking bay, Zadrus and Werrimen waited. They led the group to a lounge room where Zadrus pulled a chair around and sat facing them. Werrimen sat next to Dan, taking his hands in hers. He jumped which made Jemma smile. She was now used to the jolt from the alien clasp. Zadrus took one of her hands and one of Sean's, and she instantly felt the calm sensation charge through her body. He waited to speak until Werrimen indicated Dan had settled.

'I have not been able to speak to General Harris,' said Zadrus. 'I am informed he collapsed on learning of his son's death.'

'Understandable,' sighed Jemma.

'Of course,' he replied, staring at the ceiling before going on. 'I have spoken to your Prime Minister and I have been informed, she will not accept you back on Earth.'

'We know. The government's abandoned all of us now,' said Jemma.

'I am afraid so,' said Zadrus.

'I suppose we expected something like this,' said Jemma.

Zadrus nodded. 'Pritchard has abused their hospitality.'

'So, what do we do now?' said Sean.

'We have a couple of options,' replied Zadrus. 'I would like you to consider staying with us and joining our mission. Alternatively, we could place you on another planet, one inhabited by humans. You would be looked after, and all your needs met. I don't see returning to Anders as an option yet. There is still too much turmoil there. But if you want, I will investigate that as a possibility.'

'None of us has ever been to Anders,' said Jemma. 'I doubt that would really be a consideration for us anyway. Would you please explain your mission? It might help us to decide.'

'I cannot I am afraid,' replied Zadrus. 'I await confirmation myself. All I can say is that we were sent here to stop Earth from destroying itself. I am not confident we can do that now, having met the Council of Earth's Leaders.'

'I wish I never saw that bloody blue light,' said Sean.

'True, but you wouldn't have met me,' retorted Jemma.

He grinned. 'I guess there's a bonus to everything.' He turned to Zadrus. 'Sir, I have one request and no idea how to organise it. I need to see my mother and Dan needs to meet her.'

Mary rushed into the room before he finished. 'I just heard you're here. Are you all okay?'

'Yeah, we are,' replied Jemma, standing to give Mary her chair. 'General Hunt and Nik aren't though, and two of our people were killed.'

'Who?'

'Tom, and a sergeant you haven't met.'

'Tom Lambert?'

'Yes.'

'Oh dear,' she sighed. 'When will this all end?'

'We must find a way to end it,' said Werrimen.

Mary nodded. 'Sean, I heard your request. If you plan to go to her, I would like to go with you. She knows me. Ideally, we'd bring her back here. Zadrus, where is the nearest SCARF-type site. I believe she is in Germany.'

'Yes, she is,' said Sean.

'The nearest is Spain,' said Zadrus. 'We could land you quite close to her and have someone drive up from Spain to take you to her home.'

'I need to go too, in case she won't come back,' said Dan.

'No.' Werrimen stood and walked behind Zadrus. 'I think it might be best for Mary to go alone, give her a chance to convince your mother. If that doesn't work, then we consider an alternate plan and find a way to get you to her.'

Sean looked at each of the women. 'Alright, but she's not to be forced.'

'I would never do that, Sean,' replied Mary. 'She and I were once good friends. I believe I can talk her around.'

'Mary, I will fly you,' said Werrimen 'Now Sean, there is one scenario which may stop Mary from keeping her promise to you.'

'If Pritchard's people intervene,' murmured Jemma.

'Yes. Are you prepared to take that risk, Sean?'

'Oh God. If Pritchard were to interfere, wouldn't that mean he's watching her anyway?'

'Yes, it would.'

'Then she'd be at risk no matter what we decide?'

'Yes, that is likely.' Werrimen paused. 'You have a few hours to think about it. We must arrive at night, and it is almost morning there now. If you decide to go, Zadrus will manage surveillance and control the mission from here.'

'May I manage the surveillance?' Jemma expected Zadrus to say no, and was surprised by his answer.

'Certainly, if you are happy that I stand with you.'

'Of course.' She wanted to high-five but, given Sean and Dan's distress, she kept her hands firmly clasped on her lap.

'Would you like to control the mission too?'

She laughed. 'I'm not ready for that.'

'I disagree,' said Zadrus, turning away. 'We will talk later.'

She stared after him, unable to respond.

*   *   *

The aliens and their technology no longer shocked Sean, although he couldn't say he was happy being confined to a spaceship. He left Werrimen and Mary to work on their plan and walked arm-in-arm with Jemma to their new room. Much smaller than their apartment on SCARF, it was more like a small suite on a cruise ship. There was a large bed, with a small set of drawers on either side. An ensuite opened from the far wall. It had a shower at one end, a waterless toilet at the other, and a tiny basin in the middle. Neither of them said much as they unpacked their bags, and both jumped when a screen next to the door lit up. A Sidlown man stared down at them. 'Are you two going to dawdle? They're waiting for you.'

Sean moved closer and touched the screen. 'Who's waiting for us?'

'The other humans, of course.'

'Who are you?'

'I'm your educator.'

'Educator? Are you a real person, or artificial intelligence?'

'I'm not flesh and blood, but I'm a long way advanced on artificial intelligence.'

'How do I turn you off, so you can't just flash back on at us whenever you like?' snapped Sean.

'Well, really. Press the black button, like every other form of communicator.' The screen shut down before Sean reached the button, but he hit it anyway.

'Just like Artie,' said Jemma, laughing. 'I guess we'd better go.'

He reached out and drew her into him, holding onto her for some time before he eased back and opened the door. 'How the hell did it get to this?'

'Pritchard,' she replied, shrugging. 'We can't change it, so now we're going to have to work out how to deal with it.'

They walked slowly to their dinner, picking Dan up on the way. Mary and Eric waited, Anthony by their side, still in a wheelchair. Sean smiled; wheelchair was a bit of a misnomer. The thing floated above the floor, no wheels and he couldn't see any controls. Anthony spoke to it to make it turn towards Jemma. He seemed to stagger when Jemma ran to him and Sean ran behind to prop him up.

'Can't fall out of this thing, mate,' said Anthony. 'It grabs me and then rights itself.'

'I'm glad you're doing well,' said Sean, shaking his head. 'But it's still all so strange to me.'

'Yeah, it is, but Anthony's alive,' said Jemma, beaming. 'I had hoped you'd be up and walking by now though.'

'I know. Werrimen says I will recover fully, but apparently the virus attacked my central nervous system. I have treatments every day and I can at least feel my legs now.'

Mary cleared her throat behind them. 'We'd better have some dinner. I'll be leaving around 9am but preparations must start three to four hours before that time. We all need some sleep.'

By the time they got to Germany it would be night, and well past most people's bedtime, reducing the risk of being seen. They agreed to meet in the control room at 4 am, then

Sean led Jemma back to their room. He held onto her as they both struggled to sleep.

When they got up, Sean did his best to eat some breakfast but gave up and asked Zadrus if could visit Hunt while he waited. As they walked to the medical centre Zadrus explained Hunt's treatment but, even so, Sean wasn't expecting to see Hunt sitting up chatting to his Sidlown attendant. Structures surrounded both his shoulder and his knee to immobilise the joints. They were moulded to the joints and made it look like the injured joints were twice the size of the normal joints. Implants inserted into the bones were designed to help with regrowth and to treat the pain. His attendants checked his progress via a small computer in each of the surrounding structures and, if a bone became misshapen, they could adjust the implants remotely.

'I love these people,' said Hunt. 'I have no pain at all. I'm not being brave. I am literally free of it. They tell me my joints will be back to normal within four weeks, then all I'll have to do is exercise to get my full range of movement back. So, if you want to beat me up Bellamy, that's when you should try.'

'No, I'll wait until you're up and around, then I'll thrash the shit out of you. I still owe you for not letting me near Williamson, or that fake scientist, to strangle them.'

'You're on.'

'Zadrus has informed us we can't go home,' said Sean. 'We have to make a decision about what to do.'

'Yes, he's also filled me in. My thoughts are to stay with him. We've trusted Zadrus and Werrimen for some time now, it seems the logical thing to do, to go on trusting them.' He grinned. 'And of course, if you stay with me, I can keep training Jemma.'

'On the other hand,' said Jemma, who'd walked in on the conversation. 'I can tell you to get stuffed. If I'm not on Earth, I'm no longer in protective custody, or part of your army.'

'Your army too, don't forget. You can refuse, but I know you won't,' said Hunt, with a broad grin.

'Don't be so sure of yourself.' She turned to Sean. 'I'm going to join Werrimen and Mary in the control room. I thought, under the circumstances, I should let you know.'

'Thanks sweetheart. I'll come up in a while.'

Sean waited until she'd left to ask Hunt something that had been worrying him. 'Sir, what about your wife? Do you want me to get in contact with her, see if she wants to join us?'

A pained look formed on Hunt's face. 'No, she's better off without me. The Army will tell her I was killed in the terrorist raid, I'd say. She'll get compensation, and my insurance. And I can start fresh too.'

Sean paused, not sure if the trauma had affected Hunt's thinking. He'd wait a couple of days, then check again. He took his leave when an alert on his communicator asked him to report to the landing bay and was surprised to see several people waiting for him there, including Liam. They stood at the base of a transporter, and all looked shell-shocked. Each had been informed that they too came from Anders and they'd opted to join Sean rather than a resettlement with altered memories.

'Jemma's going to be thrilled to see you,' Sean said to Liam.

'She doesn't hate me that much, does she?'

'I don't think she hates you at all,' said Sean.

Liam laughed, 'Do you think I should suggest we start an exercise program tomorrow?'

'Only if you don't value your life,' replied Sean, grimacing.

*   *   *

Jemma was so engrossed with Werrimen as she demonstrated how to plot the route the transporter would take to Germany, that she didn't notice Zadrus walk up behind them. He tapped her on the shoulder and directed her to the control desk so he could show her how to get images like those Artie had provided at SCARF.

'Images,' said Zadrus.

Three blank squares popped up in front of Zadrus. Jemma couldn't think of any other way to describe them. They didn't have any substance, but each square was clearly visible and different from its surrounds. She wondered what else she'd have to deal with before this mission was finished.

Zadrus smiled at her expression. 'Not so different from a screen attached to your computer. Just more advanced.'

He brought up the map she'd been working on with Werrimen on one screen, the landing bay on another and the transporter Werrimen would use on a third. Then, he handed her Sean's mother's address and pointed to the route Werrimen had plotted. Next, he told her to identify the exact co-ordinates for that address and bring up an image of the house on another screen. She took a deep breath and turned to the controls knowing she had to pass this test before he'd allow her to proceed. Her hands shook but she spoke clearly, although she felt it odd to be talking to the air, and said, 'Screen.' Another screen popped up. She then told it to find the address, which it did within seconds. She zoomed in, planning to stop at the front gate. Zadrus told her to keep going but cautioned her to back out immediately if she saw anything that might compromise Sean's mother.

'Do you want me to go inside?' She looked up at him, surprised.

'Yes, you must. We need to see her and make sure we have the right person and the right place.'

'Okay, but I don't know her.'

'I understand. Remember you are controlling this mission. You must think it through.'

She stared at him and stuttered, 'No, not the mission, only the surveillance.'

'No, the mission is yours.'

'Oh my God.' She rubbed her eyes, and had to think. 'Control, show me any person inside the dwelling.'

The screen blurred for less than a second, then opened into a dining room where a woman sat by herself, at a table, reading a book. So how the hell did she identify her? She grabbed her communicator and called for Sean to come to the control room. She looked up at Zadrus who still didn't intervene, and she called for Mary asking her if she wanted to see the house before she left. Now Zadrus nodded and smiled.

Sean and Mary ran in together. 'Yes, that's mum,' said Sean.

Almost simultaneously, Mary said, 'Yes, that's Erin Bellamy.' She smiled at Sean. 'Sorry, I'm also excited to see her. We were torn apart too.'

'Thanks,' he replied.

Dan walked in behind them. 'Is that her? Is that my mother?'

Jemma looked to Sean hoping he'd offer some direction on how to proceed, but he stood with Dan, both with their eyes glued to the screen. Zadrus still didn't speak. She turned to Mary. 'Do you need anything more before you go?'

Mary smiled. 'No, dear. It's 5am. Do I have permission to commence the mission?'

'You need my permission?'

'Yes, you're the mission controller. Now give me a hug before I go.' She whispered so only Jemma could hear. 'You need to seal off the dock, so I can leave.'

Jemma waited until Mary had left the room before she turned to Zadrus. 'How do I tell everyone that a transporter is about to leave?'

'Very good,' he replied. 'First, ask Werrimen if she is ready to go. When she says yes, ask her to commence the alarm. She does that from inside the transporter. Then ask our pilot here to check that the landing bay is clear.' He pointed to a man sitting at the control desk. 'When he is satisfied, tell Werrimen she is cleared to go. Our pilot will seal the floor and open and shut the docking bay door.'

'Thank you. I know you're testing me but if I forget something please tell me.' Without waiting for a response, she contacted Werrimen and commenced the procedure. Once she'd finished, she turned back to Zadrus. 'Should I be tracking the transporter?'

'No,' he replied. 'Our pilot does that. You have done very well. Do you wish to keep going?'

'Oh yes. I would prefer to see it through.'

'Good. Pull back from the house so you can see anything approaching it. We have some time now to relax. It will take an hour for Werrimen to get to her destination, then up to another hour for our people to pick Mary up and take her to the house. One of our Prehlings can watch so we can have a talk.'

'What's a Prehling?'

'I will explain shortly.'

Jemma looked around for Sean, hoping for his support, but he and Dan must have left while she'd concentrated on getting Werrimen's flight started. She chided herself for wanting to fall back on Sean. His issues were far more important than hers right now, and she'd become far too used to having him tell her what to do. It was time to regain her independence. She suspected she knew what Zadrus wanted to talk about and braced herself as she followed him to his office. She now wore a maroon uniform, provided by the aliens, the same as the uniform worn by Sean and Dan, which signified security.

When she sat, Zadrus pulled up a chair beside her and took her hands. The familiar buzz shot through her body, and he began to explain the role of a Prehling, essentially an apprentice Trustee.

'Now that you have taken charge of a mission, I think it is time for you to be inducted as a Prehling.'

She laughed. 'You weren't just seeing if I could perform. It was the next step to convince me to train with you.'

'Yes, and I would like you to accept,' he replied.

It didn't sound like she'd have much option. She'd already been told that all the people who'd joined them from SCARF would be trained in some way and each would have their own guide. 'I would like you to wear the junior trustee crest on your uniform. We will talk more once this mission is over and you can give me your answer.'

Too stunned to reply when he rose and told her they should return to the control room, she got up and followed.

The Prehling who had been brought in to watch for Werrimen's transporter told them she'd just entered European air space.

'Oh, that is good timing,' replied Zadrus. 'But you must tell the mission controller.'

The Prehling, a young Sidlown, nodded and smiled at Jemma. 'What would you like me to do?'

She thought she must have looked like a fish as she opened and shut her mouth, but she had to say something. 'I'd like a good view of the house.' A few minutes later, she saw something behind the house. 'Control, close in on that object.'

She looked at the Prehling. 'Would you get Zadrus, please? Quickly.'

Seconds later she felt Zadrus move behind her. 'A Norellian sphere,' she said to him.

'By all the stars,' he muttered. 'This is what we feared. May I take over?'

'Of course,' she said, trying hard not to let him see her relief as she moved aside.

'Bring Sean and Dan in please,' said Zadrus. 'They should know what is happening.'

She started to run for the door, then remembered her communicator and called Sean.

'What's wrong?' said Sean.

'Your mother's fine, but there's a glitch. Can you come up please, and bring Dan with you?'

When he ran in, she pointed to the Norellian sphere that now sat above his mother's home. Zadrus had diverted Werrimen's flight to the house rather than the safe facility while they spoke.

'I will attempt to scare the sphere away,' said Werrimen.

Jemma felt Sean's hand grip hers as the transporter neared the house. The sphere moved up, but not away. She jumped as a blue light shone down from Werrimen's transporter and Mary floated down to the driveway of the house.

'All she needs is an umbrella and a carpet bag,' murmured Sean.

Jemma giggled. 'Mary Poppins. Not such a bad description for my Mary.'

'Zoom down,' said Zadrus. The image blurred for a split second then moved in so close that Jemma felt like she stood on the driveway next to Mary.

'Mary,' Erin squealed and reached out to hug her, but Mary held her back.

'Can I come in? I have a great deal to tell you, but I must do it quickly. A Norellian sphere has been watching your house.'

'Did it follow you?'

'No, it was already here. I believe it's had you under surveillance for a while, which surprises me because you don't have a tattoo.'

'Yes, I do,' said Erin quietly. 'They held me down and did it before we left Anders. I think they were worried I'd run away once we got to Earth.'

'Dear God,' sighed Mary. 'Why did we let them get away with any of this?'

Erin shrugged. 'That was the Anders way. We did as we were told. But why would they be following me now, after all this time? I was told after they caught Drick , so long as I stayed out of the way, that the kids and I would be safe.'

'He's escaped.' Mary asked her to sit, then she launched into the story telling her everything as succinctly as she could from Jemma's abduction to Patrick Harris's speech and the reuniting of Sean and Dan. 'Erin, I don't believe you are safe here. And now, more than ever, Sean and Dan need you.'

'Oh Mary, how could they accept me? I've failed them so badly, but they can't have any idea of how hard this has been. You know I tried to kill myself after Eamon died. Nobody seemed to care. They just put me in a hospital, surrounded by mentally ill people.'

'I heard, but they wouldn't let me come to you,' replied Mary quietly.

'The king ordered them to purchase the apartment in Brisbane, in my name, and I was permitted to use it twice a year so that I could see Sean and Cheryl. I had to be distant with them. There was no way they'd understand what had happened. I was never permitted to contact my other son. I didn't even know what they called him. They threatened that if I tried for more contact, they'd take the apartment and this house and leave me on the street. I didn't care about that, but they said I'd never see the children again. At least this way I saw them, and knew they were safe. Should I have ignored the security council and the guardians, Mary?'

'I don't know, Erin. I just don't know. They threatened me too if I contacted you and, like you, I was so worried about my son that I obeyed them. We must become stronger and try to right some of the wrongs. The IPL is in charge now and we'll be going to an IPL ship. No one from Anders can hurt us, so long as we get out of here safely.'

Jemma saw tears run down Mary's cheeks. 'God Sean, I knew nothing of this.'

'Neither did I,' he replied.

Suddenly, a blue light shone through the window and Werrimen's voice shouted through Mary's communicator. 'It's not ours, Mary. Hide.'

'Where?'

'Go out the front door. The bricks should shelter you long enough for me to get to you.'

The two women ran from the house and Jemma held her breath as she saw the transporter tear around the front and another blue light shoot down. Once the light had centred on them, the women rose with it at speed, not the gentle floating motion Jemma had experienced. They'd almost reached the transporter when another blue light shot across them. Both women started to fall.

Werrimen's transporter dropped down, blocking Jemma's view. She cried out, 'Where are they?'

Zadrus had his communicator out. 'Werrimen, report.'

A single word came back. 'Wait.'

Jemma stood between Sean and Dan, aware that their grip on her hands had tightened when they couldn't see either Mary or Erin.

Zadrus raised his communicator as Werrimen's voice again came through. 'I have them. I am coming in, top speed.'

'We will be ready.' Zadrus turned to his pilot. 'Evacuate the docking bay and open the door.' He tracked the transporter for fifteen minutes then shifted the image to the docking bay. Another ten minutes and the transporter shot through the open door.

'Secure the dock,' shouted Zadrus, then turned to Sean. 'Wait in my office please. Jemma and Dan, wait here. I will call you once I am satisfied Erin can cope with the introductions.'

*   *   *

Sean sat awkwardly in Zadrus's office, not sure what he planned to say to his mother or even if she'd be prepared to try to develop the relationship that he so desperately wanted with her. By the time Werrimen brought her in, he'd started marching up and down inside the room.

The colour drained from her face when she saw him, and he ran to her as she staggered, but Werrimen already had hold of her and eased her onto a chair. Sean squatted in front of her, 'Mum?'

'I'm so sorry,' she said.

He ran his fingers across her hair. 'What for? It doesn't sound like you had any control over anything. General Harris said you had a breakdown but from what you said to Mary it sounds like it was much worse than that.'

'Yes,' she whispered. 'Much worse, and I was terrified to let you know because they threatened to take you from me too.'

'Oh God, Mum.' He drew her close to him and held her until the sobs started to subside.

'Cheryl won't have anything to do with me,' she said.

'I knew that. Maybe with what I know now, I can talk her around.'

'I doubt it.'

'Would you like to meet my brother, Dan?'

'He must hate me.'

'No. He's confused. I guess I am too, and I don't know how he'll react. But Mum, we've got a chance now.'

Werrimen squatted next to them. 'Do you feel up to meeting Dan now, or would you rather wait?'

'It wouldn't be fair to ask him to wait. Will you both stay with me?'

'Of course,' said Sean.

'I will get him,' said Werrimen.

Sean helped his mother to stand, holding her close as they waited, afraid she might collapse when Dan walked in. He smiled when he saw Werrimen holding onto Dan in much the same way as they returned.

Dan stood in the doorway and looked at his mother, then Sean, then Werrimen, clearly with no idea what to do.

Sean squeezed his mother's arm, and she seemed to snap back.

'Oh Dan,' she said. 'You're so like your father.' She took a step forward, and Dan did the same, then Dan flew forward and took her in his arms.

Sean waited with Werrimen while Dan and his mother both dissolved into tears.

'Why don't you get Jemma? I'll wait here,' Werrimen whispered.

By the time he returned, Dan and his mother had sat down to talk. The conversation was quiet but friendly. Dan stood as Sean and Jemma walked in.

'Mum, I'd like you to meet my wife,' said Sean. 'Jemma, this is my mother.'

'My goodness,' said Erin, standing to look at Jemma. 'When did this happen?'

'A few weeks ago,' said Jemma. 'It's good to meet you, Mrs Bellamy.'

'I don't know what to say. I'm pleased to meet you too.'

Sean put his arm around both women, and they stood together. Dan stood opposite Sean, doing the same.

When Mary joined them, Werrimen separated the group. 'Erin, you should stay with us for a few days at least until we clear your house. After that you can decide what you'd like to do. Are you alright with that?'

'Of course. And thank you so much for helping us.'

'That is my pleasure,' said Werrimen. 'I hope you will spend some time talking to me too in the next few days.'

'I'll look forward to that,' said Erin, smiling through her tears as she looked at her sons and daughter-in-law.

A week later Sean assisted Hunt, who was now allowed to move around, although his leg was kept stiff and his pace laborious, to visit Nik. Dan sat beside her on the bed, his mother beside him when they got there. Nik had lost weight, and her muscles were wasted, but she could now sit up in bed. Her right side still had wires attached, and a machine monitored her breathing, but she seemed relaxed and happy to talk. Last time Sean had seen someone with her sort of injuries, they'd died by nightfall, but Zadrus assured them Nik would recover fully. Now they had to determine what she wanted to do.

'I'd like to stay with the team, if you're prepared to put up with me,' she said.

Dan stood when Hunt approached. 'And where she goes, I go.'

Erin stood and extended her hand. 'It's good to see you again, Alex.' When he looked confused, she added, 'I'm Erin Bellamy.'

'Oh God, Mum I'm sorry,' said Sean. 'We've got so used to you being here, I forgot the general hasn't been with us.

'And our last meeting was less friendly.' Hunt shook her extended hand.

'Yes,' she sighed. 'The only thing I wanted that day was to die.'

'I've been told the story, ma'am. I don't think you stood a chance. Maybe you can all turn it around now.'

'The boys, and my daughter-in-law, and my soon to be daughter-in-law want me to stay.' She smiled at Nik.

'I hope you will,' said Hunt. 'You all deserve it.' He turned to Nik and asked how she was.

It amused Sean when she pulled closer to Dan. Hunt had repeatedly told them their ranks had no meaning here, but none of them could act much differently, particularly towards him.

CHAPTER 27

Jemma left Sean with Hunt and Nik to respond to a call from Werrimen.

'Our fleet commander is about to join us to talk about our mission,' said Werrimen. 'We would like one of you with us, and I feel you are the most appropriate.'

'Okay, but wouldn't you prefer Sean or General Hunt?'

'You are the most intuitive of your people. Your background also makes you the leader of your people and, now that you are officially Zadrus's Prehling, I want your impression on how your group will cope.'

On their way to the landing bay Werrimen explained that she had been the Fleet Commander's guide for Trustee training, and the Commander's first post on a spaceship had been navigator for Zadrus. She'd been offered, and accepted, the role of Fleet Commander after both Werrimen and Zadrus had refused it, and they knew her well enough to believe she'd be sympathetic to the plight of the humans on board.

The Fleet Commander, who looked like a younger version of Werrimen, jumped down through the blue light and embraced Werrimen. She turned to Jemma who now wore the junior trustee crest on her uniform and pulled her into a hug. 'You must be Jemma. It's a pleasure to meet you, I've heard so much about you and I see Zadrus has convinced you to join us. Welcome.' She touched the crest on Jemma's left shoulder, then took her hand and they walked together to the meeting room, chatting like old friends. She asked many questions about the previous few months.

Jemma answered as factually as she could although she clenched her fists when she recalled their reception on Wake Island. She barely noticed Zadrus buzzing around or the large array of food set out on several tables. When she did look up, she realised that Zadrus was flustered which brought home to Jemma that the decision to be made was not just about those who'd come from the SCARF team, but it had major implications for the alien crew too.

'That was a good show you put on for me, Zadrus,' said the fleet commander, after all but he, Werrimen and Jemma had left. 'Did you think I doubted you?'

He bowed his head. 'I am sorry, I just wanted you to have as much information as I could give you.'

She laughed. 'I trust you. Both of you. And I have had information from several other sources. I know our people have begged the IPL to act many times over the last twenty Earth years. I have thought about what we should do for some time and discussed it often at the Security Council on Sidlow. Your experience has increased my resolve to act, but we must develop some clear plans, and be sure they will work. I do not want the IPL to turn on us.'

They talked well into the night and Jemma questioned their decision to bypass the leaders of both Earth and the IPL.

Like Zadrus, the commander believed Earth would destroy itself if they didn't change and, given the belligerence Jemma had witnessed, considered change unlikely. She turned to Jemma. 'Your group has been asked to wait in the lounge. Would you please return to them and relay everything we have discussed? There is something else we must discuss among ourselves before we finalise the plan. We will join you in about an hour.'

Jemma walked into a crowded lounge. Everyone, except Nik, was there, even Anthony, Petra, the scientist who'd been imprisoned with Anthony and Therese, the doctor from Costa Rica. 'Okay, everyone, you'd better sit. I've got a lot to tell you.' She recounted everything that had been said, as factually as she could remember, and had only just finished when Zadrus, Werrimen and the fleet commander walked in.

'Ladies and gentlemen,' began Zadrus. 'We have two problems. The people of Anders Major, here on Earth, have lost the support of Earth's governments, mostly due to the actions of Fredrick Pritchard, and that is why you are here and cannot return to Earth. But we have a larger problem as most of you know. We believe Earth is at risk. Earth's governments have rejected our help, and the IPL has refused to allow us to intervene. You have all stated you do not want to be placed on another planet, and we are advised that Anders is still not safe for you to return, so I will now outline our proposed mission. You may then decide whether you wish to join us or reconsider the other options.

'We plan to invite as many people from Earth as we can convince, to join us. We will move forward in time, around eighty years. If the disaster we anticipate has occurred, we will have enough people to start again to ensure the survival of Earth's human population.'

Jemma glanced at the other people in the room. They all remained still in their chairs staring at Zadrus. She stood, reaching for Sean. 'Are you serious? You're telling us you can travel through time.'

Werrimen took Jemma's hand in hers. 'Yes, my dear, we can. My people discovered it many millennia ago, when they first explored the universe. One of our craft disappeared. They knew its last co-ordinates and another ship was sent out to investigate. It also vanished. At first, they suspected a black hole, but their tracking equipment should have identified that kind of anomaly, so they dismissed the idea and banned all ships from those co-ordinates. Around fifty years later, both crafts reappeared in roughly the same area. The people on board hadn't aged. They described a rough journey, which seemed to have taken only a day or two. Some had minor injuries, but all went on to lead normal lives. Once the IPL council recognised that the co-ordinates had to be the entry to a time portal, they searched for others. Many portals have since been identified. For thousands of years we've searched for portals that could take us backwards in time to prevent wars and other disasters but have not been successful. We cannot control the amount of time we move forward; it is specific to the portal. The one we plan to use here will take us forward about eighty years.'

Jemma stared at Werrimen who stood in front of her still holding her hand. Move forward in time and start again. She giggled, then her laugh grew louder until Sean moved closer, a worried look on his face. Tears streamed down her face.

He put his arm around her shoulders, turning her to look at him. 'Are you alright?'

'I'm fine,' she gasped. 'It's just that I've spent my entire life dedicated to researching the habitats of endangered animal species, trying to prevent their extinction. Now we're being asked to travel into the future, with a race of aliens from the other side of the universe, to *prevent the extinction* of our own species.'

Sean drew her closer to him. 'So long as we're together, we can get through anything.'

They clung to each other for several minutes until Jemma felt Nik's hand edge into hers from the wheelchair. She hadn't seen Nik come in, but Erin stood behind her. Slowly others moved closer too until the entire group was huddled together.

'I think you have your answer,' said Jemma, to the fleet commander. 'Looks like we're heading into the future.'

In Review

If you enjoyed *Abandoned In Exile*, I would appreciate a review at the site where you purchased your copy.

Would like to know more about me, the author? Then sign up for my newsletter, which I send occasionally at **https://almcdonnell.com**

and I will email you a free copy of my anthology *Beyond the Exile*

Look out for Book 2

Stranded In Exile

And coming soon Book 3

Torn In Exile

9 780645 082104